SURVIVOR

Praise for *The Soul Hunters*:

The Reading Book Award 2020 – Shortlist

'A fast-paced fantasy adventure with a thrilling plot'
BookTrust

'A fantasy adventure like no other!'
LoveReading4kids

'A must-read. If we could give it more than 5 stars, we would!'
The Book Brothers

Praise for the Young Samurai series:

Great Britain Sasakawa Award 2008 – Winner

Red House Children's Book Award 2009 – Shortlist

'An adventure novel to rank among the genre's best. This book earns the literary equivalent of a black belt'
Publishers Weekly

Praise for the Bodyguard series:

Brilliant Book Award 2014 – Winner

Hampshire Book Award 2014 – Winner

'Brad

Books by Chris Bradford

The Soul Prophecy series (in reading order)

THE SOUL HUNTERS

THE SOUL PROPHECY

THE SOUL SURVIVOR

The Young Samurai series (in reading order)

THE WAY OF THE WARRIOR

THE WAY OF THE SWORD

THE WAY OF THE DRAGON

THE RING OF EARTH

THE RING OF WATER

THE RING OF FIRE

THE RING OF WIND

THE RING OF SKY

THE RETURN OF THE WARRIOR

Available as ebook

THE WAY OF FIRE

The Bodyguard series (in reading order)

HOSTAGE

RANSOM

AMBUSH

TARGET

ASSASSIN

FUGITIVE

THE SOUL SURVIVOR

CHRIS BRADFORD

PUFFIN

PUFFIN BOOKS

UK | USA | Canada | Ireland | Australia
India | New Zealand | South Africa

Puffin Books is part of the Penguin Random House group of companies
whose addresses can be found at global.penguinrandomhouse.com.

www.penguin.co.uk
www.puffin.co.uk
www.ladybird.co.uk

First published 2023

001

The quote on page 411, 'Death is but the doorway', is from the film *The Mummy*
(directed by Karl Freund, screenplay by John L. Balderston; 1932).

Set in 10.5/15.5 pt Sabon LT Std
Typeset by Jouve (UK), Milton Keynes
Printed and bound in Great Britain by Clays Ltd, Elcograf S.p.A.

The authorized representative in the EEA is Penguin Random House Ireland,
Morrison Chambers, 32 Nassau Street, Dublin D02 YH68

A CIP catalogue record for this book is available from the British Library

ISBN: 978–0–241–32674–9

All correspondence to:
Puffin Books
Penguin Random House Children's
One Embassy Gardens, 8 Viaduct Gardens
London SW11 7BW

Para mi alma de amor Marcela,
Tú eres la luz en mi vida.

1

'Keep your head down!' whispers Alhwin, forcing my face into the blood-soaked sand.

As I hide next to my Soul Protector behind the sand dune, my body trembles uncontrollably and my heart thuds so hard I swear it can be heard above the crash of the waves. The Viking Soul Hunters continue to prowl the beach, looking for any surviving First Ascendants such as myself. Their ferocious whoops and war cries send a shiver down my spine and I peek up to see their coal-black eyes glinting in the darkness. The fearsome form of their leader, Tanas, stands over the twitching body of Mercia, his bloodied axe silhouetted against the dying flames of the hallowed fire.

'What just happened?' I hiss, spitting out sand. 'Why did Mercia's Light fail her?'

'I don't know, Kendra,' mutters my Soul Protector. He reaches for his pitchfork as a Hunter draws closer to our hiding place. 'I guess she wasn't the one foretold by the Soul Prophecy after all –'

I blink away the Glimmer of myself as Kendra in my ninth-century past life and return to the present as Genna.

For a moment there's that strange sense of disembodiment as my soul adjusts to my body in its current life. Kendra's blond tresses are replaced by my familiar ringlets of light-brown hair, her milk-white skin becomes amber-brown, and her short, hardy physique so suited to her life as a farmer's daughter is exchanged for my more athletic gymnast's figure.

Although that incarnation was more than twelve hundred years ago and my soul lived in a different body, the same sense of despair that I felt then engulfs me now.

I watch my nemesis rise from the dead.

No longer an axe-wielding Viking, Tanas lives on in this life in the body of FBI agent Alex Lin. Tall, lithe and lethal, the leader of the Soul Hunters is dressed in a matt-black assault jacket. Her long dark hair falls in a sleek veil over her narrow shoulders, framing her slender, angular face and aviator sunglasses.

'Once more, your revered Soul Seer fails you,' she gloats, glancing with disdain at the injured Caleb writhing at her feet. Blood pours from the wound in his chest where the jade knife that she holds pierced him like a spear.

Spluttering blood, the white-haired and wrinkle-faced Caleb looks from Tanas to me and back again in wild-eyed confusion. 'B-b-but the Prophecy was f-f-fulfilled . . . You should be *dead*!'

Tanas shakes her head. 'Oh, Caleb. After your first feeble attempt all those centuries ago, I'd have thought you'd know better than to put your faith in false prophecies.'

'No! The Soul Prophecy is true!' he insists. 'The Soul Healer Empote and I *both* foresaw it . . . G-Genna's the one true soul . . . She ignited the spark . . . when put to the Darkest test . . .' Caleb turns towards me, eyes pleading.

I bow my head, ashamed. I feel like a charlatan. The fate of the First Ascendants rested in my hands and, when the time came, I failed to defeat our enemy. Just like Mercia, I'm not the one foretold in the Soul Prophecy.

Tanas laughs, cruel and cold. 'Won't you Ascendants ever learn? My soul cannot be killed. Only *I* have the power to destroy souls.'

After uttering the unholy incantation from her ritual – '*Rura, rkumaa, raar ard ruhrd . . .*' – she gives a final cry of '*Ra-Ka!*' then plunges the jade knife deep into Caleb's heart. Fingers of blue lightning coil round Tanas's hand and dagger. Caleb's starlit blue eyes widen in agony, burning bright for a brief moment before the Light from his soul is extinguished forever. He slumps lifeless to the floor, his lion-headed cane clattering across the white marble flagstones of Haven's shattered glass pyramid.

'NO!' I scream as a fiery pain rips through me. My fellow surviving Ascendants – Santiago, Viviana, Sun-Hi, Tasha, Thabisa and her baby son, Kagiso – all experience the same torment.

The sudden loss of Light leaves me disorientated and sick to the stomach. The starless night sky presses down on me now like a shroud and my knees give way. Phoenix, my Soul Protector, reaches out to stop me collapsing. Our Chief Protector, Goggins, drops his Maori war club and catches the elderly Viviana, while the other Protectors and Soul Warriors close ranks to help their weakened charges. Out of nowhere a grief-stricken mewling howl echoes round the pyramid as Nefertiti begins to grieve, and more wails from the other cats of Haven join her in a strained chorus for their dear departed Caleb.

Fierce tears are running down my cheeks and I glare at Tanas in hatred. 'Why didn't the Light bomb kill you? There's no way you should have survived that intensity of Light!'

Tanas gives an amused smirk. 'Do you have to ask, Genna? I haven't lived and died countless lives not to have learned from my previous mistakes.' She nods in the direction of Tarek, who is helping Thabisa with her baby. 'Tarek's previous little stunt with the Light grenade warned me of what might come, so I made suitable preparations.' She proudly pats her tactical assault jacket. Its surface is oddly flat to the eye and impossibly black, like a hole torn in the fabric of space. 'This jacket has been specially coated with a micro-thin layer of nano-carbon, which can absorb almost one hundred per cent of all light waves. And these –' she removes her sunglasses to reveal her serpent-like dark eyes – 'have a di-electric mirror layer that reflects the majority of light. Thus protecting me from your blast of Light.' She arches a thin eyebrow. 'I'll admit, though, I wasn't prepared for quite such an explosion.'

Tanas waves a hand to take in the destruction. Haven's pyramid is now a mere shell, its solar panels blown out, the glass scattered like snow. The central altar and its crystal capstone have shattered into a thousand pieces, leaving a jagged stump. Littered everywhere are bodies of the Incarnates – the nameless FBI agents, police officers, soldiers, truck drivers, farmhands and the various other unfortunate souls that Tanas managed to recruit to her Dark cause. Their weapons surround them like wreaths at a funeral.

As I gaze numbly at the devastation, still unable to believe that Tanas has managed to evade death so cunningly, I notice Damien stir. He groans and stiffly stretches his muscled limbs. The young Soul Hunter's fringe of raven-black hair lifts from his chalk-white face to reveal a pair of cracked sunglasses, their aviator design matching Tanas's shades. Dressed in the same matt-black tactical assault gear as his master, he gets unsteadily to his feet.

'Well, that was a blast!' He dusts off the fragments of glass from his jacket and hair.

'You're alive *too*?' My blood runs cold. The fact that Tanas had survived is bad enough, but knowing that my original Soul Hunter has also survived is almost more than I can bear.

Damien discards his broken sunglasses and grins at me. 'Aw, thanks. It's heart-warming to know you care so much, Genna.'

Phoenix, snatching up his Roman gladius sword from the ground, steps between us. 'Keep back, Damien, or I'll cut you down where you stand.'

Damien wags a disapproving finger. '*Tut-tut!* I wouldn't be so quick to start a fight, Phoenix. Especially when you haven't a hope in hell of winning.'

The sharpened point of a gladiator's trident is pressed against the side of Phoenix's neck. Holding the weapon's shaft is none other than Knuckleduster, the muscular young Hunter who sports a collection of vicious rings on her fingers and is the meanest of Damien's ruthless gang. I glance round to discover that other members are alive and well too – the wiry and quick Blondie and the muscular, crooked-nosed Thug. But Spider, the rake-thin girl with a black widow tattoo on her neck, isn't among them. I'm guessing she's still pinned to the wall of the Glimmer Dome by her own stiletto blade, the result of her earlier fight with Phoenix.

'Drop your weapon before I drop you,' growls Knuckleduster as she pushes harder with the trident, drawing a bead of blood from Phoenix's neck.

Reluctantly Phoenix lets go of the sword and the gladius falls to the marble floor. The noise rouses more Incarnates wearing the protective gear, namely Tanas's cloaked High Priests and a select group of FBI agents and soldiers. Despite the decimation wreaked by the Light bomb among her ranks, Tanas's motley army still outnumber us almost three to one.

'Your cause is lost,' she declares. 'The Soul Prophecy has proven to be nothing but a fairy tale. Now it's time to extinguish the Light of Humanity . . . *for eternity*!'

2

The Incarnates rise one by one, gradually encircling us. After millennia upon millennia of fighting to save the Light, we've nowhere left to run or hide. However fierce and brave our Protectors may be, the Incarnates have the advantage in terms of both numbers and weapons. They carry guns, knives and even grenades, while we're down to a handful of old swords, clubs and other antique weaponry that Phoenix managed to grab from the Glimmer Dome.

A smirk of triumph crosses Tanas's thin lips as she sees the defeat in our eyes. Her smug expression reminds me of the way one of her past incarnations looked at me and my Protector once. She has the same keen cruelty on her face as the Roman commander of the infamous Twelfth Legion when he had us trapped at the edge of a sheer cliff. Our situation then was hopeless, and in this life it seems equally so. Despairing at our options, I'm forced to come to the only possible decision.

'*Kill me*,' I whisper to Phoenix.

He stares at me, horrified. Then he firmly shakes his head.

'*Do it now!*' I insist. '*Before it's too late.*'

The Incarnates raise their weapons, eager to attack yet awaiting their master's command. Our only escape, our only way of protecting the Light of Humanity, appears to be a quick death – one that will lead to reincarnating in a new life. But Tanas seems well aware of this as she holds back on their attack. She knows that in order to perform the necessary ritual to destroy our souls and snuff out the Light she must first capture all First Ascendants alive.

'*No, I can't!*' Phoenix replies through gritted teeth. '*I vowed: never again.*'

His face contorts into a harrowing expression of guilt and abhorrence, and in his sapphire-blue eyes I recognize the same wretched look of anguish that he wore as the Roman slave Custos when he was forced to push me off that cliff to my death. But as he explained countless lives later: '*A violent or wrongful death damages the soul, weakens the Light, as well as the bond between us ... Killing you is the very* last *resort.*'

I glance around at the gathering of black-eyed Incarnates. Our current predicament surely warrants a last resort!

Damien and his gang shift like a pack of hungry wolves. The cloaked High Priests, their faces hooded, are murmuring their incantation while swaying in unison. The other Incarnates stand as still as sentry guards, weapons primed. My gaze turns to my fellow Ascendants. The all-too-young, ice-blond Tasha is weeping silently, a glistening trail of tears running down her snow-white cheeks. The irascible, bearded Santiago scowls at our foe, while Viviana, hardy as a gnarled olive tree in her old age, has found her feet and looks on defiantly. Sun-Hi and Thabisa huddle protectively round the crying Kagiso. The Soul Protectors and Warriors that stand beside them put on a brave face, but the tense manner in which they grasp their weapons betrays what they really believe: this may be our last battle.

Still, Goggins' scowl shows that he's determined to take as many Incarnates as he can down with him. 'Come on!' he growls. 'What are you waiting for?'

'There's no need for you *all* to die,' says Tanas in an insidious tone, tapping Caleb's body with her foot. 'Goggins, tell your Protectors and Warriors to lay down their arms and surrender.'

'Never, Tanas. *Never* in a million years.'

Tanas sighs. 'It's over, Goggins. Even a blind man can see that!'

My gaze drops to the slaughtered figure of Caleb. The Soul Seer had put all his belief in me. Shown me my past to prepare me for the future. By building Haven as a secret sanctuary, safe from the Incarnates, he did his utmost to protect not only me but every First Ascendant. My stomach twists into a knot of guilt. It was my error of judgement in rescuing Phoenix that has led us here, to Haven's discovery and downfall. And it is partly my fault too, I realize, that Caleb is dead.

I see now that the only way to honour his life is to keep the Light burning.

I turn to Phoenix. 'Do you trust me?' I whisper, echoing the question he asked me long ago as Custos. He nods. I look him in the eye, seeking out his soul and willing him to do the unthinkable. The deep connection that binds us – the one forged between our souls on that fateful night he first saved me from Tanas in the Great Rift Valley all those millennia ago – still burns bright and strong. I know that whatever happens that bond can never be broken . . . or, at least, I hope it can't.

'Your life with mine, as always?' I say softly, repeating the phrase that binds us.

He smiles with immense sadness, reluctantly accepting what must be done. 'Always,' he replies, his voice quavering. However, even as Phoenix prepares to take up his sword one last time and I steel myself for the pain of death, Nefertiti slips past and boldly strides up to Tanas. The Incarnate leader peers snootily down her nose at my sleek, sandy-coloured cat.

'Nefe!' I call sharply, as she sniffs at the limp and lifeless form of Caleb. Nudging the Soul Seer's wrinkled cheek with her soft nose, she gives him a tender lick. When she gets no response, her emerald eyes turn accusingly to Tanas. Hissing, Nefe bears her fangs and bristles her tail while Tanas looks on, indifferent to my cat's fierce display. Then Nefe meows in what she must imagine to be a cougar-like roar, but it comes out as a plaintive high-pitched cry.

Tanas chuckles at the pitiful challenge. 'Is that all you can offer, kitty-cat?'

Nefe, though, doesn't back down. Her call has summoned the other cats of Haven. They materialize out of the darkness, mewling their mournful lament at the death of their beloved Caleb. Bright green eyes shining and claws glinting, the feline army encircles the Incarnates.

'Well, if these are your reinforcements,' Blondie scoffs in a thin, reedy voice, 'I'd think seriously about surrendering now.' He lashes out with his boot at a ginger tom that's stalked too close. The cat nimbly evades the kick, leaps up Blondie's leg and lands on his pockmarked face. Claws out, the animal tears at the Hunter's eyes. Blondie bawls in pain, drops his nunchaku and frantically tries to pull the cat away from him, but Nefe gives another cry and, as if on command, all the other cats go on the attack. With ear-piercing screeches, they launch themselves at the Incarnates, who are quickly overwhelmed.

'FIGHT FOR THE LIGHT!' shouts Goggins, seizing on the distraction and snatching up his Maori war club.

As a black-and-white cat pounces on Knuckleduster's back, Phoenix knocks away the trident and picks up his gladius sword. I dash over to where I'd dropped my katana earlier. I see Damien rushing to intercept me but a tabby leaps on him and sinks her teeth into his neck. He shrieks and drops to his knees, wrestling with the furry beast.

With my katana in hand, I feel a sense of renewed power and join the fight against the Incarnates. I fend off a truck driver wielding a crowbar, then deflect an iron pipe aimed at my head. To my right Goggins is swinging his war club with wild abandon, knocking down Hunters like they're skittles. To my left Jude is whirling her bo staff, striking any target in range while trying her best not to hit any of the cats. Tarek is standing close beside Thabisa, lashing out with his fists and feet at a High Priest trying to snatch her baby son. The remaining Warriors – Kohsoom, Steinar and Zara – have fanned out alongside Protector Blake to tackle the High Priests who have evaded the worst of the feline ambush.

I duck as an Incarnate swipes at me with a baseball bat, then I retaliate with a slash of my samurai sword. He rapidly retreats and in the process stumbles over a Siamese cat, landing hard on his backside. Before he can rise, Phoenix slams the pommel of his gladius on top of the man's head, knocking him out cold.

'Let's get out of here!' orders Phoenix.

'But we have the advantage,' I reply as I disarm an Incarnate of her hunting knife.

'Not for long,' says Phoenix with a grunt, as he deflects a steel pipe swung at his head. 'The Incarnates still outnumber us and –'

'Get off me, you stupid cat!' screams Tanas.

I glance round to see Nefe clawing at the Incarnate leader's face, Tanas clenching her by the scruff of the neck. Leaving Phoenix's side, I dash over to save Nefe, but before I reach her Thug's imposing bulk steps into my path. He kicks me hard in the chest, the blow feeling like a battering ram. Gasping for breath, I stagger backwards and hit the jagged stump of the altar, lose my grip of the katana and sprawl across the floor. Thug lumbers forward and brings down his mace-and-chain. I scramble away just in time as the spiked iron ball shatters the remains of the altar to pieces.

'Next time, I squish *you*!' he snarls, whirling his mace faster.

I hear Nefe let out a pained cry and whip round. Tanas is wringing her neck. I cast my eyes desperately about me for a weapon – anything to stop that monster killing my cat! – and spot a smoke grenade clipped to the belt of a dead Incarnate soldier. Grabbing it, I pull the pin and toss the grenade at Tanas. It detonates with a deafening *bang* at her feet, sending up thick clouds of choking gas into the air. Eyes water, cats scatter, confusion reigns. Tanas, Nefe and Thug all disappear amid the suffocating smog.

As I crawl away, coughing and spluttering, I feel a hand seize my arm and wrench me to my feet. I go to punch my assailant in the jaw, then just manage to stop myself as Phoenix's face looms out of the mist.

'To the tunnel!' he rasps.

3

Eyes stinging and half-blind from the smoke, I stumble after Phoenix to the service hatch in the glass pyramid's floor. We meet Jude along the way.

'Get the others!' Phoenix orders her, as he thumbs the lock's fingerprint scanner and opens the hatch. She dashes off. A moment later, Tarek, Thabisa and Sun-Hi appear with Blake. The Protector, a gangly Scotsman with a short goatee, dark eyebrows and a permanent frown, is armed with a Luger pistol that looks old enough to have been used in the First World War.

Phoenix beckons urgently to Thabisa to enter the tunnel with little Kagiso, who is choking from the smoke.

'No, I'd best go first,' says Blake, cocking his antique pistol and descending the steps. As soon as he gives the all-clear, Tarek helps Thabisa down with her baby. Sun-Hi quickly follows. Phoenix is urging me to go next when Kohsoom and Zara emerge out of the fog with a wheezing Santiago and a hobbling Viviana. I let them go ahead of me. Then Jude returns with Tasha, accompanied by the bearded Norwegian Warrior Steinar. To my relief, Tasha appears unharmed, but Jude's bo staff is now broken in two from the fighting.

'Where's Goggins?' Phoenix asks as Tasha scurries down the steps with Steinar.

'Still taking out Hunters,' Jude replies. 'He's made quite a pile!'

'Does he know we're leaving?'

Jude nods and follows Tasha and Steinar into the tunnel.

Phoenix turns to me. 'Go now,' he insists. 'Before the smoke clears.'

'But Nefe . . .' I reply, my eyes desperately sweeping the battle scene for a glimpse of my cherished cat. My chest tightens at the thought of her lying broken and in pain somewhere back there. As my gaze sweeps the pyramid, I spot Goggins through the haze next to a heap of bodies. He's standing over a kneeling Damien, his Maori war club raised. Although he has the boy Hunter at his mercy, Goggins appears hesitant to strike. Then I notice the silhouette of an Incarnate creeping up behind him.

'Goggins!' I shout, my voice hoarse from the smoke. He spins round and smashes his ambusher in the head with the club, adding to his pile of groaning bodies. Then, leaving Damien still on his knees, he lumbers over to us.

'Is Viv with you?' he grunts, his eyes bloodshot from the smoke.

Phoenix nods. Goggins glances back at the horde of Incarnates furiously combing the pyramid for the disappearing First Ascendants. 'Then let's live to fight another day –'

'*Stop them!*' Tanas screeches, her dark eyes streaming as she finally spies us through the thinning smoke.

With a last, futile look for Nefe, I drop into the service tunnel, closely followed by Phoenix and then Goggins, who shuts the hatch behind us. We hurry along after the others, but all the while my thoughts are consumed by Nefe's fate. *Did she escape? Or did Tanas break her neck? What if she's injured and needs my help?* More tears prick my eyes, no longer from the smoke. I feel dreadful at having abandoned her, especially as she was the one who saved us all. Once again I owe my life to that faithful cat.

The strip lights overhead flicker as we dart down the narrow passageway. We turn left at a junction and make our way along to another set of stairs that lead up to a locked doorway. Goggins thumbs the scanner, the door slides open and we emerge into Haven's aircraft hangar. Oddly empty and quiet in comparison with the mayhem of the pyramid, the hangar houses a large, sleek white jet that gleams like a silver arrow in the gloom.

'Zara and Tarek, prep the plane. Phoenix, help me open the hangar doors,' orders Goggins. 'The rest of you, get the Ascendants on board and buckled up!'

As we hurry over to Caleb's private jet, a set of airstairs near the front lowers to the ground. Zara and Tarek mount the steps and disappear inside the cockpit. Steinar helps carry Viviana into the cabin; the others follow. There's a sudden loud, metallic screech that makes me glance round sharply. I see Goggins drawing back a heavy metal bolt and Phoenix at the hangar's control panel. The steel doors start to roll open, their rumbling noise almost as loud as the squeal of the bolt.

If Tanas and her Hunters hadn't known before where we'd disappeared to, they'd certainly know now.

The doors peel back to reveal the Mojave Desert's night sky, cloudless yet strangely starless, only the half moon casting its pale glow across the runway. The hidden valley in which Haven sits is otherwise cloaked in shadow; the five remaining pillars of red rock that once formed the sacred stone circle around the complex stand in silent witness to our frantic escape.

The jet's engines whine into life.

'Genna, get on board!' Jude urges from the bottom of the airstairs. Every other Ascendant is already safely inside. Goggins, having unlocked the hangar doors, is hurriedly clearing debris from the runway, left by an earlier Incarnate rocket attack.

I nod to Jude, then call for Phoenix to join us. He gives me the thumbs up. But as I'm about to climb the steps, I catch a flash of movement out of the corner of my eye. Peering into the darkness, I spot a sandy-coloured streak racing across Haven's training ground towards the hangar.

'NEFE!' I cry, and instinctively I turn to get her.

'No!' yells Jude, grabbing hold of my arm. 'Leave the cat. We *have* to go now.'

'But we owe her our lives – I'm *not* leaving her behind.' I shake myself free of her grip and run off.

'Genna, come back!' Jude cries. 'It's just a bloody cat!'

Ignoring her, I head out of the hangar. I've barely reached the edge of the runway, though, when my joy turns to alarm. Not far behind Nefe is an angry mob of Incarnates, Tanas leading the pack.

'There they are!' Tanas screeches, her face bleeding from the lacerations inflicted by Nefertiti's sharp claws. 'Stop that plane!'

Pulling ahead of her pursuers, Nefe bounds up to me and I gather her in my arms. Together we race back towards the plane. Zara and Tarek are already taxiing the jet on to the runway. As they pass by Goggins, he mounts the steps and clambers aboard.

'RUN!' he bawls to me and Phoenix.

With Nefe tucked under my arm, I sprint across the tarmac after the departing plane. Behind me, a muffled explosion rocks the hangar and the door to the service tunnel is blasted off its hinges. Almost immediately, through curls of smoke, Damien and his gang emerge. They spot me and Phoenix, and they charge after us.

'GO! GO! GO!' Phoenix shouts, rushing up to my side.

The jet is trundling along the runway, Goggins and the others urging us to move faster. From our left, Tanas and her Incarnates are closing in.

'We're not going to make it!' I pant, clasping Nefe closer to my chest as I struggle to keep up the pace.

'Yes, we will,' replies Phoenix, putting a hand to my back and pushing me onwards. At the same time, Blake leans out of the passenger doorway and fires his Luger into the approaching line of Incarnates. A Hunter goes down, taking two other Incarnates with him. Blake fires off several more rounds, forcing the enemy to scatter, slowing their progress . . . then the gun clicks empty. But he's given us enough time to reach the airstairs. I seize hold of the rail and jump on to the first step –

Then a hand grabs on to the small rucksack on my back.

'Where's your boarding pass, Genna?' shouts Damien over the noise of the jet's engines. He yanks me backwards and I lose my grip on the rail.

'Get off her!' Phoenix yells. He punches Damien hard in the jaw and tries to pull me free.

But Damien refuses to relinquish his hold on me. 'You don't have permission to take off!' he snarls, wrenching harder on my backpack.

With the jet continuing to pull away, a furious tug of war over me ensues between Phoenix and Damien. I attempt to shake Damien off myself, but he clings on like a pit bull terrier. It's Nefe who comes to my aid now, clawing at the Hunter's hand, scoring deep, bloody lines into his pale-white skin. With a howl of pain and rage, Damien is forced to let go and Phoenix kicks him in the knee, hobbling him.

We run on.

But the rest of Damien's gang are now breathing down our necks.

'Move!' Phoenix orders me, pushing me towards the moving plane. 'And don't look back!'

I sprint for all I'm worth. As I again approach the airstairs, the fearless Nefe leaps from my arms, up the steps and into the cabin. Then catching hold of Jude's outstretched hand, I too scramble aboard.

'*Close the door!*' screams Zara from the cockpit. 'We have to take off. *Now!*'

'No!' I cry as the jet engines begin to roar and the plane picks up speed. 'Phoenix isn't on board yet.'

I look back down the runway to see my Protector battling Knuckleduster, Thug and Blondie single-handedly. Quickly overwhelmed, he's knocked to the ground, where Tanas, raging at our escape, vents her fury on him by kicking him repeatedly in the stomach. Then, like vultures circling a kill, her High Priests close in to commence their ritual.

My first instinct is to jump from the moving jet, to run to Phoenix's aid. I try and try – but I can't move. Steinar has hold of me. Struggling furiously in his grip, I watch distraught as the door slams shut and my Protector is left to his fate.

4

'Why did you take off?' I demand angrily of Zara, bursting into the cockpit. 'Why did you leave Phoenix behind?'

'I had no choice,' she replies bluntly as the plane climbs steeply into the sky. 'Tanas was coming after us and I didn't dare delay any longer.'

'We *have* to go back,' I plead, clinging to her chair. 'Phoenix needs our help.'

'There's no going back,' insists Zara. She maintains the jet's flight path as we clear the rim of the valley.

I turn to Tarek in the co-pilot's seat. '*You* can fly a plane?'

He nods. 'I was a fighter pilot in the Second World War.'

'Then I'm begging you, Tarek – turn the plane round.'

He gives me a regretful shake of his head. 'Can't. Sorry, Genna. Zara's captain.' He fixes his gaze on the instrument panel to avoid my now furious glare.

'Don't you realize Phoenix is being sacrificed by Tanas?' I cry in frustration. 'We *have* to save him –'

'It's too late, Genna. Face it – he's gone.' Jude plants a hand on my shoulder. 'Come, leave them to fly the plane,' she says firmly, and guides me back into the main cabin where the others are seated.

I'm trembling so much that I can barely walk. I shrug off her hand.

'Look. I know you're upset,' she continues, 'but Phoenix wouldn't want you, or anyone else, to risk themselves for him. He made that abundantly clear the last time we rescued him.'

I want to argue with her, yet I know that what she says is true. Phoenix was incensed when I left the safety of Haven to break him out of the secure unit at the behavioural centre in Arizona Valley Springs. We almost all ended up dead at Tanas's hands as a result and afterwards Phoenix insisted that I never take such a risk again.

'You should be proud of him, Genna. I know I am –' Jude swallows hard, betraying her own grief at Phoenix's loss.

Steinar nods his blond head in agreement. 'He did his duty as your Soul Protector,' he says, his voice as gruff as his battle-worn appearance. 'If he hadn't stopped to take on Damien's gang, you wouldn't have made it. And, in the end, that's *all* that matters.'

I stare coolly at him. 'All that m-matters?' I question, my voice cracking. 'But *he's* all that matters to me.'

Despairing, I drop my backpack and slump into the nearest empty seat. Sensing my distress, Nefe leaps on to my lap and settles down, purring deeply in an effort to comfort me. I absently stroke her as I turn away from Steinar and Jude and gaze glumly out of the window at the black, starless night, the sky which seems even darker than before. Yet again Phoenix has sacrificed himself for me. Given up his life so that I could live. So that the Light of Humanity that I carry in my soul can continue to burn.

I curse the Light and the burden it brings. While Phoenix's death as my Protector is always a painful experience, I've usually had the small reassurance that he will reincarnate. The crucial difference this time is that I know he's *never* coming back. Phoenix won't simply be killed by Tanas. She'll rip out his soul and destroy it for eternity. No longer can I cling on to the hope of being reunited with him. Not in this life, nor in any of my future lives.

All of a sudden I'm consumed by a grief so great that I can barely breathe. It's as if the plane has depressurized and all the oxygen been sucked from the cabin. I cling on to the armrests, as I would if the jet was plummeting out of the sky. *My Soul Protector. My shield. My friend. My one true soulmate . . . gone . . . forever.*

I'm too distraught to cry. My heart feels hollowed out. My life now – and all those other lives to come – empty and utterly pointless. I let out a shuddering sob, thinking of how close Phoenix and I had come to happiness. For a brief moment, when the Light bomb appeared to have destroyed Tanas, the two of us had been free to love, to be in love, without the threat of Hunters hanging over our souls. But that moment has been snatched away all too quickly and violently.

Your life with mine, as always.

Now it would never be and I am devastated.

I gaze numbly around the cabin. The interior of the jet is brightly lit and tastefully decorated, all cream carpets, soft leather seats and wooden trims. Pristine and peaceful, it seems strangely unreal after the brutal fighting. Near the front is a high-tech computer console and display screen; towards the back, a slender dining table and a small galley kitchen complete with minibar. This is how I imagine first-class travel to be for mega-famous pop stars, presidents and tech billionaires. The contrast between those A-listers and the group of dishevelled and battle-worn passengers currently on board couldn't be any more stark.

Everyone appears shell-shocked by the surprise attack on Haven. The loss of so many Ascendants and Protectors, the unanticipated survival of Tanas and her Hunters, and our frantic escape have all taken a heavy toll. In the second row Viviana comforts a glassy-eyed Tasha, stroking her ice-blond hair with a trembling hand. Behind them, Thabisa breastfeeds Kagiso in an effort to calm his cries and soothe him to sleep. Sun-Hi is buried in the arms of her Protector, Blake, weeping softly and mourning the loss of her family. In the back row, Kohsoom and Steinar are huddled together, whispering secretively, their expressions grim and downcast. Meanwhile, Santiago has found the bar and is pouring himself a generous serving of some dark liquor.

Goggins sits at the dining table, alone, his bald head cradled in his hands.

A sudden surge of anger rises up in me. *Why didn't he kill Damien when he had the chance?* Then Phoenix might still be alive now, here with me, rather than dead by Tanas's evil hand!

'Goggins!' I shout, causing everyone to look up.

He stares vacantly at me. His face is drained, his eyes

rimmed red, his cheeks hollow. He somehow appears shrunken, as if all his muscles have withered and his once impressive frame crumpled in on itself. The Chief Protector is a shadow of the warrior he once was. I open my mouth to question him when it dawns on me that he must be deep in grief too. For Goggins hasn't just lost a Soul Protector from his ranks, he's also lost a Soul Son.

Phoenix – or as he was named in his very first life Asani – was Goggins' second-born son when he, Goggins, was the warrior chief Zuberi, the leader of the Hakala mountain tribe that first came to the rescue of the Ascendants in the Great Rift Valley eons ago. Just before the recent attack on Haven, I'd learned from Phoenix that Goggins had already lost his first-born Soul Son, Jabali, to Tanas; it was that tragic death that had fuelled the Soul Father's determination over the centuries to protect First Ascendants and defeat the Incarnate leader. Now tragedy had struck again and Tanas had taken his other Soul Son.

No wonder all the fight has gone out of him, I thought. *It's not just me. Goggins is mourning Phoenix too.*

Deciding not to question him now about Damien's survival, I mutter, 'I'm sorry for your loss.'

Goggins nods wordlessly and bows his head once more, but Santiago growls, 'You should be!'

Everyone's attention now turns to Santiago at the bar.

He eyes me with a malice that startles me as he takes another swig. 'You should be sorry, for the loss of Caleb and Fabian and Mick, of Jintao, Nam and Song . . . and of my Lena and all the other Protectors and Warriors who've lost their souls today. Thanks to *you*, Tanas found Haven and came *this* close –' he puts his thumb and forefinger together – 'to extinguishing the Light.'

My cheeks flush hot under his barrage.

'If you'd only listened to Caleb and Goggins, instead of going on your fool's errand –'

'Santiago, enough!' Viviana interrupts fiercely. 'It *isn't* Genna's fault. Tanas already knew about Haven's existence. Remember how she tortured Saul and Maddy to death trying to discover its location? It was only a matter of time before she found us.'

'Yeah, yeah, whatever!' snaps Santiago, spilling his drink over the bar. He tops his glass up. 'In my eyes she's to blame. Caleb got the Soul Prophecy wrong *again*, and we paid the price for it!'

'And Caleb paid the *ultimate* price,' Viviana reminds him sadly. At this, Thabisa murmurs a prayer in the Soul Seer's memory, which causes Sun-Hi to weep even more and Tasha to let out a gentle sob. I bite my trembling lip and blink away fresh tears of grief, this time for the tragic loss of Caleb.

Santiago scowls. 'He was an idiot to believe in that stupid Prophecy to begin with.' His burning blue eyes flick towards me. 'Genna's no saviour. She's our downfall!'

His comment stings me to my core. 'I *never* said I was your saviour,' I protest. 'I never wanted to be. I never wanted any of this.'

I struggle to maintain my composure as all the anger, frustration and grief risk bursting out of me like a breached dam. I stand up to face him, dislodging Nefe from my lap. She scurries off under the desk of the computer console.

'Only a few weeks ago I thought I was returning to my life in London as a *normal* schoolgirl,' I explain fiercely. 'I'd put my abduction by Tanas behind me. My counsellor had explained away my past life experiences as a mechanism for coping with the trauma. I was looking forward to a holiday with my mum and dad in Barbados, to visit my family there. But then –' Suddenly all the air seems sucked from my lungs, my throat tightens and I find it hard to speak as the gruesome image of two bodies sprawled on a kitchen floor flashes before my eyes. I want to scream out my grief, tear the pain from my heart. 'But then my parents were *murdered* by Damien and his Hunters!'

Viviana reaches out a hand to comfort me, but I barely feel it as I rage on. 'The Hunters were looking for *me*! I am the reason my parents are dead,' I cry. 'Can you even imagine how that feels?'

Santiago lowers his gaze, cowed by my fury. 'We've all been there,' he mumbles.

'Then you'll understand the pain I'm going through,' I snap. 'Yet again my life has been turned upside down. I was forced to go on the run, to flee England as a suspect for my *own parents'* murder. A suspect! *It sounds insane just saying it!* Not only did I have to come to terms with their deaths, I had to accept *again* that I was a First Ascendant, a reincarnated soul carrying this so-called precious Light of Humanity. And then, to top it off, Caleb proclaims *me* as the one foretold in the Soul Prophecy. The one who would overcome the Darkness and defeat Tanas. That's some responsibility. So, Santiago . . . *no, I never wanted any of this!*'

My emotional outburst spent, I slump back into my seat, my body trembling. For several seconds, no one says anything.

Then Viviana softly speaks up, 'None of us did, *mia cara*. But this is our souls' purpose. To keep the Light alive and humanity safe from Tanas and her Incarnates.'

Santiago stabs a finger at me. 'And that's something *she* has endangered.'

'Genna did her best,' Jude pipes up in my defence. She leans against the front bulkhead, her arms crossed, her spiky blond hair a mess. I offer her a grateful smile for her support, but she doesn't smile back.

'That may be so,' says Sun-Hi, sitting up and glaring at me through her tears. 'But her best wasn't good enough. It didn't save my Jintao or my precious Nam and Song.'

'Genna's idea for the Light bomb almost worked,' Tasha points out with a hopeful expression.

'"*Almost*"? "Almost" doesn't save us,' says Santiago scathingly.

An uncomfortable silence descends over us; just the background thrum of the jet's engines fills the cabin as we flee into the night. Our defeat has weakened and divided us. I don't blame Santiago for his anger. Or Sun-Hi for her resentment. I'm disappointed and angry with myself too. For a short while I *did* believe I was the one foretold in the Soul Prophecy: the one soul that shines brighter and bolder than the rest, the one that would ignite the spark when put to the Darkest test, and destroy Tanas's soul once and for all. My combat training with Phoenix in the Glimmer Dome seemed to support Empote and Caleb's belief in me, and I was emboldened by the fact that my soul shines with my First Sister Lakeisha's Light as well as my own.

But when the time came to prove myself, I still wasn't enough.

I stare out of the window at the black sky. *If I'm not the one foretold in the Soul Prophecy, then ... who is? Or is the Prophecy a lie?*

5

'What do we do now?' asks Thabisa anxiously as she cradles the sleeping Kagiso in her arms. The hum of the engines and a full stomach of milk have helped settle the young Ascendant. With Caleb gone, everyone turns to Goggins. But the Chief Protector appears to be in no state to lead us. He doesn't even seem to be aware that we're all looking at him.

'As long as we live,' says Viviana, answering for him, 'the Light of Humanity still burns.'

Santiago snorts. 'Yeah, but for how long? Tanas will be on the hunt for us. She'll use every available resource at her disposal. And as an FBI agent, she'll have access to anything she needs. We're living on borrowed time, my friends.'

'The battle may be lost, but the war is not over,' says Kohsoom, determination etched in her young, round face. She pounds a fist into her palm. 'As our Chief said, we should fight for the Light! Tanas won't be expecting us if we attack now.'

Blake shoots the Thai warrior an incredulous look. 'Have you been hit on the head, Kohsoom? We're in no position to fight. Look around you – we simply don't have enough Warriors or Protectors left to take on Tanas and her Incarnates. We barely have enough to protect our First Ascendants.'

'But this may be our best chance – our *only* chance to defeat the Incarnates in this life,' she insists. 'We just need to cut the head off the snake!'

Santiago lets out a hollow laugh. 'That would be a suicide mission!' he says scornfully, and pours himself another drink. 'Tanas has proven yet again that evil never dies.'

'So we just give up?' I counter, dismayed by his constant pessimism.

'I didn't say that,' snaps Santiago, barely looking at me. 'Our best hope now is to split up and hide.'

'Wouldn't it be better to stay *together*?' says Tasha. She clasps Viviana's hand like a lifeline.

Viviana squeezes Tasha's hand and nods in agreement. 'She's right, Santiago. There's strength in numbers.'

'*Pah!*' spits Santiago. 'It's the other way round. There's no longer any safety in numbers!'

'We could build another Haven,' suggests Steinar, his seat creaking as the heavyset Norwegian leans forward to join the conversation. 'One with better defences.'

A few people nod in agreement. I hold back on my opinion, feeling somewhat conflicted. On one hand, I found Haven to be like a gilded cage and am relieved in a small way to escape its confines. On the other, I can't deny there was a certain comfort in knowing we at least had *some* defences. Now we're pretty much defenceless.

Blake shakes his head at Steinar's idea. 'That'll take far

too long. Besides, where would we build it? And with what? This jet is pretty much all we have left.'

'Not quite true,' says Viviana. 'Caleb set up an Ascendant trust fund. We still have access to finances –'

'Forget the idea of a new Haven,' interrupts Santiago with a dismissive wave of his hand. 'Caleb's supposed sanctuary was nothing but a fool's paradise! We just made it easier for Tanas to locate us all in one go.'

'Doesn't our combined Light help to hide our presence?' I interject. 'At least that's what Caleb told me.'

'Somewhat,' Santiago admits grudgingly. 'The problem is, with every Ascendant soul destroyed, Tanas only grows stronger . . . while our Light gets weaker.'

'But if we split up, we're more vulnerable to attack,' argues Thabisa, holding Kagiso protectively to her chest.

'Maybe,' Santiago acknowledges, 'but Tanas has to find each of us first, and the odds of doing so decrease the more we're spread out across the world.'

'What about Tanas's Watchers?' says Viviana, reminding everyone of the network of Incarnate spies who keep an unconscious eye out for First Ascendants on behalf of their master. 'They're everywhere now. Isn't that right, Jude?'

'Pretty much,' replies Jude. 'They certainly were in LA.'

'More reason we should stick together,' says Thabisa firmly.

'No. Less reason,' counters Sun-Hi. 'I agree with Santiago. We need to split up.'

As a heated debate breaks out over our best strategy for survival, I withdraw and hunker down in my seat. I once more gaze out of the window at the dark clouds below to consider my own options. With Phoenix gone, I feel exposed. Unprotected. Yes, I have Jude as my Soul Warrior now. But she's no Phoenix and I don't share the same connection with her that a First Ascendant does with their Soul Protector.

I glance in Jude's direction. She has a slighter frame than Phoenix had and is a good deal shorter. Her nose ring, slanted baseball cap and mirrored glasses suggest a slacker attitude, yet I've seen her in action, and as a fighter she's almost Phoenix's equal. But I still don't know what exactly happened all those years long ago in the ancient Sumerian city of Uruk. All I do know is that she wasn't there at the crucial time my Soul Twin needed her. I don't fully trust her. *How can I, when she failed to protect my Soul Twin from Tanas? Will she fail me too?*

Of course, I could strike out on my own. I'm not entirely defenceless. During my long sessions in the Glimmer Dome and thanks to my previous past life experiences, I've acquired skills in samurai swordsmanship, karate, taiji, capoeira, the Indian martial art of Kalarippayattu and even Mongolian Bökh wrestling. But the idea of living from day to day, alone and on the run, not knowing who I can trust or who I can turn to, fills me with dread. I'd prefer to stick with the others for the comfort of company and the security of multiple warriors, even if that means relying on Jude to protect me. Besides, going it alone hasn't always worked out for the best, for me or my fellow First Ascendants.

'Goggins, what do you think?' prompts Viviana when an agreement can't be reached. Everyone falls silent as they await his answer.

He slowly looks up, the usual blue gleam in his eyes diminished. Then he rises to his feet, the effort appearing almost too much. 'You know that I, as the Chief Protector, have always been eager to take the fight to Tanas, believing offence is the best defence.'

Kohsoom nods enthusiastically, raising a clenched fist in support.

'Caleb, on the other hand, preferred a more guarded approach. Hence, his belief in Haven.'

Steinar now grunts in agreement.

'However, neither of those tactics have worked,' admits Goggins, looking each of us in the eye in turn. 'So if we're to protect the Light, the only option left to us is to run, scatter and hide.'

6

The jet touches down on a remote runway on Mexico's Yucatán Peninsula. Dawn has yet to break, the sun seeming reluctant to rise. As the plane comes to a stop, I yawn, stretch and head wearily to the galley. I've fitfully dozed on the flight, my sleep broken by nightmarish visions of Tanas rising from the dead; of Caleb sprawled on the ground, his eyes devoid of the Light; and of Phoenix being ritually sacrificed by Tanas and her High Priests. I find a bottle of water and down it in an attempt to wash away the bitter taste of those toxic memories.

'Kohsoom will be your Soul Warrior,' I hear Goggins say to Santiago as I return to my seat. Galvanized by his plan to scatter and hide Ascendants around the world, our Chief Protector seems to have regained some of his former command as he prepares for the first drop-off on our journey. 'Unless you'd prefer to have Steinar?'

'No, I'm happy with Kohsoom,' replies Santiago, his voice hoarse after a night spent drinking. 'No disrespect to Steinar, but I think Kohsoom will blend in better, and if her fighting skills are anything like my Lena's were, then she'll be more than capable.'

Hearing Lena's name, I now begin to appreciate why Santiago was so hostile yesterday. He was grieving the loss of his Soul Protector in this life.

Goggins nods. 'So be it,' he says. 'Kohsoom, gear up. There are emergency kitbags in the holding bay next to the e-jeep.'

Saluting her chief, Kohsoom disappears through a door at the rear bulkhead, returning moments later with a pre-packed rucksack. Santiago makes his way along the aisle, saying his goodbyes. He kisses Viviana's wrinkled hand, ruffles Tasha's blond hair, smiles encouragingly at Thabisa and Kagiso, and hugs Sun-Hi. When he comes to me, he stops and glares, his eyes rimmed red from lack of sleep and booze.

'I-I'm sorry –' I stutter.

'A little too late for sorry,' he cuts in. Then he lets out a weary sigh, his gruff expression softening slightly. 'I guess I was a bit harsh yesterday. The drink was doing the talking. I will forgive you, Genna, although it might take a few reincarnations – *if* we survive that long.'

'I promise I'll make amends.'

Santiago snorts. Then muttering a grudging goodbye, he pushes past me as the airstairs open out and Goggins lets his new Protector Kohsoom escort him down the steps.

In need of some fresh air myself, I make my way too towards the open door. From her makeshift bed in an overhead locker, Nefe lifts her head and peeps at me curiously. 'Don't worry, Nefe – I'm not going anywhere,' I tell her, scratching behind her ears. With a soft purr, she closes her eyes and settles back to sleep.

Standing at the top of the stairs, I'm greeted by a waft of humidity that does little to clear my head or lift my spirits. The runway is dark and deserted, the tarmac cracked. Tall bushes ring the area, the chain-link fence is rusted and the only building in view is a small, rickety shack overgrown with vines. The whole place appears abandoned.

'We'll lie low for a while,' Santiago is telling Goggins, their figures silhouetted in the pre-dawn gloom. 'Then maybe make the crossing to Cuba via sailboat. I'll feel safer in my home country.'

'Wherever you end up, best of luck,' Goggins replies, shaking hands with Santiago and then Kohsoom and bidding the two of them farewell. 'Remember to stay sharp and stay hidden.'

With a final wave to those in the plane, Santiago and Kohsoom duck through a gap in the fence and disappear into the bushes. I feel a pang of loss edged with concern. They're the first to leave us. They could also be the first to be found by Tanas and her Hunters.

As Goggins reboards the plane, I glance towards the horizon. The mantle of night still hangs heavy across the skyline.

'What time is it?' I ask him, double-checking my watch.

'Seven,' he replies.

I frown. 'Shouldn't the sun be up by now?'

From behind me, Viviana replies, 'That's Tanas's influence, I'm afraid.' I turn to see her peering out of the window in search of the dawn. 'With our Light so diminished, the world is inevitably darkening and the days are getting shorter.'

My skin goosebumps at her words. I remember the *su'mach* dream I had after I was bitten by a snake, that strange vision in which I had a premonition of an endless night. It seems to be coming true already.

'And if we don't all hide from Tanas, there are darker days to come,' Goggins warns grimly. Raising the airstairs, he gives the order to take off.

Once the jet reaches cruising altitude and we're heading to our next destination, the cockpit door opens and Tarek emerges. Having left Zara to fly the plane, he flops into the seat next to me, takes off his square-framed glasses and rubs his eyes. His wiry black hair still glitters with glass fragments from the pyramid explosion, and his polo shirt, torn and flecked with blood, reeks with the acrid stench of the smoke grenade. I'm guessing I don't smell much better either.

'How are you holding up?' I ask, handing him a bottle of water and a blanket. He looks exhausted from flying through the night.

'All right, I guess,' he replies with a stifled yawn. 'How about you?'

I shrug. 'Could be better,' I admit.

Tarek shoots me a guilty look. 'Listen, I'm sorry we couldn't go back for Phoenix, but –'

'I don't blame you,' I interrupt. 'I get why we couldn't. I just wish there'd been another way . . .' I clench a fist as a knot of anger twists in my stomach at the thought again of Tanas sacrificing Phoenix. 'Kohsoom is right when she says we need to cut the head off the snake!'

'Easier said than done,' remarks Goggins wearily. He

turns from the jet's computer console where he's plotting our course and searching for suitable places to land undetected. 'Each time we do, Tanas seems to grow another!'

'But there must be some way to kill Tanas *permanently*,' I insist. 'To destroy her soul.'

'Ah, but you're assuming she has a soul,' says Jude, passing me an energy bar from the plane's emergency ration store.

I unwrap it, not realizing how hungry I am until I take a bite, and chew ferociously. 'She *must* have one in order to reincarnate,' I argue. 'And if Tanas can destroy *our* souls for eternity, then surely we must be able to destroy *hers*?'

Goggins heaves a heavy sigh. 'Well, if there is a way, then we've yet to find it. Believe me, Caleb and I have been trying to figure that out for millennia upon millennia. Of course, Caleb had put all his faith in the Soul Prophecy.' He gives me a woeful look.

The mouthful of cereal bar suddenly seems to swell in my throat and I struggle to swallow it down. 'Can't we . . . simply copy Tanas's ritual and perform it on her?'

Goggins shakes his head. 'Only those who've been sacrificed know the full ritual, and they, of course, are dead. Besides, there seems to be more to eradicating a soul than uttering a few archaic words of dark magic. According to Caleb, in order to destroy something as pure as a soul, there has to be the *evil* intent – a Darkness in one's heart that can consume the Light.'

'Well, I certainly *intend* to kill her,' I declare fiercely as my grief for Phoenix and Caleb hardens into a vengeful resolve.

Goggins raises an eyebrow. 'Yes, but are you inherently evil? I admire your determination, Genna. Nevertheless, you've already tried and failed.' His tone isn't accusatory like Santiago's, merely factual. 'If a Light bomb won't destroy Tanas's soul, then I don't know what will.'

'Tanas is clearly weakened by the Light though,' Tarek points out.

'True,' grunts Goggins. 'However, she now has the means to shield herself from such an attack. We can no longer rely on that as our weapon.'

I angrily crumple the wrapper in my hand, get up and dump it in the bin. Then I turn back to the others. 'Surely Tanas must have *other* weaknesses we can exploit?'

'There's obsidian rock,' says Jude. 'At least, we thought so until you told us that Tanas, having been killed as the priest by Phoenix with an obsidian blade, immediately incarnated back as Agent Lin.'

'Yes, but that priest died inside a pentagram of his own dark magic,' I remind her. 'Caleb thought that was the reason his soul survived and stayed linked to the physical world. Besides, the obsidian blade wasn't the original one that first wounded Tanas and left the splinter in her heart.'

'So where's the original blade?' asks Jude.

I shrug. 'Who knows? Lost to history.'

'Then it is of no help,' says Goggins. He turns back to the computer and resumes his research, the conversation apparently over.

Frustrated by his attitude, I blurt, 'So we simply give up, do we? Like you?'

Goggins turns sharply, the old familiar fire blazing once more in his eyes. 'I haven't given up!' he snaps. 'I just recognize when a battle isn't worth the sacrifice. But maybe, just maybe, we can outrun the Incarnates. So my advice to you, Genna, is to forget revenge and focus on survival.'

7

Eighteen hours later we land at a private airstrip on the east coast of South Korea, where Sun-Hi disembarks with Blake. As soon as we've bid our farewells, and refuelled and recharged the jet's hybrid engines, we take off for our next destination: Siberia. During the flight I remember the backpack at my feet and sort through the meagre belongings I'd managed to salvage from our initial attempt to escape Haven – my passport; the envelope of US dollars that had been meant for our family holiday in Barbados; my mum's credit card; a change of clothes (thank goodness); and stuffed at the very bottom is my old fluffy bunny, Coco. I smile at my sentimental attachment to him. After all that's occurred, I feel I should have outgrown my cuddly toy, but I hug him nonetheless, gaining some comfort from his familiar smell and soft touch.

How I wish for a return to my former life! To be together at home again, watching the latest reality TV show with Mum, or eating Dad's famed brown stew chicken. Clutching Coco closer, I realize I'll never taste his cooking again. And how I desperately wish to be back with my best friends Mei and Prisha too: listening to music, making dance videos or simply chatting into the night. I'm struck by a stab of guilt as I realize I haven't contacted either of them since I fled England, deeming the risk too great. They must be worried sick – or else think I'm dead. *Some friend I am!* I think. What I'd give for my life to be *normal* again, to not have to worry about the fate of humanity . . .

Yet here I am, forced to go into hiding. To spend the rest of my life on the run. All to keep Tanas from extinguishing the Light. Whatever Goggins says, this feels like giving up. We have become the hunted once more. And I no longer have Phoenix by my side to protect me.

I squeeze Coco even harder, fighting back the tears. I feel more lonely than I've felt in centuries.

'You all right?' asks Jude, glancing over at me from the seat opposite.

'Yeah, just tired,' I lie. My relationship with Jude isn't like my connection to Phoenix. I don't feel close enough to share my innermost thoughts with her and my unresolved anger over my Soul Twin's death only adds to the distance between us. Pulling myself together, I set Coco aside and head to the toilet at the back of the plane.

Under the stark fluorescent light, the mirror's reflection comes as a shock. My hair is a mess, knotted and streaked grey with dust and glass fragments. My smooth amber-brown complexion looks strangely washed out, while my eyes are sunken and bloodshot from the after-effects of the smoke. As I examine them closer, I notice their usual starlit gleam has dulled and appears to be a darker midnight blue, which sets me off worrying. Is my soul's Light fading? Turning on the tap, I vigorously wash my face, then brush my tangle of frizzy brown hair and change into my spare clothes. When I take another look in the mirror, I'm relieved to recognize myself once more and am even more glad to see that the gleam has brightened somewhat in my eyes.

I return to my seat, feeling a little fresher and much calmer. I think about Goggins' advice: forget revenge and focus on survival. Maybe he is right. *Realistically, what other choice do we have?*

An hour or so later, we pass over the vast expanse of Lake Baikal before touching down on a bumpy airstrip thirty miles north of the Siberian city of Irkutsk.

'I've chosen this location because it's remote,' Goggins is explaining to Steinar as he lowers the airstairs, 'yet it still offers connections, should you need them, to the rest of the continent via the Trans-Siberian railway.'

'Good thinking,' grunts Steinar, hefting one of the emergency kitbags on to his back.

A large barrel-chested man in an oil-stained shirt and cap is waiting at the bottom of the steps to greet us. He doesn't look like your typical customs and immigration officer. Goggins hands him a large wad of notes, the inflated landing fee that secures our arrival and departure as an unregistered flight at this obscure airfield as well as a full tank of biofuel. A rusting fuel truck immediately pulls up alongside the right wing of the plane.

'Why can't I stay with *you*?' Tasha begs Viviana, reluctant to let go of her hand.

'I am old and slow,' Viviana explains as she hobbles off the plane with the girl to say goodbye down on the runway.

'If the Hunters find us, I'll just be a hindrance to your escape.'

'You won't be!' Tasha says fiercely. 'I'll help you to run.'

Viviana smiles and ruffles her blond hair. 'You needn't worry, *mia bambina*. Goggins will be my legs.'

Tasha throws her arms round Viviana's waist. 'But I've already lost Clara. I don't want to lose you too,' she cries, weeping for the loss of her Soul Protector.

'You have Steinar,' Viviana assures her. 'He is a great warrior.'

The muscular Norwegian lays a gentle hand upon Tasha's heaving shoulders. 'Don't worry, little one. I'll protect you.'

Feeling compelled to ease Tasha's distress, I descend the steps and present her with my fluffy bunny. 'Hey, Tasha. I want you to have Coco,' I say. 'He'll protect you too.'

A tremulous smile briefly appears on Tasha's lips. 'Thank you,' she says, gladly taking the soft toy and hugging me. For a moment, I don't think she'll let go, then she straightens, wipes her eyes and suddenly looks much older than her years. There's a resigned acceptance on her face, an understanding that comes from the hardship of many previous lives. '*Prashai*, Genna,' she says, bidding me a final farewell.

'Don't say goodbye like that,' I chide, recognizing the Russian word and its meaning from my past incarnation as the acrobat Yelena. 'We *will* meet again. If not in this life, then the next.'

Tasha gives me a look, both of us knowing that the chances of that are highly unlikely.

Leaving her in Steinar's care, we reboard the plane, which is now refuelled and ready to fly. As the jet accelerates down the potholed runway, I peer out of the window and spot Tasha waving with Coco clutched in her hand. I wave back until she disappears out of sight. Viviana sits behind me, weeping silently.

'It's for the best,' I hear Thabisa say kindly. 'We must spread ourselves out like seeds, so one of us can always survive and grow.'

Once back at cruising altitude, Tarek takes his turn at the controls while Zara catches up on some sleep. Goggins returns to the computer console, and Jude doodles distractedly in a notebook she's found. In the row behind, Thabisa cradles Kagiso, who softly gurgles in her arms. Next to her, Viviana is praying silently to herself. Everyone is in their own little world. Taking my cue from Zara, I recline my seat for the long journey to Zimbabwe. Above my head on the luggage rack, Nefe gives her paw a lazy lick before settling down for yet another nap. Lulled by the soft scratch of Jude's pencil on paper, my eyelids grow heavy and I soon drift off to sleep . . .

The scratch of the quill on parchment is loud to my ears in the heavy silence of the monastery's scriptorium. The meticulous care with which Father Benedict writes is apparent in the unusual and varying scripts that he employs, scripts of which I cannot make head nor tail.

'That doesn't look like Latin,' I whisper, venturing to break our monastic silence.

'No, it is not, Brother Wilfrid,' he replies softly, his breath misting in the chilled winter air. 'For I don't want

anyone, besides you and me, deciphering this particular manuscript.' Dipping his quill in the ink, he continues to write, yet again changing the style of the letters he forms. 'I'm recording here the locations of all the Soul Jars I can recall. These Soul Jars are the key to your survival. If I'm ever not around, seek them out. Just remember: they're not always jars – they could be wooden boxes, glass bottles, leather tubes or even the item itself. It's a matter of whatever was best to preserve and conceal them through time.'

'And what do these "jars" contain?' I ask.

'Objects that might be useful to you in this or another life. Protective charms, for example, or gold or even a weapon.'

My eyes widen in alarm and I make the sign of the cross. 'A weapon?' I question, knowing that our Order condemns violence of any sort.

'Yes, yes,' says Father Benedict, waving away my concern with the tip of his quill. 'But more importantly,' he goes on, 'some of these jars contain clues that I've gathered over the centuries with a view to destroying Tanas's soul for good. These clues, like tesserae in a mosaic, mean little on their own, but together they may form, God willing, a complete picture . . . one day.'

The candle on his desk flickers as a cold draught of air passes through the room, making me shudder. Our shadows shift on the bare stone wall seemingly with a ghostly life of their own.

'What do you mean, "not around"?' I ask, his earlier statement only now sinking in and filling me with foreboding. 'You're not intending to leave my side, are you?'

Father Benedict gently shakes his balding head. 'Not as long as there is blood in my veins, but I cannot promise –'

All of a sudden the peace of the monastery is broken by the loud bang of a door and a panicked shout. 'The Inquisition is here!'

I stare at Father Benedict in horror. 'What would the Inquisition want with our Order? We're not heretics.'

Father Benedict gives me the grimmest of looks as the bitter tang of woodsmoke seeps into the room. 'They want you,' he says starkly. 'For I daresay they're not Inquisitors, but rather Incarnates. Come – we must go.'

Hurriedly rolling up the unfinished manuscript, Father Benedict stuffs the parchment into a pot, plugs the top and seals it with wax before handing me the precious Soul Jar.

'Another piece of the puzzle,' he says with great import. 'Keep it safe, keep it secret. I'll show you the key to deciphering the scripts once we're safely out of here. Now, follow me.'

We emerge from the scriptorium to discover the monastery is ablaze. Everywhere we turn there is fire. Amid the smoke and flames, hooded figures cloaked in black habits stalk the cloisters, slaughtering our fellow brethren like lambs. As one of these devils rushes towards us with a gleaming blade, Father Benedict shows fighting skills that are remarkable and unexpected for an old monk. Dodging the lethal blade, he grabs hold of the attacker, spins him round, breaks his arm, then slams the man's head into the wall. But another black-hooded monk seizes Father Benedict from behind.

'GO!' he shouts to me as the Incarnate thrusts a blade through his chest.

I turn and run. But in my panic I trip over a loose flagstone, dropping the Soul Jar. It smashes and the parchment rolls out and into the spreading fire. I watch in horror as the manuscript begins to curl and blacken at the edges. 'No!' I cry, reaching desperately for it.

I scream as the flames envelop me too –

I wake with a start, my heart palpitating, my skin prickling painfully as if on fire. Then the sensation fades. I know I should feel unsettled by the traumatic vision, but I don't. Instead I feel a spark of hope ignite within me.

8

'The clues are in the past!' I exclaim, sitting bolt upright.

Jude glances over at me from her notebook, several pages of which she has now filled with intricate doodles and small detailed portraits of numerous faces. 'What *are* you talking about?'

'Father Benedict – he was collecting them,' I explain excitedly. 'Storing them in his Soul Jars.'

'Storing what?' asks Jude, setting aside her notebook.

'Tanas's weaknesses.'

Thabisa leans forward. 'Who's Father Benedict?'

'A Soul Seer – or at least I think he was.' I jump up and approach Goggins, who's half asleep at the console. 'I have to go back home, to London,' I announce.

Goggins squints at me. 'That's not a good idea. That'll be the first place Hunters will look for you.' He nods at the computer console on which a world map is displayed, our plane appearing as a tiny blue dot moving over Somalia. 'I'm planning on taking you to New Zealand. You and Jude can blend in with the backpacker crowd.'

'No, I need to go to London,' I insist. 'I believe there may be an important parchment in my bedroom, one from a Soul Jar.'

The Glimmer has triggered my memory of the jar Phoenix retrieved from Arundel Castle. Inside was a leather pouch which contained an obsidian blade, a Guardian Stone that proved vital in protecting me from Tanas's ritual in the crypt and . . . a sheet of parchment.

Goggins eyes me dubiously. 'What's so special about this document?'

'It lists the locations of various Soul Jars, and these may hold vital clues to destroying Tanas's soul.' I recount to him my Glimmer as Wilfrid, a Germanic monk in the fourteenth century, and what Father Benedict had said. The others on the plane listen in too.

Once I've finished, Goggins sits up straighter. 'I've already told you that Caleb and I have spent millennia trying to figure out how to destroy Tanas, so do understand, won't you, if I'm not entirely convinced by your claim. What does this parchment say *exactly*?'

'The information was encoded in various scripts,' I admit, 'and the Glimmer ended before Father Benedict gave me the key. Phoenix and I were going to ask the Soul Seer Gabriel to decipher it. Obviously, that didn't happen once we discovered he was dead.'

'And what makes you think it's the same parchment?' questions Jude. 'Didn't you just say you were caught in a fire?'

'Yes . . . I did,' I reply hesitantly, my excitement dampened by doubt. 'But in the Glimmer I only saw the parchment *begin* to burn. So it could have survived the monastery fire. I don't know yet how it got into the Soul Jar in Arundel, but, from what I recall, the parchment I have at home *is* charred at the edges. Call it a hunch, but I have to go to London and retrieve it.'

For a moment, Goggins appears to consider my request, then he shakes his bald head. 'You cannot risk your Light for something that may or may not be part of a cryptic treasure hunt for lost Soul Jars. You need to stick to the plan. After dropping off Thabisa and Kagiso, we'll head to New Zealand where Jude will keep you safe and out of sight, then –'

'No,' I say firmly. 'I'm *not* going to spend this life running and hiding.'

Goggins slams his fist on the console. 'You *don't* have a choice!' he shouts. 'Tanas and her Hunters will be scouring the earth looking for you. Your best chance of survival is to stay hidden.'

'Goggins, you're beginning to sound like Caleb!' I cry in exasperation, recalling the argument between the Chief Protector and the Soul Seer in Haven's Japanese Tea Room. 'I remember when you told him that we cannot hide forever, that it's only a matter of time before one of Tanas's Watchers finds us. Back then, it was *you* who wanted to take the fight to Tanas. What's happened to you? Have you lost your guts?'

Goggins' neck muscles tighten. He glares at me and for a moment I think he might pulverize me where I stand. Then his mighty shoulders slump. 'We took the fight to Tanas . . . and we lost.'

'That may be so, but I'm not willing to play hide-and-seek, just waiting for her Hunters to find me! Ever since I glimmered the ritual death of my Soul Twin Tishala, I vowed that I'd do whatever it takes to stop Tanas. Now that she's sacrificed Phoenix, I'm doubling down on my mission.'

'Your mission is futile,' mutters Goggins.

I narrow my eyes at the previously fearless Chief Protector. 'No battle is futile.'

He looks sharply up at me, recognizing his own words.

Then he sighs. 'Jeez, you're stubborn!'

'And you can be too, my dear Goggins,' says Viviana softly. 'It's exactly that quality that has kept you fighting all these millennia. Your dogged determination not to be beaten by Tanas.'

Goggins' eyes redden. 'But we *have* been beaten, Viviana. Tanas has taken both my Soul Sons,' he says, his voice brittle. 'I'd calloused myself against losing Phoenix. That's why I was so tough on him. Now . . . now the thing I feared most of all has happened. We cannot hope to win this war against Tanas –' He heaves a great sob.

Viviana wraps the mighty warrior in her frail arms. Only now do I appreciate how great a toll Phoenix's death has taken on our Chief Protector.

'As Empote was fond of reminding us,' says Viviana, 'hope is the only thing stronger than fear. Come now,' she says, gently patting his broad back. 'Do not lose heart, Goggins. If you can no longer carry the burden, that's fine, but allow someone else to. Give hope a fighting chance.'

After a moment's pause, Goggins nods and composes himself. He turns to me, his expression stern, his armour back on. 'I admire your do-or-die determination, Genna.

I also understand your need to avenge the deaths of your First Sister and Phoenix. The loss of my first Soul Son, Jabali, was the motivator that fuelled me. But now my sole priority must be to protect Viviana. So while I don't approve of your quest, I won't stand in your way.'

I blink, surprised. 'So you'll drop me off in London?'

'I'll do better than that,' he replies. 'Once Thabisa and Kagiso are in Zimbabwe, and I've got Viviana safely to Italy, you can take the plane.'

For a moment I stare, unable to fully comprehend his offer. '*Really?*'

He nods. 'If you're to head off on some wild goose chase around the world, then you'll need transportation.' He gives me a half-cocked grin. 'Of course, you'll also need someone to pilot the jet.'

I immediately turn to Jude. 'Don't look at me,' she says. 'I may be able to drive a car, but a jet plane is a little beyond my skill set.'

After Jude, I try Tarek. I knock on the cockpit door, hoping that once I've explained my plan to him he'll join me on my mission.

'Genna, I'd love to help you out, but –' he peers over my shoulder at Thabisa and Kagiso – 'my duty is to protect them.'

'Oh ... of course,' I reply. I'm beginning to feel that Goggins may have boxed me into a corner by offering me a plane but no pilot. 'I wouldn't want –'

'No! This is more important,' interrupts Thabisa, standing up with Kagiso in her arms. 'Tarek, you have my blessing to go with Genna.'

Tarek glances uncertainly between me and Thabisa. 'But who'll protect you and Kagiso?' he asks.

'I will,' Zara volunteers. She strides up to Thabisa's side and affectionately pinches Kagiso's cheek. The baby gurgles and gives the Brazilian Warrior a big grin.

Goggins rolls his eyes at this affection. 'Well, I guess that settles it. Kagiso seems happy with the switch. Zara will protect Thabisa and Kagiso; Tarek will join Jude in protecting Genna.'

'And Genna will be protecting us *all* if she succeeds in her mission,' declares Viviana.

Once again, I feel the impossible weight of responsibility on my shoulders. 'Viviana, I'm not the one foretold in the Soul Prophecy,' I remind her gently.

'Soul Prophecy or not, I have faith in you,' she replies with a warm, reassuring smile.

'Me too,' says Thabisa, stepping forward with Kagiso. 'Genna, you *have* to try –' she glances lovingly at her son cradled in her arms – 'for Kagiso's sake and for the sake of all humanity.'

9

I stand outside my home. A red-brick terraced house with gravel driveway and large back garden on a tree-lined residential road just off Clapham Common.

Home. At least, it used to be.

Now, dark and deserted, strips of yellow police tape still cordoning off the driveway and front door, the house appears more like a tomb under the cold light of the nearby street lamp. As I peer at it from shadows under the trees, the windows stare back at me with the blank, dead-eyed look of a skull. There's a mournful air hanging over the whole place.

All of a sudden I'm reluctant to enter. Scared of what I might find, or not find, inside. The last time I was here, I was confronted by the mutilated bodies of my mum and dad. My eyes prick with tears, and I feel the familiar yet unwelcome grip of grief. That was before the shock arrival of Detective Inspector Shaw forced me to flee. My skin crawls at the very thought of that devious, black-eyed Soul Hunter. For a long unsettling moment I wonder if she might have laid a trap . . .

'So, now that we've come all this way, are we going in?'

asks Jude, tapping her foot. Her gaze sweeps the street as she keeps an eye out for Watchers or Hunters. Like Goggins, she too was against coming to London, but since she is now my assigned Warrior she was given little choice in the matter.

'I don't like it,' mutters Tarek, who hangs back with me under cover of the trees. 'The street seems unusually quiet.' He fidgets with a tactical torch he took from the jet, its metal-edged 'strike ring' glinting in the darkness. 'Can't we enter via the back garden, so no one sees us?'

I shake my head. 'We'd have to cross several other gardens to get there. Besides, the spare key is hidden at the front.'

The rumble of a car engine alerts us to an approaching vehicle, and we retreat further behind the tree. As the car passes by, its headlights briefly illuminate my house like the sweep of a prison searchlight.

'Listen,' says Jude once the car is gone. 'Any trouble and we head straight to the jeep. From there, to the jet.' She nods towards the e-jeep she's left parked further down the road.

After landing at a private airstrip outside London, we'd taken the electric vehicle from the jet's rear cargo hold, along with torches, a laptop and other essential equipment for our mission. My thoughts turn briefly to Nefe still cooped up on board. When she started mewing plaintively, I gave her some tinned tuna to satisfy her until our return. But aside from my cat, no one is left now on the plane. Zara, Thabisa and Kagiso are in Zimbabwe, having been deposited near Victoria Falls, while Goggins and Viviana disembarked at a provincial airport outside Rome. Goggins' last words to me were, 'The sparrow should never land where the tiger roams. Be careful, Genna!'

I check the road is clear. Feeling like we're about to enter tiger territory, I adjust the straps of my backpack and build up my courage to enter the house. Our mission is simple: we enter, find the parchment and leave. And yet I hesitate.

No one knows we're here, I tell myself. Tarek hacked into the air terminal's computer system and altered the records of our flight to cover up our arrival. The jet, he says, has a stealth mode to prevent anyone tracking us by radar. What's more, it's been almost two weeks since I fled from here. Tanas and her Hunters may well be looking for me, but after such time the local police will surely have moved on to other more pressing matters.

Convincing myself the house is empty and no one is watching, I lead the way across the road. We duck under the police tape and cross the driveway, our feet crunching lightly in the gravel. Beside a rocky flowerbed, I bend down and grope around in the darkness until I find the fake stone containing the spare front-door key. With an ache in my heart, I remember the first time this phoney rock was placed here. 'In case of an emergency,' Dad had said. I never imagined I'd be using it to break into my own house.

Brushing aside the strands of police tape, I insert the key into the lock. With a soft click, the door swings open and we step inside.

There's a graveyard silence. The air is musty, tainted with the lingering acrid whiff of bleach, as well as the smell of decay. From the light spilling in from the street lamp, I spot a pile of unopened post on the window sill and a vase of dead flowers that have shed all their petals on to the carpet. At the end of the darkened hallway, the kitchen lies deep in shadow. Although the tiled floor has been polished clean, a dark stain is still visible.

'Is that where . . .?' begins Tarek in a low whisper.

I nod, swallowing hard on the grief-stricken sob threatening to burst from my throat. My parents' bodies may no longer be sprawled across the tiles, but I can still see them in my mind's eye. My mother half-hidden behind the kitchen door; my dad's hand outstretched towards her, both of them lying in a pool of their own blood . . .

I shudder at the gruesome image.

Jude, turning from shutting the door behind us, notices. 'Everything OK?' she asks.

I nod and force myself onwards down the hallway, past the family portrait with my parents' smiling faces appearing ghostly in the gloom. A sadness settles itself upon me like a heavy winter coat and I'm struck by a strange yet poignant thought: *I didn't even go to their funeral.*

A bitter tear runs down my cheek. Then I remind myself of what Phoenix told me: that my parents, although dead, would likely reincarnate and that there was every chance I'd meet them again in a future life. Wiping away the tear, I hold on to this comforting thought as I turn and head up the stairs.

Jude and Tarek follow close behind. I cross the landing and enter my room. The window that I'd once jumped out of to escape DI Shaw is closed, but the curtains are half open, letting in a shaft of pale moonlight. Gazing around,

I'm struck by how normal everything appears. Nothing has changed since that day I fled: my clothes are still scattered everywhere; my geography homework lies open and unfinished on my desk; my suitcase remains partly packed for the holiday that never happened. I glance curiously at my posters of the five band members of the Rushes . . . at the corkboard with various postcards from past family holidays . . . at my bookcase lined with historical novels, their titles now like signposts to my past. On the top shelf, taking pride of place, is my gold gymnastics trophy and beside it a framed photo of me with my parents on the day I won. Realizing this might be the last time I'm ever here in my family home, I take down the photo. There's me, dressed in my purple leotard, my hair tied back. I'm beaming a smile so wide it threatens to outshine the trophy. Yet I feel strangely detached from the memory – and all the other items in the room. The life I had here already seems like a past life to me.

'OK, this isn't just a trip down memory lane!' mutters Jude, pushing past me. 'We've already taken far too long. Let's get this parchment and go.'

I shoot her an irritable look as I slide the photo out of its frame and slip it into my back pocket. 'You can't order me around, Jude. You're not my Protector.'

'I am, now that Phoenix is gone,' she replies, twitching the curtain to peek out over the back garden.

Her words sting. 'Well, I wish you weren't,' I mumble, the words coming out of my mouth before I realize what I'm saying.

Jude slowly turns to me. 'Sorry, what was that?'

I feel the heat of her aggrieved glare in the darkness. Tarek stands by the door, motionless, sensing the sudden change in mood. 'I didn't mean it like that,' I backtrack. Hoping to move on quickly, I turn to my dresser, shrug off my backpack and busy myself with gathering some underwear and a fresh set of clothes.

But Jude doesn't let the comment drop. 'Then what *did* you mean, exactly?' she demands.

'Nothing,' I mumble. I head over to the corkboard above my bed to find the parchment. It's only thanks to my mum that I still have it. She'd rescued the artefact from my jeans pocket prior to a wash and, thinking it was an old scrap of paper and part of my history homework, she'd left it on my desk. I'd pinned the parchment to the corkboard as a keepsake from my time with Phoenix, then forgotten all about it until my Glimmer as Brother Wilfrid. I run my fingers over the layers of postcards, photos and magazine extracts attached to the board. When I come across the invite to Mei's parents' archaeology exhibition I pause for a moment, taking in the date and location, and peering at the photo of the various rare artefacts. That's where the nightmare all started for me, where I first laid eyes on the Guatemalan sacrificial jade knife – and where I first encountered the Soul Hunter Damien. I shudder at the memory and quickly move on in my search for the parchment.

'Don't think I'm not upset myself that Phoenix is gone,' says Jude tetchily. 'He was my First Brother. I feel his loss too.'

Unable to stop myself, I reply cuttingly, 'Then you'll understand how I feel about the loss of my Soul Twin.'

The atmosphere in the room seems to drop a further degree or two.

There, I've said it. The matter of my Soul Twin's death. The unspoken tragedy that has been lodged in my heart like a poisoned thorn, burying itself deeper ever since I'd learned that Jude had been her Protector.

Jude gasps. 'You know about that?' she whispers, her voice losing all its strength.

I glare at her over my shoulder. 'Phoenix told me. So forgive me if I can't have full confidence in your abilities as my Protector.'

10

'Genna . . .' Jude begins, 'this isn't really the time or place to discuss your Soul Twin's death.'

I round on her sharply. 'Then when is?'

For several long seconds, the silence in the room is so heavy that it's as if the world is on mute. I turn my back on Jude and resume my search, my grief and anger making my hands shake. The Glimmer of my twin's death all those millennia ago is seared into my soul. If I close my eyes, I can see Aya's futile struggle as she's pinned down on the marble altar. Tanas, in his incarnation as the bearded Saragon, looms over her, his golden headband gleaming in the flickering glow of the oil lamps and his white robes splattered with the blood of his previous victims. In my ears echo the bloodcurdling chants of his Incarnate followers as they kneel before their master in the vast palace chamber. I can recall my failed attempt to kill Tanas with the guard's copper-tipped spear and Aya's ear-piercing scream as Tanas's gold dagger plunges into her chest. I can still feel the excruciating wrench of our co-joined souls being torn apart; I relive the agony of witnessing my twin sister being not only killed but destroyed for eternity . . . No Soul Protector came to her rescue.

Jude swallows hard under the ferocity of my gaze. Eventually she replies, 'OK, there were circumstances beyond my control. A sandstorm had delayed my journey across the desert . . . then I couldn't find a way to get past the guards at the palace gates in time to save her.'

I lean back against my desk and study Jude's face in the half-light. Her expression is oddly strained, as though she's holding something back. 'If it were simply a case of being delayed, why would your Soul Father Goggins be so furious that he disowned you? There *has* to be more to it than that.'

Jude glances out of the window as a bat flits past, its silhouette crossing the pale crescent moon hanging in the starless sky. Continuing to avoid my glare, she replies unconvincingly, 'There were a lot of guards . . .'

'Is that so? Then how come Bashaa and I managed to escape through the palace gates?' I ask through clenched teeth. 'Oh yes, I remember – my fellow slaves had already killed the guards. You can see why I don't believe you, can't you? So tell me what *really* happened.'

Jude becomes as still as a statue, almost as if time has frozen.

Outside, a dog barks in one of the neighbour's gardens.

Tarek clears his throat. He remains at the threshold to my bedroom. 'Er, shouldn't we save this chat for the plane? I mean, we have a mission to complete and there are Soul Hunters looking for us.'

Jude bows her head. 'No, we've started, so we might as

well finish this . . .' Her stony expression cracks and her shoulders slump. 'I'm sorry, Genna . . . I truly am. I thought a half truth would be better than the whole truth. For both our sakes.' She looks over at me, her eyes now glassy. There's a vulnerability deep inside her that I've never witnessed before. 'I-I was scared. There, I admit it. Terrified by the power Tanas held over the fate of our souls. The thought of being obliterated, for eternity, filled me with dread. And I certainly didn't want to end up like Jabali.'

I can't quite interpret the look on her face. All I know from Phoenix is that Jabali, their First Brother, was killed by Tanas's hand, and his death had a huge effect on their Soul Father, Goggins.

'So, you want the truth,' Jude goes on, looking me in the eye. 'I *was* delayed by a sandstorm. I *did* have trouble getting past the guards, at least to begin with. Then, using a disguise, I managed to get inside the Lugal's palace. But – but when I found myself face to face with Tanas's High Priests and heard the screams of his tortured victims, my courage deserted me . . . and I fled.' She wrings her hands. 'Genna –'

But her confession has only angered me more. A Soul Protector is supposed to be brave, is supposed to be fearless – willing to give up their life if necessary to save their First Ascendant. Yet I hold my tongue as she continues with her story.

'That's why Phoenix no longer respected me, and my Soul Father disowned me. Rightly so. The truth is, I was a coward. I hid for the rest of that wretched life, carrying my shame to the grave. I can make all the excuses in the world – that I was too late to save Aya, whatever I did . . . that I was barely into manhood and didn't possess the strength to rescue her . . . that I'd not yet recalled any fighting skills from my previous lives to aid me –'

'So *that's* why you were so addicted to the Glimmer Dome,' remarks Tarek.

Jude nods. 'I was never going to allow myself to be under-skilled again. Believe me, Genna, as angry as you are with me, I'm furious with myself. There isn't a life that I don't wish I'd been someone else in that incarnation; someone more competent, more able, more *brave*. But I can't rewrite the past. I can't change who I was then – only who I am now.'

I glare at her. 'Too late for Aya though, isn't it?'

Jude stiffens. 'Look, I don't blame you for feeling how you do. However, since Aya's death I've done all I can to make up for my failure. In this life alone I've saved you four times over. How many more times must I prove myself for you to forgive me? Or for Goggins to accept me again? I know he grieves for Phoenix and Jabali, but he barely acknowledges *me* even though I'm still here, still fighting!' Tears well in Jude's eyes.

I've never seen her cry before, never seen her tough exterior crack.

'Jude . . . I appreciate what you've done for me, I really do,' I say, compassion dulling the edge of my fury. 'But whatever you do won't bring Aya back. I'll feel my twin's loss forever in my soul. You can't even begin to understand the magnitude of my grief – a grief that spans lifetimes.'

'How can you say that?' cries Jude. 'I truly loved your

sister and it breaks my heart every lifetime I recall her death and relive the guilt of my failure! It's like a millstone round my neck.'

'And so it should be!' I shoot back. 'Your cowardice killed her.'

Jude's eyes meet my stare in defiance, her fists clenched as if she's about to launch herself at me. 'Well, what about Phoenix?' she retorts. 'It's your fault he's dead!'

I blink. 'How so?'

'If you'd simply boarded the plane – as I'd told you to – and not gone back for your precious cat, he might be alive now,' Jude replies fiercely.

'What?' I'm stunned and my first reaction is to slap her. But I hold back, battling with my emotions, wondering if there's any truth in her accusation.

Tarek steps between us. 'Jude, that isn't fair. Phoenix was ordered to open the hangar doors; he would've been the last to board whether Genna went back for Nefe or not. And, Genna, you need to give Jude some slack. Most Soul Protectors are faced with her predicament in one life or another. Remember what I told you when I first met you: I failed to protect my First Ascendant, too.'

'You didn't run away though,' I reply, still smarting from Jude's hurtful comment. 'You had your leg blown off while trying to save your Ascendant. You've nothing to feel guilty about.'

'Maybe. Maybe not,' he replies. He pushes his glasses up his nose and appears to blink away the painful past memory. 'But since Soul Protectors are bonded to our Ascendants, we experience a similar soul separation to yours, Genna. Perhaps not as intense, because of the special link you had to your Soul Twin, but devastating nonetheless. And like you, it takes many incarnations to come to terms with our loss and failure of duty . . . if we ever do.'

I'm reminded of the loss I feel of Phoenix and wonder if I'll ever get over his death. I nod solemnly. 'Thanks, Tarek. Jude, I take back what I said. I guess my grief has blinded me to your own suffering,' I admit. 'I just find it so hard knowing that Aya *could* have been saved, if only you'd been there –'

'I said I'm sorry,' Jude replies tersely. She looks at me aggrieved.

I realize that she's yearning for forgiveness. That she's waited centuries for a reprieve. *Is that too much to ask?* I think back to the fear I felt when first running away from Damien and his Hunters. I think of my inadvertent mistake in leading the Incarnates to Haven. Of my failure to be the one foretold in the Soul Prophecy. Like Jude, I vowed to make up for those mistakes, with the same hope of being forgiven. Surely it would be hypocritical of me now not to offer my forgiveness to her?

Yet I can't. The pain is simply too great. Aya's death is seared into my very soul as if part of me died along with her.

'We should get back to the task at hand,' I mutter, and turn to the corkboard.

'Genna,' implores Jude, 'there's something else you should know . . .'

But I'm no longer listening, my hand frozen in mid-search.

'The parchment,' I say. 'It isn't here!'

11

I run my fingers over the board again, pulling off the patchwork of postcards, photos and magazine cut-outs. 'It's not where I left it!'

My search becomes ever more frantic and Tarek offers his torch. Flicking it on, I pass the bright beam over the board, then across my desk, rifling through the mess. I get on my hands and knees and look under the desk. *Nothing!*

'Could someone have taken it?' asks Tarek.

'No, why would they? I mean, who'd know what the parchment meant in the first place?' Then it dawns on me and I slump down against my desk – 'Oh, of course. DI Shaw . . . She must have searched the house after I fled. If she recognized the parchment's importance, she'll have kept it for Tanas!'

'So that's it. Mission over,' says Jude bluntly.

I stare at the carpet, the torch beam lighting a tunnel under my bed and revealing a stack of dusty school books, a lost sock, a pair of roller skates and other discarded toys. That's when I spot a fold of something old and yellowed lodged in the far corner. Scrambling under the bed, I reach with my fingertips and gently tug it free.

'I think I've found it!' I cry, waving the parchment in the air. I go over to my desk and clear a space by sweeping photos, magazines and my geography homework to the floor. I unfold the crinkled sheet and lay it flat, being careful with its charred edges.

'Well, is it?' asks Tarek breathlessly.

'Is it what?'

'Father Benedict's parchment?'

I nod excitedly. 'Yes, it is. It's somehow survived the fire. No idea how it got into the Soul Jar we found in Arundel, but who cares? This is what we're looking for.' I pass Tarek the torch. 'Hold this, will you?'

Sitting down at my desk, I study the document more closely. The parchment presents me with the same bewildering mix of ancient script and hieroglyphs that Father Benedict inscribed so many centuries ago. I rest my hands on it, feeling its age and familiar rough texture. Then I stare at it hard, willing it to give up its secrets. After several minutes of intense concentration, I lean back in my chair and rub my eyes.

'What's the problem?' asks Tarek.

'I was hoping the parchment would act as a Touchstone,' I explain. 'We need a clue as to how its messages are encoded, so I was trying to get it to trigger another Glimmer. But I'm getting nothing. I still can't make any sense of the writing.'

'So, we've wasted our time,' Jude mutters, skulking by the window. 'Risked ourselves for nothing.'

'Let me have a look,' suggests Tarek. 'There's often a logical key to breaking a code.' Passing me the torch, he takes my place at the desk. 'For example, Julius Caesar used substitution. It's a simple but effective technique. He merely shifted the alphabet three places, so D became A, E became B, and so forth. It makes the message gibberish, but it's relatively easy to break.' Peering through his glasses, he examines the parchment with the eye of a forensic scientist.

'Is that what Father Benedict's done here?' I ask hopefully.

Tarek shakes his head. 'Not by the looks of it, no. He's used a lot of different scripts, so it could be a pigpen cipher.'

'What's that?' I ask.

'It's an encrypting technique where letters are replaced with symbols. The Knights Templar employed the method during the Crusades, and Mary Queen of Scots did something similar in her plot to kill Queen Elizabeth the First –'

'Is this going to take all night?' Jude complains, peeking out of the window. 'It's just that, you know, Genna's house is not exactly the safest place to discuss the history of code-breaking.'

'Give me a little longer,' begs Tarek, holding up a finger. 'I'm close to working it out.'

Impatiently crossing her arms, Jude leans against the wall and keeps an eye on the back garden. I remain beside the desk, holding the torch while Tarek works, his head bowed over the parchment. The circle of light is over-bright in the gloom and after a while my eyes begin to ache. As the throbbing pain builds, I pinch the bridge of my nose and squeeze my eyes shut –

Tanas floats towards me, a vision of beauty turned sour. Her lean face is taut with fury, her smooth skin criss-crossed with claw marks, her thin, delicate lips twisted into a snarl, and her narrow, mesmerizing eyes burning with hate and hellfire. 'Seek Genna out. Hunt her down. Find her for me –'

'Got it!' exclaims Tarek, his eyes sparkling through his glasses. I flinch, my awareness suddenly back in the room. My heart pounds and a sheen of sweat glistens on my brow. *Did I just drift off? What was that? A vision? A nightmare?*

'In the Second World War the Americans used the Navajo language in their military codes –' Tarek stops and looks at me. 'Are you listening?'

I shake my head clear. 'Yeah, yeah, go on,' I reply, putting the unsettling vision down to stress and exhaustion.

'As I was saying, in the Second World War the Americans used the Navajo language in their military codes. It proved unbreakable because at the time relatively few people in the world spoke it. To write this text, Father Benedict needed to use a cipher that would make sense through the centuries yet remain obscure.' Tarek grins at me. 'I don't think this is necessarily encoded in the usual way, Genna. I just think it can only be read by someone who has lived many lives and knows many languages, some of them dead and forgotten.' He beckons me closer. 'Look here – this part is in ancient Arabic, this is in an obscure Latin dialect, and this is in Egyptian . . .'

As I peer over his shoulder, my past life as Princess Tiaa comes rushing back to me and, like a stormy sea becoming calm, the swirl of hieroglyphic symbols at the top of the page begins to make sense.

'You're right!' I cry. I run my finger along the lines, slowly reading out loud:

'Apep, the Eater of Souls, is to be feared.
But fear can be slain.
Seek out the hidden tomb of Hepuhotep,
where his death awaits . . .'

Tarek and I look at one another, perplexed.

'What on earth does that mean?' he says.

I shrug. 'Your guess is as good as mine. Father Benedict must have double-encoded the locations by turning them into riddles.'

'Well, does any of it make sense?' asks Jude.

'Partly. I know Pharaoh Hepuhotep was my father in a previous lifetime . . . and I think Apep is Tanas.'

Tarek nods encouragingly. 'Well, that's a start. So where's your former father's tomb?'

'Egypt, I guess, although where exactly I've no idea. I mean, I can remember from a recent Glimmer my father's pyramid being built –' All of a sudden the image of an ancient stone tablet in a display case flashes into my mind's eye. 'Wait! There was an Egyptian tablet at the archaeology exhibition that Mei's parents organized. The hieroglyphs were gibberish to me at the time, but I'm sure the display panel mentioned Pharaoh Hepuhotep and his pyramid!' I turn eagerly to Jude. 'We need to go to Mei's house, find out if the tablet's there –'

'*Shh!* Cut the light!' Jude hisses, waving at me to be quiet.

I immediately turn off the torch. 'What is it?' I whisper as I hurriedly stow the parchment in the front pocket of my backpack.

Jude beckons us over to the window. A shadowy figure is standing in next door's garden staring fixedly up at my bedroom window.

'Is that a Watcher?' Tarek asks nervously under his breath.

I squint into the shadowy night at the portly figure. 'I think it's just my neighbour, Mr Jenkins . . .'

'Whoever it is,' says Jude darkly, 'it's time we left.'

12

'Why don't we just ring the doorbell?' I suggest as Tarek tries to hack into the Harringtons' alarm system from the jeep. Having swiftly exited my own house, we'd driven straight over to Mei's on the other side of Clapham Common. We don't think anyone followed us. Still, there's always the danger that my neighbour had called the police, and Jude is now even more wary than ever.

'We can't risk alerting anyone,' she explains tersely. She leans over the steering wheel, keeping a lookout for Hunters, but it's been obvious since our argument that she's more uncomfortable in my presence and is avoiding my gaze.

I feel awkward too, aware of the unresolved tension hanging in the air. I'm still hurt by her accusation that I'm responsible for Phoenix's death . . . and worried there may be a grain of truth in it too. *Am I really to blame? Or was Jude just saying that to lash out?* Oh, how I miss having Phoenix by my side, someone whose loyalty was a given. No wonder I have this yearning to see Mei, to talk to her about it.

'Mei's my best friend,' I tell Jude. 'She'll understand. She could help us – tell us where to find the stone tablet.'

'Even more reason why we can't knock,' Jude replies. 'We can't leave a trace, otherwise the Hunters will track us.' She turns to me, her gaze severe. 'And worse: by involving your friend, you could put her in danger.'

I nod, reluctantly accepting her decision. Yet, deep down, I just want to see Mei so I can reconnect with someone I can trust.

'OK, cameras are down, entry codes reset and silent alarm disabled,' announces Tarek from the back seat. The soft glow of his tablet screen blinks out. 'Sorry it took so long, but they've got a seriously high-spec set-up.'

'Not surprising. They must have bumped up their security since Damien's break-in,' I explain. 'Mr and Mrs Harrington are famous archaeologists and keep a lot of relics and artefacts in their house.'

'Well, let's take a tour,' quips Jude, grabbing a torch from the kitbag and clambering out of the jeep.

We join her on the kerb, then cross over to the iron entrance gate. Tarek punches a code into the digital keypad, the gate unlocks and we pass through. The Harringtons' car isn't here, so there's a chance they're not at home. Mei or her brother Lee might be, though. Keeping to the shadows, we skirt the empty driveway and sneak up to the front door. All the lights are off and the curtains are closed. Tarek enters another code into another keypad and there's a soft whirr of locks. Cautiously, Jude pushes open the heavy front door and we creep inside.

I feel odd breaking into Mei's house like this. Uninvited. The entrance hall with its round Moroccan rug, polished wooden floor and wide staircase is all too familiar, yet I feel a complete stranger here. An imposter in my best friend's home.

'Leave the door unlocked in case we need to make a quick escape,' Jude whispers to Tarek. As he sets the keypad to remain open, she glances into each of the blacked-out rooms on either side of the entrance hall. Then she turns to me. 'So where's the stone tablet?'

'In there, I hope.' I point down the hallway to a door at the far end. I've only taken a glimpse into this room on a few occasions, the Harringtons' study-cum-museum being strictly out of bounds on account of the delicate nature of some of the artefacts they've discovered on their digs. I know the room is filled with their most prized treasures. What I don't know is how many pieces are kept in the house and how many are in storage or on loan to museums. I pray that the stone tablet is here on display among their private collection.

We tiptoe down the corridor, keeping to the edges to avoid the floorboards creaking. In the gloom, we pass a glazed cabinet containing a small clay statue of the Buddha, a porcelain vase and a jade ornament of a Chinese dragon.

Jude gazes at them. 'Wow. That vase is Ming dynasty. It must be priceless!' she says, her voice hushed.

'That's just the tip of the iceberg, so to speak,' I reply.

Unfortunately, however, our hopes are thwarted when Jude finds the door to the study locked.

'Old school,' he whispers, pointing to the large brass mortice lock. 'Guess they think the outside security is enough.' He glances at me. 'Do you know where the key is?'

I shake my head.

'Well, we can't break the door down,' says Jude under her breath. 'We'd wake everyone up.'

I examine the lock with the trained eye of one of my former incarnations, the Chinese cat-burglar Lihua. 'We might not need a key,' I say.

Retracing my steps to the display cabinet, I slide open one of its drawers, quickly search among the clutter of stationery items and find what I'm looking for: two large paperclips. I straighten one and bend the other into an L-shape. Then, returning to the others, I pick the lock with practised ease, listening for the soft *click* of each cylinder pin disengaging.

'Ta-da!' I whisper, swinging the door open.

Almost instantly, I grimace as the brass hinges squeak loudly. Jude and Tarek both wince too and we stand frozen in the hallway's darkness, listening hard, praying the noise hasn't woken anyone upstairs. A full minute goes by. Nothing stirs in the house. Breathing a silent sigh of relief, we step through to the study and ever so gently close the door behind us.

Jude flicks on her torch to reveal a large room the size of a small private library. It looks like one too, with its wood-panelled walls and a grand fireplace complete with Georgian mantelpiece. A solid mahogany desk holds court at the far end, wooden display cabinets line the walls down either side, while in the centre there's a long table covered with a crisp white cloth. An ancient broadsword is laid out on the white cloth like a preserved body partway through a forensic examination.

'Wow!' gasps Jude as the bright beam of her torch

sweeps over the display cases, their shelves glinting with countless artefacts brought back from all four corners of the globe. 'This is like a personal Glimmer Dome!'

I'm equally stunned by this Aladdin's cave of treasures. It's even more impressive than I remember. Upon the walls hangs art from across the ages: a Chinese silk scroll showing a pair of cranes in flight; an English tapestry of a boar hunt; an Italian oil painting of the Last Supper; and what appears to be an old treasure map with a drawing of a volcano. Above the fireplace, somewhat out of keeping with the rest of the artworks, is a modern portrait of Mr and Mrs Harrington with Mei and her older brother Lee. Her brother resembles their English father, broad-shouldered, square-jawed and tall, while Mei exhibits more of her mother's Chinese heritage in her arrow-straight black hair, svelte figure and high cheekbones.

Tarek switches on his torch and peers curiously into a display case. 'I remember using one of these . . .' he murmurs, pointing to a round brass disc with an intricate design of cogs and wheels. 'It's an astrolabe.'

While Tarek examines the ancient astronomical instrument, Jude becomes transfixed by a bronze shield in the corner of the room. She goes over and picks it up. Instantly, her body jerks slightly and her eyes roll back in her head.

'Are you OK?' I ask, worried she's having a fit.

As Jude comes back to her senses, the corners of her mouth curl into a grin. 'Yeah,' she says. 'Just had an intense Glimmer. Seems I was once an Athenian warrior.' She hefts the shield in her hand, adjusting herself to its weight, and

I'm presented with the embossed face of Medusa, the Greek monster with snakes for hair.

'Cool shield,' remarks Tarek, glancing up. 'I love the legend of Perseus. Clever how he defeated the Gorgon by using the reflection in his polished shield.'

Jude rubs her sleeve on the bronzed front. 'Well, this one could do with a bit of polish.'

I recognize the shield from the Harringtons' private exhibition and become excited. The feeling only grows when I spot a pair of white-handled samurai swords from the same display. Recalling my life as the samurai Miyoko, I get a sudden urge to take hold of them, and it's as I'm making my way over to the weapons that I also catch sight of a blue-and-white Persian vase.

'This vase was at the exhibition, and the shield and these swords too,' I say. 'The tablet must be here somewhere.'

We begin hunting through the various cabinets.

'Over here!' whispers Tarek, uncovering a rectangular object wrapped in a white gauze. The tablet rests on its own display stand next to the mahogany desk. He carefully peels back the protective material to reveal the intricate hieroglyphs etched into the stone.

Tarek focuses the beam of his torch on the tablet. 'Can you read it, Genna?'

'Yes . . . Here it mentions my father's name,' I say, pointing to the relevant symbols. As soon as my finger touches the cool stone –

I lift my gaze to admire the magnificent pyramid rising from the earth up to the crystal-blue sky. Its polished sides of gleaming white sandstone reflect the sun like a monumental mirror and I have to shield my eyes from the glare.

'My shining pyramid will look out over the great city of Shedet for all time,' declares my father with a proud sweep of his gold-bangled arm over the city and fertile landscape that lie beyond the mortuary temple's walls. Leaning heavily upon his golden sceptre, he peers over the shoulder of a scribe who is carefully chipping away at one of the stone columns lining the avenue up to the pyramid entrance. 'Fine work,' my father says softly, as the scribe puts the finishing touches to a protective spell. 'You will be rewarded in the afterlife.'

The scribe bows low, his cheeks flushing with pride at the pharaoh's praise.

My father moves on towards the pyramid's majestic entrance. I follow dutifully at his side, Nefertiti winding herself round my legs.

'Upon my death,' says my father with a reconciled smile, 'I'll be laid to rest within this tomb from where I will continue to protect my people from the heinous Apep and his Soul Eaters.'

'But what if Apep's followers ransack your tomb and desecrate your body?' I ask, recalling the fate of a previous pharaoh.

My father turns to me, his tanned face wrinkled like the dunes of the desert. 'Then they will find nothing.'

I frown, confused. 'Nothing? But I thought you just said –'

'Ah, my precious Tiaa . . .' He taps a finger on the side of his nose, a sly glint in his burning blue eyes. 'Vizier Khafra

has gone to great pains to secure my tomb. Within this pyramid are many tunnels, dead ends, false chambers and traps. Even if Apep himself should reach my sarcophagus, he will be sorely disappointed. For my body will have been placed in a secret chamber hidden beneath.' He winks playfully at me. 'Come, Tiaa, let me show you.' He beckons me to follow as he hobbles down the stone steps leading into the subterranean labyrinth of the pyramid –

'I know where the tomb is!' I gasp, coming out of my Glimmer and turning excitedly to Jude and Tarek.

'Great,' says Jude. 'Then let's take the tablet and go.'

Tarek and I wrap the stone back up in the protective gauze, but when I try to lift it off its stand I struggle. 'It's so heavy! Maybe we should just take a photo or something –'

'Genna! Is that you?'

My heart stops dead, and I almost drop the tablet as the study door creaks open and the main light is flicked on, blinding us.

Framed in the doorway stands a figure in ivory silk pyjamas . . . Mei.

13

'What the hell do you think you're doing?' she demands, her long hair in a black tangle down her back. She wears an expression of surprise mingled with mistrust.

'Erm, nice to see you too, Mei,' I reply, gingerly replacing the stone tablet on its stand. 'I was just needing to . . . to check something on this tablet.'

Her tiger-brown eyes, as piercing as ever, narrow further on noticing Jude and Tarek. 'Who are they? And how did you all get in? Our home is alarmed!'

I put a finger to my lips, then softly reply, 'Mei, please . . . this is Jude and Tarek. We, um, broke in, with Tarek's help. He's a whiz at IT stuff.'

Her jaw drops open in disbelief. 'Why didn't you just ring the bell?'

I glance sidelong at Jude with an I-told-you-so expression.

'We don't have time for catching up like this,' mutters Jude, pocketing her torch and heading for the door. 'Genna, Tarek – let's go.'

'Hold on just a minute!' says Mei, blocking the exit. She points to the bronze shield in Jude's hand. 'You're not going anywhere till you've put that back and explained what you're doing in my parents' private study.'

Seeing Jude bristle at my friend's refusal to move, I hurry over and step between them.

'Sorry we've disturbed you, Mei,' I say gently, ushering her into the room and quietly closing the door behind her. 'I know this sounds a little bizarre but I needed to examine that Egyptian stone tablet over there. It holds the key to the location of Pharaoh Hepuhotep's hidden tomb, and we hope to find a Soul Jar. It could contain a crucial clue to killing Tanas forever.'

Mei stares at me with an incredulous look. 'You're not still wrapped up in all that reincarnation fantasy, are you?'

'It's no fantasy,' I insist. 'Jude and Tarek are Soul Warriors. They're here to protect me.'

Mei now studies Jude and Tarek as if they're crazy too. There's also a flicker of fear in her gaze. 'Oh, Genna . . . what on earth have you got yourself into? I know it must be hard. Your parents' murders must have hit you so, so badly, but you didn't have to go off the rails and turn to crime –'

'We're not stealing anything,' Tarek assures her with a friendly smile.

'Really?' Mei questions sharply, her hostile look wiping the grin from his face. 'Then why is *she* taking the shield that my father found?'

Jude flinches as if offended by the accusation. 'Actually, it's *my* shield,' she replies tartly. 'I can't steal what's rightfully mine, can I?'

'*Your* shield?'

'Yes. I carried this as an Athenian warrior during the Persian Wars.'

Mei rolls her eyes and slowly shakes her head. 'Oh no, not you as well?'

'Mei, you have to believe us,' I plead. 'We're reincarnated souls, and mine is one of the few left that carry the Light of Humanity. Phoenix is dead, and I could be next unless we –'

'Are you listening to yourself, Genna?' She takes hold of my hand. 'What you're saying is *complete* nonsense!' Her grip tightens on me as if she is trying to pull me back to my senses. 'Don't you remember what Dr Larsson told you? These visions are figments of your imagination –'

'Dr Larsson was wrong! I am a First Ascendant –'

'It's as if you've been brainwashed again,' she interrupts. 'I barely recognize you.'

'Mei, I wouldn't lie to you,' I insist. 'We're best friends.'

'Are we?' she retorts, discarding my hand. Her rejection stings. Even though so many things have changed in my life, I did believe my friendship with Mei was the one constant, the one thing I could count on always being there.

Mei glares at me, her eyes ringed red with fury and hurt. 'You ghost me – and Prisha – then turn up in the middle of the night, breaking into my house . . .? And you expect me to believe you're not trying to rob the place? I've been worried sick about you, Genna! The least you could have done was contact me. I thought you were *dead*!'

'I-I'm sorry,' I stutter, her grievances both just and painful to hear. 'But I had to ditch my phone. I've been in real danger – it's true! – and I'm still in danger. In fact, the whole world is in danger unless we can find out how to destroy Tanas forever, and the first clue is in Egypt –'

I hear a loud creak from the entrance hall and I fall silent. Jude tenses by my side and Tarek's eyes widen in alarm.

'Who else is home?' Jude demands.

'My brother,' replies Mei coolly, then adds quickly, 'and my parents.'

I narrow my eyes. 'I didn't see their car in the driveway.'

Mei shrugs. 'OK,' she admits, 'they're both at some archaeological conference or other. But my brother's home.'

I strain my ears, listening to the almost silent pad of at least two sets of footsteps beyond the door. 'I know your brother sleeps like the dead, so who's in the hallway?'

'The police hopefully,' replies Mei with a smug look. 'When I heard the door, I pressed the panic button in my room. That was before I heard your voice and came downstairs.'

Jude curses. 'She's been delaying us!'

The door flies open and DI Shaw strides in. My breath freezes and horror surges through my veins. To all outward appearances, she is the epitome of a professional policewoman. Even at this time of night, she wears a crisp white blouse, a tailored blue jacket and neatly pressed trousers, and her dark hair is wrapped into a tight bun. But her smart, respectable image is no more than a facade, masking her true nature as one of Tanas's sinister Soul Hunters. While it's not apparent to most people, I can see her steel-grey eyes have dilated into oily black holes. She's flanked by two other police officers, one tall and bearded, the other squat like a wrestler. Each has the pooling eyes of an Incarnate.

'Genna!' says DI Shaw, grinning with all the warmth of an alligator. 'I've been very concerned about your whereabouts.'

'I'm sure you have,' I reply sarcastically. With our only escape route blocked, I retreat towards the fireplace with Jude and Tarek.

As the trio of Soul Hunters fan out across the room, DI Shaw sidles up to Mei. 'You did well in alerting us to your friend's return.'

'Mei, get away from them!' I cry.

'Genna, please don't try to flee again,' says Mei, oblivious to the danger she's in. 'You need help, and the police are here to help you.'

'Yes, Genna, listen to your friend,' cajoles DI Shaw, her dark eyes glinting maliciously. 'There's no need to make a scene.'

'Mei – DI Shaw is a Soul Hunter!' I cry.

My friend shakes her head. 'Oh, Genna, you've really lost it, haven't you? I'm not going to make the same mistake as last time. You need to turn yourself in. For your own good.'

'Never!' I yell, as the two officers edge towards us. Turning to the wall, I grab a white-handled katana from a rack, unsheathing it in one swift motion. The hamon on the razor-sharp steel glints like lightning and I feel Miyoko's skill with the curved blade flow through me.

'What the hell are you doing?' cries Mei. She looks on aghast as Jude snatches up a needle-pointed letter opener from the desk, and Tarek brandishes his torch like a club.

The two officers take a step back, but DI Shaw stands her ground. 'There's no need to make this any harder,' she says. 'Drop your weapons.'

'Over my dead soul,' I growl.

A devilish grin slides across her pinched face. 'It'll certainly come to that. But it would be better for all of us if you just cooperate.' She lays a hand on Mei's shoulder, her gesture benign yet the threat implicit. A flash of anger flares within me and my hands tighten round the hilt of my sword. The inspector waits a beat for us to surrender. When we don't, she adds, 'Or perhaps you need a little more persuasion.'

Opening up a display case, the detective inspector takes out a jewelled dagger.

'Hey, be careful with that!' says Mei. 'That's a rare seventeenth-century Turkish kard.'

But DI Shaw seizes my friend by the hair and puts the blade to her throat.

'Do as I say, Genna,' our enemy threatens in a cold, even tone. 'Or your friend dies!'

14

All the air seems to have been sucked out of the room. Ever since I first encountered Damien the year before, I've been attacked, hunted and almost killed by the Incarnates, but this is the first time one of my closest friends in this life has been threatened so directly. A cocktail of guilt, panic and fury grips me. But it's the fury that wins out.

'Let her go!' I demand. 'Mei's not part of this.'

'She is now,' replies DI Shaw, yanking on Mei's head to expose more of her neck. 'You should've have thought about that before coming here. And, while we're on the subject, why *here*? Not just to see your friend, I imagine,' she says, glancing suspiciously round at the numerous artefacts. 'What are you looking for?'

'Stay calm, Mei,' I tell her, ignoring the inspector's question. 'I'll get you out of this, I promise.'

Mei stares at me in wide-eyed panic. Too shocked to struggle, the knife pressed to her jugular, she stands rigid. My instinct is to cut DI Shaw down where she stands, but there's no way I can do that *and* save Mei in time. Surreptitiously, my gaze flickers left and right, towards Tarek and Jude on either side of me. *If we make a concerted attack, do we have a chance?* But the two policemen have now drawn their own weapons, the squat officer extending a wooden baton, the other whipping out a can of CS spray. The odds of rescuing Mei alive are slim at best.

'I won't say it again,' declares DI Shaw. 'Lay down your weapons or your friend dies.'

Tarek appears to be on the point of lowering his torch when, from behind her shield, Jude gives the slightest shake of her head. 'She won't kill her. Mei isn't a First Ascendant or a Protector.'

'Oh, that's where you're wrong,' replies DI Shaw, pressing the dagger's edge harder against Mei's soft skin and drawing a bead of blood. 'You see, Genna, *I* killed your parents, and I'll happily slit your friend's throat too!'

Shaw's admission hits me like a sledgehammer to the gut. I almost lose my grip on the sword as my mind tries to grapple with this new truth: It was DI Shaw, *not* Damien, who murdered my mum and dad!

'B-but why?' I stutter.

She grins. 'So you'd be alone and vulnerable of course.'

'You monster!' I yell, a tornado of rage swirling inside me. 'I won't let you get away with this.'

'Too late. I already have,' says DI Shaw with a callous laugh. 'How convenient that you're already a suspect for your own parents' murder. I can simply kill Mei and make it look like you did it. I'd get away with it again, no problem.'

I lock eyes with Mei, her fear appearing to give way to fury.

'The violent act of a deranged friend with delusions of

past lives,' continues DI Shaw. 'I'm sure I can persuade your counsellor to provide evidence of your fragile state of mind. Case closed. Now, this is your very *last* chance. Drop your weapons or –'

DI Shaw suddenly shrieks in pain as Mei bites down on her hand, forcing the inspector to let go of the dagger. The jewelled kard clatters to the floor. Without hesitation, Mei elbows the detective in the ribs, stamps on her toes and wriggles free from her grip. She dashes over to me, her eyes wild with the first gleam of understanding.

'Has the world gone mad?' she cries.

'You'd think so,' I reply, shielding my best friend behind me. 'As I told you, DI Shaw is not who or what she seems!'

The detective inspector examines the wound to her hand. 'I guess we'll just have to do this the hard way,' she snarls, picking up the broadsword from the central table.

As she advances on us both, the two uniformed officers close in on Jude and Tarek. Hefting the broadsword in her two hands, DI Shaw swings its mighty blade at our heads. There's barely any room to fight amid the display cabinets, artefacts and furniture, and Mei and I are forced to duck. The sword whistles past and smashes into a glass cabinet, sending glinting shards everywhere. She brings down the blade again, this time aiming to cleave us in two. Reacting now with Miyoko's samurai reflexes, I meet the attack with my katana. The blow is brutal and sends a bone-jarring shudder through my arm as iron and steel clash. Yet, I manage to deflect the strike and retaliate with a lightning-quick slash across the inspector's body. The tip of my blade slices through her jacket and blouse as she leaps away at the last second.

'This jacket is Georgio Armani!' she shouts in outrage. She glares at me. 'You'll pay for that!'

On the other side of the room the bearded officer attacks Jude with the CS spray, aiming for her eyes. Jude lifts her shield and the jet of blinding liquid splatters harmlessly over the bronze Medusa. Jude then charges at the officer with her shield, driving him back against the tapestry of the boar hunt. As he hits the wall, Jude plunges the letter opener into his left leg. The officer cries out and collapses to the floor, pulling the heavy tapestry down with him.

Meanwhile, Tarek is frantically bobbing and weaving as the squat officer swings his baton, demolishing a line of display cases in the process. Backed up against the fireplace, Tarek switches his torch to strobe effect and shines it in the officer's face, dazzling the man. He reels away from the glaring flashes and Tarek rams the metal strike ring on the end of the torch into the officer's chest. The officer doubles over, winded. A second strike to the back of the head stuns him and the man drops unconscious in a heap.

'Good torch, this!' remarks Tarek with a grin, flipping it round and round in his hand like a cheerleader's baton.

DI Shaw comes at me once more, the broadsword held high above her head. I grit my teeth, bracing myself for her attack. Steel and iron ring out like broken church bells. She strikes again, the weight of her sword jarring my arm and forcing me to my knees. A third blow knocks the katana from my hand. I watch in horror as it goes skittering under the desk. Left defenceless, I can only shield Mei with my body. As if it's the blade of a guillotine, DI Shaw brings her formidable weapon down for a fourth and final time.

'NO!' shouts Tarek, flicking on his torch and directing the strobe into her wide, black eyes. The blaze blinds her and her swing goes wide. She hits the mahogany desk, the massive iron blade embedding itself deep in the wood.

'Son of a –' mutters DI Shaw, wrenching furiously on the hilt. But the broadsword is stuck fast.

As she puts her foot upon the desk to yank it free, I jump up and roundhouse-kick her hard in the ribs. She crashes against the wooden stand holding the Egyptian tablet and crumples to the floor. The stand wobbles and the tablet topples off, landing with a *crunch* on DI Shaw's head. The stone cracks in half, but it has knocked the inspector out cold.

'*Ouch!*' remarks Tarek, wincing at the impact. 'Talk about a heavy read!'

'That's the least she deserves for murdering my parents.' I snatch the katana from under the desk and storm towards her.

Mei jumps between me and the comatose Soul Hunter. 'Don't do it,' she pleads.

'Out of my way!'

Mei refuses to move. 'You're not a cold-blooded killer, Genna.'

'But *she* is,' I reply, pointing my sword at the Hunter. My hand trembles so much I can barely keep the tip steady. Tears spill from my eyes, hot with grief and vengeance.

Mei holds my furious gaze. 'That doesn't mean you have to be one too.' She lays a hand upon my sword arm.

'Aren't you carrying this so-called Light of Humanity? Doesn't that mean you're supposed to act in the name of *Good*?'

Her words cut through the haze of my bloodlust and I lower the katana, my fury spent. I let the weapon drop to the floor and allow the weight of grief to replace the need for vengeance. I know my parents wouldn't want DI Shaw's blood on my hands.

She looks pretty injured anyway. Justice has been served, at least in some small way.

'Well, if you're not going to do it, then I will,' says Jude, stepping forward to claim the sword.

Mei blocks her as well. 'No! I'm not going to have anyone murdered in my house,' she says, and I can hear the steel in her voice. Her gaze sweeps over the three unconscious bodies and the wrecked room. 'Although I reckon when my parents get back they might just murder *me*.'

'Fine. If we're not going to despatch this Incarnate, then we'd best get out of here,' says Jude, turning towards the door. 'Genna, let's go. There are bound to be more Hunters on their way.'

I go to follow her, then stop at the threshold. 'What about Mei?'

'She can't come, if that's what you're thinking,' replies Jude. 'She'll be a liability.'

'But Mei's now a target too. I'm not going without her.'

Jude throws up her hands in exasperation. '*Grr!* Why do you have to make everything so difficult?' She looks over to Tarek picking his way through the devastation. 'Talk some sense into Genna, will you, T?'

Tarek steps cautiously over the wounded officer he's left moaning under the tapestry. 'Genna has a point. The Incarnates could take Mei as a hostage, just like DI Shaw tried to do just now. Then they'd have a hold over Genna.'

'Look. This isn't some school trip to Egypt, right?' argues Jude. 'What we're doing is *dangerous*. Genna, do you seriously want to put your friend at risk?'

'No, of course I don't. But, as Tarek points out, she's already at risk.'

'I want to come,' interjects Mei. She looks at us with a determined expression. 'Genna, I'm sorry. After what I've just witnessed, I believe you now and I want to help.'

'We don't need your help,' says Jude bluntly.

'I think we need all the help we can get,' I say. 'And it isn't for you to decide anyway. Mei is *my* friend.'

Jude glares at me. 'Fine, have it your way,' she mutters through clenched teeth. Turning on her heel, she strides down the hall. 'I'll bring the jeep up front. But if she isn't ready in five minutes, we're leaving without her.'

Mei dashes upstairs. Five minutes later, she rejoins me in the hall, her pyjamas replaced by jeans, a T-shirt and a green jumper, her passport in one hand and a bulging rucksack on her back. 'You never know what I might need on this little adventure,' she says with a nervous grin as she adjusts the straps.

On hearing the jeep pull into the driveway, we're heading for the front door when a sleepy voice calls down from the landing, 'Hey, sis, where are you off to?'

We glance up. Lee is rubbing his eyes and yawning, a

pair of headphones perched on his head. No wonder he didn't hear the chaos going on downstairs.

'Go back to bed, bro,' says Mei, waving him away. 'I've left a note for Mum and Dad. There's a bit of a mess in the study, so I'd stay out of there if I were you –' An impatient beep from a car horn sounds in the driveway. 'Sorry, got to go. I'm off treasure hunting with Genna. See you soon!'

15

The jet's engines thrum steadily as Tarek pilots the plane on a course south-east towards Egypt. I sit in the front row of the passenger cabin, watching with interest as he checks read-outs, flicks switches and adjusts his flight path. Nefe is curled up in my lap, ecstatic that I've returned. My backpack with the precious parchment is safely stowed in the overhead locker. Beside me is a somewhat shell-shocked Mei, the violent events of the night having finally sunk in. Jude has withdrawn to the back of the plane, the Athenian shield on the seat next to her, her head buried in her notebook as she sketches away.

Jude has been studiously ignoring Mei and me for a while. I'm not sure whether her sour mood is due to her confession regarding my Soul Twin, or our close escape from DI Shaw and her Hunters, or the fact Mei has joined us – or maybe all three. Whatever her reasons, I don't want her attitude to dampen my own elated mood. I was right in my instincts to head home and recover the parchment. With a firm destination in mind and the real possibility of uncovering a clue to help us kill Tanas, I feel for the first time in many months that I'm in control of my destiny. No longer am I blindly running for my life. I have a purpose. A mission. Even perhaps a means to ending this constant fleeing across lifetimes.

'Tell me again – where exactly is this pyramid located?' Tarek calls from the cockpit.

'Outside the city of Shedet,' I reply.

I see him pull up a map on his navigational display. He glances back at me in the cabin and frowns. 'There is no city of Shedet.'

'What?' I sit up straighter in my seat, dislodging Nefe, who gives a disgruntled mew at the disturbance. 'Are you sure?'

'Feel free to look for yourself, but it isn't on the map,' he replies.

I unbuckle my seatbelt and join him in the cockpit. My gaze scans the digital chart of Egypt. 'I'm certain my pharaoh father said Shedet.'

'Maybe you mis-remembered his words?' Tarek suggests. 'Glimmers are like memories. They can be inaccurate sometimes.'

'Or perhaps it no longer exists,' Jude mutters grumpily from the back.

I slump into the co-pilot's seat. 'How are we supposed to find my father's pyramid then?' My mood rapidly deflates. *Have we just risked our lives for nothing?*

'Shedet is the original name of Faiyum, one of Egypt's oldest cities,' Mei pipes up almost casually.

'How do you know *that*?' I ask, looking at her in surprise. I know for a fact my friend pays little attention in history classes.

Mei shrugs. 'I guess some of what my parents talk about round the dinner table sinks in occasionally.'

Tarek types *Faiyum* into the navigational computer and the city immediately pings up on his display. 'ETA about five hours. Best get some rest while you can.'

I grin at him. The mission is on again.

As I make my way back into the cabin, I catch Jude's eye. 'See?' I tell her. 'Mei's already proving helpful.'

Jude gives a noncommittal grunt and returns to her sketching. A purring Nefe winds herself between my legs as I enter the jet's small galley and open a tin of tuna for her. Then I decide to make Mei a cup of mint tea to help calm her nerves after the fight with DI Shaw and the officers.

'How are you doing?' I ask, returning to my seat and handing her the cup.

She nods and gratefully accepts the tea. 'Yeah, just coming to terms with all that's happened. I feel a bit bad for leaving my brother to sort out the mess. And I'm not sure my note will cut it with my parents. I mean, they encourage independence and all that, but running off in the middle of the night might be pushing even their boundaries!' She peers over her tea at me, her eyebrow raised and an impish grin on her lips. 'Still, they know I'm with you.'

'Is that a good thing?' I say. 'Technically, I'm on the run.'

'I explained you called and asked for some help and that, as your best friend, I needed to support you. You know, parents like that sort of stuff.' We share another smile. 'I didn't tell them, though, that it was *you* who'd actually broken into our house.'

'Thanks for covering for me.'

'I'm more worried about what the police might say.'

'There's not much we can do about that,' I reply. 'Anyway, my guess is the panic alarm went straight through to DI Shaw, judging by the speed of her arrival and the fact that no other genuine police officers turned up. I'm not sure anyone's going to believe that they were beaten up by three kids, so I think they'll want to keep this incident quiet. And, more importantly, they won't wish to draw attention to their involvement as Incarnates.'

Mei's smile fades into a guilty look. 'Genna, I'm really sorry I didn't believe you. All that stuff about First Ascendants, reincarnating souls and Soul Hunters . . . it all just seemed a little too wacky.'

'Hey, I didn't believe it myself at first either,' I reply, reaching out and squeezing her hand. 'It took Phoenix a –' I falter at the mere mention of his name, an aching grief making it hard to breathe – 'it took him a great deal to convince me.'

'It's just so *unbelievable*,' says Mei. She sips her tea, then slowly shakes her head. 'I realize DI Shaw's actions back up what you've been saying, but I'm still struggling to comprehend it all.'

'I know, it's a lot to take in,' I agree.

Having finished her food, Nefe leaps back on to my lap and settles down for a post-meal lick and wash. As I gently stroke her, I'm reminded of my first Egyptian Glimmer and the strange moment of connection between myself as Princess Tiaa and the traitor priest Ankhu – the moment I looked deep into his eyes and brought his soul back from the brink with my Light. This gives me an idea. 'Mei? Perhaps I can help you *see* the truth, if you'll allow me?'

'Sure,' she says, setting aside her tea. 'I'm up for anything that make this madness easier to understand.'

Lifting Nefe from my lap, I get up and put her back down on my seat. Then I position myself in front of Mei and lock eyes with her. Guided by instinct, I try to seek out her soul.

Mei frowns. 'Are you trying to hypnotize me?' she asks warily.

'No,' I reply, concentrating harder and staring deeper into her soul. 'I'm trying to connect with you . . .' A full minute goes by, and nothing happens.

Mei shifts uncomfortably under my intense stare. 'Is this telepathy? Cos if it is I don't think it's working.'

I shake my head. 'I'm trying to share my Light with you . . .'

Another minute passes and I'm beginning to think I'm fooling myself as to my powers. Then the faintest wisp of spectral light passes between us. As thin and insubstantial as a thread of spider's web, it's almost too slight to see. But I can distinctly feel the connection between our two souls, a tingle of vibrant energy – and it's evident by her startled expression that Mei feels it too. Seconds tick by. I see her soul grow brighter in her eyes and the bond between us is forged.

'What have you just done?' she gasps, breaking away and looking around the cabin. 'Everything's suddenly so . . . clear. And your eyes – they're bright *blue*, like starlight!' Her brow furrows in confusion. 'But haven't you've always had hazel eyes?'

'Yes, but you can now see my soul in my eyes too,' I explain. 'Having passed a little of my Light to you, I believe I've made you a Soul Sister.' I smile affectionately at her. The idea of Mei being a 'sister', even in this small yet significant way, warms the bitter-cold hollow in my heart left by my Soul Twin's death.

She blinks. 'A what?'

'A Soul Sister. Look at your reflection,' I tell her.

Turning to the window, she peers at herself and does a double take. 'Oh my . . .' Her tiger-brown eyes now softly shimmer with an ethereal light.

'While you're not a First Ascendant like me, or a Soul Warrior like Jude, from now on you're directly connected to the Light of Humanity,' I explain. 'You'll be more aware. *Awake* to what is happening. This means you'll not only recognize other First Ascendants and Protectors . . . but you should be able to spot Incarnates, Hunters and Watchers too.'

Mei nods as true understanding finally settles within her. 'I see – I finally see.' She looks at me with her gently glowing eyes. 'Genna, tell me all that's happened since I last saw you.'

I make Mei another mint tea. As we fly over Europe in the direction of Egypt, I recount to her my escape to Los Angeles and my initial fruitless search for Phoenix. Then I tell her about my fateful encounter with Jude, and our arrival at Haven, and of the joy at meeting my fellow First Ascendants. Mei's eyes widen in wonder when I explain my deep past as revealed by Caleb, and her mouth falls open in astonishment upon learning that I have a Soul family of First Ascendants.

'You have a twin sister?' she gasps.

'Had,' I correct her, and glance behind at Jude, who is hunched over her notebook, still sketching. I don't go into any further details about that, but I continue telling my friend about my past incarnations: from my very first as Tishala in the Great Rift Valley and Tanas's opening attack on the First Ascendants; on to my harsh life as the Sumerian slave girl Arwia; through my desperate escape across the Sahara Desert as the Berber Sura; and on to the time I was Yuán, a boy training in taiji at the Purple Cloud Temple in the Wudang mountains. Mei listens, rapt, as I explain my connection to Nefertiti and how she saved my life from the cobra when I was Princess Tiaa.

'So cats reincarnate too?' she asks, affectionately scratching Nefe's ear. Nefe purrs loudly in response.

'Apparently so,' I reply. 'And she continues to protect me to this day.'

'And what about your Soul Protector . . . what about Phoenix?' asks Mei hesitantly. 'Did you say he was *dead*?'

I nod and in a tremulous voice reply, 'T-Tanas killed him . . . She ritually sacrificed him so his soul will never come back.' I try to recount Phoenix's last moments, but tears fill my eyes and I begin to sob. 'It doesn't seem like he's gone . . . I can still feel him in my heart –' I press my hand to my chest where a yearning ache pulses – 'but I know that's foolish of me . . .' I break down and Mei wraps her arms round my shoulders and draws me close.

'I'm so sorry, Genna,' she says softly. 'I know how much he meant to you.'

Feeling safe in my friend's arms, I finally let go of my

grief in great, sobbing waves. The bottled-up pain of Phoenix's loss floods out. Jude glances over but says nothing. Tarek, focused on flying the jet, is unaware of my upset.

Mei holds me, saying nothing, just being there for me until my sobbing subsides and my tears dry.

'Thanks,' I say, pulling out of the hug.

'That's what friends are for,' she replies with a sad smile. Mei picks up her cup and finishes her tea. 'One thing I don't understand, though, is I thought Tanas was a man in this life.'

'She was,' I say, my grief for Phoenix now hardening into a ball of anger in my chest. 'But Tanas incarnated into a new body. It seems evil never dies,' I add bitterly.

Mei stares pensively into her cup. 'So, how will you ever defeat Tanas?'

I reach up to my backpack in the overhead locker and pull out the parchment. 'I hope this will give us the answer. It lists the locations of the Soul Jars, some of which contain clues to destroying Tanas's soul for good. And that's why we're headed to Egypt.'

'What are they, exactly, these Soul Jars?' asks Mei.

I frown thoughtfully. 'Phoenix described them as some sort of time capsules. Apart from clues, they can contain objects that might be helpful in a future life, such as gold, talismans or even weapons. Father Benedict told me that they're not always jars in the literal sense – they could be wooden boxes or glass bottles. Whatever was best to preserve them through time.'

Mei nods, taking in the information. 'OK. So what

happens if you don't find these Soul Jars? If Tanas wins and she extinguishes the Light, what happens then?'

I gaze grimly out of the window at the clouds, a storm churning them into a grey sea beneath us. 'Imagine the night sky with no stars. The day without sun. The whole of humanity enslaved in darkness for eternity, with Tanas feeding off everyone's misery like a vampire. *That* is what Tanas promises.'

Mei shudders. 'Sounds hellish!'

'It *is* hell,' I reply, recalling the nightmare world I'd foreseen in my *su'mach* vision. 'That's why we must find these Soul Jars. At all costs.'

16

'It's somewhat less impressive than I remember,' I admit, as we stand at the base of Pharaoh Hepuhotep's pyramid under the glare of the Egyptian sun. It breaks my heart to see that the polished limestone sides of my father's once magnificent monument have been plundered so thoroughly; the pillagers have left only a few slabs behind. Added to this, the harsh desert winds have sand-blasted the remains over the centuries to leave little more than an eroded mountain of dull mud bricks.

'Yes, well, it's certainly past its heyday,' agrees Jude. She cocks her head to one side. 'It's more of a blob than a pyramid.'

'My parents would find it absolutely *fascinating*,' remarks Mei. As she takes a selfie against the ancient tomb, Jude snatches the phone from her grasp.

'Hey! Give that back!' Mei yells. 'I wasn't taking a photo of *you*, if that's what you're worried about.'

Before I can intervene, Jude has picked up a rock. She promptly smashes the mobile to pieces.

Mei's jaw drops. 'What? Why on earth did you do that?'

'To stop anyone tracking us,' Jude explains. Taking out the battery, she tosses the broken remains into a ditch.

I notice a flash of anger in Mei's eyes and grab my friend before she launches herself at Jude. 'I'm sorry, Mei. My fault,' I say. 'I should have warned you. We don't carry mobiles.'

'But how am I supposed to call my parents now?' she complains. 'I told them I'd update them.'

'You don't,' Jude replies bluntly. 'In fact, you don't update anyone.'

Mei rounds on me. 'What is it with this girl? She's just smashed my phone!'

I offer Mei an apologetic smile. 'If it makes you feel any better, Jude once threw my phone under a moving truck.' I try to make light of the matter, but I'm deeply annoyed at Jude.

'No, it doesn't!' snaps Mei, going over and sifting despondently through the shattered remains of her phone. 'Why couldn't she have just turned it *off*?'

'There are ways to track a phone even when it's powered down,' explains Tarek, who is inspecting a pillar of eroded sandstone. 'We have to be really careful.'

'Careful?' questions Mei, shooting daggers at Jude. 'Well, Jude had better be more careful around me in future.'

Jude looks down her nose at Mei, remaining aloof behind her mirrored sunglasses. 'I said she should have stayed on the plane with the cat. She's a liability.'

Mei rises to her feet. Jude stiffens.

'Enough! Both of you,' I say, stepping between them. 'Jude, next time, let me handle such matters. Mei, I'm sorry.

I'll buy you a new phone when this is all over. For now, let's get on with our mission to find my father's tomb and the Soul Jar.'

The four of us begin our search of the ancient site. An archaeological dig has unearthed a few broken pots, the stump of a stone column and the cracked floor of a subterranean courtyard. Otherwise, my father's former glory is all but gone. The surrounding land is barren and flat, the arid ground strewn with rocks and patches of dry scrub. A line of scrawny palm trees marks the route of the Bahr Yussef canal, and beyond, in the distance, lies the sprawling heat haze of the city formerly known as Shedet.

'*As-salaam 'alaykum!* Would you like a tour?' asks a young boy, making us all jump out of our skins. Stepping out from behind a palm tree, he wears a long sand-coloured djellaba, white skullcap and a winning smile.

'Thank you, but I already know my way around,' I reply.

His smile momentarily drops, then returns more eagerly. 'How about a headscarf?' he offers. Like a magician, he produces a handful of colourful patterned cloths from within the folds of his robe.

Jude waves him away. 'You're wasting your time. We're not tourists.'

His face drops again. I feel sorry for the boy. There aren't many people around at all. In fact, aside from a departing minibus of half a dozen sunburned visitors, we're the only ones in sight. It appears my father's pyramid isn't a particularly popular stop on the tourist circuit.

'But it's respectful to cover your head,' insists the boy, giving his sales pitch one last shot, 'especially when entering a tomb.'

'He has a point,' agrees Tarek, who shoulders our small kitbag for our expedition into the pyramid. While we all sport sunglasses against the dazzling sunshine, only Jude wears a baseball cap, tilted stylishly atop her spiky blond hair. Having landed the jet on a small disused military airstrip outside Faiyum, we'd hurriedly opened its solar panels to charge the electric fuel cells, then driven straight here to the pyramid in the e-jeep. In our rush, we'd shamefully not given any thought to local customs.

'I'm afraid we don't have any Egyptian money,' I tell the boy.

'Not to worry. I accept American dollars,' he says with a glint in his tawny eyes. In that brief second I notice the faintest blue shimmer to his gaze. At first, I think it's only a reflection of the desert sky, then I begin to suspect he may be a Soul Brother, an inherently good soul who is unaware of their true nature, yet who intuitively helps First Ascendants like myself.

I take the time to inspect the boy's wares. The scarves are cheap polyester and he's asking way too much for them. But, after a bit of haggling, we settle on a price for four of his better samples, with Jude using hers as a neckerchief.

'You're a good salesman,' I tell the boy. Reaching into my backpack for the envelope of holiday money, I hand him several crisp notes. 'Keep the change.'

His grin widens. '*Shukran!*' he says, thanking me.

'*Ahlan wa sahlan*,' I reply.

He blinks. 'You know Arabic?'

'I used to live here,' I say as I wrap the long scarf round my head.

The boy raises an eyebrow. 'In Faiyum?'

'No, here,' I reply, pointing to the pyramid.

He gives me a perplexed look, and I laugh.

'It was a long time ago,' I explain, which makes him even more confused.

The boy stares after us, scratching his head, as we make our way over to the small dark doorway at the pyramid's base. The grand entrance once protected by a row of ram-headed sphinxes is now a pitiful sandy path lined with rubble. We stop at the threshold to take off our sunglasses and Tarek hands out torches to me, Mei and Jude. Rifling in his bag again, he then pulls out a Taser gun and surreptitiously passes the weapon to Jude. I notice the boy craning his neck, trying to make out what is in Jude's hand.

'Expecting trouble?' asks Mei.

'After our last encounter I'm not taking any risks,' Jude replies, checking the charge on the stun gun.

Mei peers anxiously into the blackness. 'Surely anyone we meet down there will be long dead.'

'Let's hope so,' says Jude, clipping the Taser to her belt. 'But it isn't mummies I'm worried about.'

'Take the left tunnel for the main burial chamber,' the boy calls after us. 'Oh, and I wouldn't stay too long. There's a sandstorm coming.' He points east.

I look to the horizon, where there is a dark smudge in the sky. It's way off. A dust trail follows in the wake of the departing minibus. Further down the road, another bus appears and the boy trots off to await its arrival in the shade beneath his palm tree.

'Let's get inside before the next lot turn up,' says Jude. She signals for me to take the lead. 'Show us the way, princess!'

I shoot her a sharp look and wonder if she's teasing me or actually referring to my former royal title. 'I think I preferred you as my guard Raneb when you couldn't talk.'

Jude mumbles something about wishing she'd been deaf as well in that life so she wouldn't have had to listen to me, but I ignore her and enter the pyramid.

As if passing through a veil, I cross the divide between sunlight and darkness. I make my way down a short flight of steps and the intense heat of the desert is replaced by the cool dankness of the stairwell. We turn on our torches. My beam sweeps the narrow passageway ahead to reveal smooth limestone walls and worn stone steps.

At the bottom, we reach a small chamber with a domed roof and a single tunnel leading off from it. Our torches cut through the gloom. The floor is littered with dirt, cigarette butts and, in one corner, the decaying remains of a rat. A musty odour drifts up as our feet disturb the dust and debris. Tarek coughs, the sound echoing off the walls and disappearing down the tunnel. The walls are decorated with faded effigies of Pharaoh Hepuhotep and his retainers meeting various animal-headed figures. I reach out, my finger tenderly tracing the outline of my father's face. All of a sudden the images appear fresh, colourful and newly painted –

'This is me greeting Ra in the afterlife,' enthuses my father, leaning upon his sceptre and peering in admiration at the artwork depicting the mighty sun god, with his falcon-shaped head and the sun-disk encircled by a cobra resting upon it. 'What do you think?'

'It's magnificent,' I reply, gazing around me in awe. Flaming torches flicker in all four corners of the chamber and cast an other-worldly glow over more of the pharaoh's depicted journey across the heavens. 'Your artists will certainly gain favour with Ra.'

My father chuckles. 'Wait until you see what they've done within my burial chamber!' He beckons me into the heart of the pyramid –

Past and present overlapping, I follow the ghost of my father into the tunnel ahead of us. Tarek, Mei and Jude trail in a procession behind me.

I hear Mei whispering, her voice echoing off the wall: 'Is Genna OK? She's acting kind of strange, like she's sleepwalking or something.'

'She's Glimmering,' Tarek replies softly. 'Following her past.'

17

The passage slopes downwards. With every echoing footfall, I feel like I'm stepping back in time. On the walls are more painted scenes. A military parade . . . an ancient battle in the land of Punt . . . a celebratory harvest festival . . . Despite their faded appearance and the flaking stone erasing large sections, I recognize them all, my ancient memory filling in the gaps.

As we carry on down the tunnel, the sense of déjà vu is overwhelming. I almost lose myself in the experience until I'm sharply brought back to the present by the sight of two fierce red eyes gleaming out from the darkness.

'Who's there?' demands Jude, drawing her Taser and training it on the looming shadow.

She yanks me away from the hidden threat and I stumble into Tarek, who drops his torch with a clatter on the stone floor. Behind me, Mei's panicked breathing is harsh and rapid within the confines of the tunnel.

Through the gloom, the two eyes continue to fix us with their unwavering glare. But we get no answer.

With an unsteady hand I raise the beam of my torch and a sunken-cheeked ebony face with a sharp nose comes into view. The chiselled figure stands stock-still, adorned with a golden headdress of a cobra's fanned collar. In one large hand is clasped a vicious-looking mace to bar our way.

I let out a sigh of relief and lower my torch. 'It's just a guardian statue.'

'Looked real to me!' mutters Jude as she holsters her Taser.

'That was the whole point, I think,' says Tarek, retrieving his torch from the floor. 'It was supposed to scare off intruders.'

'Well, it did a pretty good job,' admits Mei. 'I was almost halfway back to the jet!'

We take a moment to compose ourselves before sidestepping the pyramid's guardian, one after the other, and we head deeper underground.

We soon come to a junction of three tunnels. Tarek directs his torch down each passage; the bright beam is swallowed whole, disappearing into nothingness. 'So, which path do we take?' he whispers.

'The guide said to go left for the main burial chamber,' Mei reminds us.

I grab Jude's arm as she goes to turn left. 'No, that isn't the main one. From my memory, we need to take the right-hand tunnel.'

Jude shrugs. 'If you're certain?'

I nod and they follow me along the passageway I indicated. After twenty metres or so, we turn a corner and are forced to an abrupt halt. Ahead of us is a solid stone wall.

'It's a dead end!' mutters Jude, shooting me an irritated look.

I frown and glance back over my shoulder, then at the wall in front of us. 'But I'm sure this was the way.'

'Perhaps we'll have better luck down one of the other tunnels?' suggests Tarek, and he turns back towards the junction with Jude and Mei.

'No, wait . . .' I say, peering more closely at the wall. The blocks of limestone are faintly engraved with an effigy of the jackal-headed god Anubis, and there's a set of scales on which a heart is being weighed against a feather. 'I recognize this. Maybe I can trigger another Glimmer.'

Closing my eyes, I put my hand against the cool stone. Echoing across time, I hear my pharaoh father's voice –

'This dead end should confuse any tomb raiders,' explains my father, tapping the solid wall with the end of his sceptre. 'They'll give up and return to one of the false burial chambers down the other tunnels.'

'Where is your tomb?' I ask, as I notice Nefe sniffing curiously at the dead-end wall.

A sly grin spreads across my father's lips. 'Like Anubis, you must weigh the heart against the feather!' –

I open my eyes, feeling the same sly smile on my own lips. 'My pharaoh father said that we must weigh the heart against the feather.'

'What did he mean by that?' asks Mei.

Pocketing my torch, I run my hands down the stone wall, my fingers sweeping across the god of the underworld until I feel the faint groove round the heart and another round the feather. 'I think, if my memory serves me right, you have to press both of these at the same time, using the exact same pressure for each one.'

So, with the fingers of one hand in position on the heart and the fingers of the other on the feather, I press hard yet evenly. The stone gives slightly and there's the faintest of clicks as a counter-balance lock is released.

I turn to the others with a delighted grin. 'Help me push.'

But it turns out that I don't need their help at all. As I place my hands against the immense wall, it smoothly pivots, revealing a hidden passageway.

'This is real Indiana Jones stuff!' exclaims Mei, her eyes widening. 'I'm starting to get now why my parents love archaeology.'

We duck our heads below the low lintel and enter the passage. After rounding a corner, we emerge into a burial chamber with a high-vaulted ceiling.

Mei gasps. 'Oh my word! This is remarkable.'

Despite knowing that I've been in this chamber once before, I'm still awed into silence by the sight before us. The walls are adorned in gold leaf with the most spectacular paintings. In one sweeping, continuous piece of artwork, Pharaoh Hepuhotep is being welcomed into the afterlife by a green-skinned god – Osiris, I think, the god of the dead and rebirth. Our torch beams shimmer and bounce off the gold paint, making the room shine as if with rays of morning sun.

Set in the centre of this glorious chamber is a large granite sarcophagus, its lid pushed to one side. We go over, our footsteps echoing in the grave-like silence, and warily peer in. There's nothing but darkness and dust and a few grains of sand.

Mei sighs in disappointment. 'Oh, it's empty,' she says.

Tarek glances round the room. 'Someone must have been here before us. Taken the body and all the treasures.'

'If that's the case, then the Soul Jar is gone too,' says Jude, kicking at a loose stone. It skitters across the floor and rebounds off the wall. 'We've hit another dead end!'

'Not necessarily,' I tell her. 'My father said he would be laid to rest in a concealed chamber *beneath*. There must be another hidden door somewhere. Let's see if we can find it.'

The four of us spread out, each choosing a wall to examine. I run my hands carefully over the beautifully painted stone, seeking the faint join that will give away the presence of a hidden passageway or a concealed button.

'I've found Apep!' calls Tarek from the other side of the chamber. He points to a depiction of a large snake being beheaded with a sword. 'Remember what the parchment clue said: *Apep, the Eater of Souls, is to be feared. But fear can be slain*. We must be getting close.'

But when the walls yield no further clues, we begin to scour the floor.

'Any luck?' asks Jude as we all meet back in the centre of the room.

I shake my head, frustrated. Our hands are covered in dust and our knees sore from the hard stone, and we've still nothing to show for it.

'Can't you trigger another Glimmer?' suggests Mei.

'I'll give it a go,' I say. 'To be honest, I'm surprised I haven't had one already.'

Leaning against the sarcophagus, I place my hands upon the lid and close my eyes. A full minute goes by, but however hard I concentrate no past-life memory surfaces.

'Sorry,' I say, opening my eyes, 'I'm not getting –' I catch sight of something in the bottom of the sarcophagus. 'Hang on!' I clamber inside to get a closer look. There, carved into its stone base is a human eye topped with a thin eyebrow. A dark line extends from the corner of the eye while another ends in a small, delicate spiral.

'The Eye of Horus!' I exclaim. 'This is the exact same icon as the one on Caleb's altar in the Sun Room at Haven.'

I press my hand to the eye, feeling the cool of the stone and a prickling in my palm. All of a sudden the bottom of the sarcophagus drops away and with a startled cry I slide down the slope and into a pit of darkness. A moment later I hit the ground with a thump and lose my torch.

'Are you OK?' Mei shouts down.

'Yeah . . . fine,' I groan, rubbing my backside. Crawling over to my torch, I switch the light back on and let out another cry, this time of astonishment. 'You have to come down and see this!'

The others slide down to discover me sitting amid a pile of gold. The burial chamber is a literal treasure trove.

Set in an alcove is a large ornate throne, and next to that sits a solid gold crown upon a plinth. A long table bows under the weight of countless cups, chalices and plates, all encrusted with rubies and sapphires. Among a heap of jewellery is a polished circular mirror, an ornamental fan and a silver necklace. We stare in slack-jawed wonder at the mountain of riches. There are even silver trumpets and a golden harp, and in the far corner is a stash of shields, bows, spears and jewelled daggers. Dozens of stone jars are stacked against one wall and innumerable shabti statues line another. And at the centre of all these treasures is a polished white marble sarcophagus that gleams with ethereal light.

Overcome by my discovery, I experience a strange feeling of recognition, belonging to and yearning for a lost life. The sight of so many ancestral artefacts takes me back to my time as Princess Tiaa, to my life as the daughter of a pharaoh, and I recognize again the riches we were blessed with.

'Oh my gosh,' says Mei, running her fingers through the gold coins. 'We've hit the jackpot!'

'But how on earth are we going to find the Soul Jar in all this?' asks Tarek.

Getting to my feet, I nod at the white marble sarcophagus. 'With any luck it'll be in there.'

We gather round the pharaoh's final resting place and I ready myself to meet the remains of my long-dead father. Together, we push at the heavy lid, stone scrapping on stone. Our muscles straining, we gradually shift the sarcophagus top. A dry, dusty whiff of decay wafts up through the air and we behold a mummified body. The corpse is adorned with a golden death mask. I know the face at once and gasp, gripping the sides of the sarcophagus as my legs go weak.

'What is it?' asks Jude, peering at the surprisingly small body wrapped in white linen.

'That's not my father,' I say, barely able to breathe. 'That's *me*.'

18

The death mask is an exact copy of my face as Princess Tiaa. Almond-shaped, desert-brown eyes, a pert nose and rounded chin, the hair as black as onyx and cut into a long, straight bob. It's as if I'm staring at myself in a golden mirror but the reflection coming back at me is of an entirely different person.

'Creepy,' remarks Mei as we all gaze at the mummy of my former self. She glances from me to the mask and back again. 'That's got to feel odd, right?'

I nod. 'It's very bizarre. But what's more confusing is why I'm buried here and not my father.' I turn to Jude. 'You were my personal guard back then. Can you remember anything from when you were Raneb?'

Jude shuts her eyes and twitches slightly from an apparent Glimmer. 'From what I can recall of that time, I was injured during an attack on the pharaoh's palace by Apep's followers; I died of my wounds.' She looks at me. 'Your handmaiden, Sitre, might have known more.'

I smile grimly. Sitre was Phoenix's incarnation in that life, and whatever he knew about that time has gone with him to the grave, forever.

'So does this place still qualify as the hidden tomb of Hepuhotep if his body's not here?' asks Tarek.

'It has to,' I say, a flutter of desperation making my heart beat faster. 'It's the only tomb I know of.'

'Then we'd best start searching,' says Jude, and she begins delving into the sarcophagus. 'Remember: Apep is represented in the form of a huge serpent in Egyptian times, so shout out if you find anything with a snake on it.'

I pull back the shroud that covers my former remains and discover a mummified cat lying at the feet of my embalmed body. 'Nefertiti!' I gasp. I'm touched by her loyalty even in death; although it's strange to know her spirit has reborn and that she's now fast asleep on the jet, awaiting my return.

And yet, aside from the body of my long-dead cat and the golden death mask, the sarcophagus yields little else. We shift our attention to the piles of treasure. There's so much of it that it's hard to know where to begin.

Tarek is hunting through the rows of stone jars. He cuts the wax seal around the top of one of them with a knife and pulls out the plug. He gives the contents a sniff. 'Wine!' he says, wrinkling his nose. 'And it still smells fine, even after all this time.'

Mei is admiring herself in the round hand mirror, its handle shaped like the body and head of the solar goddess Hathor, daughter of Ra. I notice that my friend is now wearing a silver necklace of precious gemstones that glitters in the torchlight.

'This isn't a shopping trip, Mei,' I say, admonishing her.

'I realize that,' she replies, angling the mirror to get a

better view of herself. 'But you have to admit this does look good on me.'

'Could you perhaps focus on the task at hand?' Jude mutters through clenched teeth.

'Sure,' says Mei, giving herself one last admiring glance. Then she squints and peers more closely at the reflection before glancing over her shoulder. 'We're looking for a jar of some sort, right?'

'Yes, a Soul Jar,' I reply as I examine the hoard of gleaming cups and chalices on the table.

'Then what about those?' Mei points to a row of white limestone jars at the base of the sarcophagus. 'They're Canopic jars.'

Jude pauses in her search through the shabti figurines. 'How do you know what they are?'

'My parents have a set in their collection,' Mei replies as she takes off the necklace and returns it to the pile of jewellery. 'They're used in burial rituals to preserve the liver, lungs, stomach and intestines of the deceased for the afterlife.'

I regard my friend with admiration and amusement. 'You're becoming quite the archaeologist.'

She shrugs. 'I guess I'm more like my mother than I thought.' Then she frowns, appearing pensive for a moment. 'That's odd. There are five jars. According to tradition, or at least my parents, Canopic jars always numbered *four*.'

'You're right, Mei!' I exclaim, recalling this fact too from my time as Princess Tiaa. 'There wasn't a jar for the heart because the Egyptians believed it was the seat of the soul, so it was left inside the body.' I hurry over to the sarcophagus and examine each jar in turn. Engraved on the front in hieroglyphs are inscriptions asking the four sons of the god Horus to protect my organs. Their lids are carved into different shapes: the head of a man, a baboon, a jackal and a falcon. The fifth jar is topped with the head of a serpent, along with an inscription in hieroglyphs: '*Only his own death can defeat him*,' I read . . .

'This must be it,' I say in an almost reverential tone as I hold the snake-headed jar aloft for the others to see. 'Our first clue. It means the parchment is genuine!'

'Well, let's open it,' says Jude eagerly.

Carefully prising off the sealed lid, I almost drop the jar in horrified shock. Inside is a mummified hand, its skin wrinkled and as black as tar. Its bony fingers protrude like talons and its nails are pointed and sharp.

'Gross!' says Mei, grimacing as she peers over my shoulder at the gnarled hand.

Jude looks decidedly unimpressed. 'What sort of clue is *this* meant to be?'

I read the inscription on the jar again. 'Only his own death can defeat him,' I repeat, and reach in to take out the hand –

'LET HER GO!' roars Sitre as the mighty Apep hauls me away by the arm. I flail in the iron grip of the Incarnate leader, my sandalled feet slipping on the limestone floor.

The palace is in complete disarray. Apep's followers run amok through the halls and corridors, butchering whoever they meet – armed guards as well as women and slaves. Sitre tries to fight off two Incarnates at once but they drive her back.

Fear fuelling me to fight, I pummel my free fist against Apep's sides, but I might as well have been beating a drum for all the damage my blows are inflicting. Apep strides on, untroubled, the tip of his gold trident clinking on the stone steps as he mercilessly drags me towards a funeral pyre ablaze in the palace's central courtyard.

'NO! NO! NO!' I scream in terror. Amid the flames, I can see two fire-blackened bodies, which suddenly ignite in front of my eyes.

Ignoring my pleas, Apep is about to throw me upon the pyre when my personal guard, Raneb, leaps from behind a column. His bronze khopesh raised high above his head, he slices down, severing Apep's hand from his arm. The Incarnate leader howls in agony. As Raneb moves to finish him, Apep thrusts his trident into Raneb's stomach. My guard makes no sound, but the pain is bright in his starlit blue eyes. With a superhuman effort, he somehow manages a second swipe of his khopesh. Its sickle-shaped blade slices the Incarnate leader's head clean off and his body keels backwards into the funeral pyre, where it is claimed by the licking flames and burns fiercely. Yet despite his defeat, Apep's severed hand still grips my wrist, his bony fingers closing ever tighter –

I drop the embalmed hand back into the jar in horror and disgust.

'This is Apep's hand!' I stare at Jude. 'You cut it off during the attack on the palace.'

Jude eyes the dismembered body part with grim interest. 'Hmm, "his *own* death" . . . Are we meant to use Tanas's own hand from a previous life against her, do you think?'

I grimace at the idea but suspect her instinct is right. 'I guess so,' I reply, wondering *and* worrying what exactly that might entail. Securing the lid back on, I pass the jar carefully to Tarek to store in the kitbag. 'The more clues we gather, the more sense this should make – hopefully. Come on – let's go,' I say, energized by our find.

'What about all this gold? And all the treasures?' asks Mei, running her hands over the priceless artefacts. 'Your tomb is the discovery of a lifetime! My parents will totally flip out when I tell them about this. I'll be in their good books for, like, ever.'

'Mei, we have more important matters at hand,' I tell her. 'Once we've saved the world, I promise we can come back here and show your parents.'

'But what if someone else discovers the tomb before then? Steals all these treasures? I mean, this alone must be worth a fortune –' and as she reaches for the solid gold crown on the plinth I suddenly get a very bad feeling.

'Mei, *NO*!' I cry, but it's too late. She picks up the crown.

A second later the plinth on which it sat rises a full inch and a heavy *clunk* reverberates through the chamber.

'What was that?' asks Tarek, gazing anxiously around.

The *clunk* is followed by an ominous grinding of stone upon stone. We spin round to see the base of the first sarcophagus rising back up to the ceiling and closing off the secret entrance. Jude makes a dash for the opening but it seals shut before she gets there.

'You idiot!' she yells, throwing her arms up in the air. 'Now we're trapped!'

'S-sorry,' says Mei feebly, and she sheepishly returns the crown to its rightful spot. Under its weight the plinth slowly returns to its original level. To everyone's dismay, however, the slab in the ceiling doesn't reopen. Instead, more worryingly, the plinth continues to sink all the way to the floor.

Sealed inside the tomb, a suffocating silence descends on us as we nervously await whatever will happen next.

I cock my head to one side. *Is that a trickle?* It's very faint and I wonder if my ears are playing tricks on me. 'Can anyone else hear the sound of running water?'

They all nod as the trickle swells into a gentle swish, then, like an approaching wave, into an ominous roar.

'That's not water!' cries Tarek, pointing to holes opening up high in the chamber walls. 'That's sand!'

19

'Anyone who breaches this tomb will soon make it their grave too,' says Pharaoh Hepuhotep with a dark chuckle. 'For their inevitable greed will be their downfall.'

'You've thought of everything, Father,' I say, admiring the golden crown on its plinth but not daring to touch it.

'This is Vizier Khafra's cunning,' my father explains. 'For it is he who has constructed the trap.'

All too aware of the deadly sand trap, I begin to feel the walls of the tomb press in upon me. 'And there's no way out?'

My father gives me a grave look and shakes his head. 'None whatsoever –'

'We're going to be buried alive!' yells Tarek, his eyes wide with panic behind his glasses.

'I'm sorry, I'm sorry!' cries Mei as a tidal wave of sand begins to swamp the treasures and fill the tomb.

'It's my fault – I should've warned you earlier,' I say. 'But I only just recalled the trap as you reached for the crown.' I wade ankle-deep in sand over to Jude. She's standing on a table and trying to prise open the slab above our heads. 'Any luck?'

She shakes her head. 'No, it won't budge at all. It's two tonnes of solid limestone.' Giving up on the slab, Jude jumps down next to me. 'Unless we find another way out, this is going to be your tomb for a second time!' she shouts above the deafening roar of the sand.

'Surely there must be some secret passage?' replies Mei desperately. 'There's always one in the movies.'

'Sorry to break it to you, darlin', but this isn't a movie!' snaps Jude.

'Can we stop bickering and just focus on getting out of here?' I say.

Picking up a shield, Tarek heads over to the nearest wall. 'We need to block the holes!'

Following his lead, we begin grabbing plates and other large objects that might stem the flow of sand. But the pressure is simply too great and anything we try to wedge into the openings is quickly spat out.

As the sand reaches our knees, Jude turns to me. 'Think, Genna. Is there any way to reset the trap?'

I shake my head, coughing and spluttering from all the dust swirling in the air. 'Not that I can remember.'

'Then what *do* you remember?' she yells as she loses grip on a plate and is showered by a torrent of sand.

I screw my eyes shut and try to think back to my Egyptian life. But the stress of our situation is making it hard to trigger a Glimmer. I only get flashes of a memory –

My father's adviser, Vizier Khafra, enters the tomb . . .

His willowy figure bows low and presents us with a

small round mirror of beautifully polished gold, with a golden Hathor-shaped handle . . .

'The key to the door, O Great Pharaoh, for your soul must not be trapped . . .'

My questioning look at Khafra and his cryptic answer, 'With the Eye of Ra upon the throne, a way forever will be shown –'

'The mirror!' I exclaim. 'Where is it?'

Mei turns frantically around, the sand now up to her waist. 'I don't know. I've lost it!' She begins to dig furiously.

Fighting the incoming tide of sand, Jude, Tarek and I half walk, half swim over to join the search. But with every handful of sand shifted, more pours in to replace it. We become as desperate as we are determined to find the mirror. All the while the sea of sand continues to rise, threatening to reach our chests. Tarek digs deeper and disappears under a wave of sand.

'Tarek!' I cry.

Several seconds go by with no sign of him. Furiously shovelling away sand, I'm beginning to believe we've lost him for good, when he bursts to the surface, holding the precious mirror aloft. 'Got it!' he shouts, spitting out gobs of sand.

'Thank the Light you're OK,' I say as he passes me the sun-shaped mirror.

We plough our way through the sandy drifts to the alcove. Each step is a monumental effort, my legs feeling heavy as lead against the weight of sand. My lungs become tight and small as if the air is being sucked out of the room, the sense of claustrophobia only intensifying the closer the sand rises towards the ceiling. Eventually we reach the alcove. Here, mercifully, the sand isn't quite so deep.

'What do we do now?' asks Mei, her voice edged with panic.

I look at the mirror and see my own panic-stricken face reflected back at me. Etched upon the Hathor-shaped handle is an inscription. '*With the Eye of Ra upon the throne, a way forever will be shown*,' I tell her.

'And what does that mean?'

'I'm not entirely sure,' I admit, turning hopefully to the others. 'Any suggestions? All I know is that this is a key to a door.'

'Here!' says Tarek, pointing to the top of the stone throne. 'There's a hole. The mirror must go in there.'

Buffeted by the sand, I manage to slot the handle into the hole. Nothing happens.

'Turn it!' barks Jude. 'It's a key, for heaven's sake.'

I twist the mirror and a block of limestone at the rear of the alcove slides aside to reveal a narrow passageway behind.

'GO!' I shout, pushing Mei ahead of me as the sand threatens to pour into the opening and block our only escape. The four of us scramble into the tunnel, leaving behind my tomb and all its treasures buried beneath a mountain of sand.

Dark, narrow and cramped, the hidden passage seems never-ending, rising then descending, but eventually coming to an abrupt stop where a pile of boulders and mud bricks have caved in.

'Brilliant, just brilliant,' says Jude sardonically. 'Another dead end. This pyramid is determined to bury us!'

I pass my torch over the rubble, which shows that the whole tunnel is blocked. I turn to the others. 'Did anyone spot another passage along the way?'

Tarek shakes his head. 'It was pretty dark, though, so we could've missed one.'

'OK, let's retrace our steps,' I suggest.

'Hang on,' says Mei, pointing to a faint fissure of pale light shining between the rocks. 'That looks like daylight!'

Working like a chain gang, we prise apart the stones, pass them back and gradually enlarge the hole. Scrambling through, we find ourselves at the bottom of a deep shaft. High above our heads is a bright circle of blue sky.

'This day only gets better,' says Jude with a sigh. 'We're now stuck in a well!'

'HELLO?' shouts Mei. 'ANYONE THERE? HELP –'

'Will you shut up?' barks Jude, clamping a hand over Mei's mouth.

Mei angrily prises it off. 'Why? How else are we going to get out?'

'I don't know,' replies Jude through clenched teeth. 'But we don't want to draw any unwanted attention to our tomb-raiding. We can't afford to lose the Soul Jar.'

I run my hands over the rough wall, feeling for handholds. 'I might be able to climb out,' I say.

Tarek gives me an uneasy look. 'It's a long way to go . . . what if you fall?'

'I used to climb much higher things when I was the Russian acrobat Yelena,' I tell him confidently, reaching for my first handhold.

'*Allo?*'

We all look up to see a face at the top of shaft. I recognize the boy who sold us the scarves.

'*As-salaam 'alaykum!*' I shout back, waving.

'I thought I heard voices,' says the boy. 'What are you doing down there?'

'Er . . . we took a wrong turning,' I explain. 'Can you help us out?'

'Wait there,' says the boy before disappearing.

'What else does he think we're going to do?' mutters Jude.

A moment later the boy's face reappears and a snaking rope falls down towards us.

20

We emerge back into the daylight, blinking like moles. The pyramid is now several hundred metres away across a barren stretch of desert. A harsh wind whips up eddies of dust.

'*Shukran*,' I say, thanking the boy. My assumption about him was right – he must be a Soul Brother. As Phoenix once explained to me, *Sometimes they turn up in just the right place at just the right time*.

'*Afwan*,' the boy replies as he coils up the rope. Despite his friendly nature, he eyes us cautiously, clearly still trying to figure out how we ended up in the well.

'Told you there was a secret passage,' says Mei as she dusts herself down.

'You almost got us killed!' growls Jude, taking off her baseball cap and shaking out the sand from her hair.

Mei gives Jude a sheepish look. 'Sorry,' she says, then her expression turns to one of curiosity and she lowers her voice so the boy doesn't hear. 'No offence, but would that *really* matter for you? I mean, I get that no one likes dying, but you reincarnate, don't you?'

'Yes, but that's not the point,' Jude snaps back angrily

under her breath. 'Everything resets. With Phoenix gone, *I'd* have to find Genna in her new incarnation before a Soul Hunter did. And there's no guarantee I would, since I'm not her original Protector. What's more, we're on a mission to discover these clues to killing Tanas once and for all. If we die in this life, we lose that opportunity. Maybe forever. Because when we come back, there's every chance we may not remember our quest, or even be able to find the parchment again.'

Mei holds up her hands. 'OK, I get it –'

'Do you?' Jude stabs a finger at her. 'Because while *I* may reincarnate, there's no certainty *you* will.'

Mei blanches and swallows hard. 'I'll be much more careful next time, I swear.'

'*Next time* you stay on the plane –'

'Jude, we all make mistakes,' I cut in, trying to calm the situation, concerned that the boy will overhear. 'Mei did find the Soul Jar, after all. If it wasn't for her, we might have come out empty-handed.'

'I prefer empty-handed to dead,' says Jude, shoving her cap firmly back on her head. 'I told you it wasn't a good idea to –'

'Please,' says the boy, cutting her off, 'the sandstorm is coming. You need to take shelter.' He points in the direction of the pyramid.

I turn with the others to see that the earlier smudge in the sky has grown to a monstrous moving mountain of ominous darkness. It looms over the pyramid like a tsunami wave, threatening to block out even the sun.

Mei's eyes widen in horror. 'What the hell is that?'

'A simoom,' replies the boy as a gust buffets us. 'A poison wind!'

I feel my blood run cold at the sight. I recognize the threat from my deep past. A simoom is the deadliest kind of sandstorm.

'Sorry – must go.' The boy hurries off in the direction of a small ramshackle settlement. Then stops and shouts back, 'Oh, more tourists arrived. They –' But the rest of his words are whipped away by the wind.

'What did he say?' asks Tarek.

'I couldn't hear,' I reply. 'Something about more tourists.'

The wind whistles around us, and blasts of sand sting our faces.

'Back to the jeep right now!' orders Jude. 'RUN!'

We dash across the open desert, in a race to beat the storm. The tsunami of sand rushes to greet us. The wind blows harder in our faces, and dust is lifted up in swirling mini-tornadoes. Fumbling for my sunglasses, I shove them on to protect my eyes. My heart pounds and my lungs begin to burn as I breathe in the hot, dry sand-filled air.

'HURRY!' shouts Jude as we round the pyramid and the e-jeep comes into view.

In the lee of the ancient weathered tomb, the wind drops a little. We're just ahead of the storm and it looks like we're going to make it, when a hooded figure emerges from the pyramid entrance, talking to someone, their words reaching us on the breeze. '*The boy must have lied to us. There's no one down there. I'll break his scrawny neck when I find –*'

The figure stops dead and so do we. I instantly recognize the hooded figure in black aviator-style sunglasses. Lean, muscular and with a pale face as chiselled as the guardian statue in the pyramid, he's the last person I expected to see in Egypt. We stare at one another for a long, silent moment. There's just the wind howling across the desert. Then Damien grins. '*There* you are!'

The rest of his gang emerge from the pyramid.

All of a sudden a huge roar fills the air and the storm engulfs us. Like a red, raging cloud, the simoom swallows the pyramid. I'm almost blown off my feet. Coughing and struggling for breath, I wrap my headscarf round my mouth and turn to follow the others to the jeep. But they're gone, lost within the suffocating, swirling dust.

Disorientated, I fight my way through the storm in the direction that I hope is the jeep. I can hear shouts and cries above the howls of the wind, see shadows flit through the apocalyptic air. Branches of palm trees and desert scrub ripped from the ground whip past.

'GENNA!'

I spin round, trying to locate the person calling my name. The world is a whirling, chaotic nightmare and I can barely see a few metres ahead of me. Then through the blood-red cloud of dust appears a silhouette.

'GENNA!' calls the voice.

I stop dead. *Is that Damien?* I squint into the storm, readying myself to fight. But the figure appears slimmer and taller than Damien. The way they carry themself is also different. Despite the poor visibility, there's something very familiar about them. I feel a weird tug in my chest and I'm drawn to him – I'm sure now it's a him. As I take a step forward, a hand grabs my shoulder and pulls me back.

'*GENNA! This way!*' rasps Jude. She drags me off through the billowing red sand. I glance back but the storm has swallowed whoever was there.

Moments later she bundles me into the cabin of the e-jeep and slams the door shut. Immediately, the sound of the storm is quieter, although the wind buffets the jeep's sides and sand peppers the windscreen like hail. Tarek and Mei are already safely inside.

'Are you all right?' asks Mei as Jude guns the engine and drives off down the road, blindly following the rutted tracks.

I nod, numb and shocked. Pulling down my scarf, I peer out of the rear window, hoping to catch another glimpse of the silhouette.

'I'm OK, but I think I just saw . . . *Phoenix*.'

21

'I hate bloomin' sand!' says Jude as she shakes herself off in the jet, leaving a small reddish pile on the carpet.

Nefertiti is there to greet us, sniffing at our dust-laden clothes with interest. Once we've brushed ourselves down and got some refreshments, we gather round the dining table inside the cabin.

'Are you *certain* you saw Phoenix?' asks Mei as she passes me a cup of steaming mint tea.

I nod, cradling the cup to steady my hands. 'He was calling my name.'

'No, *I* was calling your name,' corrects Jude, unwrapping a protein bar and taking a hungry bite. 'You're imagining things. It was virtually impossible to see anyone in that storm. It was just sheer luck that I ran into you.'

I take a long, thoughtful sip of tea. If Phoenix is really alive, then I'm not responsible for his death. 'But he *looked* like Phoenix,' I persist.

'It was probably Damien,' says Tarek. He tears open a packet of peanuts and hands them round. 'Or else one of his gang.'

'No, it wasn't him,' I reply firmly. 'And Blondie is much

smaller, and Thug a helluva lot bigger. And you can forget Spider and Knuckleduster – I'm certain it was a boy.'

'Then perhaps it was the guide?' suggests Mei. 'He might have come back to help –'

'NO!' I shout, slamming the cup down on the table and spilling my tea. 'I tell you: I *saw* Phoenix!'

The three of them fall silent at my outburst and occupy themselves with eating their snacks. As I angrily mop up the spill with a paper napkin, I notice them sharing a concerned look. I take another sip of my tea, but the mint now tastes bitter in my mouth. 'Sorry,' I mumble.

'Genna,' says Mei softly, reaching across and laying her hand over mine, 'I know how upset you are at losing Phoenix. It's natural to want to *think* you saw him, especially when you're grieving. But everything was distorted by the sandstorm. Your eyes were likely playing tricks on you –'

'No!' I say vehemently. 'I saw him. I *felt* him in my heart. He's alive. I know it.' Hot tears well in my eyes, blurring my vision.

'Stop torturing yourself, Genna,' says Jude, her tone firm yet kind. 'You have to accept that Phoenix is dead. You and I both saw Tanas starting the ritual –'

'Yes, starting . . . but not finishing!'

Jude lets out a weary sigh, and pinches the bridge of her nose as if she has a headache. 'Genna, he was surrounded by Incarnates. Tanas and her High Priests had him at their mercy. There's no way anyone, not even Phoenix, could have escaped from that situation alive.'

I open my mouth to argue, then am forced to accept that she's right. I can't deny what I saw with my own eyes on

Haven's runway. *But if that's the case, then who* did *I see in the storm?*

We sit quietly, each of us lost in our own thoughts. I go over the scene again and again, trying to piece together what I actually saw. But the details are becoming as blurred and confused as the storm itself.

Tarek removes his glasses and begins to carefully polish them. 'What I want to know is this . . . How did Damien find us so quickly?'

We all look at one another, realizing that *that* is the question we should be concentrating on.

'That's Mei's fault,' mutters Jude. 'For bringing her phone and allowing the Hunters to track us.'

'Well, I'm *sorry*,' Mei replies, 'but how was I to know?'

'You weren't,' I say.

Tarek shakes his head. 'Jude's theory still doesn't explain how Damien and his gang got to the pyramid so quickly. Since this is Caleb's jet, the cabin is electro-magnetically shielded. That means Mei's phone could only have been tracked once we'd landed and disembarked.'

'Then DI Shaw must have overheard us talking back at Mei's house and informed Damien,' I suggest. 'I mean, the clue to the location of the pyramid literally landed on her head!'

'That stone tablet will have put her in hospital,' says Jude. 'I'd be surprised if DI Shaw even remembers her name, let alone what we were talking about.'

Tarek doesn't look fully convinced. Frowning, he holds his glasses up to the light before putting them back on. 'That possibly explains it. Anyway, however they knew where to find us, we need to be more vigilant going forward.'

'I agree,' says Jude. 'We can't allow Damien and his gang to derail our mission or take us by surprise like that again –' There's a spitting *hiss* at our feet and we all glance down.

Nefe has her teeth bared and her back arched, her beige fur on end. Her emerald-green eyes are fixed on the snake peeking out of Tarek's kitbag. Before Nefe can pounce, Tarek picks up the serpent-headed Soul Jar and puts it on the table. 'I guess Nefe doesn't like snakes.'

'Or what's inside them,' I reply, as my cat jumps up but continues to warily eye the jar containing Apep's mummified hand. I prise off the lid to examine our find. Nefe hisses once more and swipes at it with her claws. Tarek shifts uncomfortably in his seat and a sickly look steals over Mei's face. I feel nauseous too, repulsed by the blackened skin and sharp talons. The disembodied hand seems to emanate evil, the spirit of Tanas seeping from the Canopic jar like toxic fumes.

'Put the lid back on, will you?' says Jude, grimacing. 'That hand is creeping me out.'

I seal up the malignant relic once more. 'Where shall we keep it?'

'Give it here,' says Jude. Going over to the minibar, she opens the glass-fronted cabinet, pulls out the bottles of spirits and stows the jar inside.

'So, what else do we need besides *that* thing to kill Tanas?' asks Mei.

'Hopefully, the parchment should tell us,' I reply. Retrieving the precious document from my backpack, I lay it out flat on the table and the others lean in. 'If we can translate it, that is,' I add.

'Well, that part looks to be in Old Chinese,' says Mei. She points to a small hand-drawn image of a Buddha with a column of ancient Chinese characters.

'Can you read it?' I ask eagerly. Although I was once the Chinese thief Lihua in a former life, I'd been illiterate.

Mei peers closer, her brow wrinkling in concentration. 'There are some characters that are different from modern Chinese, but I think I get the gist.' She runs her finger down the text and reads out the second riddle: '*Upon the Silk Road where a thousand Buddhas meet is one that holds enlightenment within.*'

She glances up, bemused. 'Why does everything have to be so cryptic?'

'Father Benedict didn't want an Incarnate finding and destroying the knowledge he'd acquired over the centuries,' I explain. 'So he was being careful to keep the locations of the Soul Jars secret.'

'Well, he could've been a *bit* more specific,' moans Jude. 'The Silk Road was over four thousand miles long!'

'And it wasn't even a road,' corrects Tarek. 'Traders used a network of routes over the course of some thousand years or more.'

'Then how on earth are we supposed to locate this Soul Jar based on *that* clue?' Mei says, exasperated.

We stare blankly at the Chinese script and the little drawing of the Buddha. I notice a doodle of an interconnected triple spiral on his forehead. The symbol is familiar, yet I can't immediately place where I've seen it before.

‘Where would a thousand Buddhas meet?’ asks Mei.

Tarek frowns. ‘A temple?’

‘It would have to be a pretty big one,’ remarks Jude.

‘Well, maybe that helps narrow it down,’ I say. ‘What large famous temples were built along the Silk Road?’

Jude shrugs. ‘It was a pilgrimage route, so there’s bound to have been tens of thousands of temples. We’d probably have more luck finding a four-leaf clover!’

‘There are ways to find four-leaf clovers,’ says Tarek, getting up from his seat and heading over to the jet’s computer console. He types in a search for a ‘thousand Buddha temple’ and scans the results. ‘Top hit is the Garden of One Thousand Buddhas, but that’s in Montana, nowhere near the Silk Road.’ He continues down the list. ‘Ah, this is more promising . . . in Hong Kong we have the Ten Thousand Buddhas Monastery, except that was constructed in the mid-twentieth century.’ He clicks to the next page and scrolls through several more results. ‘Most of the hits relate to the Hong Kong temple. There’s nothing about a thousand-Buddha temple.’

‘Keep looking,’ I insist. ‘There *has* to be something.’

‘Perhaps the temple doesn’t exist any more,’ suggests Jude. ‘Or maybe the clue doesn’t refer to a temple at all. We need to rethink –’

Mei clicks her fingers. ‘Hang on! Genna, remember that clay statue of the Buddha in my hallway?’ I nod vaguely. ‘My mother gave that to my father as a gift after a trip home to China. She’d visited an archaeological site in Gansu province and was raving about the thousand clay Buddhas that had been discovered there.’

I sit up straighter. 'What is this place called? Can you remember?'

Mei's brow wrinkles. 'I think . . . the Muguo – no! – the Mogao Caves.'

Tarek types the name into the search bar. 'Bingo!' He reads off the screen: '"The Mogao Caves – or the Caves of the Thousand Buddhas – lie near the city of Dunhuang in Gansu province, western China. The caves, comprising a unique complex of five hundred temples, became an important religious site on the ancient trading routes known collectively as the Silk Road."'

'That has to be it,' I say, with a triumphant grin. Then the grin is replaced by a grimace of pain. The cabin darkens, my body spasms and –

I writhe and thrash against the wooden stake, my skin burning, my flesh flaming. I want to scream but my throat is scorched by the searing smoke. Beyond the flames, hooded figures lurk in the darkness, swaying and chanting. My eyes blister in the heat as I look upon the charred body of my Soul Protector Blake bound to another stake, already consumed by fire. Then a slim, porcelain face, terrifying in its cold beauty, leans into my warped vision and mutters, 'Uur ra uhrdar bourkad, RA-KA!' *and I feel a piercing stab as a red-hot poker is driven through my chest, and my soul burns –*

'No!' I cry as the apparition vanishes and the burning sensation fades to a needle-like prickling.

'Genna, are you OK?' asks Mei, her voice strangely distant. She kneels beside me, cradling my head.

My focus returns and I see my friend close to me. She's

crouching over me, along with Jude and Tarek, their faces creased with concern. Mei helps me sit up. As my mind clears, I realize what's just happened – I'd soul-linked with Sun-Hi and felt the extinguishing of her Light.

'Tanas . . . has found Sun-Hi . . . and Blake,' I croak, my throat sore as if I'd inhaled the smoke myself. 'She's ritually killed them by burning them alive!'

Tarek exchanges a deeply uneasy look with Jude. 'The days have just got darker.'

She nods grimly and glances out of the cabin window at the blood-red sky, an eerie aftermath of the sandstorm. 'And our time shorter. Tarek, you need to get us to China – fast. Before Tanas hunts down and kills any more Ascendants.'

22

The next day, in the late afternoon, we touch down at the small provincial airport of Dunhuang and taxi to the terminal. After waiting for the jet to be refuelled, we disembark for security checks. Jude is forced to leave her Taser on board and there's no way to avoid passport control, but Tarek has at least managed to forge student visas for us all and a digital landing permit for the jet. Our fake names are logged into the system, and we can only hope that we won't be staying in the country long enough for Damien and his Soul Hunters to track us down.

We use the jeep's satnav to guide us along the short stretch of highway towards the Mogao Caves. Jude has the radio on and a Mandarin Chinese pop song is playing, its jaunty beat and high-energy vocals in stark contrast to the tense atmosphere. Despite Jude's objections, Mei has joined us on our mission after I argued that she was the only one who spoke fluent Mandarin. I sit in the back with my friend, staring out at the arid landscape. A flat, barren plain ends abruptly at a ridge of yellow sandstone mountains. Hundreds of small caves have been carved into the steep cliff faces that rise from the dry bed of the Dachuan river, and inside one of those caves lies another clue to killing Tanas. At least, I hope so.

But which cave?

'Can we change station?' asks Tarek.

'By all means,' says Jude as the song ends and the presenters come back on and start talking.

As Tarek reaches for the radio, however, Mei sits up sharply. 'No, wait!' Listening intently to the broadcast, she starts translating for us: 'There's been a massive cyberattack on Germany . . . All Berlin's core infrastructure is down – energy, water and telecommunications.' She looks at me in alarm. 'They say it isn't terrorism. Germany are saying it's an act of war.'

I feel a dark sense of foreboding, a tightness in my chest. 'Who by?'

She listens again. 'They don't know who's behind it yet.'

'It's Tanas's influence,' says Tarek, voicing my own fear. 'This is another sign of her growing power. The more the Light fades, the more the world is plunged into chaos and darkness.'

'Then we'd better find all the Soul Jars before she finds us,' says Jude, pulling into the car park at the entrance to the caves.

With an even greater sense of urgency, we clamber out of the jeep and make our way towards the cliffs. At the entrance gate, Mei pays the fee and hands us our tickets. 'We have to join that guided tour over there,' she says, pointing to a small gathering of tourists clustered round a smartly dressed woman wearing thin glasses and carrying a small red flag.

'*Must* we?' complains Jude. 'That'll slow us down. Can't we explore the site alone?'

Mei shakes her head. 'It's impossible to access the caves otherwise.'

The guide beckons us impatiently with a wave of her flag and points at her watch.

'Looks like we don't have any other choice,' says Tarek.

'Who knows – maybe we'll learn something that can help us find this next Soul Jar,' I say as we reluctantly join the group. Tagging along at the rear, we cross the wide footbridge over the river and enter the ancient temple complex.

'The construction of the Mogao Caves began in the fourth century AD after a monk named Lè Zūn had a vision of a thousand Buddhas bathed in golden light,' explains the tour guide. She holds her flag aloft for us to follow her through the other groups of tourists. 'This inspired him to dig a cave here, where the first rays of the rising sun meet the cliffs. Lè Zūn was soon joined by a second monk, Faliang, and over time the site gradually grew. By the Tang Dynasty, the number of caves had reached over a thousand . . .'

'A thousand!' blurts Tarek. He glances sidelong at me. 'Looks like we've got our work cut out then.'

I nod, wondering where on earth we should start our search.

As we approach a towering, saffron-coloured pagoda built into the side of the cliff, the tour guide announces, 'The nine-storey building ahead is Mogao's crowning glory. Inside is cave ninety-six, which contains the second-largest stone Buddha statue in the world.'

She ushers us through the orange wooden doors and there's a collective gasp from the group. Rising in front of us like a gentle giant is the biggest, most monumental statue I've ever laid eyes on. We have to crane our necks just to see the underside of the chin of the colossal Buddha.

'Constructed in the year 695 under the edicts of Empress Wu Zetian, the statue is more than thirty-five metres tall,' the tour guide explains. 'Made of clay stucco over a solid sandstone frame, the statue is so big that the cave had to be dug starting from the top of the cliff. Large earthquakes in the tenth century destroyed all the original murals and wooden structures surrounding it. However, the Buddha's image remained –'

Jude stifles a yawn. 'All this is very interesting,' she murmurs, as the guide carries on with her well-rehearsed script, 'but it doesn't help us find what we're looking for.'

'And what *are* we looking for exactly?' asks Mei, gazing round the pagoda and at the colourful murals on the cave walls. 'I don't see any jars anywhere.'

'The clue said a Buddha "that holds enlightenment within",' I reply. 'So I guess we're looking for a Buddha.'

Tarek peers up at the mighty statue. 'Then do you think this is it? I mean, it's pretty darn big, so it could contain *a lot* of enlightenment!'

I shrug. 'I don't see why not.'

'This statue is just one of the two thousand, four hundred surviving clay statues at the site,' continues the tour guide, 'although, of course, this is the most impressive.'

Mei's jaw drops. 'Did she just say two thousand, four hundred statues?'

I nod and give her a pained smile.

Jude rolls her eyes. 'Then our search could take us days, if not weeks!'

I shrug. 'Well, we'd best get on with it then. Shall we start with this one?' I pat the Buddha's stone foot with my hand and –

I cling on as the ground trembles beneath my feet. There's a roar like an ancient beast awakening from the bowels of the earth and the cave walls begin to crack and crumble around us.

'Zuoren!' I cry, fearing for my life.

My fellow monk breaks from his deep meditation and rushes to my side. He throws his sinewy arms over my shaven head, shielding me against the debris cascading from the roof. He shouts into my ear over the thundering noise, 'DAQIAN! We need to –'

The ground heaves like the deck of a ship and we both struggle to stay standing. The wooden pagoda creaks; joists split apart and rafters start to fall around us. Zuoren grabs my arm and drags me out. We've barely made it into the open when, with a tremendous crash and rush of noise, the temple tumbles down the cliff face in an avalanche of wood and dust. Zuoren pulls me aside to avoid being crushed beneath the landslide.

'Are you hurt?' he asks, dusting off my saffron robes and checking for injuries.

Blinking away the dirt, I shake my head and look up. Through swirling clouds of dust appears the serene face of the Buddha, his half-closed eyes seeming to gaze upon the destruction in stoic resignation.

'What just happened?' I ask, my body now trembling as much as the ground had done.

Zuoren helps me back to my feet. 'It's an omen, Daqian. The invaders are coming.'

I stare into his blazing blue eyes, suddenly even more afraid. 'Incarnates?'

He nods. 'Tanas and his Hunters will surely be among them, feeding off the chaos. I've heard that the Karakhanids have vanquished the kingdom of Khotan. They've destroyed all the Buddhist temples. We must preserve what we can, while we can. Above all, we must keep safe what we've discovered about Tanas. We cannot –'

Another quake hits. As the ground shudders, boulders tumble down the cliff face, trees are uprooted and the wooden footbridge over the river buckles. Monks run for their lives, others fall to their knees praying to the Buddha, and a few can be seen still in their caves, determinedly meditating in spite of the disaster befalling our order.

'We don't have long,' says Zuoren. He leads me through the mayhem and up a wooden ladder to a platform built high on the cliff face. We dash along it to a cave at the far end and enter a shrine exquisitely decorated with rows of seated Buddha figures upon the walls. Flying apsaras adorn the ceiling, the beautiful, nymph-like beings dancing among the painted clouds. As another tremor rocks the cliff, some of the apsaras fall away with the thin layer of plaster and smash upon the floor.

'Not a good omen,' Zuoren mutters as we head further into the cave. Here, the shrine opens out into a larger chamber where the walls have been carved with deep

shelves stacked with numerous scrolls, paintings and manuscripts. Zuoren hurriedly sifts through them.

'These are for the abbot,' he says, shoving a bunch of manuscripts into my arms. 'I'll meet you back outside. There's just one more scroll that we need.'

I carefully make my way to the entrance and wait for Zuoren. Outside, the world is still in turmoil and the wooden platform attached to the cliff is now hanging at a precarious angle. In the far distance, on the horizon of the desert plain, I spy what at first appears to be a caravan of traders travelling along the road to the oasis of Dunhuang. But I soon realize they are moving too fast and can only be warriors on horseback.

'Hurry, Zuoren!' I urge, as more apsaras drop from the ceiling, their images disintegrating into dust.

Zuoren delves into the darkest corner of the cave. 'Got it!' he shouts, holding up a scroll bound with dark red silk.

However, as he turns to rejoin me at the entrance, a massive aftershock strikes. The whole cliff face seems to shift and the roof is brought down in one go.

'Zuoren!' I yell, as he's buried beneath the rubble. Discarding the manuscripts, I dash back into the cave. But I don't get far. As the dust settles, I discover the shrine is completely blocked, the chamber sealed off. Spluttering, I stagger back out to call for help, but suddenly the wooden platform gives way beneath my feet and –

23

'Don't touch the Buddha!' snaps the tour guide, glaring furiously at me.

'Sorry,' I mumble, obediently moving away from the statue. I sway slightly on my feet, still feeling the tremors of the earthquake from my Glimmer.

Mei reaches out a hand to steady me. 'Are you OK?' she asks.

'Fine. Just had a Glimmer, that's all.'

The guide gestures with her flag for everyone to follow her out of the cave. We trail behind the rest of the group again, even as the guide watches us like a hawk.

'Let's ditch this tour,' mutters Jude under her breath. 'Our guide is getting on my nerves.'

'With a thousand caves to search, perhaps we should split up?' suggests Tarek.

'No need,' I reply as we emerge from the pagoda into the late-afternoon sunlight. 'I know which cave we're looking for. I used to be a monk here.'

Mei stares at me. 'That's a lucky coincidence!'

'I'm beginning to think coincidence has nothing to do with it,' I reply. 'First, we find a Soul Jar in my own tomb in Egypt and now the second is in a monastery I used to pray at. Maybe Father Benedict planned it this way.'

I quickly recount my Glimmer to the others as we follow our guide to the next cave on the tour. Despite the renovations and modern walkways, I can still envisage the Mogao Caves as they were all those centuries ago, with their rickety ladders, timber-framed platforms and wooden porches. I point to a cave halfway up the cliff face, in the opposite direction to where our tour guide is going. 'I believe what we're looking for is in there.'

'Then let's go and check it out,' says Jude eagerly.

'Hold on!' I reply, grabbing her arm. I crane my neck to see if the guide still has her eye on us. She's busy answering a question from a small, tubby man with a bucket hat and a video camera, but her sharp gaze remains ever watchful. We wait until she is preoccupied with introducing the next cave, then quietly split off from the group as they follow her inside.

'We'd best hurry,' I say. 'I get the sense she won't miss us for long.'

I lead the way up a set of steps, then along a concrete walkway until we reach a metal barrier with a yellow warning sign. 'What does it say?' asks Tarek.

'Restricted area,' I translate. 'Closed for restoration and repair.'

Mei frowns at me. 'I thought you couldn't read Chinese?'

'I can now,' I say with a grin. 'My Glimmer as the monk Daqian has refreshed my memory.'

'Well,' says Jude, 'it's a shame *I* can't read Chinese!' and she promptly ducks under the barrier.

With a quick check that no one is watching us, I follow her. 'It's the third cave along.'

Skirting past a pile of workmen's tools, we slink inside the entrance only to find our way blocked by a pair of metal doors, intended, no doubt, to preserve the cave from the public. Jude tries the handle but the doors are locked.

'What do we do now?' asks Mei.

I kneel down and peer at the keyhole. 'Anyone got a hairclip or paperclip on them? I might be able to pick the lock.'

Tarek shakes his head and Mei searches her pockets but comes up with nothing.

'I've an idea,' says Jude. She disappears back outside, then returns with a pickaxe.

I laugh. 'That's not the sort of "pick" I mean!'

'I know,' she replies, waving me aside. 'But I think this will be more effective.'

As I step out of the way, Mei asks in a dubious tone, 'You're not going to *dig* your way in, are you, Jude?'

'No. That'll be Plan B if this doesn't work.' She fits the flattened end of the pickaxe into the slim gap between the two doors, then throws her full body weight against the tool's handle. The door frame gives a protesting creak, before the bolt breaks and the doors pop open.

'Ta-da!' says Jude ceremoniously. 'Who needs a key?'

'Good work, Jude,' I say.

'All part of the service,' she replies, as she ushers us inside.

Entering the dark, hall-like cave, Tarek switches on his torch and we're greeted by a large Buddha seated in an alcove at the far end. The statue is guarded by two small, stone Chinese lions. On the ceiling are colourful geometric patterns in gold, turquoise and blue – but there are no dancing apsaras or clouds. The walls are still decorated with rows of stencilled Buddha figures, but, unlike the paintings we've see before, these are painted in bright saffron-orange rather than a more subdued brown, and they are accompanied by scenes of a wonderful paradise.

'*WOW!* These paintings of the Pure Land are amazing!' Tarek lets out an appreciative whistle as his torch beam sweeps over the ancient Buddhist art before he lets it rest on the intricately carved statue. 'So this is the Buddha we're seeking.'

I gaze round in puzzlement. The murals are unfamiliar. 'I'm not entirely sure,' I say. 'This doesn't look like Zuoren's cave – at least, it's not as I remember it. There should be apsaras on the ceiling and a manuscript chamber back there where the statue is.'

'Perhaps we're in the wrong cave?' suggests Mei. 'I mean, with so many, it would be easy to make a mistake.'

Jude hefts the pickaxe to her shoulder. 'OK. Let's try the next one then. See if we have any better luck.'

Disorientated by the strange surroundings, I turn and follow the others, but Tarek lingers behind, examining the breath-taking artwork.

'Are you coming?' I ask.

'Just a moment . . .' he says, and focuses his torch beam on the ceiling. 'It looks like these scenes have been done more recently. I think the original murals have been painted over.' He points to a small section of the ceiling that's still to be renovated. Part of the clay plaster has fallen away to reveal the faded image of a celestial female figure flying among the clouds. I recognize the apsara immediately.

'Of course!' I cry. 'After the earthquake, the damaged murals must have been replaced.' A rush of euphoria floods through me as I realize that this is the right cave after all. I turn slowly round on the spot. 'But then . . . where's the manuscript chamber?'

'Maybe it was relocated following the earthquake?' suggests Jude, coming back in with Mei.

'Possibly. The ceiling did collapse . . .' I stare at the Buddha statue, seeking the enlightenment that it supposedly promises. It returns my pensive gaze with an enigmatic, almost amused look. My eyes are then drawn to a triple spiral in gold leaf upon its forehead. 'Does anyone recognize that symbol?' I ask. 'It looks familiar.'

Tarek peers at the Buddha. 'That's the symbol for reincarnation. Caleb often used it around Haven.'

An image of the marble altar in the Sun Room flashes up in my mind and I realize I've seen the symbol somewhere else very recently too. 'Yes, you're right – that's where I know it from!' Pulling the parchment from my backpack, I hold up the little hand-drawn image of the Buddha and compare the symbols. 'Look, they match!'

Like a veil being pulled back from my eyes, I now notice the same spiral design in the geometric patterns on the ceiling. The whole cave is a shrine to reincarnation! There are even murals depicting the previous lives of the Buddha.

I turn excitedly to the others. 'This is definitely the Buddha we're seeking. And the clue says that one Buddha holds enlightenment *within*.'

Everyone's gaze drifts towards the statue. I tentatively reach out and rap the Buddha's belly with my knuckles. There's a hollow sound.

'That's odd. Didn't the guide say the statues were made of solid sandstone?' questions Tarek.

Jude steps forward and lifts her pickaxe. 'Then what are we waiting for?'

'Whoa, stop!' yells Mei, leaping in front of Jude and holding up her hands. 'You can't destroy a religious idol.'

'But we need to get inside,' insists Jude. 'I think the fate of the world is a little more important than a statue.'

'That may be so, but we still need to show some respect,' insists Mei. 'This is a UNESCO World Heritage Site, after all.'

'How about here, instead?' suggests Tarek, pointing to a larger triple spiral in the mural behind the Buddha. He taps the wall and there's a dull, hollow thud. 'I think this is a false wall.'

'Some sacrifices have to be made,' I say when Mei still looks uncomfortable. 'Besides, it technically isn't the *original* wall anyway. At least, not from what I remember.'

Jude moves into position and swings the pickaxe. Mei winces as the iron tip strikes the wall. There's a heavy *clunk*, the clay layer breaks away, and the sandstone crumbles to reveal . . . a small black hole.

Tarek shines his torch at the hole and peers inside. 'There's a hidden chamber behind!'

Jude works hard to open up the hole and soon the gap is large enough for us to squeeze through. The air inside is cold and stale and I feel as if I've entered a tomb rather than a manuscript room. Piles of rubble are strewn across the floor. The ceiling has lost all its plaster and is partly caved in. The shelves in the walls are stacked high with dusty manuscripts, faded paintings and ancient scrolls. They appear untouched, the bone-dry atmosphere having preserved them through the centuries. The others stand quietly beside me, seeming to sense they're in an ancient library.

Tarek sweeps his torch slowly round the chamber. 'I don't see any Soul Jars,' he says.

'We're not looking for an *actual* jar this time,' I explain. 'We're looking for a scroll.'

'Any idea which scroll?' asks Jude. 'There's quite a few of them here.'

'One that's bound with dark red silk,' I reply.

Together, we start sifting through the aged documents. As we move from shelf to shelf, we discover old books of prayers, Buddhist sutras, Taoist poems and even a manual to playing the game of Go. But none with a dark red silk binding or anything that appears to offer a clue to killing Tanas. I begin to wonder whether the artefact we're looking for is still even here.

Mei blows a layer of dust from a rolled-up parchment and catches Jude full in the face with it.

'Sorry!' says Mei as Jude sneezes hard and stumbles backwards over a rock. She lands with a thud on a pile of rubble, dislodging some of the stones. She gives a startled cry as a bony foot suddenly pokes out.

'Ugh, dead body!' she exclaims, scrambling away and dislodging more stones in the process, and uncovering more bones – what looks like a human shin bone and maybe part of a hand.

We glance at one another, greatly unsettled by this discovery, but we clear away the rest of the rocks to reveal a complete human skeleton. Clasped in its bony hand is a scroll . . . with, yes, a dark red silk binding.

'That's Zuoren,' I say, bowing my head in respect. Presented with such a stark reminder of the monk's death centuries ago, I think of my Soul Protector and I feel once more a sharp pang of grief for the loss of Phoenix.

'I suppose we should thank the Light for small blessings,' says Jude as she gently prises apart Zuoren's fingers and tugs the scroll from his grasp. 'At least we've found the scroll.' She hands it to me.

With Tarek holding the beam of his torch steady, I carefully undo the silk binding and unroll the ancient document. We all stare at a seemingly random array of dots and lines.

'What does it mean?' asks Mei, her face creasing in bafflement.

'I've no idea,' I reply as I turn the scroll upside down in an attempt to make sense of the drawing.

'Looks like a game of join-the-dots to me,' remarks Jude.

Tarek rubs his chin. 'There's something familiar about the patterns,' he murmurs, 'but I can't quite put my finger on it.'

'Come on,' I say. 'Let's see if we can work it out back on the jet.'

Stowing the scroll in my backpack, we clamber out through the hole, dust ourselves down and start heading away from the cave. But we're stopped in our tracks as we find ourselves surrounded by black-shirted security guards, two police officers with expressions as stern as their starched blue uniforms, and one very irate tour guide.

She points her red flag at us. 'That's them!'

24

Our holding cell consists of breeze-block walls, harsh strip lighting, a cold grey floor and a single bolted-down bench. Tarek and Mei sit together on the hard bench: Mei biting her fingernails; Tarek, his head bowed as if in deep prayer. Jude leans against the rear wall, arms crossed, staring off into nothing, while I pace up and down the small cell, feeling like a caged animal. There are no windows, just a single locked metal door.

'How much longer are they going to keep us waiting?' I mutter, glaring at the door as if willpower alone might open it.

Since our arrest and transfer to the local Dunhuang police station, all our belongings have been confiscated, including my backpack with the parchment and the precious scroll. We've been denied access to a phone, a lawyer and even food and water. I shake my head in frustration. *We'd been making such good progress with the clues on the parchment too*, I think. Each find had felt like a small victory against Tanas. But now it looks as if our mission is suddenly over, with our arrest for trespassing and damaging a World Heritage Site! I kick the door in annoyance, then wince in pain, immediately wishing I hadn't.

'Why don't you just sit down and save your energy?' suggests Jude, leaning nonchalantly against the wall.

'How can you be so relaxed?' I snap. 'The longer we're locked in this cell, the greater the chance of Tanas or her Soul Hunters tracking us down!'

Jude puts a finger to her lips, then glances up at the right-hand corner of the cell. A small lens gives away the presence of a CCTV camera.

'I'm aware of the danger,' she replies quietly under her breath. 'But there's little we can do while we're trapped in here, aside from conserving our energies.'

'And what about Nefe?' I whisper. 'Who's going to feed her? She's stuck on the jet.'

'That darn cat of yours is the least of our worries,' mutters Jude. 'I'll be more worried if the jet gets impounded. We'd be well and truly stuck then.'

'Don't worry about Nefe, Genna. I put down extra food for her before we left,' says Mei. 'And I'm sure she's figured out how to use the water fountain. I found her playing with the tap.'

I stop my pacing and sit down beside my friend on the bench. 'Thank you. At least one of us can eat and drink while they're locked up.' I turn to Mei with an apologetic smile. 'I'm sorry for getting you into all this trouble. I bet being arrested was the last thing you expected.'

'Hey, what are friends for?' she says with a half-hearted shrug. 'Besides, it isn't the first time –'

The door buzzes open and a police officer strides in.

White-gloved, with a pressed blue shirt, navy tie and peaked cap, the man has a look on his face that's as blank and unyielding as the breeze-block walls. He sifts through the four passports in his hand, flips one open and calls out, 'Mei Zhang Harrington!'

Startled, Mei springs to her feet and the officer swiftly escorts her out.

'Hey! Where are you taking h–' My question is cut short by the metal clang of the cell door as it closes behind them. I turn to the others in a panic.

'She'll be fine,' Jude assures me.

'Will she? Why's she been separated from us?'

'They probably want to interview us individually to see if our stories match,' explains Tarek, but his drawn expression suggests he's as worried as I am.

'And what is our story?' I slump down on the bench and cradle my head. 'Poor Mei, she must be freaking out. I shouldn't have let her come with us.'

'No, you shouldn't,' Jude agrees bluntly. 'But don't worry. It isn't as if Mei's killed anyone.'

I glance up. 'No, but I supposedly have, thanks to DI Shaw!' I hiss, keeping my voice low. 'How long until they trace who I really am and discover I'm wanted for murdering my own parents?'

'We'll deal with that if we come to it,' replies Jude. She perches herself on the bench and leans in close to me. 'In the meantime,' she continues quietly, 'we need to work out how to get through a locked door, a security-coded gate and past four armed police officers.'

'What?' Then I realize why Jude had carefully positioned

herself against the rear wall. She'd stood there in order to get the best view down the corridor when the door opened, and to figure out an escape route. I sit up straighter, energized by her cunning. I glance at the steel door. 'I can't pick that lock. It's electronic,' I whisper.

'No need to,' replies Jude softly. 'We wait until the officer returns with Mei. He has a key card in his breast pocket – I'm hoping that opens the gate. He carries an electric stun baton on his right hip. I'll disarm him of that while you get the key card. Tarek, you keep the door open for us.' Jude glances up at the camera in the corner of the cell. 'They'll be watching us, so we'll have to be quick. We need to appear casual and unprepared when he enters. So wait for my signal before attacking. I'll cough twice, OK?'

I nod. 'Can't Tarek do something about the camera?'

Tarek looks up, a blank expression on his face. 'Huh?'

I frown at him. 'Have you been listening to anything Jude's just said?'

Tarek shakes his head. 'Er, no, sorry ... my mind's a little preoccupied.'

'With what?'

'The scroll,' he replies, then the corner of his mouth twitches into a grin. 'I think I may have worked out what it is.' He produces a stub of pencil from his jeans pocket and begins to draw on the cell wall, replicating the dots and lines from the scroll. When he's finished, he stands back. What he's drawn looks to be an exact copy of what was on the scroll.

'How do you remember it so accurately?' I ask, amazed.

'I've a photographic memory,' he explains.

'Still looks like a join-the-dots to me,' remarks Jude.

'No, it's actually a star chart,' says Tarek. His finger traces a line of three dots. 'Here is Orion's belt . . . This the constellation of Virgo . . . and *this* represents a rare alignment of the five closest planets in our solar system: Mercury, Venus, Mars, Jupiter and Saturn.'

The star map begins to take shape before my eyes. 'How do you know all this?' I ask.

Tarek gives a modest shrug. 'I used to be an astronomer in a past life under the patronage of Ulugh Beg, the Timurid sultan of Samarkand.'

'Impressive,' says Jude, 'but keep your voice down!'

He nods, and I ask quietly, 'How does a star chart help us in our fight against Tanas?'

Tarek pushes his glasses up his nose. 'To be honest, I've no idea. My best guess is that this alignment indicates the optimum timing to destroy Tanas's soul.'

'And when is that?' presses Jude.

Tarek rubs his chin thoughtfully. 'If I had access to a computer, I could tell you more or less straight away. As I haven't, you'll have to give me a moment.' He starts scribbling mathematical equations on the wall. A moment turns into five minutes, which turns into fifteen . . . and then thirty. All the while I'm worrying about what has become of Mei.

Then Tarek puts down his pencil. 'If my calculations are correct, this conjunction of the planets next occurs in roughly seven days.'

'*Seven days!*' I exclaim, forgetting the CCTV camera.

'Shh!' hisses Jude.

'But we could be held here for a week, if not longer,' I whisper.

'The conjunction will happen again,' assures Tarek.

'Oh, thank goodness,' I say, and let out a sigh of relief. 'When?'

With a strained smile, Tarek replies, 'In about a hundred years.'

'What? That's in another lifetime!' I leap up from the bench, the urgency of our mission now even more pressing than I could have imagined. 'Our souls might not even make it to the next incarnation! We have to –'

'It's a trap!' shrieks Kohsoom, as a gunshot goes off.

She urges me onwards. We run for the sailing boat tethered to the shoreline, our feet splashing in the wet sand. My lungs burn and my heart pounds hard from the sudden exertion. I shouldn't have been such a drinker in this life. I'm just not fit enough.

More gunfire!

I hear Kohsoom cry out. Then a bullet hits me in the back and I go down too. Pain sears through me and I begin to feel as if I'm slowly drowning. But the boat is near . . . I crawl frantically towards it across the sand.

Tanas steps in front of me, her gleeful face lit by a watery dawn sun. Her narrow, dark gaze delights in my desperation as I try to claw my way over the last few metres to the boat that'll take me to Cuba. She plants a foot in my side and rolls me over on to my back. I catch sight of Kohsoom lying further down the beach, the waves washing over her lifeless body.

'This will be the last dawn you'll ever see,' gloats Tanas

as she takes out a jade-green knife and puts the tip to my chest.

I spit into her face. 'The sun will always rise!'

She scowls at me and wipes away my phlegm. 'Not when the last of the Light is extinguished.'

I splutter for breath, blood filling my lungs. 'You'll never . . . find us all.'

Tanas laughs cruelly as her High Priests close in for the ritual. 'Oh, that's where you're wrong, Santiago – so very wrong. The darker the days get, the easier it is to spot your Light –'

'Genna!' calls Jude, bringing me back to my senses. I'm on the floor of the cell. She crouches in front of me, clasping my shoulders. 'What happened?'

I shake my head and sit up. 'I had . . . another soul link.'

'Who with this time?'

'S-Santiago,' I reply, my voice hitching in my throat. 'Tanas tracked him and Kohsoom down.'

Tarek swallows hard, his eyes suddenly wet behind his glasses. 'No! Are they –'

I nod again. I put the palm of my hand to my chest and try to rub away the throbbing pain. While Santiago and I had our differences, his death still hurts; the loss of his Light is a devastating blow.

Tarek goes over to the wall and stares numbly at his calculations. 'What's the point of any of this? Tanas is winning and we're trapped in a prison cell!' He sinks down on to the bench. 'I should *never* have left Thabisa and Kagiso,' he says, his voice racked with guilt. 'They're too vulnerable without me.'

'Zara is a fine Warrior,' assures Jude. 'Thabisa and Kagiso will be safe in her hands.'

Tarek shakes his head. 'Just as Santiago should've been safe with Kohsoom? Sun-Hi with Blake? But they're dead! *All dead!* How long until Tanas finds Thabisa and Kagiso and sacrifices them too?'

I stand up and face Tarek. 'The only way to save Thabisa, Kagiso and the others is by stopping Tanas,' I tell him. 'I vowed to Santiago that I would do my best to protect the Light, to make amends, and that's what I intend to do. We'll get out of here and we will –'

The cell door clangs loudly and we all turn, expecting, hoping to see Mei. But it's just the hatch being opened. A tray is shoved through with three bowls of watery soup.

'*Wǎncān!*' barks the officer on the other side of the door, announcing dinner.

'*Méi zài nǎlǐ?*' I say, demanding in Chinese where my friend is.

The officer bends down and looks through the hatch. 'Don't worry about your friend,' he replies. He treats me to a smile as thin and unappetizing as the soup. 'It's *you* who should be worried. The Hunters are on their way.'

Only now, as the officer peers through the hatch, do I see that his eyes have dilated into the inky pools of a Watcher. Then, before closing the hatch, he deliberately spits into each of the bowls and grins at us. 'Enjoy your last meal!'

25

The night passes excruciatingly slowly. The cell walls press in on us, making it hard to breathe. Fear seeps into my bones. Hungry as we are, the three bowls of soup lie untouched on the floor. I get no sleep, knowing that Tanas's Soul Hunters are closing in. The loss of Santiago and Kohsoom is yet another blow to our already fading hopes. Now the Light of Humanity is being kept burning only by a handful of First Ascendant souls – and Tanas has us all in her sights.

Time is running out . . . fast.

And where is Mei? My best friend! What's become of her? Has she been released? Or is she being interrogated? Or . . . tortured even? I shudder. In the semi-dark, I think the worst. Imprisoned in this police cell, I am powerless. I cannot run, cannot hide. I cannot even help my sweet friend. And it's all my fault.

The stress of our situation is getting to Tarek and Jude too. Tarek continues to berate himself for leaving Thabisa and Kagiso's side, while Jude sits silent and coiled tight as a spring in the corner of the cell. Our plan is to fight our way out. But for that we have to wait for the cell door to open and, when it does, we might be confronted by Hunters rather than police officers. In the gloom of the windowless cell, we lose all track of time. I take out the photo of my parents and gaze at their faces, wishing they were still alive and that none of this had happened.

At some point though I must have fallen asleep, since I wake with a jerk when the cell door bangs open and two police officers appear in the doorway. Tarek sits bolt upright, his glasses askew. Jude springs to her feet, alert and ready.

'OUT!' orders the lead officer with a wave of his baton. He isn't the Watcher who served us dinner – neither is the other officer. They don't possess the pooling eyes of a Hunter or a Watcher but they do both carry stun batons and wear stern expressions.

We're marched down the corridor in single file. I keep my eyes trained on Jude just ahead of me, waiting for her signal to attack. The officer at the front enters the code to the gate and it buzzes open. Directed along a short hallway, we're herded into an interrogation room. One of the original arresting officers stands behind a table, eyeing us critically as we enter. Strewn over the table are all our belongings: our passports, backpacks, money, torches, the keys to the jeep, the parchment and even the star chart. I glance at Jude: this seems the moment to make our move. There are three officers and three of us. We even have our possessions within our grasp. I tense, readying myself for Jude's signal.

Then the police officer announces in English, 'You're free to go.'

We stare at him, momentarily dumbstruck. This is *not* what any of us expected.

'What about Mei?' I demand. 'Is she free to go too?'

'Your friend has been released,' replies the officer without breaking his stern expression. He gestures towards the door on his right. 'She's waiting for you outside.'

I look over at the door promising us our freedom. It seems too good to be true. Warily gathering up our belongings, we head towards the door. As Jude takes hold of the handle, she hesitates and I know what she's thinking. *What awaits us on the other side?* Have the Hunters engineered our release in order to capture us without making a scene?

But when we emerge into the police station foyer, it's empty save for Mei sitting nervously on one of the hard plastic chairs. She looks exhausted, but unharmed.

I dash over to her, and she greets with me with a hurried hug.

'Let's go,' she says, 'before that creepy Watcher officer returns to the reception desk. The jeep's outside – they brought it over this morning.'

Without needing to be told twice, we head outside and across the car park.

'What happened? How come we've been released?' asks Tarek as the four of us clamber into the vehicle.

'The police allowed me one call,' Mei explains, seating herself in the back with me. 'So I called my mother.'

Jude glances in the rear-view mirror at Mei. 'Your *mother*? She must have been darn persuasive to get us out of that situation.'

'My mother's furious,' Mei replies curtly. 'So is my father.

If it wasn't for our discoveries at the cave yesterday and in Egypt, I think I'd be grounded for the rest of my life! But, thanks to my mother's family connections and her reputation as a world-renowned archaeologist, she does have some influence in these matters –'

'HEY!' comes an angry shout from outside.

We turn to see the Watcher officer striding out of the police station towards us.

'GO! GO! GO!' says Tarek as the officer begins to run, his baton raised.

Jude guns the engine and speeds out of the car park.

Once we're clear of the police station and certain that the Watcher hasn't jumped into a car to follow us, I turn to Mei, a heavy guilt weighing upon my shoulders. 'I'm really sorry I dragged you and your family into this.'

'Don't blame yourself, Genna. It was my decision to come with you,' insists Mei. 'But I can't lie – I'm on very thin ice with my parents. You can imagine how angry they are that I went off without discussing it with them first, and they're even more anxious now that there's been that cyberattack on Berlin and all the talk of a possible war in the news. But as soon as I mentioned the vast treasures we found in Pharaoh Hepuhotep's hidden tomb, my mum's mood quickly changed.'

'Yeah, I bet it did!' says Jude, turning on to the main road. 'There's a king's ransom in that pyramid.'

'Well, her upbeat mood didn't last long. I had to tell her we'd been arrested. In China.' Mei grimaces. 'My mother completely lost it. She was so angry. At least, she was until I told her about Zuoren's manuscript chamber. She couldn't believe her ears! She was comparing our discovery to those of Tutankhamun and the Dead Sea Scrolls. Anyway, once she'd finally calmed down, she contacted the director of the Mogao Caves – turns out he's an old friend from Beijing University. Which is kind of lucky for us. And, in light of our extraordinary find, he agreed to create official permits, backdated to cover our *unofficial* archaeological dig. Then he arranged for the charges to be dropped and secured our release. I'm just sorry it took all night.'

'Gosh, don't be sorry,' says Tarek. 'You've saved our skins!'

'There's one condition though,' Mei informs us. 'We've four hours to leave the country, otherwise we'll be back in jail.'

'Oh, don't worry – we've no intention of staying any longer,' replies Jude. 'There are Soul Hunters on the way.'

As we speed along the highway towards the airport, I take Mei's hand. 'I've been thinking. Maybe we should drop you back in England with your parents. This is becoming far too dangerous.'

Mei vehemently shakes her head. 'I'm not leaving you.'

'But I can't have you risking your life like this. I worried all night about you.'

'I know, Genna, but I can look after myself,' she replies. 'Besides, you need me. You'd still be in jail if it wasn't for me. And if what you say about Tanas is true, then I'm in grave danger whether I'm with you or not.'

'Surely, after what's just happened, your parents want you home,' I argue.

'Not yet,' Mei says. 'I explained we're following clues from an ancient scroll that could lead us to even greater treasures. It took a bit of persuasion, but they eventually agreed I could stay with you, on the condition I updated them immediately with any more finds. I guess they're happy that I'm finally showing an interest in archaeology!' she adds with a laugh.

Realizing I won't be able to dissuade my friend, I find myself laughing too. Then I feel a strange, faint pulsing in my chest, the sensation swelling like the throb of a bass speaker. I glance out of the window as a black car speeds by on the other side of the road and the laughter dies in my throat as I catch a glimpse of pale skin and raven-coloured hair in the front passenger seat.

'That was *Damien*!' I gasp, the throb fading the further the distance gets between us and the black car.

Jude floors the accelerator. 'Then we don't have long before he reaches the police station and discovers we've been released.'

Cornering hard into the airport, we pull up at the entrance gate and show our documents. After a slight delay, we're given clearance and waved through. Jude heads over to our waiting jet at the far end of the runway. The rear door automatically opens at the jeep's approach and Jude drives up the ramp and into the cargo hold. Once the door closes behind us, we leap out, dash through to the cabin and buckle ourselves into our seats. Nefe peeps out from her bolthole under the computer console but has the good sense to stay where she is..

'OK, let's go,' calls Jude impatiently to Tarek.

'We can't. We don't have permission to take off yet,' replies Tarek from the cockpit.

Feeling the vague pulsating in my chest return, I peer out of the window and spot a black car skidding on to the tarmac. 'Damien's found us! We can't wait for permission!'

Cursing, Tarek pushes forward the throttle and the jet moves on to the runway. Even from the cabin I can hear the protests of the air traffic controller leaking from Tarek's headphones. But Tarek ignores them as he increases speed. Damien's black car races up alongside us. The passenger window rolls down and his vampire-pale face appears. His black eyes blaze with fury when he spots me on board. The next thing I know, he has a hand gun and is pointing it at the undercarriage of the plane.

'Damien's trying to shoot out the wheels!' I exclaim.

'We're not yet at take-off velocity,' Tarek replies, holding his course.

The shouting through his headset becomes even louder as we continue our desperate escape down the runway.

'Air traffic control seem a little annoyed,' comments Jude.

'They should be,' replies Tarek through gritted teeth. 'Another plane is coming into land!'

Mei shoots me a panic-stricken look and grips the arms of her seat in terror. I glance out again and see Damien still taking pot shots at our landing gear. Then Tarek pulls up hard on the joystick. The jet's engines strain, the fuselage shudders and the wheels lift off the ground. Behind me, I hear Jude's shield come loose from its seat and hit the rear bulkhead with a crash. Through the cockpit door I spy the other plane heading directly towards us and let out a startled shriek. Tarek fights the controls, pushing the jet to its limit. At the last moment, we pass over the other aircraft, barely clearing its tail fin. It roars beneath us and our whole jet shudders in the turbulence.

Then it's open sky ahead.

I look out through the cabin window again at the airfield below and watch as Damien's car is forced off the runway, almost crushed by the other plane landing. The car skids to a stop as we soar away into the clear sky.

26

'That was close, too close,' Mei gasps, releasing her death grip on the armrests.

I too settle back in my seat with a sigh of relief. 'Nice flying, Tarek!'

'I wasn't flying – I was praying!' he replies, still gripping the control stick so hard that the whites of his knuckles are showing. 'I might just lose my pilot's licence for pulling off that little stunt!'

'Don't worry – the other plane landed safely,' says Jude.

Once the jet reaches cruising altitude and levels out, Mei unbuckles her seatbelt and heads to the galley. 'I need a mint tea,' she says. 'Anyone else want one?'

Jude and Tarek both decline. 'I'll have one,' I say, my stomach feeling a touch queasy after the perilous take-off.

Emerging now from her bolthole, Nefe winds herself round my legs and mews hungrily. Evidently our stressful escape hasn't affected her appetite. I get up and join Mei in the galley. Finding a tin of tuna in a cupboard, I open it and spoon the contents into Nefe's bowl, and as she tucks in I realize just how famished I am.

'That Damien is certainly hellbent on killing us all, isn't

he?' remarks Mei, her hand visibly trembling as she dunks the teabags in our cups. 'If he'd managed to shoot the wheels out, we'd have crashed for certain.'

'Damien doesn't want to kill us,' I correct her. 'He just wants to capture us for his master.' I delve into another cupboard and find a box of protein bars. I take it out and put it on the table. 'Breakfast!' I call to the others, then turn back to Mei. 'After that, Tanas will sacrifice us and destroy our souls forever, along with the Light of Humanity.'

'Great,' says Mei, tossing the teabags into the bin. 'Something to look forward to!'

She hands me my cup. We clink our drinks together in a solemn toast. I take a sip of herbal tea and feel the tension in my stomach ease slightly. Sitting down at the dining table, we unwrap a protein bar each and hungrily devour our scant breakfast.

'That's the *second* time Damien's caught up with us,' remarks Jude crossly, as she retrieves her shield from the floor and looks for a better place to stow it. 'It's like he's planted a tracker on us or something.'

'That Watcher officer at the police station must have informed him. The Incarnate network seem to have infiltrated *everywhere*.' I rub away the lingering ache in my chest, wondering what caused it. *Stress? Anxiety? Damien's presence?* I take another sip of tea to calm my nerves.

'Or else Damien simply traced our passports,' Mei suggests, 'when we went through immigration control.'

Jude secures her shield behind the minibar, then joins us at the table. She helps herself to a protein bar and in three quick bites polishes it off. 'Even so, Damien got to China worryingly quickly.' She turns to the cockpit and calls, 'Are you certain they can't track this plane, Tarek?'

'As certain as I can be,' he replies. 'I've been using the jet's stealth mode when entering new airspaces and been careful to wipe its ID registration from any landing records.'

'Well, I still don't like how fast we're being hunted down,' says Jude, selecting a second bar from the box. 'It's as if they already know where we're going.'

'Then we need to complete this Soul Jar quest before Damien finds us again,' I say. Setting my tea down, I get my backpack and take out the parchment and star chart and place them on the table. 'According to Tarek's calculations, we've less than six days until the conjunction of the five planets. And so far we've only got a mummified hand and a deadline.'

'So what's the next clue?' asks Mei.

As Tarek emerges from the cockpit to join us for our poor excuse of a breakfast, I smooth out Father Benedict's cryptic manuscript flat on the polished wooden surface for all to see.

Mei points to a curving script at the bottom of the page. 'Is that in Arabic?'

Tarek reaches for the box of protein bars and glances across. 'No. Looks similar, though.'

Mei looks up at him, somewhat alarmed. 'Who's flying the plane?'

'Don't worry,' he says, smiling. 'It's on autopilot.'

I study the script a little closer. 'I think that might be . . . Sanskrit?' I say, vaguely recognizing the language from my incarnation as Aarush. I recall my reading lessons under the tutelage of my strict and ancient martial arts guru. After each long training session in Kalarippayattu, we'd sit in the shade of a mango tree in our village of Aranmula and she'd make me study the Hindu holy scripture, the Bhagavad Gita. She told me that each Sanskrit word had its own consciousness, and that pronouncing a word perfectly allowed one to tap into that consciousness – '*No other language in the world can translate the divine word like Sanskrit*,' she would say. At times, her reading lessons felt harder and more painful than the Kalari training she'd put me through!

'Can you read what it says?' asks Jude, finishing off her third bar and tossing the wrapper in the bin.

I frown deeply. 'I'm not sure. Sanskrit's mainly used for the sacred texts of Hinduism. The letters here are similar to Aarush's mother tongue of Malayalam, but the words are slightly different.' I run my finger along the script as if trying to feel my way into the past. 'There's something about a river's banks . . . a city and . . . *mṛtyu*.'

'What's that?' asks Tarek, helping himself to a soda from the fridge.

I look up from the intricate string of Sanskrit characters with a grim expression. 'Death.'

Tarek dryly swallows his food, then takes a gulp of his drink.

'Sounds inviting,' remarks Jude. 'Any other cheery clues?'

The script fades into the charred bottom edge of the parchment. I flip the page over, hoping to find the rest of the clue, but the other side is blank. 'Looks like it's been burned away.'

'Then it's not much help,' says Jude. 'We'll have to skip that Soul Jar.'

'We can't,' I say. 'Father Benedict said each jar is vital to stopping Tanas.'

'Well, what else do you suggest? How are we supposed to –'

Without warning, the jet shudders, then drops so suddenly that we're lifted from our seats.

'Turbulence!' cries Tarek, dashing back to the cockpit. Nefe flees for her bolthole beneath the console, while Mei, losing grip on her cup, sloshes tea over the table. The scalding water splashes across the parchment and my hands. I cry out in pain –

My skin blisters as I pull the parchment from the fire. In desperation, I smother the document with my monk's habit, putting out the licks of flame along its edge. But the inferno consuming the monastery rages on. The screams of my fellow brethren echo through the burning cloisters and the blaze roars in my ears like a hot wind.

The hooded figure in the black habit tugs out his vile blade from Father Benedict's body and leaves it to slump to the floor. He advances towards me, his gaunt face red in the firelight, his sunken eyes glinting with murderous intent.

I scramble away across the flagstones but I'm surrounded on all sides by flames. Smoke swirls in the air and I choke from the acrid stench close to my face of the fire singeing my hair. As the hooded Incarnate bears down on me I know I'm about to die, and wonder if it will be the fire or his blade that gets me first. Keeping the parchment safe inside the folds of my habit, I pray for salvation.

The hooded Incarnate lets out a hoarse laugh. 'No use praying now. Your soul is mine!'

All of a sudden the burning door is kicked off its hinges and an ice-cold wind cuts through the inferno. Amid a blizzard of snow a knight in battle-worn armour strides into the monastery. He marches in our direction, dispatching the black-cloaked monks with wide sweeps of his iron broadsword as if scything down barley in a field. The hooded Incarnate standing over me turns and thrusts his blade at the approaching knight, but his weapon is no match for the knight's chain mail. As the blade glances off him, the knight slams an iron-clad fist into the Incarnate's face. There's a crunch of bone as his nose breaks. Writhing in pain, he drops to the floor. Above us, the burning roof timbers start to come crashing down. The knight grabs my arm and hauls me out of the open door, leaving the injured Incarnate to be crushed beneath a pile of blazing beams.

Outside the night is dark and cold, the land thickly blanketed in white. The knight bundles me into a snowdrift, rolls me over, extinguishing the flames that lap at my sleeves and the hem of my habit.

'Who are you?' I rasp, my throat sore from smoke. I relish the welcome coolness of the snow upon my scorched skin.

The knight flips back the visor of his helmet and I'm startled to see that my rescuer is not a man but a young woman with a rose-white face and eyes like sapphires. 'Don't look so surprised, young Wilfrid! Lady Eleanor Fitzalan at your service, daughter of the Earl of Arundel, and your Soul Protector in this life.' She offers me her hand.

'I'm as skilled with a sword as any knight and as brave, and I am here to escort you to England.'

'England?' I reply, even more confused.

Lady Eleanor pulls me out of the snowdrift. 'Yes, it will be far safer for you there.'

I turn in despair to my former sanctuary, the monastery now a flaming funeral pyre for Father Benedict and my fellow monks. As Lady Eleanor untethers a horse from a tree nearby, I gingerly take out Father Benedict's parchment from the folds of my habit. To my relief the document is still intact; only the bottom edge is burned. I can still just make out the strange script that Father Benedict wrote there and hurriedly commit that piece to memory before the charred edge crumbles into ash and is lost in the snow –

'Sorry,' says Mei as she mops up the mess. 'How's your hand?'

'No need to be sorry,' I say, blinking away the vision. 'You helped trigger a Glimmer. I now know how the parchment got to England. More importantly, I remember the rest of the script!'

Tarek once more has the jet under his control, so I get up and go over to the computer console. 'Of course, I couldn't make sense of it at the time,' I explain, pulling up a virtual keyboard on the screen, 'but following my incarnation as Aarush, I can now recognize the Sanskrit characters.'

I switch the keyboard setting to Sanskrit and painstakingly type in the words I'd committed to memory. Then I press translate and the complete clue appears in English on the screen. I read it out loud so Tarek can hear too:

'*Upon a holy river's banks an ancient City of Light*

expands. Here, where life to death is turned, a flame eternal forever burns. Take from this fire to fuel your fight, and in so doing save day from night.'

'Well, that clears things up nicely!' snorts Jude, joining me at the console. 'Another blindingly obvious clue.'

'Are you sure that's translated correctly?' questions Mei.

'I'll double-check,' I say, and pass the script through a second translation program, only to get the same result. 'So, if I'm interpreting this right, it seems we have to find an eternal flame and use it to fight Tanas.'

Jude nods. 'But first we need to figure out where this City of Light is. Any idea?'

I frown, racking my brain, sure I've heard this phrase somewhere before . . .

'Paris is known as the City of Light,' says Mei.

'Is it? You're certainly proving to be a fountain of knowledge, Mei,' I remark, looking my friend up and down. 'You were never like this at school. Where did you get that nugget of information from?'

'I was there last summer with my mother,' she replies. 'To be honest, I'd hoped it was going to be a shopping trip, but it ended up being another of her "fascinating" history trips.' She rolls her eyes. 'I had a full lecture on how Paris was a centre of the Enlightenment during the eighteenth century and one of the first cities to start using street lights during the Great Exhibition of 1889.'

'That's all very interesting,' says Jude. 'The only problem is that Paris isn't on a holy river.'

'You're right,' I say, pulling up a map of Paris and the River Seine on the screen. 'So, what holy rivers are there?'

'The Jordan,' calls Tarek from the cockpit.

'This clue is written in Sanskrit though,' points out Jude. 'I assumed the river would be more likely to be located somewhere in South Asia.'

'The Ganges then?' he suggests.

I nod, sensing that this is somehow right. 'And what ancient City of Light is on the Ganges?'

'Delhi? Mumbai?' proposes Jude.

I call up a map of India. 'No, I don't think so. Delhi is too far west, and Mumbai is on the coast.'

'I bet Prisha would know,' says Mei as we all peer at the map.

The mention of our friend jogs a memory. I think of our last sleepover together at Prisha's house in celebration of her birthday, and then I remember where I heard the phrase 'City of Light' used before. 'Prisha *does* know!' I exclaim. 'In fact, we both know too, Mei. What did Prisha's father give her for her birthday?'

Mei gives me a bemused look. 'Er . . . tickets to see the Rushes?'

I laugh. 'Yes – but also a once-in-a-lifetime pilgrimage trip to Varanasi in India.'

Mei now mirrors my excited expression. 'Of course! Mr Sharma called it the sacred City of Light.'

I zoom in on Varanasi on the flight map and send Tarek the coordinates. 'It's time to go on a pilgrimage of our own.'

27

The dawn sun casts a reddish hue upon the mirror-like surface of the Ganges as our rickety rowing boat slowly makes its way up the river.

Having landed at a disused airstrip an hour outside Varanasi, we'd attempted to drive into the ancient city, but had been defeated by the potholed roads and the tangle of traffic – rickshaws fending off taxis, buses barging aside lorries, and sacred cows blocking Varanasi's narrow streets. Moving at a snail's pace and feeling oppressed by the humidity, we'd eventually given up and hired a boatman to take us via the river instead. Just one of countless people plying their trade along the banks of the Ganges, he'd offered us the best price for our journey up to the city, and he had helped us change some dollars for rupees too. True, he didn't own the best boat there was, but when Mahul had introduced himself I'd noticed the faintest blue sheen to his eyes and sensed he may be a Soul Brother. I got a good feeling about hiring him, anyway.

Now, Mahul's sinewy brown arms strain against the current, and his wooden oars creak as his paddles plop in and out of the muddy waters. To one side of us, where the sun is rising, the land is a vast, flat and empty marshland. On the other, the bank is lit golden by the sun's rays and is crammed with a bewildering jumble of temples, ashrams, royal palaces and crumbling hotels. Morning prayers and the chiming of bells echo across the waking city, smoke hangs like mist in the sultry air, and countless fires smoulder along the river's banks where piles of wood are stacked almost as high as the temples.

'What's that smell?' asks Mei, wrinkling her nose as we draw closer to the city.

I almost retch as well at the overpowering stench. It's a sickening mix of burning plastic, rotting rubbish and cow dung. A faint aroma of spices, jasmine and incense wafts in the air too, along with something else I can't quite identify, but I daren't breathe in too deep for fear of being sick.

Mahul grins, revealing a row of bone-white teeth. 'Welcome to Varanasi!' he says, noticing our queasy expressions. 'You'll soon get used to the smell.'

'I very much hope so,' mumbles Jude, covering her mouth and nose while she tries and fails to keep her feet out of the brown slurry of water washing around in the bottom of the boat.

'What are all the fires for?' asks Tarek, who perches at the stern of the rocking vessel.

'Cremations,' replies Mahul. 'This city is where many Hindus come to die.'

'It's certainly a popular spot for it,' Mei remarks, gazing in astonishment at the large groups hosting multiple funeral ceremonies on the ghats leading down to the river. Crowds of people of all ages line these stone steps, either praying, mourning or bathing in the holy waters of the Ganges.

'You've arrived at a busy time,' explains Mahul, turning towards the bank. 'This is the start of Diwali, the festival of lights.'

Rows of earthenware lamps line the buildings along the waterfront, and strings of festive lights hang between the roofs like colourful cobwebs. As we approach, a cluster of children let off firecrackers among the crowd. There are delighted squeals and good-natured exclamations of shock.

Mahul pulls up at a wide, stone-stepped dock and helps us to disembark. 'I hope this Diwali brings light into your lives!' he calls.

'And yours too,' I say with a smile, adding a generous tip for his services. Stepping on to the dock, I experience an odd yet familiar tingling in my limbs. Although it could be the warmth of the rising sun on my skin, I can't help but feel that we've arrived in the right place. I sense a strong presence of the Light, similar to that which I felt in Haven.

As soon as our boatman departs, though, that sense of peace is shattered as we're quickly surrounded by touts, beseeching beggars and excited children.

'For the goddess Ganga,' urges one round-faced little girl, thrusting a small candle into my hand. I examine it, intrigued to discover the wax has been moulded into a star shape. Believing this to be a lucky sign, I offer her some rupees in return and she runs off happily.

I carefully pocket the candle, then a rangy old man seizes my wrist and holds out his open palm. 'Donation for old people's home,' he croaks, his tone more a demand than a request. Slightly alarmed by his aggressive approach, I pull away. His bony grip on me tightens.

A slick-haired, younger man steps in and disentangles me from the beggar, shooing him off. 'You need an English-speaking guide?' he asks, flashing me a winning smile. Then another young man jumps in, offering his services too. Jostled by the eager crowd, I feel like a cork bobbing in a storm.

'What do you reckon, Jude? Do we need a guide?' I ask, as more and more touts vie for our business.

'We have to be careful,' says Jude, waving away a man with a bushy beard and bad breath. 'We can't trust anyone.'

'But we do need a guide,' I insist.

Jude shakes her head. 'Not necessarily. Not for what we're looking for.'

I frown. 'Then how are we going to find this eternal flame without help –'

'You want to see the eternal flame?'

I turn sharply to the would-be guide with the winning smile. 'You know where it is?' I ask him.

He nods enthusiastically. 'Come, come – I can show you.' And, before we know it, we're being shepherded up the steps.

'Your first time in India?' he asks. His black hair is as smooth as his smile, his prominent teeth somewhat over bright. His pink shirt is pressed and remarkably clean despite the ash floating in the air.

'Not really,' I reply, reckoning that my former life as Aarush in Kerala counts as my first time in this land. Although that incarnation was in the far south of India, and my Glimmer was restricted to my time learning the ancient martial art of Kalarippayattu, it familiarized me enough with the vibrant culture of the country.

'Then your first time in Varanasi?'

'For me it is,' says Mei, looking around in awe at the rainbow of colourful, crumbling buildings.

'Good. Then let me tell you all about it,' he says, weaving expertly between the throngs of mourners and festival-goers. 'Varanasi – or the City of Light as it is known during Diwali – is one of the oldest settlements in the world. In fact, some people consider it an immortal city. For Hindus, it is the holiest of cities, a crossing point between earth and heaven.'

He leads us up to a platform overlooking the largest of the cremation grounds. A funeral pyre has been readied for the arrival of the corpse. A stream of mourners trail behind four men bearing a body swathed in saffron-coloured robes.

'Manikarnika Ghat,' announces our guide with a majestic sweep of his hand. 'This place is so sacred that to die here helps the soul achieve *moksha* – the breaking of the soul's endless cycle of death and rebirth – thus ensuring entry into heaven.'

I exchange a hopeful look with Tarek. 'Seems like we've come to the right place to end Tanas's rebirth,' he says, keeping his voice down, and I nod in agreement.

We watch as, below us, the body of the deceased is carefully washed in the waters of the Ganges before being embalmed and wrapped in white linen. Finally it is laid to rest on the funeral pyre, and a priest in a white dhoti emerges from a nearby building carrying a smouldering stick. He slowly circles the pyre fives time before setting the wood alight. The fire quickly takes hold, and the body is consumed by the flames.

Jude looks around and taps the guide on the shoulder. 'So, where's this eternal flame you promised us?'

'Close, very close,' our guide replies earnestly. 'Come this way.'

With the smell of sandalwood thick in our nostrils, we follow him down a narrow, twisting backstreet. I notice Jude's hand is in the pocket of her cargo pants, no doubt clasping her Taser gun. However, I'm more excited at the prospect of finding our next Soul Jar than worried by our guide – while his eyes may be dark brown, they show no signs of having a Watcher's or Hunter's over-dilated pupils.

We turn a corner into an alley, and I glimpse a sandy-coloured cat atop a nearby roof. For a moment I think it's Nefe, until I realize this one's a stray, although I wouldn't have been surprised if Nefe had indeed escaped the jet and followed us. She's becoming quite irritable from being cooped up all the time, and I don't blame her, but we can't allow her to roam free. We never know when we might have to make a quick getaway.

We turn another corner and find our way blocked by a cow coming the other way. The guide shoos the animal to one side. After squeezing past, we duck through a low door into a small, smoky temple to the rear of the ghat, where we are proudly shown a smouldering fire of six or so small logs in a plain stone hearth.

'The eternal flame!' declares our guide.

We stand around the pitiful fire in underwhelmed silence.

Our guide beams at us. 'I can see you are all suitably awed!'

'Not really,' says Jude, speaking for all of us. 'To be honest, it doesn't look very eternal. In fact, it looks like it's going out.'

'No, no! Don't let appearances deceive you,' he insists, wafting a piece of cardboard at the flames. 'This fire has been kept burning for more than three thousand, five hundred years. It contains the eternal flame created by Lord Shiva himself. Without it the funeral pyres cannot be lit.'

Jude still looks dubious, but my hopes are relit.

'If what he says is true,' I whisper to Tarek, 'then this is the fire we need to fight Tanas!'

'But how are we going to take it with us?' asks Tarek, eyeing the small pile of burning logs.

'Using this,' I say, pulling the candle from my pocket. 'If it's eternal, we just need the flame.' I turn to our guide. 'I've someone's death I wish to honour. May I light this candle from the fire?'

The guide inclines his head. 'A donation is usually expected.'

'Of course,' I reply, taking out my purse and handing him some notes.

With a quick flash of a smile, he pockets the money. But, as I go to put away my purse, his expression sags. 'Each cremation is so expensive,' he says with an almost theatrical sigh. 'Just one kilogram of wood costs more than a week's wages for many people, and each pyre requires tens of kilograms. It's desperately sad that many poor people cannot afford the wood and therefore won't achieve *moksha*. They're waiting here to die, without hope.'

Mei puts a hand to her mouth. 'Oh, that's awful.'

'I know,' agrees our guide. 'I, however, represent a local charity that funds cremations for the poor. So if you would care to make another donation?' He holds out his hand.

'Sure . . .' I reach into my purse and make another generous contribution.

The winning smile returns. Then, as he counts the notes, it is replaced by a scowl. 'There's four of you. You need to donate more!'

'I'm sorry?' I reply. 'More?'

'Yes! You need to donate *all* your money,' he insists as several shifty-looking accomplices suddenly emerge from the shadows. I curse under my breath. We've been tricked!

28

The fake guide and his gang close in on the four of us, blocking our escape to the door.

'Stay back!' warns Jude, and she draws her Taser.

The guide stops, then cocks his head to one side and smirks at her. 'That's a Taser, not a handgun, so you can only shoot one of us. Now stop playing games and hand over your money.'

His expression hardens and he pulls out a butterfly knife and flicks open the handle to reveal a shiny blade. His accomplices unsheathe an array of equally vicious weapons, including one very nasty-looking machete.

I barely have time to register the danger we're in when there's a deafening *BANG* and the fire explodes in a burst of bright white light. The guide is thrown backwards by the force of the blast; the rest of his gang are dazed and blinded. Yet oddly I only feel a wave of heat through my body. My sight remains unaffected. Jude, Tarek and Mei also appear untouched by the blast and observe the strange scene with bemused expressions.

Clearing the smoke from my face, I notice an old man standing at the back of the room. He leans upon a tall wooden staff as thin and gnarled as his own body. Dressed like a guru who's wandered in off the street, he wears a saffron-coloured loin cloth round his waist, several strings of beads round his neck, and wooden bangles on his scrawny arms. His greying hair hangs long and lank down his back, while the tip of his beard almost reaches his protruding belly button. His dark brown face is cast in shadow and his eyes are so sunken they can't be seen.

'Be gone!' the old man orders, in a voice that is surprisingly strong.

The guide and his accomplices tremble before the apparition and stagger half-blindly out of the temple. For a moment we stand motionless too, then, unnerved by this skeletal holy man, we make a bolt for the door ourselves.

'No, not you!' he commands.

We stop dead in our tracks. Turning slowly back, we all bow our respects.

'We're grateful for your help,' I say. Feeling the candle still in my hand, I ask, 'Could we take a light from this fire? We need to break a soul's cycle of rebirth.'

The guru clicks his tongue disapprovingly and wags a bony finger. I lower the candle, disappointed. Then to my surprise he announces, 'That is not the fire you seek.'

Jude is at once on her guard, her Taser levelled at him. 'How do you know which fire we're looking for?'

The guru raises his hands.

'Ow!' yelps Jude, dropping her weapon. As it hits the ground, the Taser sparks.

'What's wrong?' asks Tarek. 'What happened?'

Jude massages her hand. 'I'm OK. The gun short-circuited on me, that's all. Must have got wet on board the boat.' She nudges the Taser with her foot before gingerly picking it back up.

From the corner of the room, the guru lets out a quiet chuckle and I suspect that there's more to the malfunction than water damage. 'You haven't answered our question,' I remind him. 'How do you know which fire we're looking for?'

'This fire is for tourists,' he replies with a dismissive wave of his staff. 'If you wish to find the flame that burns eternal, then follow me.'

The holy man steps out of the shadows and Mei stifles a gasp. I stiffen in surprise, for his face looks as old as time itself, his cheeks hollow and his skin wrinkled like worn leather, but what's most shocking are his eyes – the sockets of which are empty, like dark caves. Despite his apparent lack of sight, he strides easily between us and out through the door.

'We're not going to follow him, are we?' whispers Mei. 'He looks like Gandalf!'

I point to the pile of logs, their flames slowly dying. 'What other option do we have?'

Jude shakes her head. 'I'm with Mei,' she says, which surprises me, because they don't often agree. 'This feels like another scam. I don't fancy getting mugged a second time.'

'But the guru saved us,' I argue. 'And he seems to know about our quest.'

'All the more reason not to go with him,' says Jude. 'Because he doesn't have eyes, we can't tell if he's an Incarnate or not.'

'Well, I'm with Genna on this. I don't see we have much choice,' says Tarek. 'Unless you two know where to find another eternal flame?'

Jude looks despondently at the smouldering logs and shakes her head.

Having Tarek's backing, I glance towards the door. 'Come on,' I urge. 'We're going to lose him otherwise.'

Jude resets her Taser and sighs. 'I guess it's out of the frying pan and into the fire then.'

Dashing out of the temple, we catch sight of the guru vanishing round a bend and we hurry after him. The alleyway twists and turns, the guru always one step ahead of us.

'What does this guy have for breakfast?' Mei pants, as we push past another cow. 'For such an old man, he sure does move fast.'

'There's something unusual about him, that's for certain,' I reply.

'*Unusual?*' says Jude, narrowly missing treading in a pile of dung. 'I'd say dangerous!'

All of a sudden the alleyway ends and we spill out on to a busy street jam-packed with festival-goers and mourners. Car horns blare, bells ring and firecrackers burst at our feet.

'Where is he?' shouts Tarek, standing on the tips of his toes to look over the heads of the crowd.

'There!' cries Mei. She points to the carved tip of the guru's staff wending its way through the market. We dive into the crowd. As we battle our way through the tide of oncoming people, I hear a shout over the hubbub. 'Genna?'

I spin round, thinking it's Jude who's calling me, but who should appear out of the melee, her father in tow, but Prisha.

'Genna! It *is* you.' My friend is wearing a purple sari, her long black hair tied back and her bindi dot a bright red. 'And Mei! What on earth are you two doing here? And who are your friends?'

I embrace Prisha warmly, delighted and amazed our paths have crossed. 'Prisha, this is Jude, and this is Tarek,' I say. 'Jude, Tarek – this is our friend Prisha Sharma and her father.' They all shake hands. 'We're on a pilgrimage,' I explain. 'Of sorts.'

'A pilgrimage!' exclaims Mr Sharma, his bushy moustache curling upwards with his grin. 'Genna, I must say it's good to see you finding your way after you got so lost, metaphorically speaking.'

As Mei and Prisha become immersed in conversation, I crane my neck to look for the guru and am relieved to see he's waiting by the entrance to a narrow lane. Mr Sharma leans close to me, his smile softening.

'I'm so sorry about the passing of your parents, Genna,' he says in a hushed tone. 'I didn't believe for one second that preposterous suggestion of you being involved in their deaths. But please try not to grieve too bitterly for them. As it is written in the Bhagavad Gita: "Death is certain for one who has been born, and rebirth is inevitable for one who has died. Therefore you should not lament over the inevitable."'

'It isn't simply their deaths I grieve, Mr Sharma,' I reply, feeling a sharp pang in my heart. 'It's that their lives were cut so cruelly short.'

Mr Sharma presses his palms together and bows his head. 'You're quite right, Genna. As a Hindu, though, I believe they'll be reborn and will have the chance to live again. I sincerely hope you can find some solace in that.'

'I believe that too –'

'Father, can I join my friends on their pilgrimage?' asks Prisha, out of the blue.

Jude catches my eye and gives me a firm shake of the head.

Mr Sharma purses his lips, his moustache bristling. 'I don't see why not, my petal, at least for a little while –'

'No, we mustn't disturb your special holiday together,' I interrupt.

'But I can help you, Genna,' insists Prisha, fixing me with a meaningful stare. 'Mei has told me *all* about your pilgrimage and how important it is.'

I shoot Mei a disbelieving look. Surely she'd know that, following our arrest in China, I wouldn't wish to draw another of my friends into direct danger? 'Has she now?' I say primly. 'Well, Prisha, you'll understand what's at stake then.'

'Helping another in their pilgrimage is a laudable endeavour,' remarks Mr Sharma, gently patting Prisha on the shoulder. 'It certainly gets one closer to achieving *moksha*.'

'But, Mr Sharma, I know you've been looking forward to spending time with Prisha –'

'Oh no, it works out well, in fact. I've an important business meeting I must attend and was wondering how to entertain my daughter. This is ideal! Prisha, enjoy your time with your friends. I'll see you back at the hotel at eight. Remember, it's the first night of Diwali and the festival will be at its best and brightest. Be careful not to get lost, though – Varanasi is a real rabbit warren.'

'Yes, Father,' replies Prisha, ushering us away before I can protest any further. As soon as we're out of earshot of her father, Prisha turns to me. 'So, your Glimmers *are* real? Everything you told us is true then?'

I'm still upset with Mei for disclosing our mission but I'm more worried for Prisha. She has no idea what she's just got herself into. As glad as I am to see my friend, I'll be relieved when she is safely back with her father this evening. And, by the disgruntled look on Jude's face, I can tell she feels the same.

'Yes,' I reply tersely. 'It was all true.'

'I knew it!' Prisha cries, clapping her hands together. She looks me up and down. 'So you *were* a Kalari warrior?'

'Apparently so.'

She grins. 'And a Russian acrobat? And a Cheyenne? And a samurai? And you now have all those skills?'

I nod, unable to stop myself smiling now at her unbridled enthusiasm for my past lives. She was, after all, the only one of my friends who expressed any belief in my claims of reincarnation. Until very recently, not even Mei would contemplate such a possibility. It helps that Prisha is Hindu, but her willingness to listen first gave me some hope I wasn't going totally crazy. So I guess that if anyone is going to join our so-called pilgrimage, then Prisha deserves her place among us – even if Jude looks to be still against it.

'I suppose that also means you're a First Ascendant,' says Prisha, her tone almost reverential. Then the excitement drains from her face to be replaced by a look of dread. 'And that Tanas and his Soul Hunters are really after you?'

'Unfortunately, yes.' I snatch a glance over my shoulder, suddenly feeling Tanas's shadow looming over me, but the crowd is oblivious to us. I turn my attention back to Prisha. 'That's why we're here in Varanasi and why you must be careful. Any sign of trouble and you go straight back to your father. You see, we're seeking the eternal flame that will help us destroy Tanas's soul forever.'

Prisha looks in the direction of the guru still waiting for us up ahead, his staff tapping impatiently. 'And that guru claims to know where the flame is?' she says, her tone sceptical.

'He's our only lead.'

Suddenly, his patience clearly run dry, the guru turns on his heel and strides off down the narrow lane. We hurry after him, Jude taking the lead, followed by me next, then Prisha, Mei and Tarek. Once more, the guru moves nimbly, his beads rattling, wooden staff clicking upon the road. As predicted by Mr Sharma, the backstreets and alleyways prove to be a complete labyrinth. Some of the lanes are so narrow that not even sunlight can penetrate. Moving through the heavy gloom, we leave the light behind and enter a shadowy backstreet world full of stray dogs, beggars and open sewers. The deeper we go, the more unsettled I become.

Beginning to suspect that this holy man is leading us on a wild goose chase, I ask him, 'How much further?'

'It depends how far you want to go,' he replies, 'but that which you're seeking is right here.'

He stops outside a narrow wooden door to a poorly kept building. Hidden away from the rest of the city, the temple is a three-storey block of crumbling stonework, leaning worryingly to one side. The blue paint on the door is peeling badly and the gold of the dome atop the roof is flaking off. There isn't a name plate, just a small brass bell hanging to the right-hand side of the entrance and the image of a single flame engraved into the warped wood.

'Welcome to Jwala Temple,' announces the guru. 'The home of the true eternal flame.'

29

The guru touches the end of his staff to the flame symbol by the door. There's a faint glow, followed by an almost imperceptible click of a lock, and the door swings open. He disappears inside, melting into the shadows. One by one, we cautiously follow him into the mysterious temple. A dark, narrow corridor stretches out before us. As we make our way along, the heat of the city is replaced by the coolness of ancient stone, the sounds of the street become muffled and strangely distant, and the pungent smells of the alleyways fade beneath the familiar scent of sandalwood incense. Ahead, the guru reaches out and lights the lamps upon the wall. He touches each wick in turn and they flicker to life. He uses no match or lighter as far as I can tell.

Mei exchanges an uneasy glance with me.

'If you're blind, why light the lamps?' she asks.

'They're not for me, they're for you,' the guru replies. 'I can see just as well in the darkness as I can in the light.'

My step falters at his reply. With their black, pooling eyes, Incarnates don't need much light – if any – to see. Worried now that we're being led into a trap, I clench my hands, readying for a fight.

Our shadows ripple across the uneven walls of the temple and we enter a round, domed chamber with a stone-flagged floor. The ornate ceiling is decorated with carvings of Hindu gods and there are four entrances, each cloaked in darkness. At the chamber's centre sits a circular hearth where a strange blue flame burns, rising straight out of a pile of gleaming black rocks. We stand around the fire, awed by its almost supernatural appearance.

'Now this looks more like an eternal flame,' murmurs Jude.

The guru leans proudly upon his staff. 'As created by Lord Shiva himself.'

'Lord Shiva? You're kidding!' Prisha appears to become mesmerized by the dancing flame at the mention of the Hindu god. 'Is that why it's so *blue*?'

The guru nods. 'The flame burns hot with magic.'

'What sort of magic?' asks Prisha, her eyes widening and reflecting the flickers.

The guru's beard twitches with the slightest of smiles. 'This flame was first lit by a spark of Light,' he explains, 'and it therefore will never go out.'

On hearing the holy man mention the Light, I relax my guard. Whoever he is, he seems more aligned with the Light than the Darkness. I take the star-shaped candle from my pocket, eager to collect the eternal flame before Damien and his Hunters catch up with us again. 'May I light this candle please?'

'By all means, but you may wish to transfer the flame to one of my oil lamps.' He gestures to a brass lamp with a glass cover nestled in an alcove. 'It will make carrying the flame easier.'

Thanking the guru, I take down the lamp and kneel by the fire. I can feel its warmth on my skin – an energizing, healing heat. I light the candle and carefully transfer its blue flame to the lamp, then blow out the candle. Almost immediately its wick bursts back into life. I blow it out again and the same thing happens.

'It's called an eternal flame for a reason,' says the guru, chuckling at my futile efforts, 'which is why I hope it will help break the cycle of Tanas's reincarnation.'

I tense, a chill running through me at the mention of the Incarnate leader's name. 'I didn't say who the fire was for,' I say.

'Why else would you be seeking it?' the guru replies matter-of-factly. 'Since the Great Evil cannot simply be killed, his blackened soul has to be destroyed permanently, otherwise the cycle will simply repeat and the wheel will turn yet again. His soul's eternity must end.'

Jude draws her Taser. 'Who are you?' she challenges.

The guru turns to her. 'You don't want to electrocute yourself again, do you?' His words are more of a threat than a warning, and Jude reholsters her weapon.

Then he returns his attention to me. His eyeless sockets now appear to glow a starlit blue in the reflected light of the eternal flame.

'Who am I?' he asks rhetorically. 'I've been many people over many incarnations – so many that I honestly can't remember them all. And for a long while I was lost in the Darkness. But I believe –' he seems to stare at me – 'I was once a father to you in a previous life.'

I study the guru's lined face, searching for our shared past. But without his eyes I cannot easily access his soul. Then I experience the briefest flash of a pyramid and a golden sceptre and I instinctively sink to one knee. 'Pharaoh Hepuhotep!'

The guru throws back his head and laughs. 'No, I'm far more humble than that particular First Ascendant. And I'm not that sort of father either.'

Mystified, I stand up and peer once more into his glowing eyeless sockets. This time, I glimpse a monk's brown habit, hear cries of panic amid the roar of flames, smell the acrid stench of smoke. 'Father . . . Benedict?'

The guru inclines his head. 'I was once that man. Now I am Vihan, a guru of the Light. The last of the Soul Seers.'

I gasp in astonishment at our strange reunion. I feel a warmth flood through my heart on learning that Father Benedict's soul survived. What a comfort it is to know that my friend and mentor has returned, that our paths have crossed in this life. 'Then you know how to destroy Tanas!' I exclaim.

Vihan chuckles, but this time there's no humour to his laugh. 'What makes you think that?'

'I have your instructions here!' I reply, taking the parchment from my backpack. 'Your list of Soul Jars that contain the clues to destroying his soul.'

Vihan raises both eyebrows, lending himself a haunted look. 'I wondered where that had got to.' The guru regards me with his empty sockets. Then he murmurs: '*One Soul shines brighter and bolder than the rest; this one must ignite the spark when put to the Darkest test.'*

Hearing him recite the Soul Prophecy, I suddenly feel the unwanted weight of expectation.

'Come,' he says, beckoning us deeper into the temple. 'We have much to discuss.'

30

Vihan leads us up a flight of narrow stairs to the highest roof terrace of the temple. From here we have a view over the city. The sun is high in the smog-filled sky; the air is hot, laced with the smell of incense and the acrid tang of woodsmoke from funeral pyres. The heart of Varanasi beats below us in a distant yet incessant thrum of market chatter, barking dogs and chanting priests. The bursts of firecrackers punctuate the air as Diwali is celebrated. Like some geometric puzzle, a confusing tangle of rooftops stretches off towards the horizon, bound only by the long, lazy bend of the Ganges. Monkeys leap from building to building, stealing scraps of food and fighting among themselves, while atop a nearby house a woman hangs out laundry to dry, her baby asleep on a rug next to her.

Shooing away a monkey perched on the wall, the guru invites us to sit down under a flimsy bedsheet, erected as an awning over our heads to shade us from the heat of the sun. We each take a threadbare cushion and settle around a low table. Setting aside his staff, Vihan kneels stiffly beside a makeshift stove and gathers together some kindling to start a fire. 'So what's your name in this life?' he asks me.

'Genna,' I reply.

'And is this your Soul Protector?' he asks, nodding in Jude's direction.

'No, Jude's just a Warrior,' I reply, immediately regretting my choice of words. I go on quickly as I notice Jude's lips narrow into a vexed scowl. 'My Soul Protector was Phoenix. He was killed by Tanas.'

'I'm sorry to hear that,' says Vihan. He regards Jude. 'You're not *just* a Warrior, though, are you? You're Zuberi's Soul Daughter.'

Jude nods. 'For what it's worth.'

'It's worth a great deal, in my opinion.' He finishes arranging the kindling into a neat pyramid. 'And who are your other companions?'

I introduce Tarek, Mei and Prisha.

'Do you need any help?' offers Prisha, as the guru reaches up to a rickety shelf stacked with teacups and plates.

'Thank you. You can set out the cups, if you'd be so kind,' replies Vihan, and, leaving Prisha to lay the table, he turns his attention back to me. 'Now, tell me, Genna, which Soul Jars have you managed to collect so far?'

'We have the Canopic jar that contains Apep's mummified hand,' I reply.

Vihan's mouth curls in distaste. 'Ah, yes. I remember placing *that* particular relic in your tomb. Nasty business. I had to seal the jar with a protective spell to stop his evil polluting your soul in the afterlife.'

'*You* put it there?' I ask, stunned.

Vihan nods. 'It seemed the most secure place to preserve

such crucial remains down through the centuries. You see, following the passing of Khafra, your Soul Father's chief counsellor, I became your vizier when you were Princess Tiaa.'

I lean across the low table towards him. 'Do you know what happened to my Soul Father, Pharaoh Hepuhotep? Why was I buried in his tomb?'

'You don't remember?' A mournful look passes across his lined face. 'Tragically, he was sacrificed by Apep. His body was burned during the ritual. That's why you took over his throne – as well as his pyramid upon your death.'

'So my Soul Father is dead, his soul destroyed?'

'Yes, I'm afraid so.' Vihan bows his head. 'Along with your Soul Mother. She was sacrificed in the same fire.'

I gaze out across the heat haze of Varanasi's rooftops, saddened but not surprised at this news. I'd suspected for some time my Soul parents were gone, since they weren't at Haven and Caleb did not mention them to me. Varanasi blurs as tears well in my eyes. Memories, like fragments of sunlight, glisten then fade: my Soul Mother's gentle touch as she combed my hair when I was a young girl; my Soul Father telling me stories about the great sun god Ra, and of sailing together in the royal barge upon the life-giving waters of the Nile . . . then the waters turn to flames and I once more hear the screams of my Soul Mother and Father as they burned alive upon the pyre. I clench my fists in rage. Even though their deaths were more than four millennia ago, my grief is as bitter and raw as what I felt for the recent murder of my present-life parents. *This torment never seems to end!*

Mei gently touches my arm. 'Are you OK?' she asks.

I nod, feeling the grief harden into a fierce determination. 'I will be – once we've put an end to Tanas. For good.'

'So, you have the Canopic jar. What else have you recovered from the list?' asks Vihan.

Recomposing myself, I turn to him. 'The star chart from the Cave of a Thousand Buddhas.'

'Excellent! So the scroll survived the cave's collapse. Have you been able to interpret it yet?'

'Yes,' I say. 'Tarek figured it out.'

Tarek adjusts his glasses and clears his throat. 'I recognized the planetary alignment of Mercury, Venus, Mars, Jupiter and Saturn. I assume that the conjunction somehow weakens Tanas's soul?'

Vihan nods. 'That's my hope, at least. When the planets appear at their brightest, Tanas's soul will be at its weakest. As Abbot of that Buddhist monastery, it took me almost my entire life to work out the timing and significance of that conjunction. Do you know when the next one will occur?'

'Yes. In four days.'

'Hmm, less than we would want, but more than we could hope for,' responds the guru thoughtfully. 'At least it is within this lifetime. Have you collected any of the other Soul Jars?'

'Just the eternal flame from you,' I reply with a glance at the blue flame flickering inside the lamp Tarek holds on his lap.

'You've done well to get this far,' Vihan commends. 'That leaves only two items left to acquire. The first one is the glass vial I gave you in Sijilmasa.'

'What vial?' I ask. 'And where on earth is Sijilmasa?'

'It's in Morocco,' he replies. 'The city is now a ruin, but back in its heyday Sijilmasa was a thriving settlement on the trans-Saharan trade route. We met there briefly when I was a mage and you were a young Berber going by the name of Sura, if my memory serves me correctly.'

I furrow my brow. 'Yes, I recall being Sura . . . but I don't remember ever meeting you.'

'Maybe this will help.' He reaches across the table and lightly presses the palm of his wrinkled hand to my forehead. All of sudden I feel a burst of warmth on my skin and a Glimmer stirs in my mind *of a narrow dusty backstreet . . . of a glass-beaded door curtain leading into a smoky, incense-laden room . . . of a mysterious, bearded figure, dressed in purple robes, sitting behind a counter of crystal vials, each gleaming like a polished jewel in the flickering light of an oil lamp . . . then being handed a teardrop-shaped vial containing a silvery liquid –*

I nod vaguely. 'I remember now . . . There was some liquid, like mercury, inside.'

'Soulsilver,' says Vihan.

Mei frowns. 'What's Soulsilver?'

'In essence, it's the fabric of a soul,' explains the guru. 'Very rare, for it usually doesn't exist in physical form.' He turns to me. 'So I hope you can recall what you did with the vial. Can you?'

I close my eyes, trying to chase the fading Glimmer, but I only see myself walking out of the door, through the glass-beaded curtain, and back into the hot glare of the Saharan sun. 'No . . . sorry, I don't know what I did with it.'

The guru's wrinkled brow deepens with concern. 'You *need* to remember, Genna,' he insists. 'That's the last vial of Soulsilver I know of in existence. The first vial was lost during the reign of Emperor Commodus in Rome; the second sank to the bottom of the South China Sea aboard a Vietnamese trading ship in the seventh century; and the third and last is the one I gave to you in Sijilmasa.'

I massage my temples, trying to will my memory back. I shake my head in frustration. 'Nothing is coming!'

'Keep trying, Genna,' insists Vihan. 'The contents of that vial are *crucial* to the ritual you must perform.'

'And what ritual is that?' asks Prisha as she turns from finishing laying the table.

'One that I've spent many lifetimes devising,' Vihan replies. 'One that I hope will destroy Tanas's soul, just like he destroys ours.'

31

We all wait on tenterhooks as the guru draws in a long, deep breath. He interlaces his fingers and regards each of us with his eyeless sockets. 'Destroying a soul is unnatural. It goes against the very laws of nature. As such, it is no easy task.'

A dog howls plaintively in a far-off street. The bedsheet over our heads ripples in the oven-hot breeze, the sun's oppressive glare seeming to intensify as we sit in silence listening to the guru.

'The ritual requires a unique combination of factors. It must be performed on the Day of Alignment, when the planets are at their brightest and Tanas's soul is at its weakest. Tanas must consume the Soulsilver to separate her dark soul from her present-life body. The hand needs to be burned in her presence, for, as we know, only her own death can defeat her. It must be set alight using the eternal flame, the flame that will never go out or allow her to incarnate again in physical form. Finally, to complete the ritual and seal the spell, you must end her present life with the obsidian blade that first wounded her soul. That knife is the final item we must acquire.'

For several moments, no one speaks. Just the eerie screech of a monkey across the rooftops, and the distant hum of Varanasi's traffic can be heard.

Tarek is first to break the silence. He blows out his cheeks. 'Sounds like a piece of cake!'

'Sounds impossible,' mutters Jude. 'We're fighting for our lives every time we encounter Tanas. I can't see her lying down quietly and allowing us to perform this ritual on her.'

'Ah, I didn't say it would be easy,' admits Vihan. 'But it may be our only chance of stopping the Darkness enveloping the world.'

'Vihan, even if we could somehow complete this ritual, we've no idea where the obsidian blade is,' I point out. 'It's lost to history.'

'I once thought so too,' the guru replies. 'But after much searching, across many lifetimes, I began hearing rumours, when I was a Spanish conquistador, of an ancient lost city in the jungles of what was called in those days the New World. Most explorers were seeking the legend of El Dorado, but I knew that the lost city I was looking for contained something far more valuable than gold . . . the obsidian blade!'

'Where is this lost city?' asks Mei.

'In Guatemala.'

'Can you be any more specific than that?' presses Jude. 'Guatemala's a big country.'

Vihan gives a slightly impatient sigh. 'Yes, *more specifically*, in the jungle near to the Diablofuego volcano.' He reaches for his staff, twists the wooden shaft and pulls it apart to reveal a hidden compartment. Inside is a scroll of yellowed paper. 'The location is marked on this map,' he says, handing me the scroll.

I unroll it and study the paper, turning it over and over in my hand. 'Vihan, you must be mistaken,' I say, bemused. 'There isn't any map. It's blank.'

The corner of Vihan's bearded mouth curls into a sly grin. 'Some fires can be good for paper. Hold it over the eternal flame.'

Tarek opens up the oil lamp and I carefully present the yellowed paper to the flame. Almost immediately the heat causes faint outlines to appear on the paper: of a river, a crude compass, a volcano, and then a city, and, there, a small cross . . .

Prisha gasps. 'Invisible ink!'

'You've got to be kidding me!' exclaims Jude with a roll of her eyes. 'We'd never have worked that out. Why make everything so cryptic? Why hide the map?'

'Just imagine if an Incarnate were to get their hands on this map, or the parchment you have,' explains Vihan. 'They would seek out and destroy the Soul Jars. That's why I had to conceal their locations in riddles and with deception. Besides, the obsidian blade was carefully hidden and then apparently forgotten by the Incarnates themselves. I have no desire to jog their memories.'

Mei peers over at the map. 'Where did you get this?' she asks.

'From a Soul Jar that I'd buried in a past life,' replies Vihan. 'It's a copy of the original. Why do you ask?'

Mei frowns. 'Oh, no reason. Just curious, that's all.'

As Vihan reconnects his staff and I stow the map carefully in my backpack, Prisha clears her throat. 'May I ask why this ritual of yours hasn't ever been attempted before? I mean, wouldn't it have solved a lot of problems?'

'Because until now the Soul Jars were scattered far and wide, in both time and place,' explains Vihan. 'I also needed personal insight into Tanas's ritual in order to work out our own version. So I gave Tanas the opportunity to ritually destroy my soul. It was a highly risky and tortuous strategy. He even plucked out my eyes! Mercifully, and as I planned, I died before the ritual was *fully* complete. Nevertheless, my soul was lost for many generations in the Darkness.' The wrinkles on his worn face seem to deepen into craggy valleys at the painful memory. 'Eventually I managed to find my way back to the Light and I returned in this life. Alas, as a consequence of Tanas's ritual, and also of being lost in the Darkness for so long, I was born without eyes.'

'That's awful,' says Prisha.

'Not so awful,' he replies, returning his attention to prepping the fire. 'In fact, it's proven to be a blessing in disguise. Not having eyes has kept my presence hidden from Watchers and Hunters. Moreover, I am now able to perceive the world in a very different way, sensing the Light in all living and non-living things. For I can see a person's true nature by the aura of their Light, or lack thereof. So, you see, this ability has kept me safe and concealed over the years, allowing me to protect the eternal flame from the Incarnates.'

The guru holds his hand over the pile of kindling he's arranged. After a few seconds, the wood smoulders, then bursts into flame. He then picks up a battered tin kettle, fills it with water from a bucket and hangs it on a hook over the fire.

'How do you do *that*?' I ask, astonished.

Vihan frowns. 'What? Make tea?'

'No, ignite the fire without a match or lighter!'

'Ah! By wielding the Light,' he explains matter-of-factly.

My jaw falls open. 'You can *channel* the Light to start a fire?'

The guru nods. 'I can channel it to do many things. The Light is what sustains me in my old age and gives me strength.'

I smile to myself. That explains why Vihan can move so nimbly for such a frail man. I recall how Caleb's limp would disappear in the Sun Room back at Haven, and how our wounds were healed with the explosion of Light during the battle against the Incarnates. In Vihan's case, the guru *himself* is the source.

Jude regards the holy man more closely, her expression now one of admiration. 'So it was *you* who made my Taser short-circuit earlier?'

Vihan holds up a bony hand. 'Guilty as charged.'

Tarek laughs. 'And you caused the fire to explode with Light too, didn't you?'

The guru offers a modest shrug. 'That takes a little more effort.' He lifts the kettle off the fire and adds tea leaves to the steaming water. He then passes round a plate of seeded biscuits. 'Please, help yourself to a jeera cookie. They're very tasty.'

As I take one, Vihan says, 'I can teach you to be a Wielder of the Light, if you so desire.'

I almost drop my biscuit in my lap. 'Teach *me*?'

'Yes. I can see that your aura is special – I might even say different from other First Ascendants. Your soul burns very bright. In fact, judging by your *nadi* lines, you should have little trouble channelling the Light.'

'I don't think we have the time,' I reply, almost fearful of his offer. The guru pours out the tea. 'Tanas could track us down at any moment,' I continue. 'And we've less than four days until the planets align.'

'You always have time,' replies Vihan, handing me a cup. 'It's what you decide to do with that time that counts.'

32

I stare into my cup, watching the tea leaves settle as though I'm a fortune teller hoping to see the answer in their patterns. The idea of being able to wield the Light is enticing but also daunting. After my previous attempt back at Haven to channel the Light, I've little confidence in my abilities. Earlier, Vihan had quoted the Soul Prophecy and I'm worried he may have mistakenly put his faith in me, just like Caleb did.

'I'm not the one foretold in the Prophecy, if that's what you think, Vihan,' I tell him.

'I never said you were. But if we're to have any hope of defeating Tanas, then you need to be able to wield the Light,' he insists.

'I've already tried that and failed,' I admit. Haven's downfall weighs heavy on my heart.

He dismisses my objection with a wave of his hand. 'Failure is merely a stepping stone to success,' he declares.

'Or a faster way of getting yourself killed,' mutters Jude.

Rising with the help of his staff, Vihan beckons me to join him in the centre of the roof terrace.

'Go on!' Mei coaxes, giving me a gentle push. 'Imagine if you could do it – you'd be like a real-life superhero!'

I shift awkwardly on my cushion and contemplate my cup. The question is, do I *want* to be a superhero? Do I want to risk failing again? *'Mia cara, this is our souls' purpose. To keep the Light alive and humanity safe from Tanas and her Incarnates.'* Viviana's words come back to me and I realize I don't have much choice. I vowed to Santiago that I would do my best to protect the Light, that I'd make amends. So, reluctantly, I step out from beneath the shade of the canopy and into the full glare of the sun.

'At its essence, the Light is energy,' explains the guru as I stand opposite him. 'Which means you can channel it and even transform it into another state, whether that be heat, sound or even electrical energy, as when I disrupted your friend's weapon.'

Vihan holds out an open palm and circles it in front of me. A halo of shimmering silver light appears out of thin air. I hear a collective gasp from Mei and the others.

'This is a Light shield,' says the guru as I stare at him in stunned silence. 'It acts like a mirror to the Darkness and can be used to deflect attacks. Go on – touch it.'

I cautiously reach out. 'Ow!' I cry, receiving an electric shock and immediately retracting my hand.

'The Light has super-charged the atoms in the air,' explains Vihan. 'Now, you try. Imagine the Light flowing from your fingertips, stirring the air into a whirlpool.'

I motion my right hand in a circular pattern, just like he did. But nothing happens. Furrowing my brow, I circle my hand faster and faster. I begin to work up quite a sweat. Slowly and gradually a distinct warmth builds in my palm and the tips of my fingers tingle –

'I think I saw a spark,' says Jude, peering over the top of her sunglasses.

'*Really?*' I say excitedly, circling ever faster.

'No,' Jude replies flatly.

I lower my hand, feeling a complete idiot. *Who am I to believe I can channel the Light?* I've already proven I'm not the one foretold in the Soul Prophecy.

'Listen, Vihan,' I say. 'I think this is a waste of our time. Time we don't really have. I'm not my Soul Twin. She's the one who could channel the Light.'

Vihan stares hard at me, or at least that's what it seems like. He reaches out and caresses the air around me. 'So that explains what I'm seeing . . . A double aura.'

'A double *what*?'

I wait for a reply, but he just continues to study me intently. I shift uncomfortably under his eyeless gaze.

'The Soul Seer Caleb once told me that I carry some of my sister's Light,' I hesitantly volunteer.

'Uh-huh,' he murmurs distractedly.

'We were born of the same spark and shared each other's souls,' I go on. 'Caleb believes that, when Tanas sacrificed her, some of her essence passed over to me.'

'Yes, yes,' says the guru, nodding. 'The silver aura appears to be yours and the golden aura your sister's. They're entwined like a double helix . . .' He twirls a finger through his long beard, wrapping and unwrapping it repeatedly. 'Mmm, that may just work.' He gestures for me to rejoin the others under the makeshift awning. Relieved to be out of the sun, I sit back down on my cushion.

Vihan kneels opposite me. 'Let's try something on a

smaller scale,' he suggests, placing a tiny clay diya lamp upon the table, its wick poking up like a stray hair. 'Hold your hand over this lamp.'

'OK. Now what?' I ask.

'Use the Light within you to ignite the wick. Concentrate its energy into the centre of your palm. But this time I want you to visualize a *golden* light pouring forth.'

'Golden? OK.' I close my eyes and send the Light along my arm, imagining it as a golden beam, focusing it into my palm.

'Is it working?' I hear Prisha whisper after a minute has gone by.

'Patience,' replies the guru softly. 'I'm hoping that by focusing on her golden Light Genna can untangle her auras, allowing her sister's to flow free. If her Soul Twin was truly capable of channelling the Light, then this is the aura that must dominate.'

Another minute passes. I'm about to suggest giving up when I feel a prickle in my palm followed by a sudden intense heat. Yelping, I pull my hand away and open my eyes. The candle wick has burst into flame! *Did I really do that?*

Prisha claps a hand over her mouth and Mei applauds.

'Congratulations!' says Tarek, patting me on the back. 'You're a natural Wielder.'

Jude is less impressed. 'That's going to be great if we're stuck in the woods without a match, but what use will that little magic trick really be against Tanas?'

The guru holds up the candle. 'From a spark, great fires can be lit!'

33

My hands are numb and my arms ache so much I can barely raise them. Having spent most of the morning learning to light candles and ignite fires at will, I'm back to attempting a Light shield. However, this is proving far more of a challenge. As yet another weak halo of Light crackles and fades like a dying sparkler, I drop my hands in frustration. 'I can't do this!'

'Can't? Can? Whatever you believe will be,' replies Vihan. He sits upon a straw mat in the lotus position while I'm made to train under the merciless Indian sun. 'Your Light is dispersing too quickly, that's all. You need to polarize it so that the Light vibrates only in one plane.'

'Polarize?' I stare at him, bewildered. He's beginning to sound like my physics teacher and I never understood half of what she was saying either. 'How do I do that?'

'Think like you're polishing a mirror. Visualize your energy being reflected by the air.'

'OK . . .' I say uncertainly.

Wiping the sweat from my brow, I shake out my hands and massage the feeling back into my fingertips. Then I circle both my palms and focus on the golden element of my aura. Imagining the energy flowing out and being reflected, I windmill my arms, change direction, spin them faster . . .

I hear a muffled laugh. 'You look like the Karate Kid,' remarks Mei. '*Wax on, wax off!*'

She reclines on a pair of cushions under the canopy, her feet propped up. Jude is dozing beside her, her baseball cap over her face. Tarek and Prisha meanwhile have gone off to buy some lunch for us all.

'Very funny!' I reply.

Mei's comment, though, reminds me of my life as the samurai Miyoko-san and her use of *chi* in martial arts. I wonder if wielding the Light is a similar technique. Drawing upon Miyoko's skills, I imagine not Light but *chi* flowing through my fingertips instead.

A spark appears . . .

Then a faint ring of golden light . . .

Mei sits up. 'You're doing it!' she cries.

Jude peeks out from beneath her cap in sleepy curiosity. I grin as a surge of warm energy floods my body and the ring becomes more and more solid.

'You're right. I am!' All of a sudden I feel dizzy and my legs go weak. I lose concentration, sway sideways and the ring fades.

In an instant Vihan's by my side, holding my arm. 'Steady,' he says.

'I'm . . . fine,' I insist, finding my feet again. 'Just a little light-headed, that's all. I think it must be the heat.'

The guru checks my pulse and lays a hand on my

forehead. 'The Light may be limitless, but the body has its limits,' he says. 'Time to take a break.'

At that very moment, Prisha and Tarek appear at the top of the stairs. 'Lunch!' calls Prisha.

Helped by Vihan, I flop down on to my cushion, glad to be out of the searing sun. Jude rouses herself as Prisha lays out vegetable curry, rice and samosas on the table. A delicious aroma fills the air. Tarek hands each of us a fresh lassi drink. I down mine in one go, the iced yogurt quickly reviving me.

'And we have mangoes for dessert!' announces Prisha. She takes a small knife from the crockery shelf and begins to dice the fruit, but the knife slips and she cuts her hand. 'Ow!' she cries, the blood beginning to ooze.

Prisha winces and Tarek inspects the wound. 'It's deep. Vihan, have you got a plaster or a bandage?'

He shakes his head. 'I have something better,' he says, and takes Prisha's injured hand between his own.

Prisha flinches in his grasp. 'Whoa, your hands are hot!'

'Don't worry, it's perfectly normal –' Vihan grins – 'for me at least.'

When he lets go, the bleeding has stopped and the cut is completely healed.

Prisha stares at her hand in amazement.

'How did you do that?' Mei gasps.

'The Light heals,' explains Vihan simply. He picks up a bowl and begins to help himself to some curry. 'Now, I don't know about the rest of you, but I'm famished.'

With Prisha healed, we exchange an amazed glance

before turning our attention to the food. I tuck into the curry and samosas, the mouth-watering mix of Indian spices immediately familiar from my former life as Aarush.

'There was a TV in the restaurant and I'm afraid there's a bit of worrying news,' announces Tarek. Immediately, we all stop eating. 'Prisha, why don't you tell them? You understood the report.'

My friend sets aside her spoon, her expression grim. 'A massive tsunami has hit the coast of Japan. It was triggered by an unexpected earthquake in the Pacific. For some reason, the tsunami warning system supposedly didn't go off. Thousands of people are feared missing or dead.'

I put my bowl down. I no longer feel so hungry. 'That's terrible,' I say.

Vihan puts his palms together in prayer. 'I'm afraid this is the world Tanas promises us. A world of war, chaos and natural disaster.'

Jude carries on wolfing down her lunch. 'Then how much longer will Genna's Light training take?'

The guru takes another spoonful of rice. He chews slowly. 'It is hard to say . . . It took me three incarnations, prior to this one, to master wielding the Light.'

Jude almost chokes on her curry. 'Three lives? That's no good to us! So we'll just hang around here for a couple of generations? Great! I'm sure Tanas will be happy to wait.'

Vihan raises a bony finger. 'Ah! But remember that I had no one to teach me. Genna has progressed much faster than I ever did. It took me a whole lifetime just to learn to light a candle!'

'We don't have the luxury of three lives, Vihan,' I say, echoing Jude's sentiment. 'To be honest, I'll be lucky to survive much longer in this one!'

The guru takes a long, steady sip of his lassi, seemingly untroubled. 'Don't worry – you've got more than enough time.'

Tarek frowns. 'But you just said it took you three incarnations to master the skill.'

Vihan smiles. 'To *master*. Not to learn.'

After I've exhausted myself conjuring a Light shield, Vihan decides to change tack for the afternoon and has me focusing on blasting out bursts of Light, like he did to scare off the fake tour guide and his accomplices. But this technique proves even harder than the shield. I can't even produce a decent spark, let alone a blast.

As I struggle on under the heat of the sun, Jude wanders over to the balustrade at the edge of the roof terrace and peers down into the street below. She's becoming noticeably more nervy with each passing hour. She turns to me. 'This training is taking far too long. Damien and his Hunters could track us down at any moment.'

I lower my hands, which now throb from my efforts. 'Jude's right, Vihan. I think we should stop,' I say. 'I'm not making much progress here anyway.'

'Nonsense!' chides Vihan. 'You're so close to wielding the Light.'

'Can't she practise on the move?' questions Tarek. 'While we track down the last two Soul Jars?'

'Yes, that would be possible . . . but I'd advise *against*

attempting Light blasts in a jet flying at forty thousand feet,' replies Vihan. 'Besides, Varanasi is a city rich with the Light. It's makes wielding easier here.' He shuffles over to the balustrade and sets a porcelain teacup down on the edge. 'Humour me, Genna. Try one more time.'

Despite Jude's impatience, I position myself in the middle of the terrace opposite the teacup.

'Imagine that you're a river, like the Ganges,' instructs Vihan. 'But, rather than water, pure Light is flowing through you. Visualize all the tributaries running in and the current surging up to a great dam.'

The hot Indian sun beats down upon me as I raise my hands and imagine that I'm a river of energy.

The guru nods encouragingly. 'Good, good! I can see the Light building. Let it spread through your body, flow through your system, flood your *nadi* lines.'

Closing my eyes, I try to picture my twin sister's golden aura expanding, growing, brightening. At first nothing happens. Then suddenly I get a vision of Aya's face and I feel a surge of power. Rivulets of sweat begin to run down my back. But it's the heat *within* me rather than the sun that causes me to perspire. My whole body thrums, my skin becomes electric and the hairs on my arms rise.

'Now focus all that energy into your hands,' cries the guru excitedly. 'Target the cup and let the dam burst!'

My eyes snap open, I thrust out both arms at the teacup. There's a searing *crackle* in the air and a bright flash of golden light streaks out from my palms. The cup explodes in a hail of shattered porcelain. Close by, a pair of monkeys shriek in terror and flee across the rooftops.

I gape, open-mouthed, at my hands, almost fearful of their power. The others stare at me, equally startled. 'Did I *really* do that?' I ask, breathless.

The guru nods. I turn shakily to my friends.

'I can wield the Light!' I exclaim. Then everything goes black –

34

I hear voices, distant and distorted. My soul seems separated from my body. Everything feels numb. *Am I dead again? Did the Incarnates find us?*

An odd prickling of pins-and-needles sweeps through me and I feel myself reconnect with my physical form. The voices draw nearer, echoing in my ears.

'She's breathing . . .'

'Her hands are really cold . . .'

'Will she be all right?'

I recognize Mei's voice. My eyes flicker open. The sun filters through a coloured shawl, a light, warm breeze making it flap. I'm stretched out under the shady awning on the terrace. My head is propped up on several cushions and a cool, wet cloth has been laid across my brow.

'She'll be fine,' answers Vihan, his leathery face and beard appearing in my vision. I can feel his fingers pressed against my temples, a healing heat emanating from his touch.

Jude and Tarek stand nearby, arms crossed, a deep concern etched across their faces. Prisha, noticing my eyes are open, helps me take a sip of water. My head slowly clears.

'What happened?' I ask.

'Just as an electrical circuit can overheat, so can the body,' Vihan explains. 'It's merely a consequence of wielding the Light.'

'So will that always happen?' asks Prisha.

Vihan shakes his head. 'The more Genna practises, the more resilient she'll become.' He lifts his fingers from my temples, and I feel recharged. He pats my shoulder. 'But be careful not to burn yourself out like that again.'

I sit up, my bones buzzing, my skin tingling all over. 'Why?'

Vihan gives me a grave look. 'Imagine a light bulb exploding and you get the picture!'

Dusk has fallen by the time I'm able to leave the temple rooftop. The idea of exploding like a light bulb doesn't fill me with the greatest of confidence in my newly acquired skill, but Vihan has promised he can train me to recognize the signs of a potential burn-out. And the fact that he's volunteered to join us on our mission sets my mind more at rest. Still, the power in the palms of my hands is somewhat daunting. While it is a much-needed weapon in our fight against Tanas, I question how much control I actually have over it. As we make our way out of the temple, I notice my friends glance at me with a mixture of awe and fear.

After closing the door on the Jwala Temple and sealing it with a spell to protect the eternal flame, Vihan guides us through Varanasi's serpentine side streets in the direction of the ghats. From there we hope to hire a boat to ferry us back to the jet. The blue glow from the oil lamp in Tarek's hand glances off the dark alley walls, making our shadows loom large. The narrow lanes are quieter than before and we soon discover why. As we emerge from the backstreets, we're engulfed by an explosion of blinding lights and a mass of people who are partying.

The Festival of Diwali is in full swing, and with it Varanasi is ablaze. The ground is carpeted in flickering flames, as though a million stars have fallen from the sky. Countless candles are arranged in intricate flowering patterns; rows of diya lamps line the pavements, window sills and rooftops; and laser beams shoot up to the heavens. A haze of smoke hangs in the humid air, adding an air of mystique to the vibrant celebrations. Incense burns everywhere in a heady cocktail of jasmine, sandalwood and exotic spices. Priests wail in prayer, bells chime, and firecrackers burst at our feet as excited children squeal around us in mischievous delight.

'Now I can see why they call Varanasi the City of Light,' marvels Mei.

'Diwali is a celebration of the triumph of good over evil and light over darkness,' Vihan tells us above the clamour of the crowd. 'For some, it commemorates the return of Lord Rama from exile and his vanquishing of the demon-king Ravana. For others, it represents the killing of the evil demon Narakasura by Krishna's wife, Satyabhama. For me, it is a reminder that even in the darkest times a glimmer of hope prevails.'

He glances over his shoulder and fixes me with his eyeless sockets. I sense he's seeing the double aura of my

Light and its unspoken potential to help us in our fight against the Incarnates.

From out of the throng, a woman in a vivid purple sari comes up and gifts me a garland of bright orange marigolds. 'The flower of the soul!' she says with a sunshine smile, placing the fragrant chain over my head. 'May your Diwali be free from darkness and abundant with light!'

'*Dhanyavaad*,' I reply in Hindi, pressing my palms together in gratitude as she generously presents the others with garlands before disappearing back into the crowd.

A street vendor passes by, and Prisha buys half a dozen dumplings from him and hands them round.

'What are these?' Mei asks, examining the sticky, deep-fried balls.

'Gulab jamun,' she replies. 'Indian doughnuts.'

'Wow! This is good,' says Tarek, devouring his in a couple of bites.

I take a tentative bite and am treated to the most intense sugar hit, flavoured with rose water. 'Mmm, delicious!'

Prisha bows her head. 'May these sweets sweeten your success.'

Buoyed by the celebrations, I feel my hopes rise. Whether I'm the one foretold in the Soul Prophecy or not, this unique double aura of mine may just give us an edge over the Incarnates. Once I've mastered my newly acquired ability to wield the Light, I believe that we do have a chance – albeit a slim one – of defeating Tanas. And once we have the remaining Soul Jars in our possession, we will have the means of extinguishing her evil soul forever.

'As wonderful as these celebrations are,' says Jude,

finishing off her gulab jamun, 'we really should get going. In a festival this big, there are bound to be Watchers.'

The guru nods in agreement and ploughs on ahead. Following his staff, we thread our way through the crowds towards the ghats. When the route becomes too congested, Vihan leaves the main procession and turns down a quieter side street leading to a small public park.

'I know this place,' says Prisha as we pass under an old iron gateway and enter a garden of low hedges, patchy grass lawns and mango trees. 'This is the Garden of Shiva. My hotel is just down the next street.'

'Then we'll drop you off on the way,' I say, glancing at my watch. 'It's almost eight. Your dad will be waiting.'

The park is quiet compared to the rest of the city, with only a handful of festival-goers strolling through the grounds. At its centre is a six-sided temple of ivory-white marble with an onion-shaped dome and a golden spire that gleams in the night. A statue of Lord Shiva can be seen within the inner chamber, lit by the orange glow of candlelight. But what makes the park magical are the hundreds of tiny diya lamps laid out in concentric circles round the temple. As we stop in front of the statue, the effect is like standing in a swirling whirlpool of light.

'It makes you realize how beautiful yet fragile this world is,' says Prisha.

I nod, equally mesmerized. Then I get an odd sense of foreboding, a subtle shift in the tranquil atmosphere, like the turning of a tide. Once more I feel the strange pulsing in my chest, like a double heartbeat. Looking round, I realize the park has mysteriously emptied of people. Vihan seems to sense the change too. He has his head cocked to one side, listening hard.

'What is it?' I ask.

'I hear footsteps. Many of them,' he replies.

'No surprise there,' says Jude. 'There's a full-on festival happening.'

'No, these steps are lighter, more deliberate in their approach.'

Listening closely, I can't hear any footsteps but I notice that the celebrations sound oddly distant, almost muffled. Then the circles of diya lamps begin to flicker, their tiny flames trembling as if they are afraid. The hairs on the back of my neck rise.

'Vihan's right,' I say, tensing. 'Someone's coming.'

The night air turns unnaturally still. All of a sudden it's as if an unfelt gust of wind passes through the park. The diya lamps go out, their flames extinguished in a rolling wave . . . until the only light left burning is the eternal flame inside the old brass lamp.

35

A hooded figure appears in the sudden darkness, followed by another, then another, and another . . . fanning out until they surround us.

While the Diwali celebrations continue brightly in the background, we stand silent, facing one another in the gloom. A deathly chill runs through me, despite the humidity of the night. *They've found us!*

Instinctively, I recoil as Tanas throws back her hood. Her face is more serpentine and soulless than ever. Her sable black hair is pulled into a tight ponytail; her cheekbones are more razor-like, her chin more pointed, her lips thinner. Once flawless, her skin is now marred with a light criss-crossing of scars where Nefertiti's claws have left their mark. Underneath her cloak she wears the matt-black assault jacket with its thin coating of nano-carbon and her aviator sunglasses shield her pooling eyes.

Her Hunters are similarly attired, their identities concealed by their hoods and dark glasses. Yet I still recognize Damien and most of his gang by their bearing and build – Damien, confident in his swagger and muscular beneath his cloak; Knuckleduster, fierce as a pit bull and just as stocky; Thug, cumbersome and oversized like a teenage giant; Blondie, fidgety and wiry; Spider, hunched from her knife wounds yet as dangerous as an injured viper.

Fear and adrenaline course through my veins. I want to flee these black-eyed Hunters, but there's a burning anger that impels me to stay and attack, to avenge the murder of Phoenix. And beneath the fury, that nagging question . . . *How did they find us?* For yet again we've been hunted down in remarkably quick time. *Was it a Watcher who spotted us? Did we stay too long in one place? Are they somehow tracking the jet? Or is it as Tanas boasted to Santiago: 'The darker the days get, the easier it is to spot your Light'?*

However they've found us, we're now in serious danger – and so too are Mei and Prisha.

Tanas's cold gaze slowly sweeps the park where from each of the extinguished candles a last gasp of smoke spirals into the still air like a crowd of departing spirits. Her upper lip curls. 'What a pointless celebration. Don't they realize that the Darkness is destined to overwhelm the Light?'

'Not every light!' shoots back Tarek. A blue halo radiates from the lamp in his hand, bathing us in its protective glow.

'So that's why you're here in Varanasi,' Tanas sneers. 'For the so-called eternal flame. Well, let's put that claim to the test, shall we?'

She cuts the edge of her hand through the air in a sharp gesture. A second later, I give an involuntary shudder as a chill spears me; the others appear to experience the same sickening sensation too, judging by their involuntary shudders.

The flame in the lamp blinks out.

Fearfully, I peer into the pitch-black night. Tanas's cold, cruel laugh echoes round the garden. 'Ha! Not so eternal now, is it?'

Then, just as suddenly as it died, the flame bursts back into life.

In its determined glow, Tanas's malevolent grin cracks into a scowl of fury.

'Varanasi isn't your domain, Tanas,' declares Vihan, stepping forward from the entrance to the temple. 'The Light here is strong, which makes you weak.'

Tanas laughs, trying to brush off her symbolic defeat. 'You can talk!' she scoffs. 'When we first met upon this earth, Chibuzo, you were a mighty chieftain. Now look at you! Little more than a beggar, all skin and bones. You don't even have eyes in this pathetic incarnation of yours.'

'I don't need eyes to see the evil that you are, Tanas,' retorts the guru. With a majestic sweep of his arm, Vihan sends an arc of Light towards the Incarnate leader. Like a curved blade, it scythes through the air, crackling with static.

Tanas ducks, barely avoiding the attack. The Incarnate standing behind her, though, isn't so quick. The arc of Light strikes him just above the neckline of his assault jacket and he judders as if electrocuted and drops to the ground, the Incarnate's dark soul severed from his earthly body.

I'm stunned at the brutal effectiveness of Vihan's Light-wielding. *Do I possess this sort of power too?* I wonder.

Tanas stares in outrage at her fallen Hunter.

'Two can play at that game!' she snarls. Punching out a fist, a dense ball of Darkness surges in the guru's direction.

Vihan deflects it with a hastily made Light shield, but the force of the attack knocks him back against the trunk of a mango tree. Mei and I rush to his side but he waves us off and gets to his feet with the aid of his staff.

'It is nothing. I lost my balance,' he explains calmly.

I'm not sure I completely believe him, however, and I'm shaking with shock. Panic courses through my veins at this supernatural show of power. *Tanas just used the Darkness as a weapon!* I know I shouldn't be too surprised by that. *If an Ascendant can wield the Light, then why wouldn't an Incarnate be able to wield the Darkness?* The realization changes everything: the winning edge I thought we had is now gone.

'W-when did Tanas learn that trick?' stutters Tarek, eyes bulging behind his glasses.

'I wish I'd brought my shield with me now,' mutters Jude as she looks towards the temple for cover.

'Tanas has been strengthened by her ritual sacrificing of First Ascendants,' the guru mutters under his breath. 'And, judging by the nature of that attack, she must have absorbed the power of a Soul Seer.'

I cast my mind back to Caleb's death and recall the brief flash of lightning entwining itself round Tanas's hand . . . I realize that *that's* when she must have gained the ability to wield.

'Your days are numbered,' declares Tanas, relishing our stunned expressions. She raises her hands and balls them into fists. 'Night is about to fall forever –'

'WAIT!' I cry. 'Let my friends go. They've got nothing to do with our fight.'

Lowering her hands, Tanas regards Mei and Prisha with a pitying look. 'Oh, but they have *everything* to do with it. For these pathetic souls that you try to protect with your Light will soon become my slaves –' She flings out her arms, this time sending two dagger-like shards of Darkness shooting towards Mei and Prisha.

Instantly, I leap in front of my friends, frantically circling my hands. *Wax on, wax off!* I think desperately. A pair of spirals – one golden, one silver – crackle in the air. I sustain them just long enough to block the shards.

The shards disappear.

Tanas's mouth falls open in disbelief. I gaze at my hands, astonished to have created not one but *two* Light shields at once.

Vihan grins at this miraculous feat. 'Genna, somehow you're tapping into *both* your auras.'

Emboldened, I stand straighter and face Tanas.

Tanas fumes. 'Impressive as that little trick of yours is, Genna, the Darkness is all powerful.' She turns to her Hunters. 'Subdue them!'

The Incarnates surge forward.

Jude immediately stuns one with her Taser, then roundhouse-kicks another in the head. Vihan sends arcs of Light spinning out like silver shurikens into the darkness. Two Incarnates fall where they stand. Thug is hit in the chest by one of the silver stars, the Light piercing his nano-carbonized jacket. He drops to his knees.

Tanas barks out an order to seize the eternal flame and Knuckleduster and Blondie charge straight for Tarek. Tarek does his best to fend them off, but their combined blows hammer him to the ground. They kick and punch him as he clings to the lamp.

'I'm going to pound your face to a pulp unless you let go!' snarls Knuckleduster.

I fire off a burst of Light, knocking Blondie aside. But when I try to blast Knuckleduster nothing comes out. I try again, but it seems my wielding ability is depleted after the day's training.

'Mei! Prisha! Get inside the temple,' I shout as I rush to Tarek's aid. He's trying to defend himself against the metal-ringed fists of Knuckleduster, but, before I can reach him, Damien leaps into my path.

'Genna, somehow we keep missing each other,' he quips, gracing me with a roguish smile.

'Well, this won't miss!' I throw a hook punch. The strike lands square across Damien's jaw, whipping his head to one side. Angered but not out, he counters with a vicious jab to my gut. I double over, pain flaring inside me, and gasp for air, all the wind knocked out of my lungs. Before I can recover, he rips the garland of flowers from my neck, grabs my throat and pins me against the trunk of a mango tree.

'That wasn't a particularly friendly greeting,' he says, spitting blood on to the ground.

'We're not friends, that's why.'

Our fierce gazes lock. In his dark Hunter eyes, I see a world of hate. But then I glimpse the briefest gleam of blue in their murky depths, like a single silk thread swimming in oil. I've seen this gleam once before, back at the mental health facility in Arizona. At the time, I thought it was merely a reflection of my own Light in Damien's eyes. But now I'm not so sure.

Focusing hard, I search deep into his corrupted soul for this slender sliver of Light, wondering who he is – or, rather, *was* in a past life. I get a Glimmer of an ancient burning city, blood running in rivers through its dusty streets. I hear the clashing of swords and the screams of battle. A soldier stands before a warrior king with black eyes, a sabre held to the throat of an unarmed young woman on her knees –

Damien breaks away from my intense stare. 'Don't pry, Genna,' he snaps. 'You may not like what you see.' Arm muscles flexing, he lifts my feet off the ground. I struggle in his grip and begin to choke. My heart pounds, the double beat more intense than ever. 'Night-night, Genna,' he gloats as I clutch weakly at his hands.

I catch sight of Mei and Prisha leaving the shelter of the temple to come to my rescue. But Blondie intercepts them, grabbing Prisha by the hair. Darkness seeps into my vision, and I feel myself slipping away. Then a familiar figure strides from the shadows towards me . . .

'*Phoenix!*' I splutter, reaching out in desperation. And desperate I am, for I know my Soul Protector is dead and that this vision is a figment of my oxygen-starved mind. Yet it *does* look like him – chestnut-brown hair, an olive tan, slender frame . . . I call out his name again and the figure steps towards me, his face revealed in the eternal flame's wildly swaying light.

It is Phoenix!

Revitalized by a surge of hope, I pull myself back from the brink. Cupping my hand against Damien's side, I summon up what little energy I have left and concentrate a burst of Light into my palm, just as if I was igniting a candle. A moment later, Damien shrieks in panic as his cloak bursts into flames. He leaps away and slaps at the spreading fire, tearing at his cloak.

Freed from his grip, I dash towards Phoenix and the protection he promises. He opens his arms to welcome me.

My heart throbs for him, the familiar magnetism drawing us together. Then I stop dead in my tracks. Yes, he may look like Phoenix but his eyes are no longer starlit.

They're pitch-black!

36

'Genna, what's the matter?' he says, wearing a grin about as trustworthy as a wolf's. 'It's me.'

I recoil at his approach. 'Ph-Phoenix,' I stutter, 'what's happened to you?'

He blinks, seemingly bemused.

'Your eyes,' I say, taking another step away. 'They've pooled into a Hunter's.'

'Oh, that.' He laughs coldly. 'I guess I finally saw the light! Or rather should I say . . . the Darkness.'

My mind seizes up. *How can this be? How can his soul have turned?* 'I thought you were dead!' I cry.

'I was certainly left for dead –' his dark eyes narrow – 'by you and the others.'

'NO! No, that's not how it was,' I protest, shaking my head. Flashes of light burst in the gloom of the garden, silhouetting scenes of frantic fighting around us. 'I *wanted* to go back for you. But the jet had to take off. We had no choice –'

'Excuses, excuses,' he snarls, his lip curling. 'All those wasted lives of mine that I sacrificed protecting you. And for what? To be abandoned, discarded, forgotten!

What makes you so special, anyway? You're nothing but –'

'Phoenix, stop!' I plead, my heart breaking at his cruel words. 'How can you say such things?'

Damien, his cloak now a smouldering heap on the ground, strides up and puts an arm round his former adversary. He smirks at me. 'How? Oh, that's easy. Because he's given his soul to Tanas!'

My hopes shatter like glass. 'Phoenix is an . . . *Incarnate*?'

'Yup. All signed up, a fully fledged member!' says Damien, smirking.

I stand motionless in the middle of the park as around me the fight rages on. But in my mind the battle is already lost. My Soul Protector is now my Hunter. Even as Jude takes down Spider . . . as Mei courageously sweep-kicks Blondie to protect Prisha . . . and, as Vihan stuns yet another Incarnate, I wonder whether there's any point in fighting on. Tanas has won. She's taken the most precious soul that I know – Phoenix – and turned him against me.

'Be good, Phoenix, and restrain Genna,' orders Damien. 'She can be a little hot to handle.'

Obediently Phoenix advances towards me.

I raise my hands, warning him off. 'I don't want to fight you.'

'Then don't,' he replies.

He makes a sudden lunge for me. I twist away. He seizes hold of my backpack and almost jerks me off my feet. As I struggle to break free, I hear a *rip* of fabric. I spin round to punch him. Phoenix blocks my attack and grabs my wrist. I raise my other fist as he raises his.

'Phoenix, don't make us do this,' I plead, searching in his fierce gaze for the Phoenix I once knew. But he's no longer there. His soul is dark and distorted. An immense sadness wells up inside me and I struggle to find the will to fight him.

Miyoko-san, your friend is now your enemy, says a voice from my past in my head. I hear the words of my old sensei: *Don't let your emotions cloud your warrior mind. Even the slightest hesitation in your attack could be your undoing.*

Shutting off my emotions, I force myself to accept that Phoenix is dead to me and is now my enemy. With a roar of fury, I call upon Miyoko-san's jujitsu skills and go on the attack. I trap his arm into a crippling lock. He grunts in pain. Just as the bone is on the point of breaking, he counters with his own jujitsu move – he rolls out of the armbar and hurls me to the ground in a sacrifice throw. I hit the ground hard, my bones jarring with the impact.

'Nice try, Miyoko-san,' says Phoenix, springing to his feet as I lie gasping. 'But you forget: as Takeo, I was always better at jujitsu than you.'

Realizing I can't beat him in that martial art, I draw on Aarush's Kalarippayattu skills instead. Flipping back to my feet, I attack with a series of high leaps and ferocious kicks: a straight kick leads to an outside kick and then to a pendulum kick. Phoenix bends from side to side like a reed in the wind, deftly dodging each one.

Frustrated, I change tactics again. This time I drop into a low, wide capoeira stance and begin to sway just as I would have done as the Brazilian slave Sabina. Immediately Phoenix imitates my stance, clearly remembering his life as my training partner Gana.

'This should be fun,' he says with a grin. 'We've not practised capoeira for a while.'

We whirl and spin round one another in a deadly dance. He adapts like a mirror to my every move. He knows me too well. We've lived so many lives together, trained in so many martial arts together, fought in so many battles together that we are an equal match.

I switch fighting styles yet again, calling upon my time as the Mongolian warrior Buri. But he catches me with an unexpected upper cut to my chin. Stars burst before my eyes, and I reel backwards. Phoenix moves in fast to restrain my arms behind my back in a double lock. With my limbs pinned, Damien sidles up to me, a fiendish grin on his pale face.

'Stop struggling!' he tells me. 'Just look around you, Genna – you're fighting a losing a battle.'

I gaze at the desperate scene before me. Tarek is on the ground, being pummelled by Knuckleduster. She sits astride him, her ringed fingers beating him to a pulp. His glasses are shattered, his face bleeding and bruised. The lamp lies discarded on its side, Tanas's order to seize it forgotten in her bloodlust. The flame inside is spluttering, seemingly on the edge of going out.

Prisha's screams fill my ears as two High Priests drag my friend across the concrete towards an old bench. Mei is valiantly trying to stop them, but her beginner-level kung-fu is having little effect.

On the other side of the garden, Jude is fighting tooth-and-nail against three Incarnates. She takes a kick to the ribs, then a punch to the head. Yet somehow she remains standing.

Meanwhile, Vihan and Tanas are locked in a furious exchange of Light and Darkness. Their supernatural attacks decimate the park. The temple shudders as chunks of marble explode and vaporize. My hopes lift when Vihan hits Tanas directly in the chest with an arc of Light. The Incarnate leader howls in pain and staggers into the trunk of a tree. But she recovers quickly, the nano-carbon coating of her jacket having absorbed the worst of the attack, and almost immediately she retaliates with a spinning orb of Darkness. Vihan summons up a Light shield. The dark orb disintegrates, but a dart of Darkness hidden within its core drills its way through the shield and pierces the guru.

'*No!*' I cry as Vihan slumps at the base of Lord Shiva's statue. I writhe in Phoenix's iron grip and Damien laughs.

'It's game over,' he gloats, as we watch his master advance on the fallen guru.

Slow and assured, Tanas fashions a spear of Darkness in her hands, carefully shaping the dark energy into a long shaft with a pointed tip. Vihan's head lolls to one side, his expression one of resigned defeat. His lips move rapidly as if mumbling a mantra.

'No use in praying, Chibuzo,' Tanas declares. 'Your little Light show is over.'

'Not quite,' gasps the guru as his eye sockets start to glow. 'Genna, remember all the darkness in the world cannot extinguish the light of a single candle!'

Like a filament in an electric bulb, Vihan's skin begins to radiate a fire-orange hue until his whole body becomes incandescent. Tanas rushes forward and drives the spear of Darkness into the guru's heart just as the guru explodes into Light. Burning brighter than a star, his body illuminates the entire park for one brilliant moment. Even with their protective gear, the Incarnates are blown off their feet. Damien is thrown backwards. Phoenix's grip on me loosens and he slumps to the ground. In the neighbouring streets, people cheer and applaud, clearly believing the fantastical light display to be part of the Diwali celebrations.

As for me, I know that was the final breath of the last Soul Seer on earth. I clutch my chest with both hands as an excruciating emptiness seems to hollow out my heart. I never anticipated *this*. Vihan warned me to not burn myself out – yet he's done precisely that to himself and on purpose too, in an act of supreme self-sacrifice. To save *us*.

When the glare of the Light fades, all that is left of Vihan is a lifeless shell. I feel a loss so profound that I wonder if I'll ever recover. If the world will ever recover. The Light of Humanity has once more dimmed; Tanas has caused another Ascendant soul to be extinguished *forever*. Near to Vihan, his adversary Tanas lies sprawled on the ground, unmoving yet not dead. I know the layer of nano-carbon on her assault jacket will have protected her.

'Genna!' calls Jude, waving to me. 'I need your help.' She kneels beside Tarek, who is bleeding badly. As I hurry over, Mei and Prisha join me.

'Are you two OK?' I ask.

To my relief, they both nod. 'Shaken,' says Prisha, clearly downplaying her shock, 'but otherwise unhurt.'

'H-how's Tarek?' asks Mei, letting out a little gasp when she sees his battered face.

'He's in pretty bad shape,' Jude reports as she examines

the multiple cuts left by Knuckleduster's rings. 'No thanks to *her*.' She glares at the fallen Soul Hunter a few feet away, face down in the grass. The brass lamp lies beside her, the eternal flame again burning bright and strong, as if Vihan's burst of Light has refuelled it.

'It's OK. I'm ... jus' a little ... punch-drunk,' slurs Tarek, blood oozing from his split lip.

'We need to get you back on the jet and patched up,' I say, helping him to his feet. 'Prisha, get the lamp.'

'What about Vihan?' she asks. 'We can't leave his body here.'

We all turn to the body, slumped at the base of Lord Shiva's statue. In the darkness and with no visible wounds, the guru could be sleeping peacefully. He looks at rest. Nearby, Tanas groans and begins to come round.

'I'm afraid we don't have a choice,' says Jude. 'Let's go!'

I utter a quick prayer for Vihan, bidding my teacher and mentor a final and tearful goodbye. Then, with Tarek supported between Jude and myself, we hurry across the park for the exit. Along the way, we pass another prone body on the ground.

'Isn't that your Phoenix?' asks Mei in surprise.

'No,' I reply stiffly, barely able to look at him. 'Not any more.'

37

Rejoining the Diwali celebrations, we dive into the crowd and hide ourselves among the multitude of candles, lamps and decorations. It feels better – *safer* – to be back in the light, Tanas's ambush now only a passing nightmare. The festivities are in full swing. Drums pound, cymbals crash and people dance. Everyone is too caught up in their revels to notice five teenagers, one bruised and bleeding, pushing their way through the throng.

As we head in the direction of the ghats, we pass Prisha's hotel and I spot Mr Sharma checking his watch, waiting impatiently at the entrance. I hurriedly embrace Prisha. 'Stay with your father and stay in the light,' I tell her.

'But what about you?' she asks, gripping my hand tightly.

'We have four days to find the last two Soul Jars and end this,' I reply. 'Vihan has given us a map to the obsidian blade and told us the ritual. I just need to remember the location of the vial of Soulsilver. If all goes well, the next time we encounter Tanas we'll be ready to destroy her soul.'

'And what if you aren't ready?'

I glance at the people around us laughing, dancing and smiling. It strikes me just how fragile this existence is. I can feel the weight of responsibility upon our shoulders and the immensity of the task ahead of us. 'Then all is lost.'

Prisha bites her lower lip, then looks at the lamp in her hand. Contemplating the blue flame inside, she seems to come to a decision. 'Well, in that case, I'm coming with you.'

I blink in shock. 'What? No! You've seen how dangerous it is.'

She nods, apparently unfazed. 'If the fate of the world really is in your hands, then – as one of your best friends – I'm not going to hide in the shadows. I'm standing right by your side, Genna. In the light.'

I shake my head. 'This isn't negotiable.'

Prisha's determined gaze flicks from me to Mei. 'I know you're trying to protect me, but if Mei is with you, then I am with you too,' she insists. 'Besides, I have the eternal flame.' She holds up the guru's dented lamp.

I go to take it from her, but she pulls it out of reach.

'Please, just give me the lamp,' I beg.

'No, not unless you let me come with you.'

'We don't have time to debate this,' says Jude. She glances back in the direction of the park. 'Tanas will be coming after us any minute.'

'Am I in or out?' asks Prisha.

'OK, fine,' I say. 'You can join us, but *only* if your father allows you to. Go and ask him.'

Prisha darts off, the eternal flame still in her possession.

'What is it with your friends and their death wishes?' Jude remarks to me as she struggles to support Tarek.

'We're loyal,' replies Mei, her eyes glimmering with the blue sheen of a Soul Sister. 'Just like you, we want to help and protect Genna.'

'You're crazy, more like!' says Jude with a snort. 'Then again, I suppose I must be too.'

I smile at them both, amused at their growing camaraderie. 'Crazy or committed, I appreciate your –'

'Let's go!' says Prisha, returning with the lamp.

I do a double take. I had *not* expected Mr Sharma to give her his permission. Actually, I was counting on the fact he wouldn't. 'What did you say to him?' I ask as we hurry down the street.

'I asked if I could join you on your pilgrimage for the next four days.'

'And he let you?'

Prisha gives me a peculiar look. 'That's the odd thing. He seemed to sense there was much more at stake than I was telling him. He gave me his blessing, kissed me goodbye, and told me to pass on a prayer to you. It goes like this: *From what is not, lead me to what is; from darkness, lead me to light; from death, lead me to what is undying*.'

I glance back over the crowd to see Prisha's father standing on the steps of the hotel, his hands pressed together in prayer, his gaze fixed upon us. His eyes seem to gleam like stars – whether from tears, the light of the Diwali celebrations, or something more spiritual I cannot tell. All I know is that his soul seems more aligned with our cause than he ever let on.

Then my blood runs cold as I notice waves of lamps going out further up the road and hear shouts of confusion and alarm sweep through the crowd. Tanas and her Hunters are on to us.

'RUN!' I shout, pushing Mei and Prisha ahead.

'Follow me,' cries Prisha. 'I know how to get to the ghats from here.'

We dash down the street. Jude trails behind, weighed down by Tarek. I take his other arm and we carry him through the crowd. Emerging on to the ghats, we're overwhelmed by a seething mass of people and so many lights that we have to shade our eyes. Diwali is at its brightest and loudest here. The stones steps are lined with row upon row of lamps. Countless candles flicker along the paths and float upon the Ganges as if the sky has rained fire. Funeral pyres burn fiercely. Fireworks burst in the night. The air billows with smoke and the heavy scent of incense, while drums and chanting blast from multiple speakers, threatening to deafen us all.

As we slowly make our way down to the docks, I glance back to see Tanas and her Hunters at the top of the ghats. Their arms are raised to shield their faces against the barrage of light. It appears they've lost us in the crowd. At least for the time being.

'Come on, quick! Let's find a boat,' I say.

But when we reach the water's edge, we discover all the boats have been hired for the celebrations. Flotillas of little craft bob upon the Ganges, their festival-going occupants gazing starry-eyed at the firework display.

'Great!' mutters Jude, struggling to hold Tarek up. 'How are we supposed to get back to the plane now? We can't exactly swim there!'

'What about a taxi?' suggests Mei.

'Good luck getting one on Diwali night,' says Prisha.

'Everywhere is clogged with people, anyway,' I say, looking up and down the river. 'We wouldn't get far.'

'Well, we can't make a run for it either,' says Jude. 'Tarek is barely able to walk.'

I turn to look at Tarek. His head lolls to one side and already his left eye is almost swollen shut. Blood dribbles from his mouth.

'They've spotted us!' warns Mei.

I glance over my shoulder. Tanas and her Hunters are shoving their way through the crowd. They leave a trail of darkness in their wake, lamps and candles being snuffed out around them. A yell over the noise of the celebrations snaps my attention back to the river. Mahul, our friendly boatman, is moored up at the far end of a rickety wooden jetty, waving to us. It's the only vessel there. I raise my eyes to the heavens in thanks.

Sometimes they turn up in just the right place at just the right time. Mahul's fortuitous appearance is evidence if any were needed that he is a Soul Brother.

Manhandling Tarek along the jetty, all five of us clamber into Mahul's boat. He casts off and takes up the oars. Tanas and her Hunters come racing along the dock, their feet pounding on the warped planks. But the boatman's powerful strokes ferry us quickly away . . . our little boat surrounded by shoals of floating candles as we escape down the Ganges.

38

'Tarek's in no fit state to fly a plane,' I say as we lay him across a row of seats at the back of the jet. The blood has soaked his shirt and his face looks as though it's been used as a punchbag.

'How are we going to take off?' asks Jude, hurriedly closing the airstairs. 'The Incarnates won't be far behind.'

'I'll be . . . f-fine,' slurs Tarek, peering at us with his one good eye. 'Jus' need to . . .'

'No!' I say, putting my hand on his shoulder as he tries to rise. 'You can barely see, let alone stand.'

I quickly assess his injuries, grateful yet again for my medical skills as a former Second World War nurse. His wounds include a split lip, heavy bruising and multiple cuts. I'm concerned about his left eye and the risk of concussion. I pull out an emergency first-aid box from an overhead locker, disturbing Nefe in the process. She gives me a disgruntled flick of the tail. Then she notices Tarek and, seeming to sense his pain, springs down and settles beside him, purring softly. I ask Mei to get some towels and hot water and begin to tend to Tarek's wounds.

Jude peers out of the cabin window. 'We're sitting ducks on this runway. We should take the e-jeep and head north into the mountains.'

'We can't leave the jet,' I argue. 'We need it if we're going to complete our mission.'

'Then how do you propose we escape Tanas?' retorts Jude. 'I've certainly never flown a plane – not in this life, nor any other!'

'I've no idea!' I snap as I tear open a dressing and apply it to a deep cut over Tarek's brow. 'But if Tarek attempts take-off in his current condition, we risk crashing.'

'I know how to fly a plane,' Prisha volunteers as she's stowing the lamp away in the minibar.

We all turn and stare at her. Prisha suddenly looks awkward. She closes the cabinet door. 'Well . . . when I say I can "fly" . . . I've only ever done it in a simulator,' she backtracks.

'Good enough f'me,' says Tarek, nodding weakly. 'If Prisha can handle the controls . . . I can instruct her . . . Then we sh'd be OK.' He rises stiffly from his seat and takes Prisha's arm for support.

'"OK"? What do you mean, "OK"? You don't even have your glasses!' I protest as he hobbles down the aisle.

He waves away my concern. 'There's a s-spare pair . . . in the cockpit.'

'I didn't sign up for this!' says Mei, strapping herself tightly into the nearest seat. 'World travel, treasure hunting and the odd bit of hand-to-hand combat, yes. But a suicidal take-off in a plane with Prisha as the pilot? No!'

Seeming to sense the danger, Nefe darts into her bolthole

beneath the computer console. Hurriedly taking my place beside Mei, I secure my own seatbelt, as does Jude. The jet's engines kick into life and I clasp on to the armrests.

'Engine run-up checks complete,' I hear Tarek say from the cockpit. 'Adjus' the flaps . . . to ten degrees.'

Through the open cockpit doorway I can see Prisha's trembling hands flicking switches and pressing buttons. I glance doubtfully at Jude. 'Do you really think this is a good idea?'

Jude shakes her head. 'Not at all. But we don't have any other choice.' She nods for me to look though the cabin window. A convoy of vehicles is speeding down the road toward the disused airstrip. 'Tanas has already caught up with us!'

'Push the throttle forward,' Tarek instructs. The whole jet lurches and we're rocked in our seats. '*Gently!*' exclaims Tarek.

From a juddering start, the jet gradually picks up speed, the landing gears rumbling beneath us. 'Good, keep her steady . . . Now increase velocity . . . to one hundred and twenty knots.'

The jet's engines roar louder and the plane rockets down the runway, my heart rate racing along with it. I glance back through the window. Tanas's convoy has turned on to the old runway. From the cockpit I hear Prisha's panicked cry, 'We're running out of tarmac!'

I close my eyes, unable to watch any more. Next to me, I can hear Mei muttering a prayer. I feel the nose of the jet lift. The rumble of the wheels fades and the engines settle into a steady thrum. I release my death grip and open my eyes. By some miracle, we're all still alive.

'Way to go, Prisha!' I shout. She gives me a thumbs up.

'Yeah, good work, Prisha,' agrees Mei, her face pale. 'Although I think I left my stomach in India,' she mumbles.

'You can s-switch to autopilot now,' says Tarek. Then he high-fives Prisha before slumping across the controls.

'Tarek!' I unbuckle my seatbelt and dash into the cockpit. Together with Jude, I carry a semi-conscious Tarek back into the cabin and lay him across some seats.

'I'm fine . . . jus' a little woozy,' he groans.

'You're concussed,' I say. 'You need to rest.' I take his temperature and check his pulse, then finish tending to his wounds and give him medicine to dull the pain. Within moments, he's asleep.

I look down at his battered face and want to cry. Knuckleduster really did some damage. Recalling how Vihan healed Prisha's cut, I'm impelled to try the same on Tarek. I gently lay my hands on his injured brow and cheek, and channel some of my Light into him. A warmth emanates from my palms and I visualize healing his wounds. After a few minutes, I stop and place an icepack over his bruised eye before joining Mei and Jude round the small table in the rear of the cabin.

'Will he be all right?' asks Mei.

I nod. 'He should sleep for a good few hours. Hopefully the swelling on his face will go down in that time. But we'll need to keep tending his eye, and I'll attempt some more healing.'

'That Knuckleduster *really* laid into him,' says Jude. 'If I ever see her again, I'll –' She clenches her fist and grinds her knuckles into an open palm.

'I think I can guarantee we'll run into them again,' I reply. 'You see, I know how the Hunters are tracking us.'

39

Jude looks up and regards me across the table. 'How?'

'Through my soul link with Ph– with Phoenix.' I swallow hard. His name sticks like a bone in my throat. His metamorphosis into an Incarnate seems impossible, unreal, *unnatural*. After all our lives together, the unwavering devotion he's shown me . . . the many battles we've fought side by side . . . and the love we've declared for one another, I can't really believe he's become my mortal enemy.

I lower my gaze guiltily to the table. 'I should have recognized it. That faint throb in my chest, that sensation of a double heartbeat. What was once our blessing is now our curse,' I say. 'Just as he could find me when he was my Protector, he's using that same ability to locate me now he's with them. Wherever I hide, he will find me.'

Jude curses. 'That's all we need. As if it isn't hard enough evading Watchers and Hunters at the best of times. What chance do we have now of ever keeping you safe? Or, for that matter, of saving the Light of Humanity?'

A heavy silence descends over the dining table as the jet continues on its course into the night.

'What I don't understand is how Phoenix could have

been turned,' I say, my voice brittle with emotion. 'Surely that isn't even possible for a Protector.'

Jude clears her throat. 'I'm afraid it is.'

I look up sharply. 'How do you know?'

She gives me a pained look. 'Because it's happened before.'

I stare at her. 'Before? To whom?'

'To Jabali.'

Mei looks between us. 'Who's Jabali?'

Jude lets out a heavy sigh. 'My First Brother. From when we were first born upon this earth. We were raised in the same Hakalan warrior tribe. He is Phoenix's First Brother too.'

I narrow my eyes at Jude. 'But Phoenix said Jabali was dead, by Tanas's hand.'

Jude gives a dismissive snort. 'He would say that, for Jabali was certainly dead to him after what happened. But Jabali wasn't killed by Tanas.'

'So . . . what did happen to him?' asks Mei.

Jude pauses and looks at me. 'You don't remember, Genna?'

I shake my head. 'I may have known in a past life. But in this one I didn't even know you and Phoenix were soul-related until very recently. I certainly didn't know anything about your First Brother.'

'Well, let me jog your memory.' Jude goes over to another seat and pulls her notebook, the one she's been doodling in, out of the pocket. She flips to a page and lays it flat on the table. Among the various sketches are a collection of small, detailed portraits.

Mei leans across the table. 'Wow, they're good!'

Jude gives a modest shrug. 'I was an artist in a previous life.'

Mei glances up at her. 'Who are these?'

'Faces from the past.' She points to one with a broad nose, full lips and a strong warrior's brow. 'That's Jabali –'

The fire burns fierce and warm, sending sparks into the vast expanse of night sky. Drums pound in a hypnotic rhythm and I gyrate to their beat, my limbs bathed orange in the glow of the flames. As I dance round the fire with the other women of our Ascendant tribe, I feel eyes upon me. Glancing over my shoulder, I expect to see Asani, my Soul Protector, waiting his turn to join the ceremonial dance. But it's his elder brother, Jabali, who's watching me. Standing outside the circle of men, he grins at me. Then Asani leaps into the firelight, blocking his older brother from view, and I'm whisked away to the throb of drums –

'I remember him!' I exclaim. A wistful smile plays round my lips at my Glimmer of the fire dance in the Great Rift Valley all those millennia ago.

Jude points to another face on the page. 'Do you know who this is?'

I turn the notebook towards me to get a better look. This time the picture is of a young man with a prominent nose. My brow furrows. 'No . . .'

'That's Jabali too, in a later incarnation,' reveals Jude. 'In fact, that's who he was when he was turned by Tanas. During the battle of Ashur in ancient Mesopotamia, we were losing heavily to the Incarnates. The city was burning, the streets ran red with blood. Jabali – or Naram as he was called in that life – switched sides and offered his soul and service to Tanas.' Jude scowls as if she's just swallowed something very bitter.

I study the portrait again, now seeing the face of a traitor. 'So, Jabali sold his soul to the devil?'

'Apparently so. We didn't know that at the time. We thought he'd died protecting his First Ascendant, when in fact he'd sacrificed her to prove himself to Tanas.' Jude narrows her eyes. 'And to think our Soul Father gave him a hero's funeral!' She turns the page and taps her finger on a portrait of a bearded face with pooling, coal-black pupils. 'This is Jabali in his next incarnation as the High Priest Adamen.'

I let out a gasp. 'I recognize him!'

'And so you should,' says Jude. 'He would have been among those present at your Soul Twin's sacrifice.'

A surge of anger courses through me as I recall the very same bearded priest pinning down one of Aya's limbs on the blood-stained marble altar, in readiness for Tanas's barbaric ritual.

'In fact,' Jude goes on, 'he's the primary reason I lost courage and failed to save Aya. You see, when I sneaked into the Lugal's palace, I was met by Jabali – or Adamen. The discovery that my First Brother had not only survived but was now an Incarnate shocked me to the core. *Terrified* me. To my mind, that's a fate worse than oblivion. He offered me the opportunity to join the Darkness. I refused. I didn't want to turn out like him. Yet I couldn't bring myself to kill my own brother either, even if he was an Incarnate. So –' her voice trembles – 'so I fled.'

I regard Jude in a new light. 'Why didn't you tell me this before?'

'I did try,' Jude replies. 'Back at your house in London, but the parchment took priority.'

'Jude, if only I'd known . . .' I shake my head and sigh. 'I could have understood better. I faced the same struggle when fighting Phoenix.'

Jude gives a weary shrug. 'Perhaps the hardest battles are with yourself.'

I nod and realize that I need to let go of the bitterness surrounding Aya's death. The hot coal of blame has been hurting me as much as Jude.

'Jude, I should have said this a long time ago. I can't forgive you –' Her face drops. 'I can't forgive you,' I continue, 'because there's nothing to forgive.' She looks up at me now, surprised. 'My Soul Twin's death wasn't your fault. It never was. The only one to blame is Tanas.'

Jude looks as if she might cry. 'Thank you, Genna,' she says. 'That lifts a great burden from my heart. If only my Soul Father would see things the way you do. He still refuses to believe that Jabali turned of his own free will; he views me as the coward, the failure.'

'I'm sure if we complete our mission and destroy Tanas's soul, then Goggins will change his mind about you.' Flipping over the pages of her notebook, I notice there are other portraits too of faces with pooling eyes like a Hunter's. 'Are these all of Jabali?'

Jude nods. 'It's my way of tracking him through his incarnations. It helps me come to terms with who he has become.'

I turn to the last page and gasp in shock. I'm confronted by a very familiar face. Lean, chiselled and chalk-white, with a low fringe of raven-black hair.

Damien.

40

I stare glumly out of the cabin window, with Nefe curled up on my lap. The land far below us is shrouded in darkness; only a few disparate patches of light indicate the odd town here and there, like islands in a black sea. I feel numb, unable to comprehend everything that's occurred in the last few hours.

It's hard enough dealing with the heartbreak and shock of Phoenix's conversion into a Hunter. But the revelation that Damien is *Jabali*, a former Soul Protector and the First Brother to Phoenix, is a devastating double blow. Yet, if I'm honest, I already suspected something was amiss with Damien. That faint blue shimmer I saw hidden in the depths of his dark eyes – that has to be a fragment of his original Protector soul. It dawns on me now that this must have been the reason why Goggins couldn't kill Damien in the final battle for Haven. He must have recognized his own Soul Son. *And what father could slay his own child?* I think.

Now Phoenix has joined his First Brother in the Darkness. I can't believe for one second that my Phoenix *chose* that path. Surely he must have been forced into it against his will? Nonetheless, his conversion feels like the ultimate betrayal. In fact, it would be easier if Phoenix was dead, his soul destroyed.

My lip trembles at the bitter thought and I fight back tears. Only a few hours before, I would have been elated to discover that Phoenix had survived. Now, I'm desperately wishing he hadn't. Tanas has managed to turn the one soul closest to me against me, made my friend into my enemy. My Protector into my Hunter.

My thoughts spiral further into despair. Peering out of the window again, the world seems darker than it's ever been. A night without stars. I absently stroke Nefe but it gives me no comfort. I just want to close my eyes, fall asleep and awake to discover that this is all some terrible nightmare. What I would give to find myself back at home! To be in my cosy little bedroom in Clapham, my parents still alive, the smell of bacon and eggs being cooked by Mum wafting up from the kitchen, the sound of Dad's off-key singing drifting in from the bathroom . . .

But I realize that world has gone forever.

I hear a groan in the row behind me and I turn to see Tarek stirring. He sits up and puts a hand to his head.

'How are you feeling?' I ask.

'Like someone's used my head as a football?' he groans.

I pass him a bottle of water and a couple of headache tablets. 'I did some healing on you while you slept. I'm not as practised as Vihan, but it seems to have done some good at least. The swelling round your eye has gone down, and the cuts have closed up, but it'll be a few days before the bruising fades.'

'Thanks,' says Tarek, knocking back the tablets and taking a swig of water. I hand him his glasses and he inspects his reflection in the cabin window. 'Oh . . . I was hoping my face felt worse than it looked, but I guess I was wrong.'

'You don't look *that* bad,' assures Mei kindly.

Tarek offers her a lopsided grin. 'I guess it's a miracle any of us made it out of Varanasi alive.' Gently, he shakes his head. 'I still can't believe Vihan turned himself into a human Light bomb.'

A tear rolls down my cheek. 'He burned himself out to save us,' I say, the guru's loss only adding to the weight of my grief.

'It's a pity that he didn't burn Tanas out too!' mutters Jude. She sits at the dining table, meticulously polishing her Medusa shield as if trying to rub out her anger.

'If not for her protective gear, I'm certain it would have,' says Tarek. His pained expression turns thoughtful. 'We need to figure out how to overcome her body armour. The Light can't penetrate her jacket or her sunglasses.'

'Could we set her jacket on fire?' I suggest. 'Damage it in some way?'

'Possibly. Although I suspect the material will be fire-resistant and stab proof.'

'Then somehow we need to get her to take them off.'

'Good luck with that,' says Jude. She sets aside her shield, the bronze now so burnished it shines like a mirror. 'However, Tanas's body armour is the least of our problems. What troubles me most is that she can now wield the Darkness as a weapon. I've never known Tanas be able to do this in any previous incarnation. How on earth are we supposed to fight her now?'

'We have Genna,' Mei points out. 'She can wield the Light.'

I hold up my hands. 'I hate to disappoint you, but if Vihan with all his mastery couldn't defeat Tanas, what chance do I have? Besides, how am I supposed to master wielding the Light without Vihan to teach me any more?'

'You just need to keep practising,' encourages Tarek. 'You're our best hope.'

'No,' I say. 'Our best hope is to find the last two Soul Jars and bring an end to Tanas's soul.' I reach for my backpack – and suddenly feel sick. The front pocket has been torn open! My heart thumping, I thrust my hand in, but of course the pocket's empty. My stomach plunges and I stare aghast at the others. 'The map – I've lost it!'

'What? Genna, you *idiot*!' exclaims Jude. 'It had the location for the obsidian blade.'

'I know!' I snap, frantically searching the bag. 'The parchment's gone too! They must have fallen out when Phoenix ripped my backpack.' A cold dread runs through me. 'Oh no, what if Tanas found them . . .?'

Jude curses and slams her fist into the wall. 'That's it! We've no way of stopping her now.'

Tarek cradles his head in his hands. 'It's over. The ritual can't be completed. Tanas has won.'

Furious at myself, I throw my backpack across the cabin, causing its contents to spill across the floor and startling Nefe. She caterwauls indignantly and hightails it to the far end of the jet.

Mei's gaze flicks between our crestfallen expressions. 'But can't you still kill Tanas?'

'Sure,' replies Jude with a half-hearted shrug. 'But you've seen how powerful she's become. Even if we somehow managed to kill her, she'd simply reincarnate and continue her hunt for the last few surviving First Ascendants.'

Tarek groans. 'It's inevitable . . . the Darkness will conquer the Light.'

I swear out loud and slump into a nearby seat, feeling weighed down by defeat and despair.

Prisha enters the cabin. 'My father once told me that it's better to light a candle than to curse the darkness.' She points to the lamp behind the door of the cabinet, its flame shining through the glass and casting a blueish hue within the cabin. 'So, while this eternal flame burns, there is always hope, always a way.'

'And what way is that?' I ask miserably.

'We find the last two Soul Jars.'

'Prisha, we don't know where they are!' cries Jude in exasperation.

'That's not entirely true.' She seats herself at the computer. 'Vihan said the obsidian blade was in Guatemala, near to Diablofuego volcano.' She pulls up a map of Guatemala on the screen and zooms in on a volcano.

'And where exactly do you propose we begin?' challenges Jude, waving a hand at the swathe of green on the monitor. 'The area is thick with jungle. A search could take us weeks. And we've little more than three days until the alignment of the planets.'

'Then we'd better get started,' urges Prisha, refusing to

be put off. 'Look, there's a local airport near this town called –' she peers closer at the screen – 'Barbarena.'

'I'm sorry, Prisha, but I'm with Jude on this,' I interject. 'Without more to go on, such a search could be a huge waste of the precious little time we have left. It'll be like looking for a needle in a haystack –'

'Hang on!' cries Mei, jumping up from her seat. 'What town did you say?'

'Barbarena,' replies Prisha.

Mei joins her at the console and stares at the map. She taps the screen with her finger. 'I've heard of this town. I'm sure my parents stayed there during one of their archaeological expeditions. In fact, I remember them talking about the Devil's Fire volcano. Isn't that what Diablofuego means in English?' She turns excitedly to me. 'I knew I'd seen Vihan's map somewhere before! I just couldn't quite place it. Genna, I think my parents have the same one on their wall.'

'Really?' I frown, trying to visualize their study. I can picture the Chinese silk scroll and the tapestry of the boar hunt, also the portrait of the Harringtons, and beside that . . . a framed antique treasure map with a drawing of a volcano!

'You're right!' I cry. 'Isn't that where they discovered the ceremonial jade knife?'

Mei nods. 'I think so, although you paid more attention to their finds than I ever did.'

'Then if anyone knows where to find an ancient site in a Guatemalan jungle, they should,' says Prisha, joining in with the excitement. 'Mei, give them a call.'

Mei throws Jude a dirty look. 'I would, but Jude here broke my phone.'

'Then use mine,' offers Prisha, pulling out her mobile.

I snatch it from her before Jude can. 'I'm afraid it won't work in here,' I say, powering the phone down. 'The cabin is electromagnetically shielded. And it's best to leave it here so we can't be tracked.'

'Then how do we get in touch with Mei's parents?' asks Prisha.

'She can message them from this computer,' says Tarek. 'It's encrypted.'

'And what about the other jar?' questions Jude, as Mei sits at the console and begins to type an email. 'The vial containing the Soulsilver.'

Prisha looks at me. 'That's still down to Genna to remember.'

I pinch the bridge of my nose and think hard. 'Sorry, but I still don't recall anything more about my past life as Sura. I remember the mage handing me the vial in Sijilmasa, but after that I've no idea what I did with it.'

Prisha sits down next to me and takes my hand in hers. 'Vihan managed to prompt your memory. Is there any way to do that again? You once explained to me that Glimmers can be triggered by Touchstones or a particular place, smell or taste. So what might trigger your memory of being Sura?'

'I'm not sure . . . I was on a plane flying to LA when I had my first Glimmer as Sura.'

Prisha leans forward. 'And what were you doing?'

I think back to my frantic escape from England,

remembering my concern that the plane wouldn't be allowed to take off, then my encounter with the passenger Rose who turned out to be a Soul Sister. I recall being preoccupied by the brutal murder of my parents, and my attempt to keep my mind off my grief by watching a movie –

'I started watching a film,' I tell Prisha.

'OK, good. And what was it about?'

I close my eyes and recall the opening scene. 'The film was set in the desert. The heroine was fleeing across the dunes from a group of bandits on camels. As I watched, I became thirsty, really thirsty –'

. . . desperate for a drink in a sun-scorched land. A vast, dry salt lake ripples in the heat haze, giving the cruel illusion of water. I lie weak and dying in the meagre shade of a crumbling salt-built mosque, the only building still standing amid the ruins of the ransacked mining village. A loose heap of bleached bones on the barren ground offers a grim vision of my impending fate. Amastan, little more than a skeleton himself in his indigo robes, lowers the jar into the well with the last of his strength. I can hear his rasping voice over the hot desert wind. 'Remember this Soul Jar in –'

My eyes snap open.

'Taghaza!'

41

'There's nothing down there,' says Jude, peering out of the cockpit window at the vast, endless desert some twelve hours later. 'Tarek, are you certain we're in the right place?'

With the celestial alignment looming, Tarek had plotted the fastest route to our final two Soul Jars – the Sahara worked out to be closer than Guatemala, so the desert was to be the first stop.

Tarek nods. 'According to the flight coordinates, we're directly above it.'

'Well, if Taghaza was here, it no longer exists.'

'There wasn't much there to begin with,' I explain. 'We need to land and get a closer look around.'

'We can't land on sand dunes,' says Tarek.

'How about a salt flat?' I point east to a glinting area of exposed rock. 'That was solid, from what I can recall.'

Tarek exchanges a doubtful look with his new co-pilot Prisha. 'It's highly risky . . . but I guess we can't be too choosy. Strap yourselves in. It's going to be a bumpy landing!'

Jude and I join Mei in the rear cabin and we buckle ourselves into our seats. Sensing the danger, Nefe scurries into her bolthole again beneath the console. The jet banks left, then levels out for the approach. As the undercarriage touches down, the plane shudders violently and there's a heavy rumble of wheels. I'm tossed about in my seat so hard I fear my bones may break. The jet's fuselage groans under the strain before we come to a juddering halt at the end of the ancient dried-up lake.

'We've . . . landed,' Tarek announces in a tremulous, relieved voice. 'And let's just hope we can take off again!'

As the jet's airstairs open out on to the desert, we're hit by a blast of intense heat. The temperature rockets, the air is baked bone-dry and I immediately start perspiring as if I'm in a sauna. Donning sunglasses against the glare of the sun, I descend the stairs and step down on to the arid ground, my feet crunching on the glittering flakes of salt. I gaze around; the desert is even more harsh and hostile than I remember. There's nothing but salt, sand and more sand. Beyond the margins of the dried-out lake, fire-orange dunes rise and fall in peaks and troughs the size of mountains. A heat haze distorts the hellish horizon, giving the appearance that the world is melting like candlewax.

'Anyone got any suntan lotion?' asks Mei, clearly wilting under the scorching rays of the Saharan sun. She pulls out one of the scarves we bought in Egypt from her pocket and covers her face and neck. I do the same.

'I think cooking oil would be more appropriate,' remarks Prisha. 'It feels like we're in an oven!'

She helps Tarek as he limps down the airstairs. Tarek has thankfully recovered from his beating, at least enough to join us on our expedition to find the Soulsilver. Although his face is still marred by cuts and bruises, the icepacks together with my Light healing have reduced the swelling, while ten hours of solid sleep have countered the worst effects of his concussion. Behind him, our jet looks to be in a similar state to Tarek – functioning yet rather worse for wear. Its once sleek white exterior is now coated in dust, bullet holes pockmark its fuselage, and dents from the stones kicked up by our landing pepper its wings.

Jude appears at the jet's door, shouldering a rucksack packed with water bottles, a coil of rope and a collapsible shovel taken from the jet's emergency stores. 'Then let's find this Soul Jar before we get cooked to a crisp,' she says, the desert dunes reflected in her round mirrored sunglasses.

She gives me the nod and I lead the way across the dried-out lake bed. Vaguely recalling the layout of the land from my Glimmer, I aim for a small cluster of mounds at its edge. The heat quickly sapping our energy and our conversation, we trek in silence, with only the brittle crunch of our footsteps in the salt-encrusted ground to be heard. We pass wide, shallow indentations in the ground, the sand-filled remnants of deep holes that slaves once dug to mine the salt.

After what seems an age, we reach the strange collection of mounds I spotted in the haze. Now rubble, worn away by the wind and time, it's hard to imagine that these were once houses, the meagre and mean dwellings of the miners, built of salt-brick and roofed with camel skin. Set in formal rows, the eroded walls now look like misshapen tombstones.

'I think this is Taghaza,' I say uncertainly, 'or at least

what's left of it.' I glance around at the desolate site but struggle to get my bearings. Even the mosque is gone, lost long ago to the desert.

'How could anyone survive out here?' Prisha asks in disbelief.

'More to the point, why would anyone *want* to be out here?' says Mei.

'For the salt,' I reply, picking up a chunk from the ground and tossing it to her. 'Back when I was Sura, salt was worth its weight in gold.'

Mei examines the off-white crystal, then discards it. 'No amount of salt or gold would convince me to live here. It's a hellhole!'

Tarek glances sidelong at her. 'I don't think the inhabitants had much choice.'

Mei waves off a fly buzzing round her head. 'Well, then I'd have escaped and run away.'

'Good luck with that!' I say, mopping at my brow as I wander through the site. 'Amastan, my Soul Protector, told me it was ten nights on foot to the nearest settlement, Oualata. With no water en route, you'd die of thirst before you'd even got halfway.'

'I'm *already* dying of thirst,' says Jude, taking some water from the rucksack and passing the bottle round. 'Now where's this well we're looking for?'

'It should be next to the mosque,' I reply. I turn full circle. 'But I can't tell, for the life of me, which ruin was the mosque. They all look the same.'

The others spread out and help search. They scour the area but there's no sign of any well.

'It must have filled up with sand,' says Prisha as she wafts herself with her hat.

Jude sets aside the shovel. 'Well, I'm not digging random holes in the desert in the hope of finding it.'

Hot and bothered, I slump down on one of the mounds. 'If only we could identify the mosque, then at least we'd have a good idea where to start.'

'Are you sure we're even in the right place?' asks Mei.

'As sure as I can be . . .' I scan the horizon, seeking out any other unusual formations, but the heat haze warps the landscape, making everything appear odd. 'There doesn't seem to be any other –'

'Hold on!' says Tarek, cocking his head to one side and studying the ruins again. 'All these remains are facing south-east, away from the prevailing wind. A mosque, though, would face towards Mecca.' He glances at his watch, then up at the sky as he judges the position of the sun. 'We need to look for a mound pointing directly east from here. That way.' He points in the direction the jet lies in.

Sweeping through the site again, it only takes a minute or so before Prisha cries, 'Found it!'

The mound is now obvious, its orientation clearly different to the others.

'I still don't see any well,' says Jude, kicking at a loose stone and sending it skittering across the barren ground.

'It has to be around here somewhere,' I insist, as I try to recall my Glimmer and match it to the current setting. 'I know I was slumped in the mosque's shade . . .' I walk round to the side away from the sun, but to my frustration I find nothing to indicate a well.

'Remember, the side the shade is on depends on the time of day,' says Tarek. 'Was it morning or afternoon?'

I frown, thinking back to the Glimmer. 'I can't really remember. I was barely alive at the time.'

'Where the hell do all these flies come from?' asks Mei, batting at the cloud of insects hovering over her head and taking a step back. 'We're in the middle of a –'

Suddenly the ground beneath her gives way and the desert swallows her. I can only watch in horror as she drops like a stone and disappears before our eyes.

42

'MEI!' I yell, dashing over with the others to the gaping hole. 'Mei?' I kneel down and peer anxiously into its dark depths.

For one long, worrying moment there's deathly silence, then a disgruntled voice drifts up. 'I've found your well, anyway.'

Jude raises an eyebrow. 'I guess your friend *has* come in useful after all.'

I shoot Jude a look. 'Don't tell me you're finally concerned about her. Just do something useful, can you, and get the rope?'

'Sure,' she replies with a smirk.

I turn back to the hole. 'Mei, we're going to pull you out, but first can you see if the Soul Jar's down there?'

We hear the sound of scrabbling and a faint splash, then Mei's voice echoes up from the well: 'Yuck! There's water but I don't think you'd want to drink it. Looks like goat's pee! Hang on . . . I think I've found –'

A shriek pierces the desert's silence.

'*What's happened?*' I cry.

'Just get me out of here!' comes Mei's panicked reply.

Jude hurriedly throws down the rope and together we haul Mei up. She emerges from the well, dirty and dishevelled. Her black hair is orange with sand, her clothes smeared white with salt, and her trainers are damp from a yellow slurry of stagnant water. Under one arm she clasps a large clay jar.

'Here you go,' she says, handing me the jar.

'Are you OK?' I ask. 'You look like you've seen a ghost.'

She nods. 'I'm fine. Something startled me, that's all.'

'Well, your parents would be proud of your tomb-raider skills,' I say. 'You were a natural, falling into that hole.'

'Thanks. Takes practice to be that elegant!' Mei shakes her head and a cloud of sand billows off her.

'What spooked you?' asks Prisha, passing her a bottle of water.

Mei takes a long swig, then gives her a grim look. 'A human skeleton.'

Prisha gasps and I feel a chill run down my spine, despite the intense heat of the desert.

'Who could it have belonged to?' asks Tarek. He peers apprehensively into the gaping mouth of the well as if he's half expecting the skeleton to come crawling out of its ancient tomb.

A faint memory is stirred in my mind, but it fails to fully surface.

'Probably some unfortunate miner,' says Jude. 'Now let's get this Soul Jar open and see if Mei's treasure-hunting exploits have been worth the effort.'

I rest the clay jar down on one of the salt-brick walls and Jude cracks open the lid with the edge of her spade.

She reaches inside and pulls out a worn leather carrying tube.

'That was Amastan's!' I say. She passes me the tube and I feel an immediate warmth in my heart upon holding a relic of my Soul Protector's desert life after so many centuries. Acting as a Touchstone, it triggers a flurry of ancient memories: *wandering the dunes barefoot together in the early dawn light . . . the thrill of racing our camels to an oasis . . . his tender smile as he watched me bake flatbread upon a hot stone . . . his voice as he chanted poetry by the fire while I lay upon my rug gazing at the myriad stars.* A bittersweet smile graces my lips, then fades when I weigh such happy moments in that former life against the pain of Phoenix's treachery in this. With a regretful sigh at all that's been lost, I prise open the top of Amastan's tube and carefully pour out its contents.

A nugget of gold rolls into the palm of my hand, where it glitters under the hot Saharan sun.

Mei's eyes widen until they gleam almost as bright as the gold. 'Is that what I think it is?'

I nod and toss her the nugget. 'Here, buy yourself a new phone.'

'Are you serious?' she gasps, her jaw dropping. 'This'll buy me twenty new phones!'

'Your cut for finding the well,' I say. I upend the tube again and this time a teardrop-shaped vial slides into my hand. Now my eyes light up.

'Is that the vial Vihan gave you in Sijilmasa?' Tarek asks eagerly, mopping the sweat from his bruised brow.

'Yes!' I hold the glass vial to the sun, admiring its gleam.

We've done it! Here it is, the last vial of precious Soulsilver! Now all we need to do is get Tanas to swallow it and then . . . And then I give the vial a gentle shake. When I see nothing move, my excitement fizzles into sickening dismay. 'I-I don't believe it . . .' I whisper. 'It's empty!'

Tarek takes the vial from me and teases out the stopper. 'Looks like the seal wasn't airtight. The Soulsilver must have evaporated over the centuries.'

Inside, I feel as dry and empty as the vial. Our mission has derailed, once again.

There's a dreadful moment when no one says anything, then Jude tosses aside her spade and curses. 'Just our luck!'

Mei pockets the gold nugget and stares at us. 'So, what do we do now?'

I slump down beside the mosque, the heat of the desert hammering me. I'm at a loss as to what to tell them. Without the Soulsilver, we cannot separate Tanas's soul from her body. There's no way to complete the ritual.

'Is there anything else in the tube maybe? Another vial perhaps?' asks Prisha.

I give the leather tube another shake and hear something rattle. My hopes lift. I tap the end firmly and a large crystal of salt drops out on to the ground.

'Oh,' says Prisha, in a tone as deflated as I now feel. 'Not quite what I was hoping for.'

Frowning, I pick the crystal up. It wasn't what I was expecting either –

Emerging out of the shimmering heat, the black-robed bandits draw ever closer, appearing to float across the dried-out salt lake towards us. The sorcerer, Makoud, leads the caravan, the pace of his camel steady yet unhurried. He knows we're too weak to run, and there's nowhere for us to go anyway.

As we await our fate, slumped together in the scant shade of the mosque, the flies buzz over us as though we're already dead. I feebly reach out and clasp Amastan's hand for comfort.

'We did well . . . to get this far,' I rasp, my throat raw and parched.

'Our journey together isn't over yet, Sura . . .' insists Amastan. His voice trails away, his eyes close and his grip on my hand loosens.

'Amastan?' I croak, but I get no response.

Entering Taghaza, Makoud and his bandits dismount beside the well. One of the Soul Hunters approaches us and kneels down beside Amastan's lifeless body.

'Master, we're too late,' he calls back to Makoud. 'The desert has claimed this one –'

All of a sudden Amastan's starlit eyes open wide as he draws his telek dagger from the sleeve of his indigo robes and plunges it into the Hunter's neck. Then, seeming to rise from the dead, Amastan hurls himself at the other bandits. A whirl of blade and blue robes, he manages to take down three more – his will to defend me overcoming his enfeebled state – before the remaining two Hunters run him through with their swords.

'No –' I cry as my Protector staggers backwards, mortally wounded. He makes one last, wild swing of his dagger at Makoud, but the sorcerer mercilessly kicks him away. Amastan stumbles towards the well, teeters on the

edge, then with a final desperate glance in my direction, plunges into its depths.

'Don't drink all the water,' mutters Makoud spitefully.

With my Soul Protector gone, Makoud turns his attention to me. He can see that I'm at the limit between life and death and immediately commences his ritual. Kneeling down beside me in the shade, he draws a curved green blade of pure jade from his belt and begins to chant: 'Rura, rkumaa, raar ard ruhrd, Qmourar ruq rouhk ur darchraqq . . .'

As I lie there frail and helpless, I feel something hard in the palm of my hand. I realize it's a large salt crystal I'd picked up before Makoud's arrival. With the very last of my strength, I bring up my arm and slam the crystal into Makoud's face. I'm too weak to hit him with any force, yet he screams as if I've struck him with a branding iron. Dropping the knife, he lurches away.

The sharp smell of burning flesh wafts through the dry desert air.

Staggering over to the saddlebag on his camel, Makoud pulls out his waterskin and pours the water over his head, paying no heed to how much he spills. As he leans against the camel, trying to recover his strength, I feel my own ebbing, my heartbeat slowing and my breathing become more laboured.

With his pain relieved by the water yet his temper enraged by his injury, Makoud stalks back over to me. His right cheek now bears a vicious red welt where the salt has seared his skin.

'You'll suffer for that,' he growls harshly, picking up the jade knife.

Even though my attack won't have stopped Makoud from performing his ritual, the delay has given me all the precious time I needed.

'Not in this life . . .' I croak, managing the faintest smile as I let out my last breath and slip away –

'The salt hurts Tanas!' I exclaim, staring in astonishment at the crystal in my hand. 'I remember now how I used it to burn her once before. It maybe even weakened Tanas's powers.'

'That would make sense,' says Prisha. 'Salt supposedly absorbs negative energy. Traditionally, it's used in magic for purification and protection.'

'If that's the case, then we should take some for *our* protection,' says Tarek, slipping the empty vial into a side pocket of his rucksack and picking up a shard of salt from the ground. 'We're going to need it now we can't perform the ritual.'

Jude kicks off a block from a salt-brick wall. 'Do you think we can use this to counter Tanas's wielding of the Darkness?'

'Only one way to find out,' I reply.

Toiling under the scorching sun like the Taghaza miners of old, we gather up as much as we can and stow the salt crystals in Tarek's rucksack. Once the bag is full, we take a few moments to pay our respects to Amastan's remains in the well before returning to the jet.

The trek back is slow and arduous, each of us taking turns to carry the pack. Sweaty and thirsty, we're halfway across the salt flat when I begin to feel a sense of foreboding. I stop and stare into the heat haze.

'What's wrong?' asks Jude, suddenly on guard.

'Don't you see it?' I ask, pointing into the distance. 'The mirage.'

A city with towers and domes, tall umbrella pines and what looks to be the ruins of an immense colosseum shimmers upon the horizon. It fades in and out of focus.

Jude shakes her head. 'I only see the jet.'

The image suddenly sharpens. I see the city's labyrinth of streets and, amid them, I can make out two figures – one large and limping, the other small and slow – making their way towards the ruin, apparently fleeing from several dark shapes coming behind them.

'Then, if only I can see it, it isn't a mirage,' I reply, feeling a stab of panic and breaking into a run. 'Tanas is hunting down Goggins and Viviana.'

43

'Maybe it was just a mirage?' says Jude, panting hard from our sprint across the salt flat back to the jet. 'I mean, I wouldn't be surprised if we haven't all got heatstroke!'

'No, the vision was more than that,' I insist, urging Tarek, Mei and Prisha to hurry up the airstairs and into the plane. 'It was like a soul link with Phoenix . . . a glimpse through his eyes . . . or maybe even a premonition. I don't know. But what I do know is that we have to go there and save them.'

'Go where?' asks Tarek. Dumping the heavy backpack down on the floor, his shirt soaked through with sweat, he collapses into the nearest seat. I close the airstairs and the cabin's air conditioning kicks in.

'Rome,' I reply, as Prisha hands out fresh bottles of water. 'I recognized the Colosseum. That's where they were headed.' I glug my water down in one go.

'Goggins is more than capable of protecting Viviana,' says Jude.

'He was limping,' I explain. 'He's obviously injured. He needs our help.'

'If Tanas and her Hunters are in Rome, then that's

exactly where we *shouldn't* go,' argues Jude. 'It would be like heading into the lion's den.'

I glare at her. 'So we simply let Goggins and Viviana fend for themselves, is that it?'

'I'm afraid we've no choice in the matter,' she replies flatly. 'Without the Soulsilver, we no longer have a way of destroying Tanas's soul forever, so my priority as your Soul Warrior is to keep you hidden and your Light safe.'

'But what about Viviana's Light?'

'That's Goggins' concern, not mine.'

Mei clears her throat. 'Wouldn't saving Viviana help save the Light, though?'

'Yes,' concedes Jude, 'but we'd be risking both Genna and Viviana's Light by going to their rescue.'

'That's a risk I'm willing to take,' I declare. Nefe appears and rubs herself against my legs. I pick her up and stroke her. She purrs loudly as if in agreement with me.

Jude regards us both with annoyance. 'Need I remind you, Genna, that you've taken similar risks before, and they've cost us dearly?'

Her words prick at my conscience, causing a sharp pang of guilt, but also a hardening of my resolve. 'Tanas and her Hunters are picking us off one by one. There are so few of us left now that every First Ascendant soul is more precious and more vital than ever. We have to at least *try* to save them. Besides, Tanas won't expect us to come to her. With the element of surprise, we'll have the advantage.'

'Not for long, though,' argues Jude. 'We'll be heavily outnumbered.'

'We always are. Goggins is your Soul Father – doesn't that mean anything to you?'

Jude's jaw tightens and she becomes tight-lipped, then she lets out a sigh. 'Jeez, you're stubborn. Sometimes I wonder whether you were born a Warrior rather than a First Ascendant in this life.' She turns to Tarek. 'How long will it take us to fly to Rome?'

Tarek sits down at the computer console and inputs the destination. 'Five hours, maybe a little less.'

Jude glances back at me. 'It could all be over by the time we get there.'

'Then we shouldn't waste another second discussing it!' I reply, and head to my seat for take-off.

Five hours later, the mirage I saw from the Sahara Desert comes into view for real through the cockpit's windscreen. Peering over Tarek and Prisha's shoulders as they fly us across the city, I gaze in awe at Rome's beautiful skyline of domes and monuments shining bright and golden in the light of the setting sun.

'There!' I say when I spot the crumbling limestone walls of the Colosseum, Rome's huge oval amphitheatre, in the distance. 'That's where they were headed.'

We land in the north of the city at a private airport. Tarek almost has a heart attack over the exorbitant landing fees and fuel charges. 'It's lucky Caleb was a multimillionaire!' he mutters as he pays with the jet's crypto-card. I'm just glad we're only five miles from our destination.

Leaving the hybrid jet to be refuelled, we take the e-jeep into the centre of the city. Jude weaves through the traffic at breakneck speed, driving like one of the local taxi drivers. 'Bloody tourists!' she mutters as she honks the horn and swerves to avoid a party of snap-happy holiday-makers spilling off the pavement.

When the Colosseum comes into view, Jude turns into a side street and skids to a halt in an empty parking bay. We pile out and dash across the road. In the growing dusk, spotlights illuminate the multiple arches of the ancient gladiatorial arena, the monument's imposing walls towering over us.

We run up to the main visitor entrance and find it closed for the night.

I shake the iron gates in frustration. 'We'll have to find another way in.'

'But if the site is shut, then surely Goggins and Viviana won't be here,' Prisha points out.

'I can sense Viviana's Light,' I reply, feeling a subtle pull on my soul. 'It's weak, but it's definitely close by.' I set about frantically seeking another entrance along the row of arches. Security fences run the perimeter of the Colosseum but halfway round I notice a side gate, the lock broken open. 'There!'

We dart through the gate and under a stone archway into the immense amphitheatre. Three tiers of seating, worn down by time and the elements, encircle a vast oval arena. Much of this space is exposed, revealing the hypogeum – a network of tunnels and chambers that would have been beneath the arena floor. At the far end, a wide platform has been reconstructed from wood and sand, showing how the arena would have looked in Roman times. And its authenticity is made all the more chilling by the fact that a full-blown battle is playing out upon this platform.

'There's Goggins!' I shout, pointing to one of several figures who are fighting tooth and nail like real-life gladiators. Bald-headed and with the muscular build of an ox, Goggins is easily distinguishable from the hooded pack of Soul Hunters. Dread fills me as I scan the rest of the arena. 'I don't see Viviana, though.'

'Come on!' orders Jude, drawing her Taser. 'Goggins needs our help.'

Forced to follow the walkway that skirts the open hypogeum, we sprint round the edge of the amphitheatre. All the while, Goggins puts up a heroic fight against impossible odds. The Hunters appear to have armed themselves with weapons from the Colosseum's museum. One has a gladius sword, another a dagger, two wield wooden clubs, and the last carries a net and trident.

As we race towards the platform, Goggins dodges a lethal sword thrust, disarms a Hunter of their knife, and knocks another out with a single punch. But then he becomes ensnared in the net. Struck across the back of the head with a club, he goes down, disappearing beneath a rain of brutal blows.

Jude screams, charging on to the sand-strewn platform. She tasers the Hunter who holds the club. Immobilized, the woman drops her weapon and collapses to the ground. Meanwhile, I pick up a handful of sand and throw it into the eyes of the Hunter with the sword. Blinded, the Incarnate makes a wild swing with his weapon. I duck beneath it and kick up hard in his chest. He stumbles backwards, hits the platform rail and tumbles over the side.

Tarek dashes over to help disentangle Goggins from the net. Dazed and bloody, Goggins rises up to rejoin the fight. But the Hunter with the trident charges forward, and spears him through the gut. Goggins roars in pain, the barbs driving deep.

Reacting instinctively, I tap into my twin sister's golden aura, channelling the energy along my *nadi* lines, down my arm and out through my right hand, just as Vihan had taught me. The air crackles and a blast of pure Light shoots from my open palm. Like a lightning bolt, it hits the trident Hunter in the back and he collapses to the sand.

I stare at my hand, astounded. *Tarek was right*, I think. *I just need a little more practice.*

As the tasered Hunter recovers and reaches for her club, I fire out another bolt of Light. It strikes her and she flops back down to the ground. I turn to the last remaining Hunter, who flees through an open archway and disappears into the darkness.

'Chicken!' shouts Mei after him. She still has her fists raised ready to fight.

Prisha regards me with wide, almost fearful eyes. 'Be careful not to burn yourself out.'

I rub my hands together, feeling a frisson like static electricity in my palms. My whole body buzzes, but I'm not light-headed this time.

'Genna!' calls Tarek, and I turn to see Goggins sprawled on the arena floor in a spreading pool of his own blood. We dash over. Holstering her Taser, Jude drops to her knees beside her Soul Father. For a moment, Goggins appears too dazed to recognize her, then he splutters, 'J-Jude! What are you doing here?'

'We came to help you,' she replies. Tarek, who has been examining the Chief Protector's wounds, looks up gravely at us and shakes his head.

'You shouldn't have!' Goggins barks at Jude. 'You've risked Genna's soul.' His furious stare flicks to me. 'Genna, you need to get out of here. Tanas is close –'

'Where's Viviana?' I ask, fearing the worst.

Goggins averts his gaze, ashamed even as he lies dying. 'They've taken her!'

'Where?'

'I-I don't know. I tried to stop them, but there were too many . . .' He coughs up more blood. 'Tanas tricked me! She knew my Achilles heel.' His eyes suddenly gain a sharp, angry focus. 'Did you know that Phoenix lives and is now one of them?'

Jude pauses, then nods. 'Yes. We've been reunited, so to speak.'

Goggins swallows hard, fighting for breath. 'Tanas sent both my Soul Sons to me, Damien and Phoenix. She knew I'd hesitate to kill them, and I've paid the price for it –'

Jude cradles her Soul Father's head in her lap as he spasms with pain. 'Hush, now. It'll be all right,' she says, running a soothing hand across his broad forehead. 'They didn't complete the ritual on you. You'll get another chance. You'll get payback.'

A tear spills from the corner of his eye. 'No, no – I failed her. I failed my Viviana!'

'You didn't fail anyone,' insists Jude. 'You've fought for her to the bitter end. You did your duty as her Soul Protector. You'll come back in another life.'

Goggins shakes his head regretfully. 'There's nothing left for me to reincarnate for . . .' He looks up to the dark sky, then directs his faltering gaze to me once more, as if suddenly remembering something important. 'Did you . . . find your parchment?'

I nod.

'And does it tell you how to destroy Tanas?'

I nod again. Realizing he's close to death, I can't bring myself to speak, emotion choking any words I may have had.

Goggins manages a blood-soaked smile. 'Good, then there's still some glimmer of hope . . .'

I force a smile in reply. I don't have the heart to tell him that the parchment is lost, that one of the key elements – the Soulsilver – is gone, and that there's consequently no way of completing the ritual. There would be no benefit for him in him knowing such details in these final moments of this life.

'Jude . . .' murmurs Goggins, reaching for her hand, 'my Soul Daughter. I've been too hard on you . . . As your Soul Father I want you to know . . .' But the starlit glow to his eyes fades; he loses grip on her hand and his head lolls to one side in her lap.

'I know, F-Father,' she says, her voice breaking. 'I know.'

We stand round the Chief Protector's lifeless body, our heads bowed in grief. The silence in the Colosseum is strange yet somehow appropriate for honouring such a great warrior. Jude lets out a quiet sob. Mei offers her a tissue from her pocket, but Jude refuses it, too hardened by her warrior lives to cry.

Blinking back my own tears, I gaze round at the amphitheatre, for the first time really taking the ancient arena in. 'I remember this place,' I murmur as the distant sounds of a roaring crowd echo in my ears.

44

Thousands upon thousands of spectators bay for our blood, their thirst for violence only matched by the ferocity of the fighting in the arena. Emperor Commodus watches from his box at the north end as we are led into the centre of the Colosseum.

I stand among my fellow Christians, trembling with dread. Dressed in a simple white gown, I'm unarmed and as defenceless as my brethren. The body of a gladiator lies nearby, a victim of an earlier match. Blood stains the sand in dark red patches around him and the air reeks of sweat and fear.

The emperor raises a hand and the crowd falls silent. Then he drops his arm, the pits open and the beasts are released. Our priest, Father Lucius, holds up a small wooden cross and begins to recite the Lord's prayer, blessing each of us and preparing us to meet our maker. As the tigers stalk towards us, two of our group lose their nerve and flee, running for the barred gate through which we entered, but this only entices the hungry animals. They bound after their prey.

I screw my eyes shut, but I can still hear the savage

growls of the tigers and the men's agonized screams, at least until the cheers and whoops of the crowd drown them out. Dropping to my knees, I pray for a quick death. The roar of the crowd grows louder, laughter mixing with taunts and whistles.

Then the frenzied shouting gradually peters out into groans of boredom and disdain. I feel a hand lightly touch my shoulder and open my eyes to see Father Lucius standing before me. 'God has spared us, Laetitia,' he says.

In disbelief, I gaze around me. Half of my fellow Christians have been torn to pieces, but, with the tigers' appetites now sated, the animals show little interest in those of us left alive.

The crowd boos and jeers, dissatisfied by our reprieve. Then a gate opens and an armour-clad gladiator strides into the arena. A great cheer goes up from the spectators when they recognize the gold-masked gladiator: Titus – the reigning champion of the Colosseum.

The colour drains from Father Lucius's face. With a trembling hand, he raises his wooden cross before him. 'May this blessed cross and the relic within protect our souls.'

Walking barefoot, the cross held out like a shield, Father Lucius goes to meet the approaching gladiator. Without even breaking his stride, Titus calmly runs his unarmed body through with his sword. The priest slumps to the ground and the gladiator stamps the wooden cross into the blood-soaked sand.

The brutal killing of our priest, a good man, sends the

remnants of his flock into a blind panic. One woman bolts for the open gate. Titus cuts her down before she's barely taken a step. Another begs for mercy and is rewarded with a strike in the heart. The others cluster together on their knees, weeping, their hands clasped in prayer. The fearsome gladiator decapitates them one by one, to the elated applause of the crowd.

Finding from somewhere a hidden reserve of courage, I'm impelled to act. As Titus takes a swing at my head, I snatch up the dead gladiator's shield from the ground and deflect his sword. The clash of steel rings out loud round the arena and the crowd gasps at my daring.

Titus is taken aback and strikes again. I hold up my shield, buckling under the heavy blow as the blade glances off. The gladiator roars in fury and brings his weapon down a third time. I roll out of the way, picking up a discarded sword as I go. Instinctively I seem to know how to fight, as if I've done this before in a previous life.

Fending off the gladiator's attacks, I retaliate with cuts and thrusts. The crowd starts to turn in my favour, cheering at each of my strikes. Caught off guard, Titus is forced to retreat. I even manage to land a blow and draw first blood. The crowd erupts with cheers and wolf whistles. But then Titus tricks me with a feint and I feel his blade cut into my side. Gasping in pain, I crumple to the ground.

Titus looms over me, sword raised, eager to restore his dignity. Glaring at me through his mask, his eyes appear to pool into tar-black holes and there's a flicker of recognition in his ferocious gaze. He lowers his sword and, for a moment, I believe he's going to show mercy. Then he grabs me by the scruff of my robe. 'You're one for the emperor himself,' he snarls.

Badly wounded, I struggle in Titus's strong grip as he drags me towards the north box and dumps me before the emperor.

'Hail, Commodus!' bawls Titus, raising a fist in salute. 'What is your judgement on this Ascendant soul?'

From his box the emperor looks down at me, his eyes dark and contemptuous. He holds out his fist and, much to the delight of the crowd, turns his thumb down. A trapdoor springs open in the arena and a lioness leaps out. It's me she's meant for, I'm sure, but instead the beast pounces on Titus. He tries to fend her off, but his sword arm gets caught in her jaws and he falls to the ground under the animal's weight.

As Titus wrestles with the powerful lioness, a young beast-master appears from the pit. He dashes over to me. 'Can you stand?'

I nod weakly and clasp my bleeding side. As he helps me to my feet, I notice the boy's eyes gleam like starlight. 'Who are you?' I ask.

'Your Soul Protector,' he replies. He glances towards a gate through which several soldiers are spilling out. 'No time to explain. Nefe, come!'

The lioness releases the gladiator, who lies limp and still upon the blood-stained sand. The wild cat obediently follows us as we head for the trapdoor and the tunnel beneath. The crowd, whipped into a frenzy by the sudden turn of events, cheers us on as soldiers pursue us. Spotting Father Lucius's wooden cross along the way, I snatch it up.

It's broken in half and now reveals the gleam of the relic inside –

I feel a tug on my elbow and come back to the present.

'Genna! We need to go,' says Tarek urgently.

Mei and Prisha are huddled together, their eyes watchful of the Colosseum's darkened archways.

Jude still kneels beside Goggins' body, her face no longer strained with grief but set in a mask of vengeful determination. 'Have you any idea where they've taken Viviana?' she asks.

Still a little disorientated from my Glimmer, I close my eyes and feel for the Light. Viviana's presence is faint, as if receding or – worse – dying. Then I get a flash of . . . *ancient stone steps, marble columns and a circle of hooded High Priests in an old Corinthian temple.*

'She's close.' I try to home in on the location when an excruciating stab of pain pierces my heart. I gasp and grab hold of Tarek's arm for support. The agony is brief, brutal and final. The spotlights round the Colosseum flicker and go out, plunging us into darkness. I drop to my knees, my energy suddenly drained. Feeling cold and hollow to my core, I let out a shuddering breath. 'Viviana is dead!'

'What? No!' cries Tarek.

'Tanas has taken her soul.'

'That can't be true,' he pleads. 'Not Viviana!'

As the lights round the Colosseum hesitantly return, Tarek wanders in a daze over to the platform barrier and clings to the rail as if he's on the pitching deck of a ship in a storm. Mei goes to comfort him.

I feel strangely off balance too, as if the Light of

Humanity is on the brink of a precipice. Of all the First Ascendants, Viviana was perhaps the one I felt closest to. A wise and reassuring presence, she was the one who understood me most, defended me, comforted me. The one Light I hoped would never go out.

Prisha puts an arm round me. 'Oh, Genna . . . I'm so sorry for your loss.'

'Our loss,' I reply, through a stifled sob. 'Without Viviana's soul, there are only four Ascendants left to carry the Light of Humanity. Thabisa, Kagiso, Tasha . . . and me.'

'Then we've no further reason to stay here,' says Jude, resting her hand upon Goggins' broad chest for the last time and standing up. 'We should go before the Hunters regroup and return.'

'We can't go yet,' I say.

Jude looks at me. 'Why ever not?'

'Because I believe I know where there's another vial of Soulsilver.'

45

Descending the steps into the sunken grounds of the Colosseum, I experience a strange double vision where I can see the arena's tunnels and cages of the past overlaid on the ruins of the present.

As we skirt along the outer passage in the darkness, the ghosts of gladiators and slaves pass me by, and the snarls and growls of wild animals echo in my ears. These sounds are accompanied by the grinding and creaking of all the elevators, pulleys and machinery that move the scenery, beasts and fighters up to and down from the battle arena. In my nostrils I can even smell the sour stench of fear, sweat and blood –

'Out of our way!' yells my Soul Protector as we flee along the torchlit tunnel.

None of the Colosseum workers need to be told twice. The lioness, Nefe, bounds ahead, teeth bared and growling. I limp along in her wake, the wooden cross clasped in my hand, my wound leaving a trail of blood behind us. Taking a side tunnel, we pass under the stands of the amphitheatre, the cheers of the crowd fading to a distant murmur . . . but the shouts of soldiers are growing louder –

'Down here,' I say, guiding Jude and the others into an unlit side tunnel.

'Where exactly are we going?' Jude asks, as Tarek rummages in his backpack and hands out torches. 'Now that Viviana is dead, Tanas will surely be on the hunt for you – we don't have long.' She reloads her Taser with a new cartridge.

'I'm not entirely sure,' I admit, directing my torch down the passage, its beam disappearing into emptiness. 'I'm following my memories of Laetitia, as and when they surface. I fled this way with the relic.'

'And this relic contains Soulsilver?' asks Mei.

I nod. 'It looks exactly the same as the one I recalled in Sijilmasa. And Vihan said there were three vials: the one in Sijilmasa, which we found but turned out to be empty; another that was sunk on a seventh-century Vietnamese trading ship in the South China Sea; and one that was lost during the reign of Emperor Commodus in Rome. That's the vial we're seeking now.'

I stop as we come to a padlocked gate barring our way –

'CASSIUS!' A leather-strapped bear of a man with battle scars and a missing eye blocks the tunnel ahead. He wields a large club and shows no fear of Nefe. He seizes a torch and holds her at bay with the flame. 'What in Jupiter's name do you think you're doing? You release this wild cat, then save a condemned Christian – have you gone mad?'

'Magnus, just let us pass,' appeals my Soul Protector. 'This girl has earned her freedom. She defended herself with honour and drew first blood in a duel with Titus.'

The man raises a bushy eyebrow. 'Is that so?' He gives

me an appraising look with his single eye, which shines with a faint reassuring gleam, then grins to reveal a mouth of missing teeth. 'I never did like that arrogant gladiator,' he says, standing aside to allow us through. 'I'll hold the soldiers off for as long as I can, Cassius, but don't expect that to be very long.'

I make quick work of the padlock, picking it with a hairpin from Prisha and the expertise I inherited from the Chinese thief Lihua. We follow the tunnel deeper underground. Our footsteps echo in the darkness and our distended shadows play upon the rough stone walls. Eventually we come to a junction, and I bear left.

'My Soul Protector, Cassius, took me this way,' I say.

The tunnel gently slopes upwards until it reaches a large chamber with several long stone tables and a number of passages leading off from it. There's a chill in the air that makes my skin crawl.

'What is this place?' asks Prisha, wrapping her arms tightly round herself. An involuntary shudder runs through me as I recall the room –

The stone floor is slick with blood, the bodies of butchered gladiators, limbless slaves and mauled Christians piled high. Those of the gladiators are being laid upon the tables in turn and stripped of their armour and weapons. Weak from loss of blood, I lose my footing and Cassius catches me in his arms.

'Are you hurt badly?' he asks.

Hearing the shouts of the soldiers not far behind, I know we cannot afford to delay. 'Just slipped, that's all,' I lie.

Nefe rubs against me, seeming to sense my pain. Cassius

grabs a lit torch from the wall and carries me towards a doorway in the corner. As we skirt the piles of bodies, I press the broken cross to my chest and murmur a prayer –

'The spoliarium,' I reply. 'It's where they stripped the armour from the dead gladiators and disposed of their bodies.'

'Nice,' says Mei. 'Remind me to take a holiday in Rome with my parents. They'd love it here!'

Ignoring the main passages, I cross the room to a narrow, easily overlooked doorway in the far corner. 'Stay close.'

We duck under the stone arch and descend a set of stone steps, going deep into the earth. At the bottom, we follow a long passageway into a gallery of interconnecting tunnels. Countless alcoves and niches are dug into the volcanic rock walls, some carved out in columns of three or more high. They stretch on as far as our torch beams will go and beyond.

'Where are we now?' asks Tarek.

'The catacombs,' I reply.

'How lovely,' says Mei, with a nervous laugh. 'Another picturesque tourist spot!'

'It's where Christians buried their dead during Roman times,' I explain. 'The tunnels run on for miles. It's a place where it's easy to get lost, but it's also somewhere where it's easy to lose your pursuers –'

By the flickering flame of the torch, we hasten through the catacombs. Nefe pads along silently at our side as Cassius seems to take random turns and tunnels. Then I notice that at every junction he pauses briefly to look for a small groove cut into the rock, a sign that marks the passageways he chooses. As we head ever deeper underground, passing the many graves of the dead, the sounds of the soldiers behind us become more and more distant. And I become slower and slower.

'I need to rest,' I gasp, clutching my side.

Cassius stops in a burial chamber with a low ceiling. He leans me against the wall and looks back down the tunnel the way we've come. 'Good. I think we've lost them,' he says.

I smile, clutching the cross, then slowly slip to the ground –

Following the trail of grooves left by Cassius, I guide Jude and the others through the labyrinth of passages, galleries and burial chambers. Many of the alcoves are empty, some are blocked off with baked clay or marble, and others are filled with ancient bones wrapped in the remnants of cloth. We go further and deeper until we reach a chamber with a low ceiling and multiple tunnels leading off from it.

Prisha turns slowly on the spot. 'How did you ever get out of here?'

'I didn't,' I reply as I stop beside a grave in the wall filled with clay. A single name is engraved into the stone beside it: LAETITIA.

46

'We seem to be making a habit of digging up your dead body, Genna!' says Mei as Tarek chips away at the clay with the reinforced strike ring on the end of his tactical torch.

Prisha's face screws up. 'What? You've done this sort of thing before?'

Mei nods. 'Yeah, in a pyramid in Egypt. We found her mummy in an old tomb. The place was full of treasures.'

'And traps!' reminds Jude.

Tarek pauses in his task and glances up at me, eyes flashing with concern behind his glasses. 'You don't think there are any traps here, do you?'

I offer him a strained smile. 'Hopefully not. It isn't as if there are many treasures in these catacombs. I'm guessing I died of my wounds and Cassius buried me here out of respect.'

'Or else to hide the fact that you had died,' says Jude, who is now examining a large pile of bones stacked against the far wall of the chamber. They've been arranged in a neat rectangular block and topped with skulls, the macabre sculpture a chilling altar to death. 'If Emperor Commodus –

who I assume was Tanas – thought you were still alive, then he'd have invested time and resources into searching for you rather than for other First Ascendants. So maybe it was a trick. It would have been a good diversion tactic by Cassius.'

'I'm through!' says Tarek as he knocks a hole in the clay.

We all gather round and help pull chunks away to reveal the burial alcove behind. Inside is a skeleton, its arms crossed over its chest.

Prisha peers with grim fascination at the skull. 'Is that *really* you?' she asks.

'Must be,' I reply, my voice sounding hollow in the chamber. 'My name's on the wall.'

It feels bizarre to see my dead self again and an uneasy sensation creeps into me.

'Looks like you've lost a bit weight!' jests Mei, trying to lighten the mood.

'OK, let's get this over with,' I say, ignoring the tension in my chest. 'We're looking for a small wooden cross.'

We search the alcove and my body, but there's no sign of it.

Tarek gives the alcove another sweep of his torch. 'The wood likely decayed centuries ago.'

'Or else Cassius took it,' I reply. 'In which case, the vial is truly lost.'

'Hang on!' says Prisha. 'What's that?' She points to a gleam of glass, picked up by Tarek's torch, just visible between Laetitia's skeletal fingers.

Carefully, I prise apart the bones and – oh joy! – find the relic intact.

'This is it!' I exclaim, handing the glass vial to Tarek as carefully as if it were a newborn baby. 'Is the seal OK?'

He closely examines the stopper and gives the vial a gentle shake. A silvery liquid swirls inside. He smiles. 'Yes, the seal is good,' he says, and he picks up his rucksack to stow the vial away.

'I'll have that, thank you very much –'

The five of us freeze. The condescending, self-important voice is like a razor down my back. I don't even need to turn round to know who it is. I curse myself for letting my guard down, for not paying attention to the thrumming in my chest. For allowing myself to get distracted by our search for the vial. My heart beats hard as I ready myself for the fight to come.

From the darkened tunnel opposite us steps Damien, a smug grin on his lips. In the setting of the catacombs, his marble-white complexion and chiselled looks make him appear like a handsome vampire risen from his crypt.

Mei recoils. 'How on earth did he find us down here?' she whispers.

Phoenix steps from the shadows and, immediately, the answer is obvious.

'Phoenix,' I say, 'when he was Cassius – buried me in these catacombs. He knew exactly where we'd be.'

I feel a crushing ache in my heart on seeing my former Soul Protector. To all appearances, he is still my Phoenix. Chestnut hair, olive-tan skin and a lean physique. But his eyes are pools of inky black, empty of warmth and humanity. They drain all the goodness and Light from him.

'Phoenix, you're my Protector, not my Hunter!' I plead.

'Come back to the Light.' I hold out my hand, but he stares at me with cold disdain.

Damien snorts a derisive laugh at my wounded expression. 'How pitiful! You still think he cares about you? You're nothing to him now. Only the Darkness matters.'

I turn on Damien. 'I don't believe you. Deep down in his soul, he is still my Phoenix. And deep down, I know who you are . . . Jabali!'

Damien recoils at the use of his soul name. 'I'm no longer *Jabali*!' he snaps. 'Jabali's soul died a long time ago. Thanks to you,' he adds bitterly.

I flinch as if I've been slapped. 'W-what do you mean?'

Damien regards me with a strange combination of hurt and hate. 'Why am I not surprised you don't remember? You never did pay me much attention, did you? None of that matters now, anyhow,' he growls. 'Enough of this wasted talk! Tanas is waiting.' He turns to Tarek. 'Hand over that vial.'

Tarek closes his fist round the relic. 'You'll have to prise it from my cold, dead fingers.'

Damien shrugs. 'If that's what you really want.' He lets out a whistle and Thug materializes from the tunnel behind Tarek, ensnaring him in his bulging arms. Before we can react, the rest of his gang emerge from the other tunnels to surround us. The chamber suddenly feels very small and tight. I can barely breathe. Prisha and Mei shrink away, backing themselves up against the alcove as far as they can go. Jude reaches for her Taser, but Spider puts a knife to her back and she freezes mid-draw.

'I see that Jessica has made a good start on your face,'

Damien remarks, eyeing with satisfaction the mass of purple bruising disfiguring Tarek. 'I think we should let her finish off her handiwork, don't you?'

Knuckleduster cracks her ringed knuckles and approaches Tarek. She carefully removes his glasses and puts them in his shirt pocket. 'We don't break these, do we? Just your face.'

Tarek's eyes widen. 'Here, have it!' he says desperately, tossing Damien the vial. It lands at Damien's feet. Rather than picking it up, Damien stamps on the vial. The glass splinters like a bone.

'NO!' I cry as the vial of Soulsilver is ground into the dirt . . . and, with it, the last hope we had of destroying Tanas. My instinct is to scream. Instead, I focus all my frustration and fury into the palms of my hands. Feeling the heat build beneath my skin, I cast a blast of Light at Damien.

But he's quick to react. He ducks and the Light pulse hits the bone altar instead. It explodes in a hailstorm of skulls and bony limbs. They ricochet off the walls and everyone dives for cover.

'Follow me!' I yell to the others.

With the Hunters blinded by the intense flash of Light, we disappear down the nearest tunnel. Our feet pounding in the darkness, our torch beams wavering, we sprint with no real idea of where we're headed. Behind us, the furious shouts of Damien and his Hunters echo: '*Which way did they go?*' Then: '*Split up!*'

I turn left, then right, then right again, along a narrow corridor, then cut through a chamber and up a sloping passage. At the top, I reach a junction and stop, all of a sudden realizing I've left everyone behind. I can hear their nervous whispers and uncertain footsteps echoing from the other passageways; my friends are close yet equally lost in the labyrinth. Holding my torch steady, I turn full circle, trying to locate them and get my bearings. I spot a groove in the wall. *Cassius's trail mark!* Recognizing where I am, I turn round and call quietly to my friends, 'This way!'

I shriek as Phoenix's black-eyed face looms out of the shadows and into the beam of my torch. 'Thanks, Genna,' he says with a cold smile. 'But I know my way through these catacombs.'

Almost dropping my torch, I turn and run. Following Cassius's grooves, I retrace my steps to the surface, finding the stairs, then the spoliarium and finally the tunnel out. Ahead I can see the pale yellow glow of the Colosseum's spotlights. Phoenix's footsteps close in on me. I reach the gate and slam it on him, snapping shut the padlock.

Phoenix reaches through the bars for me as I back away.

'Genna, don't go!' he pleads. 'It's so dark . . . so empty . . . so lonely in my soul . . .'

I stop. His eyes are still pooled, but his malevolent expression has softened into one of genuine desperation and his voice is more his own. 'P-please, Genna, I beg you! I need you . . . help me!'

I find myself drawn to him, unable to resist. My heart yearns for the Phoenix I once knew – and there he is, or, at least, there is a fragment of his former self. As I stand before the gate, I'm barely aware of him taking my hand. His skin, though, is unnaturally cold to the touch.

'Phoenix, I want to help you,' I say, my eyes meeting his, seeking out his true soul. 'Just tell me *how*.'

He presses his face against the bars. 'Genna, there is a way for us to be reunited . . .' His voice becomes barely a whisper and I have to lean in to hear him. 'All you need to do is embrace the inevitable. Join me in the Darkness.'

Held fast by his mesmerizing gaze, I feel my resistance weaken. His pooling eyes seem to expand, becoming my entire world. In their reflection I see us both together, hand in hand, entwined for eternity. *Would that be so bad . . .?* The temptation to surrender to the Darkness becomes overwhelming –

No! No! Fight this! I tell myself.

But look how happy you would be, says a voice in my head. *The Darkness is a gift, not a burden.* The voice is powerful and persuasive.

Don't be fooled! I force myself to think.

It would be so easy to join him in the –

I blink hard, breaking the connection. 'No, no!' I say, shaking my head fiercely. 'You come back to the Light.'

Phoenix gives me a bemused look. 'Why on earth would I want to do that?'

'Because you're my Protector!' I reply. 'Our souls are linked. Your life with mine, as always. Remember?'

He stares at me, indifferent to the point of cruelty.

'Because you *love* me,' I cry in desperation.

'I never loved you.' His face contorts into a dark hatred and he seizes hold of my throat. 'Join me or your soul will perish!' he rasps, his voice sounding demonic.

'NEVER!' I yell, slapping him hard across the cheek

with my free hand. For a moment, he is stunned. Then he begins to squeeze his fingers.

'Phoenix – don't!' I gasp, as my windpipe is crushed. 'I beg you, don't do this –'

Suddenly Phoenix convulses. There's the faintest recognition in his eyes, the briefest gleam of blue, before the curtain falls again on his soul. His grip on my throat loosens and he slumps to the floor. Behind him in the tunnel stands Jude, a discharged Taser in her hand.

47

'I saw it, I tell you – I saw the Light in his soul!' I cry as we speed through Rome's streets in the e-jeep, trying to put as much distance between ourselves and Damien and his Hunters as possible. We'd managed to lose them in the maze-like tunnels of the catacombs, but it had been a close call.

Mei and Prisha sit either side of me, panting hard from the mad sprint to the e-jeep. In the front passenger seat, Tarek clutches his backpack like the world depends upon it, while Jude's eyes are firmly fixed on the road ahead.

'My Phoenix lives!' I declare. 'Deep down in his soul's darkest depths, a trace of his true self still exists.'

Two police cars, sirens blaring, shoot by in the opposite direction towards the Colosseum. They're no doubt responding to the report of a dead man found in the arena, or else an old woman lying murdered upon an altar in an ancient Corinthian temple.

'Don't get your hopes up, Genna,' says Jude, glancing in the rear-view mirror, first at the police cars and then at me. 'It was probably just the effects of the Taser.' She waves her gun. 'This thing delivers *one hundred thousand* volts. No wonder his eyes lit up!'

I shake my head. 'No, it was more than that,' I insist. 'It was a starlit gleam. I think there's a chance we can bring him back.'

Mei and Prisha both turn to me, surprised. 'Is that possible?' Mei asks.

'Remember, Mei, I made you a Soul Sister by sharing some of my Light with you. I believe it's the same principle –'

'Forget it!' says Jude dismissively. 'Once Tanas has her hold on your soul, there's no coming back.'

'That's not entirely true,' I argue. 'Jude, remember that Egyptian priest, Ankhu? I brought his soul back from the brink by sharing my Light.'

Jude frowns. 'That priest was weak-minded and a lowly Watcher. Phoenix is a full-blown Hunter. Tanas's soul grip on him will be far stronger.'

I clench my fists. 'Then we need to somehow kill Tanas before trying to free Phoenix's soul.'

'What difference would that make?' asks Prisha, as we pull up at the entrance gate to the private airport. Tarek flashes our entry pass and we head over to our jet.

'When Tanas dies, so does her hold over her followers,' I explain. 'At least for the remainder of that life.'

'That wouldn't solve the problem, though,' says Jude, the jet's bay door automatically opening at our approach. She drives the e-jeep up the ramp and into the cargo hold. 'Having previously been a Protector, Phoenix would be left a shell of his former self, essentially a soul zombie. The same would happen to Damien.' Parking the jeep, she switches off the engine and turns to me. 'Don't think I haven't tried to recover Jabali's soul in previous lives. There's nothing there to save. Besides, they'll just come back as Hunters in the next incarnation. The only way to stop the cycle is to destroy Tanas's soul. And since Damien has smashed the only vial of Soulsilver, that's now impossible.'

She clambers out of the jeep and slams the door shut with finality.

I leap out after her. 'No, it *is* still possible. That wasn't the only vial. There's one more at the bottom of the South China Sea.'

Jude shoots me a disbelieving look. 'Do you know how big the South China Sea is? If Vihan didn't know where the shipwreck lay, then there's little hope of us ever finding it, let alone recovering a tiny bottle of Soulsilver from the seabed. And certainly not in time for the alignment anyway!'

I open my mouth to argue, but no words come. It's obvious how ridiculous my suggestion is. My desperation to save Phoenix is making me clutch at straws.

Tarek emerges from the jeep, his backpack in hand and a strange smile on his bruised face.

'What are you so cheery about?' I ask flatly.

'No need for us to go deep-sea diving just yet.' And as if from nowhere he produces a glass vial of silvery liquid.

I gape in astonishment.

Mei jumps out of the jeep, with Prisha close behind her. 'B-but we all saw you throw the vial to Damien and him stamp on it! How's this possible?'

'A little sleight of hand,' Tarek explains, his eyes glinting mischievously behind his glasses. 'I switched vials and threw him the empty one we found in Taghaza.'

I rush over and embrace him. 'Oh, Tarek! You're a genius!'

'Careful!' he replies as he extricates himself from my hug. 'We can't afford to lose this one.' He passes me the vial and I cradle it in my palm. The Soulsilver seems to pulse as if it has a heartbeat.

Jude punches the button to close the cargo-bay door and exclaims, 'Well, I guess our mission to destroy Tanas's soul is back on!'

As soon as I enter the jet's cabin, Nefe runs up to me, demanding food. Trying not to trip over her, I open the minibar cabinet and stow the vial carefully alongside the mummified hand, the star chart and the oil lamp containing the eternal flame. Then I take a tin of tuna and empty it into Nefe's bowl.

'There you go, my little lioness,' I say, stroking her sleek, sandy-coloured fur. 'Thanks for saving me at the Colosseum all those centuries ago.' She responds with a rolling purr before tucking into her food.

'That poor cat must be getting fed up with being stuck on this jet,' remarks Jude. 'I know I would.'

'Well, hopefully she won't have to be cooped up for much longer,' I reply, hunting in the galley for some food for myself. 'We've only the obsidian blade to go. Mei, any word from your parents yet?'

'I'll check,' says Mei.

While Mei seats herself at the computer console, Tarek and Prisha head to the cockpit to prepare for take-off. I dig out a bag of roasted peanuts from the cupboard and offer them to Jude. As we share our meagre snack, I'm plagued by a nagging thought.

'What did Damien mean,' I say, 'about his soul dying thanks to me?'

Jude shrugs. 'No idea. Maybe he was playing mind games with you.'

I shake my head. 'It seemed more personal than that. Like I'd wounded him somehow –'

'Hey,' says Mei, interrupting us, 'I've got an email from my parents!'

Jude and I hurriedly join her at the console and peer over her shoulder at the screen:

> Hello, my bǎobèi, we're so relieved to hear from you. After the 'incident' in Dunhuang, we were worried, but we're also super proud of your treasure-hunting exploits.
>
> Guatemala, hey? You're correct! We did find the ceremonial jade knife near Diablofuego volcano. That was one of our most exciting yet challenging archaeological expeditions. The jungle there is almost impenetrable! You need to take great care and must have a trustworthy guide. So we've taken the liberty of calling Pablo in Barbarena. He was our lead guide and is expecting you. This is not negotiable – we'd feel safer knowing that you are accompanied into the jungle. Pablo's contact details are below.
>
> We've also attached a copy of the original treasure map,

along with the coordinates of where we discovered the knife. According to our research, there should be an ancient lost city in the region, but we never found it.

Good luck in your expedition. While we've always encouraged an adventurous spirit in you, do stay safe and don't take any unnecessary risks.

Love, Mum and Dad

Mei glances at us. '*Don't take any unnecessary risks*? That's a laugh!'

'At least we have a copy of the map again,' says Jude, printing one off.

'And a local guide,' I point out. 'That should help speed up our search.' I call to Tarek in the cockpit. 'How long to get to Guatemala?'

'Thirteen hours direct,' he replies.

'And how long does that leave us to find the blade and kill Tanas?'

Tarek turns in his seat to give me a strained look. 'It's going to be tight. I've double-checked my calculations for the star chart on the jet's computer system. Once we land in Guatemala, we'll have exactly one day, twenty-three hours and thirty-two minutes left.'

48

'This is as far as the road goes,' announces our guide, Pablo, stopping the engine of his battered jeep. 'Road' is being generous, to say the least. For the last five or so miles, it has been little more than a rutted dirt track with thick jungle on both sides.

Feeling as battered and bruised as his jeep, we gladly clamber out and stretch our aching limbs. Immediately the heat and humidity of the jungle drench us in sweat. The air is thick with the smell of rotting vegetation. Insects whir in the bushes, the screeches of howler monkeys echo through the trees, and exotic birds call from high up in the canopy.

I glance at my watch. We've been driving for almost three hours. Combined with the journey into the town of Barbarena from the airport, and the time it took us to locate our guide and prepare for our expedition, almost twelve hours have passed since landing in Guatemala. By Tarek's calculations, that means we've less than a day and a half to locate the obsidian blade and complete the ritual on Tanas. The task ahead feels almost impossible and with each passing second the pressure only builds.

'Time is tight!' says Jude, clapping her hands. 'Let's get going.'

We hurriedly unload the jeep. Each of us has a backpack with food, water, a mosquito net and a hammock. Prisha is in charge of the first-aid kit, while Mei has been given a sat phone and GPS unit by Pablo in case we get lost in the jungle. Jude unlocks a small black plastic case containing a Taser and a set of loaded cartridges. She holsters the gun and pockets the extra cartridges, then she reaches into the back of the jeep and pulls out her Athenian shield.

'Do you really need to take that?' asks Mei. 'It's not exactly jungle gear.'

Jude slings the shield across her backpack. 'If this is to be our final battle, I'm going to need every bit of protection I can get.'

Throughout our preparations, our guide says nothing. He watches us with amused curiosity, clearly considering this to be some sort of eccentric school trip rather than a life-or-death expedition. A small, stocky man with a pencil-thin moustache and a row of uneven yellow teeth, he wears a brightly coloured, zigzag-patterned shirt, faded blue jeans and a white cowboy hat. While we gather the last of our things, he leans against the jeep, rolling a cigarette between his fingers, as if there is all the time in the world.

Yet I know full well that the world is fast running out of time.

The final item in the back of the jeep is a large duffel bag containing the relics from the Soul Jars we've collected so far. Tarek goes to pick it up when something inside moves. He looks at me, startled. The bag twitches again.

'You don't think Apep's mummified hand has come back to life, do you?' he asks, eyeing the suspect bag.

'I certainly hope not!' I reach over and cautiously unzip it. A sandy-coloured head with whiskers and a rather indignant expression pops up, followed by a sleek tail.

'Nefe!' I cry as she leaps out.

'What's she doing here?' exclaims Jude. Pablo smirks in amusement at our surprise hitch-hiker.

'She must have snuck in while we weren't looking,' says Mei.

I bend down to pick Nefe up. 'Well, I don't blame her for making an escape attempt,' I say. 'She's been confined to the jet for far too long. We can't take her back to the plane now, and she can't stay locked in the jeep . . . so I guess she'll just have to come with us.'

'But what if we lose her in the jungle?' asks Prisha, giving Nefe's cheek a tender rub. At that moment, a large tropical butterfly flutters past and Nefe springs out of my arms and bounds after it. She disappears among the bushes, clearly relishing her new-found freedom. I call after her. For several seconds I think I have lost her, then in a tree overhead there's a violent rustle of leaves, a mad flapping of wings and a panicked squawk, before Nefe eventually re-emerges. She sits down on the path and grooms herself. I note there's a small green feather now caught in her whiskers.

'I have a feeling she'll survive,' I say.

With our mystery stowaway revealed, Tarek distributes the rest of the duffel bag's contents. He hands round some of the salt crystals we collected from Taghaza, giving the surplus to Mei to carry in her pack; Prisha volunteers to look after the lamp containing the eternal flame; Tarek keeps hold of the star chart; and I carefully slip the Soulsilver into a padded side pocket of my backpack. The Egyptian Canopic jar, however, remains untouched in the bag, no one particularly wanting to claim it. All eyes turn to Jude, who gives a weary sigh.

'I guess I'll be taking Apep's cursed hand then,' she says, reluctantly picking up the jar and depositing it into her pack.

'*Listo?*' asks Pablo through a puff of smoke.

I nod. 'As ready as we'll ever be.'

He tosses aside his cigarette stub. Shouldering a small canvas rucksack with a machete strapped to the side, Pablo leads the way over to the head of a trail where there's a wooden sign in both Spanish and English. It appears to have been recently erected.

DIABLOFUEGO VOLCÁN

WARNING: THIS IS AN ACTIVE VOLCANO

HIGH RISK ZONE!

DANGER TO LIFE!

TRAIL CLOSED

'Great! That's all we need,' says Mei, peering at the smoking peak in the near distance. 'A live volcano!'

I glance at Pablo. 'Should we be worried?'

He takes off his hat and wafts himself casually with it. 'Diablofuego has always rumbled, since I was a boy, but she's yet to lose her temper. As long as we don't anger the ancient fire god, we should be fine.' Popping his hat back on his head, he saunters off down the trail. We follow in single file behind him.

For the first hour we walk in silence, the load of our backpacks and the burden of our mission weighing heavily upon us. The jungle seems to sense our purpose. The birds fall quiet, and at first only the buzz of mosquitoes accompanies us. The heat is oppressive, and the light is blocked by the thick canopy overhead. We walk through a shadowy world. Occasionally shafts of sunlight spear their way down to the jungle floor. Through these gaps in the canopy, the jagged peak of Diablofuego thrusts upwards. Grey smoke rises from its crater into the azure-blue sky. Every so often, we hear a low rumble like distant thunder, but the sound soon fades and the volcano settles back into a malevolent silence.

Pablo stops along the trail where a tree has fallen and calls for a water break. While he smokes another cigarette, I take a much-needed swig from my bottle, the water warm and unappetizing. My top clings to me like a wet towel.

'And I thought the Sahara was hot,' says Mei, mopping her brow. 'This humidity is ridiculous. I'm showering in my own sweat!' She ties her shirt around her midriff and rolls up her sleeves.

'I'd keep your shirt rolled down if I were you,' Pablo advises. He wears a thicker shirt than any of us, yet has hardly broken a sweat. 'You don't want to cut yourself on any leaves in the jungle. Or, worse, have a botfly lay its eggs under your skin.'

'Ew, gross!' squeals Mei. She quickly pulls down her sleeves and securely tucks in her shirt.

'And I wouldn't sit there,' Pablo warns Prisha, as she goes to settle herself on the fallen log.

'Why not?' she asks, instantly freezing in her position, the lamp swinging in her hand, its blue flame casting a halo of light on the ground.

'Army ants.' He points to an undulating river of brown insects flowing across the forest floor and over the log. Prisha leaps away and shakes herself free of ants.

'And careful by that tree, Tarek,' adds Pablo casually. 'There's a poison dart frog on the branch above you. Its skin is toxic to the touch.'

Tarek peers nervously up at a tiny yellow-and-black frog over his head, then shifts ever so carefully to one side.

Mei gives me a horrified look. 'This place is going to eat us alive!'

We set off again, more alert now to the jungle's dangers. I glimpse movement to my left and spot Nefe leaping from branch to branch like a jaguar, easily keeping pace with us and avoiding the forest floor. I sense she's more at home than us in this jungle so I wouldn't be surprised if she'd had a previous life here before. However, as we trek deeper and deeper, the undergrowth and vines thicken and seem to want to choke us. When our way becomes blocked, Pablo is forced to get out his machete and cut a path through. Our progress slows dramatically.

'How much further, do you think?' asks Tarek, slapping at a mosquito on his neck.

'A couple more kilometres, judging by the GPS,' replies

Mei. She leans against a tree, then thinks better of it when she spots a giant spider's web beside her.

Jude adjusts the shield on her back. 'At this pace, it could take us until nightfall to reach our destination.'

'Then we'd best help Pablo with the machete,' I suggest. 'It looks like even he's tiring in this heat.'

Eventually, after three hours of relentless hacking, we emerge into a large and unexpected clearing. Here, the trees have been cut back and the ground dug into deep trenches. The area is about half the size of a football pitch, but vines are already encroaching, the jungle creeping back to reclaim its land. Ahead, the forest slopes steeply up towards Diablofuego, which now looms over us like a slumbering giant. To the west, in the reddening sky, the sun hangs low and sickly above a ridge as if struggling to fight off the impending night.

Pablo guides us over to a large pit in the centre of the clearing. The excavation has revealed a tall upright slab of volcanic stone with a carving of a strange face featuring wide blank eyes, rounded ears, a beak-like nose and a gaping mouth. The carved head is crowned with a ring of fire. Hieroglyphs and images of ritual sacrifice decorate the pillar on all its sides. In front of this ancient monument sits a low circular stone altar, its surface scored with numerous, ominous grooves.

'This is where the jade knife was found,' announces Pablo, 'and where human sacrifices were made.'

49

We stand round the stone monolith in silence, sensing the presence of death in the air. The voices of ghosts long dead seem to whisper in the trees, and an unnatural chill permeates the air despite the heavy heat of the jungle. As we gaze upon the ancient monument and its sacrificial altar, I notice a peculiar aspect to the carved face. When I'm not looking directly at it, its features seem to twitch to life, the mouth curling into a devilish grin and its gaze narrowing into malevolent intent. But each time I glance back, the face remains set as stone, its square eyes staring blankly at me. I notice Nefe keeping a wary distance. She mews plaintively far from the edge of the pit, her sixth sense seeming to warn her off – and I don't blame her.

'Let's spread out,' I instruct the others, shrugging off the uneasy sensation. 'See if we can find any other ancient stones that may lead to the obsidian blade.'

We put down our backpacks and begin to scour the area. Each of the archaeological trenches is marked with a small wooden post, a number and letter engraved on the side. Over in one corner are the remains of a camp and in another a large heap of discarded earth. The jungle presses in on all sides, forming a dense wall of vines, bushes and trees. Our first sweep of the clearing results in little more than a few fragments of stone and a small collection of human bones uncovered by the most recent archaeological dig.

'The Harringtons searched this site for months,' says Pablo, sitting on the lip of a trench while he smokes a hand-rolled cigarette. 'I assure you, there's nothing else significant to find here.'

'They must have missed something,' I insist. 'Vihan was adamant that the obsidian blade is located in this area.' I take out the printed copy of the guru's treasure map and lay it on the ground. 'See! The volcano on here matches Diablofuego. And that ridge to the west must be this one –' I point to a jagged line on the paper. Then I plant my finger in the middle of the map. 'This pyramid marks where the lost city is.'

Pablo squints at the map through a haze of smoke. 'Maybe so, but I know of no pyramid in this area. Besides, this is a very big jungle. Even a slight miscalculation could put us miles out.'

'Isn't there any way we can narrow the search down?' I ask.

Pablo draws thoughtfully on his cigarette before tossing the stub into the trench. 'Maybe,' he grunts. Delving into his canvas rucksack, he pulls out a compass and a tattered geological map. He orientates his map and compares it to the treasure map, then takes a bearing on each of the landmarks and draws a pair of lines on his map. 'We'll need a third marker to triangulate the exact location.'

'What about that?' asks Tarek, pointing to a river drawn on the treasure map.

He shakes his head. 'Too imprecise to take a bearing.'

'Then how about this lake?' I ask, indicating an oval-shaped expanse of water.

Pablo frowns. 'That must have drained away long ago. It isn't on my map, and as far as I'm aware it no longer exists.' He sets aside his compass. 'Without a third definitive landmark, I'm afraid I don't hold out much hope of locating this city. If it is a lost city, then it is well and truly lost.'

I sigh and fold Vihan's treasure map. 'We've come this far,' I say, 'we can't give up yet.' I glance at my watch and see the time ticking relentlessly away. I turn to the others, who have been taking the opportunity to rest and drink some water. 'We need to search again.'

As we scour the site for a second time, the daylight fading, I can feel the pillar's stony gaze following our every move, mocking us in our attempts to find the obsidian blade. Yet I sense we are *so* close. In fact, I'm sure that's the reason the face taunts us so much. It knows the blade is maddeningly within our reach.

After a third unsuccessful sweep, we decide to expand our search area beyond the borders of the clearing. We split up into pairs. Tarek goes with Pablo towards the volcano; Prisha with Mei in the opposite direction; and Jude and I head west towards the early-evening sun, now dipping below the ridge. As we enter the jungle perimeter, I start to feel light-headed and wonder if I'm dehydrated. I take a long draught from my bottle. But the dizziness doesn't go away. I hear the sound of rushing water. I didn't think the river was this close –

I clutch Kagiso to me as we're forced on to the ledge

jutting out over the thundering waterfall. The air is swirling with mist so thick it looks like smoke. Far below, the Zambezi river is churned up into a white, writhing monster, jagged rocks poking up out of it like shipwrecks. In the shallows and upon the banks I can see crocodiles basking in the hot African sun, their saw-toothed jaws wide open.

'Not Kagiso,' I plead, terror taking me. 'Spare his soul!'

But the High Priests ignore me as they bind our bodies tightly and weigh us down with stones. Amid the haze and roar of the waterfall, I hear Tanas commence her ritual. I stand trembling and afraid, Kagiso crying in my arms.

The incantation ends and for a moment there is only the thunder of the falls. Then we're shoved violently over the edge. We plunge downwards ... falling ... falling ... falling ... until we hit the river below, the brutal impact knocking all the air from my lungs. Dragged under the churning waves, Kagiso's cries are drowned out and I gasp for breath, only to swallow cold, suffocating gulps of water. I can't breathe! I can't –

'Genna! Genna!'

I open my eyes to discover I'm lying in one of the jungle trenches, my arms and legs flailing. Jude kneels beside me, trying to control my limbs. 'Calm down! You fell in. Are you hurt?'

'I-I'm fine,' I reply groggily, and stop kicking. Slowly sitting up, I take a minute to breathe in the warm, welcome air of the jungle and wait for the painful pressure in my lungs to ease.

Prisha dashes over with Mei. Tarek and Pablo appear seconds later on the other side of the trench.

'What happened?' asks Mei, as Jude and I are helped out of the trench. 'Did you trip up or something?'

'N-no,' I reply, still trembling from the experience. 'I had a soul link.' I glance over at Pablo, fighting to keep my composure. 'Would you give us a moment, please?'

'Sure,' he says with a shrug. 'I'll be over by the altar.'

Once our guide is out of earshot, I allow the tears to cascade down my face. 'Thabisa and Kagiso have just been sacrificed. Thrown off Victoria Falls!'

Tarek's eyes widen in horror. 'NO!' he cries, dropping to his knees. He balls his hands into fists and pounds the earth. 'No! No! No!'

'Kagiso is dead?' questions Mei in disbelief. 'Are you saying Tanas killed a *baby*?'

I nod grimly, feeling sick at the thought. 'She's the devil incarnate.'

'I should never have left them,' wails Tarek. 'They were too vulnerable. It's my fault. It's all my fault –'

'Tarek, don't say that. It isn't your fault,' says Jude, putting a hand on his shoulder.

He shrugs her off. 'But I left them!' he cries. 'Abandoned them. And for what? Some crazy quest to find Soul Jars. And look where it's got us! Stuck in a jungle in the middle of nowhere!'

I turn to him and wipe the tears from my eyes, more determined than ever. 'But this is the only way to destroy Tanas's soul. The only way to gain justice for their deaths,' I remind him. 'Once we have the obsidian blade –'

'What blade? Where is it? Do you see it?' Tarek shouts at me. 'Face it, Genna – it's not here! It's lost. *Forever*.

We've no chance of destroying Tanas. This has been a fool's quest from the very start. Why did I ever agree to come? I've failed in my duty to protect Thabisa and Kagiso's souls . . . and now they're gone!'

He sobs loudly. I feel his pain, raw and angry like a hot coal in the pit of my stomach. Guilt also weighs heavy on my heart for taking him away from the two souls he'd vowed to protect. *Maybe Tarek is right*, I think. I've been leading all of them on with a false hope – a lie potentially as empty and as hollow as the Soul Prophecy itself. Rather than seeking Soul Jars, we should have been seeking safety, hiding from Tanas's Hunters to preserve the Light. As a result of my reckless quest, there are now just two of us in the whole world – me and Tasha, somewhere in Siberia – the only First Ascendants left carrying the Light of Humanity. A bleak despair floods through me and I begin to wish the ground would swallow me up. The sky above appears darker than ever before and I sense the Light failing like a guttering candle in the wind. The loss of two more Ascendants – one but a baby – seems too much for the world to bear.

All of a sudden there's a deafening explosion. The ground trembles. Trees shake. Birds squawk in alarm and take flight.

Over by the altar, Pablo's eyes widen and the cigarette drops from his lips.

Another detonation rocks the jungle. The earth beneath our feet heaves, throwing us to the ground. Trees protest in ear-splitting creaks as they begin toppling. The volcano roars again, this time belching smoke and ash, sending billowing black clouds into the sky and blocking out the sun.

'What's happening?' cries Prisha.

'Diablofuego is waking up!' yells Pablo, taking cover behind the stone monolith.

As the volcano erupts, a great crack in the earth snakes through the clearing, opening up a huge fissure in the jungle ahead. Earth, trees and bushes fall into the abyss. We cling to one another while the ground around us breaks apart.

'Tanas's grip on the world is tightening,' shouts Tarek over the thunderous roar of the volcano. His face is taut with fear.

I exchange a terrified glance with Mei and seize hold of her hand, afraid this may be the end . . . and the beginning of Tanas's reign of Darkness.

50

As suddenly as it started, the earthquake subsides and Diablofuego falls into a grumbling doze. I release my grip on Mei's hand, the immediate danger appearing to be over. Cautiously, we pick ourselves up and gaze in awe at the sight before us.

The jungle has been peeled back, like the skin of an overripe fruit, to reveal the ruins of an ancient city. A cracked, paved plaza edged on either side by a long line of stone monoliths leads to a colossal stepped pyramid. Guarding the entrance to the city are a pair of forbidding statues with cat-like eyes and snarling jaws. They each clasp a spear tipped with shards of obsidian. Pablo peeks out from behind the upright stone where he'd been sheltering, takes off his hat and holds it to his chest, before dropping to the ground and prostrating himself at the feet of one of the fearsome statues.

Struck by an overwhelming sense of déjà vu, I stand as still as the two statues. I've seen this place before.

'Th-this is where it all started for me,' I say, my voice quavering. 'My first full Glimmer.'

My gaze sweeps across the cracked plaza where I fled

from Tanas all those millennia ago as Zianya, a young girl of the Omitl tribe. I had my Soul Protector with me, Necalli, his face embellished with swirling tribal tattoos. On our heels was a host of savage Tletl warriors and, while I escaped, thanks to Necalli, he was killed by a poisoned arrow.

Slowly retracing those frantic steps of long ago, I enter the ancient city and pass down the avenue of carved stone pillars. The others follow in a slow procession, awed into silence by the row of menacing faces and the intimidating temple ahead.

I stop at the foot of an immense flight of steps running up the side of the pyramid. The same steps that Necalli and I slid down on the stolen ceremonial shield to escape. The same steps that I'd been dragged up, before Necalli's daring rescue, to be sacrificed in the name of Ra-Ka, Lord of the Underworld.

In the name of Tanas, in other words.

As if drawn by Ra-Ka's dark power, I slowly ascend the steps. I'm powerless to resist. The others appear to be caught up in the spell too, for they follow in mute obedience, flanking me like mourners at a funeral.

After a long, steep climb we reach the peak of the pyramid – a wide, flat ceremonial platform overlooking the jungle, which stretches out like a dark green sea. The sun is low now as it struggles to stay above the horizon, its rays as red as spilled blood in the twilit, ash-filled sky. Diablofuego fumes in the near distance, its crater rimmed with fresh lava, veins of molten rock oozing down its sides like open sores.

Before us stands a monolithic statue of the jaguar-headed god that was once worshipped here. The one at whose feet Tanas fell when Necalli pierced his chest with the obsidian blade, leaving a splinter in his heart. A wound that the Incarnate leader carries from incarnation to incarnation. The weakness we desperately hope to exploit in our ritual.

As before, Pablo prostates himself before this statue too. Mei and Prisha huddle close together, their eyes haunted in the blue glow of the eternal flame. Tarek glares at the godhead.

'In the names of Thabisa and Kagiso,' he declares, 'we're going to find this blade and finish Tanas.' Then, like a bloodhound having caught the scent, he begins to search the ceremonial platform.

Jude remains at my side, her shield gleaming in the last rays of the dying sun. I swallow hard, trying to dislodge the lump of fear in my throat. This was the exact same moment in time – the thin divide between day and night – when Tanas attempted to sacrifice me in my past life as Zianya.

At the centre of the platform is the sacrificial altar, a rectangular slab of cold stone. I find myself inexplicably drawn to it . . . As I touch the rough stone –

I see the jade knife poised to strike, the sun's dying rays reflected in its polished green surface. Ceremonial drums pound in time with the quickening beat of my heart. The chants of 'RA – KA! RA – KA! RA – KA!' *from the frenzied crowd in the plaza below grow ever more feverish. Bewitched into a trance, I lie limp and helpless upon the blood-soaked stone of the altar. The High Priest stares down at me with his fathomless black eyes, their infinite depths of darkness terrifying to behold –*

'Genna? Are you OK?' asks Mei, noticing my ashen face and trembling hand.

I nod and take my hand away, trying to steady my nerves. 'This isn't a place I expected to ever visit again, nor ever wanted to,' I say. I gaze numbly round at the platform and down at the plaza far below. 'In fact, I can scarcely believe that the place where it all started for me in this life may also be where it all ends.'

'Well, let's hope it's the end for Tanas,' says Jude. 'Any idea where this obsidian blade might be?'

I point at the jaguar godhead. 'That's where Tanas pulled the blade from his chest, and that's the last time I ever saw it. From my memory, he dropped it at the foot of the statue.'

Jude goes over and begins a thorough search. Tarek joins her.

'What's this?' asks Prisha.

I turn to see my friend pointing to a wide oblong slab in the platform's stone floor. 'That opens up to a lava pit,' I reply, recalling the fate of my friend Meztli. 'It's where the bodies were thrown after they'd been sacrificed.'

Prisha recoils. Mei grimaces. 'What? Wasn't killing them once enough?'

'It was part of the ritual, an offering to appease the fire god,' I say.

Mei casts an apprehensive glance at the rumbling, lava-streaked volcano. 'Well, it doesn't appear very appeased at the moment. I sure hope the fire god doesn't require *my* sacrifice.' She treads carefully around the fateful trapdoor.

I notice Nefe keeping her distance too. She sits statue-like at one corner of the platform, quietly watching Pablo, who is now staring glassy-eyed at the dying sun.

'I've found some steps!' calls Tarek from behind the colossal godhead.

Going round to join him, we discover Tarek beside an opening in the back of the monolith. A flight of stone stairs runs straight down into the bowels of the pyramid. The descent looks dark, dangerous and deeply uninviting.

'So, who wants to go first?' asks Tarek in a forced jaunty tone.

'I will,' says Jude, drawing her Taser. Prisha goes next with the lamp, followed by Mei, then me, then Tarek and finally Pablo. Nefe quietly pads alongside me, her green eyes luminous in the light of the eternal flame. The passageway is tight and claustrophobic, the steps unnervingly steep.

Suddenly Nefe zips ahead and I hear Jude swear. 'Will you keep your cat under control? I almost tripped!' she snaps as we're brought to a sudden halt.

Nefe meows insistently at Jude. Then I hear a shocked gasp.

'I think she was warning you,' says Prisha, holding up the lamp.

Ahead, the passageway abruptly ends and opens out into an abyss of darkness. We cautiously edge forward. The staircase continues down, running along the inner wall of the pyramid. However, there's nothing to our right, just a deadly drop.

Risking a look down, I can see we've entered a vast chamber. Far below is a wavering orange glow. At first,

I wonder where the light is coming from, then I get a nauseating whiff of sulphur.

'Careful!' I tell the others. 'We don't want anyone falling into the lava.'

'That's the understatement of the century!' says Mei, flattening herself against the wall.

The rotten-egg smell only grows stronger and the glow more intense the deeper we go. Our footsteps echo in the ever-expanding lofty chamber. When we finally reach the bottom, we step out on to an expansive stone floor through which runs a river of lava. A narrow stone bridge leads to a small island. At its centre is a circular pool glowing red hot with bubbling magma.

Tarek holds up a hand to shield his face against the blast of heat. 'Wow! Talk about a descent into hell . . .'

Mei pinches her nose. 'It sure smells like Satan's underworld!'

But I'm no longer aware of the noxious odour or the cloying heat. Erected in front of the magma pool stands a mighty obelisk with a profusion of jaguar-like faces carved into its stone. Their fanged mouths gape open and, through the numerous holes, glinting darkly at the heart of the obelisk, can be seen . . . the obsidian blade!

51

'We've found it!' I cry. Caught up in the excitement of our discovery, I dash across the bridge. I'm about to thrust my arm into one of the jaguar mouths to claim our prize when Jude comes racing after me.

'STOP!' she yells, grabbing my arm.

I stare at her, bewildered. She nods to the other side of the obelisk. A skeleton lies slumped on the floor. I was so focused on retrieving the blade that I hadn't seen it.

'Someone's been here before us,' says Jude, releasing my arm and holstering her Taser.

The others warily cross the bridge and join us beside the skeleton. A few ragged tatters of clothing remain preserved on its bones, along with a Spanish conquistador sword. Lying next to this is a leather tube, as grey and wrinkled as the skin of a corpse. Kneeling down, Jude picks up the tube and prises off the end cap. Inside she finds a wrinkled scroll of parchment. Ever so gently, she unravels it to reveal a hand-drawn treasure map.

I gasp. 'That's an exact copy of the ones Vihan and Mei's parents gave us!'

Prisha holds up the lamp and Tarek peers curiously over

my shoulder. 'No, I think *we* have the copies,' he says. 'This is the original.'

I drop my gaze to the skeleton at my feet. 'So these are the remains of Vihan from a past life?'

Tarek nods. 'How else would he have known that the obsidian blade was hidden inside this temple, unless he'd seen it with his own eyes?'

'Then why didn't he take the blade?' asks Prisha, her face shining blue in the light of the eternal flame.

'I think he tried,' replies Jude. 'Haven't any of you noticed what's odd about his skeleton?'

'He's missing a hand,' says Mei.

'It isn't missing,' corrects Jude. 'It's in there.' She points to the obelisk, where the stump of a skeletal hand is trapped between the jaws of one of the many jaguar mouths.

'The altar is booby-trapped,' Pablo explains, his voice echoing through the chamber, the lava's hellish glow reflected in his glazed eyes. 'Only the temple's High Priest knows which mouth it is safe to take the blade from, the holy blade that is imbued with the blood of Ra-Ka himself, Lord of the Underworld.'

Prisha lets out a nervous laugh. 'Pablo, you're scaring me.'

'No need to be afraid,' he says flatly, turning his gaze upon her. 'As long as you respect Ra-Ka.'

I frown, wondering whether the sulphurous fumes are affecting our guide. He's beginning to act and sound a little strange. Then again, the whole experience of an ancient lost city rising from beneath the jungle is enough to unsettle anyone.

'So, without this High Priest, how are we going to extract the obsidian blade?' asks Tarek.

'Easy,' says Jude. 'We borrow Vihan's sword.'

She picks up the conquistador sword and, choosing the mouth nearest to her, she slowly inserts the steel blade. The weapon is halfway in when the jaguar's jaws snap shut, biting the steel in half. Jude stares aghast at the stump in her hand. 'Er, anyone got another sword?'

Shocked at the jaguar's brutal bite, I look around and my gaze falls upon the skeleton. 'Apologies, Vihan, but I'm sure you won't mind helping us out.'

Taking one of his leg bones, I tentatively slide it into the nearest mouth. It's barely entered the obelisk when the jaguar's jaws crunch down hard. I flinch as the bone shatters, splinters flying.

'I guess it isn't that mouth either,' I say.

I try again, a different hole with another bone. This time my hand is almost inside when the jaws again clamp shut. Startled, I leap away.

'It seems they close at random points,' remarks Mei.

'No kidding, Sherlock!' I reply, my heart still racing.

'My turn,' says Tarek, picking up a bone and walking round to the other side of the obelisk. A moment later, we hear a *crack!* as another pair of stone jaws snaps shut. Mei and Prisha both have a go too, and they too are left with stumps of bone in their hands. We keep trying until we run out of long bones.

Tarek wipes his brow of sweat, the lava like a furnace inside the chamber. 'Only three mouths left. What are we going to use now?'

Jude glances at Pablo. 'Can we borrow your machete?'

Pablo shakes his head. 'I need it for the jungle.'

'How about the spears the two statues in the plaza are holding?' suggests Prisha.

'Good idea!' says Tarek. 'I'll get them –'

But straight away Pablo pulls a handgun from beneath his shirt and points it at him. 'You're not going anywhere!'

'Pablo!' cries Mei. 'What are you doing?'

As Pablo waves his gun at us, we each take a sharp step back. Now his face appears demonic in the red glow of the lava. 'You –' he snarls, jutting his chin out at Mei, 'your parents call themselves archaeologists, but they're thieves!' He spits on the ground. 'They claim to have "found" the jade knife, but they stole it! Took all the fame and fortune for themselves. That knife belongs to the Tletl people. I won't allow my ancestral treasures to be plundered by foreigners again.'

'Pablo, we don't want to take the knife out of Guatemala,' I explain hurriedly. 'We only need it for a day or so. You can have the knife back once we've finished. You can claim *you* found it, if you like, take all the fame and fortune for yourself.'

Pablo sucks on his uneven, tobacco-stained teeth, appearing to consider the offer. 'OK,' he replies with a sly grin. 'We have a deal . . . if you put your hand in and get the knife yourself.'

'What? Are you insane?' I think the fumes must have gone to his head. 'I could lose an arm.'

He grins. 'Better yours than mine, eh?'

All of a sudden a deep rumble sounds underground like

the passing of a huge train. The lava in the river seethes and boils, sending up clouds of sulphurous smoke. The pyramid's foundations begin to quake; the bridge trembles.

'Do it now! Time is short!' Pablo snaps, as dirt and debris shower down upon us. He points the gun at Mei's head. 'Or your friend dies.'

I exchange a panic-stricken look with Mei. My instinct is to tackle Pablo, but there's no way I'll reach him before he pulls the trigger. I can't risk Mei's life. Nefe arches her back, hissing at our guide. Prisha clutches the lamp close to her, nervously eyeing the rising lava. To my right, Jude exchanges a subtle glance with Tarek and I notice her reach for her Taser.

'Uh-uh!' warns Pablo, wagging a finger at Jude. 'Put your hands in the air.'

Jude slowly and reluctantly raises her arms.

'OK, Pablo. I guess you leave me no choice,' I say.

As I approach the obelisk, the pyramid continues to quake. The lava roils and rumbles, threatening to swamp our little island.

'Genna – let me do it,' volunteers Tarek. 'You need to be able to wield the Light against Tanas, and that'll take *both* your hands.'

'I can wield the Light with one,' I say with forced bravado. 'Besides, Mei's my friend, so this is my responsibility.'

'No!' Tarek insists, stepping in front of me. 'If you die now and reincarnate, everything we've achieved to date will count for nothing. Our lives will reset and we'll lose this one opportunity to destroy Tanas's soul –'

'I'm waiting,' growls Pablo, cocking his weapon. Mei

flinches at the sharp *click!* and I realize we've had our last warning.

'I hear what you're saying, Tarek,' I tell him, 'but we're running out of time and we need that obsidian blade.'

I step round him and examine the three remaining mouths on the great obelisk. Each jaguar is carved slightly differently – one has pointed ears, another sharp fangs and the third a long, lolling tongue. None looks particularly promising. The first jaguar, though, is the only one to have its pupils inlaid with black obsidian, which helps make it the most menacing of the three. I reason that if I was a High Priest of Ra-Ka, this is the one I'd choose. Taking a deep breath, my hand trembling, I prepare to insert my arm – when all of sudden Nefe leaps up on my shoulder and jumps into the jaguar's mouth. '*No, Nefe!*' I cry as the jaws snap shut on her.

52

At first I can only stare at the obelisk, listening to Nefe's pained mews, too shocked to move. Then I snap out of my paralysis, grab the broken conquistador sword and wedge it between the jaguar's teeth. Tarek rushes to help me lever the mouth open, but the jaws are locked tight. Nefe's cries slowly trail off and all goes quiet.

I let out a choking sob and drop the broken sword. Tears stream down my cheeks. 'Oh Nefe! N-not my Nefe . . . !'

Tarek catches me up in an embrace. 'That's one loyal little cat. Her actions saved you.'

Behind us Pablo sniggers. Angrily, I round on him.

'What's there to laugh about?'

'Don't you realize yet?' he says, unable to suppress a yellow-toothed grin. '*All* the jaguar mouths are booby-trapped!'

I glare at him. 'Then why force me to put my arm in?'

Pablo shrugs. 'It's just an 'armless joke!' he replies. He lets out a mad cackle, his laughter echoing through the temple's chamber. In the wavering light of the lava, I see his eyes pool into those of a Watcher, his pupils expanding until they fill his sockets like black holes drilled into his head.

Why had I not noticed the change sooner? His odd behaviour since we discovered the lost city now makes complete sense. Furious, I stride towards him, my fists clenched.

'Not so fast,' he says, pressing the gun into Mei's temple and stopping me in my tracks.

The rumbling of the volcano turns to a muffled roar and the pyramid shudders violently. Debris rains down and the ground beneath us lurches. We struggle to stay on our feet.

'You'll never take the obsidian blade from Ra-Ka's temple!' Pablo shouts. 'And you'll never leave his temple alive!' Pushing Mei away from him but keeping the gun trained on her, Pablo hurriedly retreats across the bridge. Multiple cracks snake across the stone walkway.

'The bridge!' cries Prisha.

'RUN!' Jude orders as soon as our guide turns his back to flee, and we all make a dash for the bridge. But Pablo lets off a wild gunshot behind him. Mei ducks and the bullet ricochets off the obelisk. A second later the bridge splits apart and collapses into the boiling river of lava. We watch helplessly as we're left behind, trapped on the island.

Slipping his gun into his belt, Pablo taunts us by tipping his hat in salute, then ascends the flight of stairs. As we watch him vanish into the darkness above, the rumbling dies down, the pyramid stops quaking and Diablofuego once more settles into its uneasy slumber.

'What a snake in the grass!' spits Mei. She turns to us with a furious expression. 'I can't believe my parents trusted him.'

'It isn't their fault,' I tell her. 'Pablo must have had a past life in this ancient city as one of the Tletl tribe. I guess seeing the were-jaguar statues again triggered his soul's memory of being a follower of Ra-Ka.'

Jude kicks at a loose rock. It goes skittering into the lava. 'Why the hell didn't any of us spot that sooner?'

'Because we were all too wrapped up in discovering the city and the blade,' replies Tarek.

'So . . . what are we going to do now?' asks Prisha. She looks down in alarm at the river of lava flowing around us. 'With the bridge gone, there's no way we can cross *that*.'

It takes us less than a minute to explore the small island we're stranded on.

'We're cut off in all directions!' announces Jude. She dumps her pack on the ground and slumps down next to it, her shield clanging loudly on the volcanic rock. 'Now Tanas has us right where she wants us!'

'But we can't just sit here and wait for Tanas to turn up,' protests Mei.

'Then what do you suggest?' mutters Jude. 'Unless one of us can fly, it looks like we're stuck!'

'Genna,' says Mei, 'weren't you once Yelena, the Flying Firebird? Can't you use your acrobatic skills to cross the river?'

I stare at the bubbling lava, terror filling my stomach. 'Being a Russian acrobat in a circus tent is one thing, but leaping a river of molten rock is something entirely different,' I reply, though that doesn't stop me from edging as close as I dare to assess the jump. The heat singes the hairs on my arms and I am forced back. 'I don't know . . .

it's touch-and-go,' I admit. 'I definitely need a bigger run-up. And I can tell you one thing – if I don't make it, I really will become a firebird!'

'No, Genna, it's far too risky,' argues Jude. 'We can't have you barbecuing yourself.'

'Any other bright ideas then?' I ask.

'Not yet, but I'm working on it,' she replies, staring hard at the disintegrated bridge.

We fall into a despondent silence. As each of us tries to figure out a way off the island, I glance at my watch. There's less than twenty-four hours until the planets align. Infuriated, I turn to the towering obelisk and glare at the jaguar-mouthed symbol of Ra-Ka, Lord of the Underworld. After all our sacrifices, we've been stopped at the final hurdle by a lowly Watcher.

'Genna, don't torture yourself,' says Prisha, seeing me looking at the stone. 'Nefe is gone from this life.'

I feel my grief and anger bubble away, just like the lava that surrounds us. My dear Nefe . . . she sacrificed herself for me. The obsidian blade still glints inside the obelisk like a winking black eye, maddeningly within my reach yet impossible to take. And even if we could somehow manage to extract it without losing a limb, we'd still be trapped on this island –

I kick the obelisk in frustration. There's a muted cry of protest. For a second, I think my ears are playing tricks on me, but then I'm not so sure.

'Did you hear that?' I ask the others.

'Hear what?' asks Prisha.

Leaning in closer, I put my ear to the obelisk and can

make out a faint scraping inside. Suddenly a streak of sandy-coloured hair bursts from an open mouth, the stone jaws clamping shut a fraction of a second later. I recoil in surprise as my cat lands, paws splayed, on the ground beside me. In her mouth she clasps the smooth black blade of the obsidian knife.

Relief floods my heart. 'Nefe!' I gasp. 'You're back from the dead!'

I'm gladdened by her presence, but she looks decidedly the worse for wear. Not only is her fur matted with patches of blood but the tip of her tail is actually missing. Cautiously, I approach her and she drops the blade at my feet as if presenting me with a dead mouse.

'Good girl!' I say, rubbing her cheek.

'Let me tend to Nefe,' offers Prisha. Kneeling beside her, Prisha opens the first-aid kit, finds some wipes and dressings and begins to clean the blood from her fur and see to her injuries. Nefe tolerates the attention, but as soon as Prisha has finished bandaging her tail she scampers off to a safe distance and preens herself, her unfamiliarly white-tipped tail flicking irritably.

'Well, that's one problem solved,' I say, picking up the blade and slipping it into my belt. 'Now to get off this island!'

Tarek cocks his head to one side and examines the obelisk. 'Look here,' he says, pointing to the base. 'There's a crack.'

'So?' questions Mei.

'I noticed the obelisk shift slightly when Genna kicked it. I think the quake caused the stone to break.' He casts his eye up and down the column, then at the lava. 'If we can push the obelisk over, it might just span the river.'

'It's worth a shot,' says Jude, getting to her feet.

We all huddle on one side of the obelisk.

'On the count of three, push,' instructs Tarek. 'One, two . . . three!'

Straining and groaning, we shove as hard as we can. The obelisk wobbles but doesn't topple.

'We need more leverage,' says Tarek. He gets out the rope from his backpack and lassoes the top of the column. Then eventually, between pushing and pulling, we manage to unseat the obelisk. We give a great cheer as it falls across the river and the other end lands on the opposite bank.

However, our sense of achievement quickly fades as the obelisk begins to crack from the intense heat of the lava.

'Quick, we've got to get across it – go, go, GO!' I shout.

Jude tests the way, running the gauntlet first before turning back to help the rest of us. Nefe is across in a few leaps and bounds. I urge my friends ahead of me. Arms spread wide, Mei makes a nervous tightrope walk across, the obelisk bridge becoming more and more precarious with each passing second. Clutching the lamp to her chest, Prisha totters over and almost falls as the stone slumps, but Jude pulls her to safety.

'You next,' I tell Tarek.

'No, you should go first –'

'We've no time to argue,' I say, pushing him ahead as the obelisk continues to disintegrate.

Shouldering his backpack, Tarek dashes across. A moment later, our makeshift bridge breaks apart into several small floating islands of stone.

'Genna!' shouts Mei in despair as I'm left stranded.

The waves of heat from the river of lava remind me of the Flaming Hoops of Hell from my time in the circus as Yelena. Recalling her acrobatic agility, I jump for the first block, then leap to the next, using each one as a stepping stone. But the blocks are sinking fast. I'm halfway across, with two more blocks between me and the bank on the far side, when, to my horror, I see the last section of obelisk disappear beneath the molten rock. There's no going back, however, so I jump to the next and only remaining block. Then, before that sinks too, I launch myself into the air and somersault over the bubbling magma to land on the opposite bank. *Just*. My feet slip on the edge and I cartwheel my arms manically, trying to regain my balance.

At the last second a hand grabs me and pulls me upright. I hear applause from my friends at my daredevil acrobatics and see Jude's grinning face. 'Nine points for style and eight point five for complexity. Three for the landing.'

53

We ascend the stone stairway and emerge from the temple into an almost starless black night. I'm glad to be back in the open air and away from the lava. The jungle around us is an impenetrable curtain of darkness, making it impossible for us to follow the trail back to the main road without our guide. The city ruins are too creepy to contemplate staying in those, so we decide to pitch camp for the night on the site of the archaeological dig bordering the ruins.

Once we've hitched up our hammocks, I use my Light-wielding ability to ignite a campfire, holding my hand over the tinder and focusing the energy until the heat in my palm sets the wood alight. Prisha heats up some beans and rice from our supplies over the flames, while we huddle close, not for the fire's warmth but for the comfort and security of its flickering, defiant glow.

Looming over us is the ever-present Diablofuego, a shadowy giant against the coal-black sky, its lava-rimmed peak looking like a fiendish grin. The volcano rumbles ominously, threatening to wake again at any moment, and I find myself clasping the handle of the obsidian blade. I sense danger everywhere as the night presses in upon us.

Just beyond the light of the fire, countless unseen insects crawl and buzz around our makeshift camp. The hiss of a snake nearby causes Nefe to bristle and arch her back; thankfully, the slithering beast doesn't approach the fire. Then we all flinch at the sudden *crack* of a branch in the canopy. The unfamiliar jungle has come alive in the night and its hidden threats set us on edge.

'What do you think has become of Pablo?' whispers Mei, keeping close beside Tarek.

'He's likely headed back to his jeep,' Jude replies. 'He'll be eager to inform Tanas of his loyal service in capturing us.' She snorts a laugh.

'I'm counting on him doing so,' I say. 'We're running out of time and need Tanas to come to us. The temple is where Tanas's soul was first wounded and where we must make our final stand.'

Prisha dishes out the beans and rice into bowls and hands them round. We eat quietly, our solemn silence broken only by the scrape of our spoons and the crackle of the fire. My friends' faces, warped orange by the flames, appear grave and tense. The idea of confronting Tanas clearly scares them. It fills me with fear too. Tendrils of dread twist and tighten round my stomach. My instinct has always been to run from the Incarnate leader. To flee, to hide. Yet now I actually *want* Tanas to find me.

I throw another log on to the fire, sending sparks into the night. The pinpricks of light glow like fireflies.

'*This one must ignite the spark when put to the Darkest test*,' murmurs Tarek.

'I'm not the One,' I remind him.

'But there are only two of you First Ascendants left,' he says. 'You and Tasha. And you have the ability to wield the Light. That must count for something.'

I peer into the impenetrable night, sensing but not seeing the temple of Ra-Ka, and realize the Darkest test may already be upon us. 'The Soul Prophecy, whether true or not, can't be about one lone soul. Because I can't do this alone. We'll need *all* five of us if we're to succeed.'

'So what's our plan?' asks Prisha.

'If Vihan was right, then we now have all the necessary relics to destroy Tanas's soul,' I reply. 'The obsidian blade –' I pat the chiselled shard of black volcanic rock in my belt – 'Apep's hand, the eternal flame, a vial of Soulsilver, some salt crystals to protect us, and, crucially, the timing for the ritual.' My gaze sweeps round the fire, meeting each of my friend's nervous glances in turn. 'Tarek, since you're the astronomer among us, and the one who worked out the star chart, will you tell us when to commence the ritual? We need Tanas to die at the point her soul is at its weakest.'

Tarek nods. His face still mottled with bruising, he casts an anxious eye up at the almost starless sky, the smoke and ash from the volcano suffocating the little light there is. 'I just hope I can see the alignment,' he says.

'Whatever is happening at the time, you'll have to give us a signal to begin,' I insist. 'Mei, I'll need your help to get the Soulsilver into Tanas.'

Mei swallows hard. '*Me?* And how are we going to do that?'

'We'll use the salt from Taghaza,' I explain. 'You'll make

some salt bombs to throw in her face. With any luck, this will wound and distract her long enough for me administer the Soulsilver.'

Jude pokes her spoon at her rice. 'And what about her Hunters? They're not exactly going to sit back and watch as we pin down their leader on the altar, are they?'

'That'll be yours and Tarek's job – to hold them off,' I reply, 'using the spears from the guardian statues.'

'But Tarek is watching the skies,' she points out.

'I'm afraid he'll have to manage both tasks.'

'This plan sounds rather . . . risky,' remarks Mei. 'We barely survived Varanasi, don't forget. What makes you think we can defeat Tanas's Hunters now?'

'We don't need to defeat them,' I explain. 'Just hold them off long enough for me to get Tanas to swallow the Soulsilver.'

'And what if she refuses or spits it out?' asks Jude. 'I mean, we can't exactly go up to her and say, *Hi, Tanas, nice of you to join us. Here's a cold, refreshing drink of Soulsilver. Bottoms up!*'

'Who says Tanas has to swallow it?' interjects Prisha.

We all turn to her. 'What do you mean?' I ask.

She holds up a needle-tipped syringe. 'I found this in the first-aid kit when tending to Nefe. If you can get close enough, you can inject it into Tanas.'

'Great idea, Prisha!' I exclaim, feeling the plan coming together. 'Now, once we've got the Soulsilver into Tanas . . . Prisha, you'll need to burn the mummified hand with the eternal flame. Then I'll complete the ritual by using the blade to end her present life.'

'Easy-peasy,' says Jude, spooning in another mouthful of her beans and rice. 'But we still have the little issue of Tanas's Hunters and High Priests to deal with. After our last encounter, she's bound to bring more Incarnates with her.'

'Then we set some booby traps of our own,' I reply. 'Even up the numbers. It's time for the Hunters to be become the hunted.'

I add another log to the fire and a cloud of sparks ascends into the night . . .

The moon casts a watery light across the ancient plaza as I stand alone at the foot of Ra-Ka's mighty temple. On either side of me the macabre faces on the pillars appear to be asleep, their eyes cloaked in shadow. Beyond the city, the jungle is strangely silent, even the drone of insects absent.

Out of the darkness strides a hooded figure. As they cross the plaza, their footsteps echo loudly. I wait, my hand resting upon the cold, hard handle of the obsidian blade, sheathed in my belt.

The figure stops before me and throws back their hood.

'I knew you'd come,' I say.

Phoenix smiles. 'You know I can't resist you. Our souls are drawn to one another.'

He glances up at the peak of the pyramid. 'Why here?'

'Because this was my first Glimmer. My first full memory of you as my Soul Protector.'

Phoenix raises an eyebrow. 'You realize this place will only make Tanas more powerful.'

My grip tightens on the blade's handle. 'But this is where you saved me, and where I intend to save you.'

Phoenix laughs, a strange hollow sound in the silence of the plaza. 'Genna, I assure you, I don't need saving.'

I put a hand gently to his cheek and meet his gaze. His eyes are unnaturally dark, yet in their depths is the faintest gleam of Light. 'Phoenix, come back to me.'

Phoenix wraps an arm round my waist and draws me closer to him. I feel our connection, our soul link strengthen.

'Genna,' he says, as my hopes rise, 'I'm sorry –'

All of a sudden his face contorts into the angular features of Tanas, his round eyes narrowing, his cheekbones sharpening, his lips thinning and his hair fanning out in a black curtain over his shoulders. 'But I'm not!' snarls Tanas.

I feel a sharp stab of pain and look down to see the obsidian blade buried in my own heart –

I wake with a jerk. Nefe is curled up next to me in the hammock, but Phoenix is gone, our connection severed. The hilt of the obsidian blade is digging into my side. Disturbing Nefe, I clamber out of my hammock and reposition the blade in my belt. The fire has burned itself out overnight; only a frail wisp of smoke rises from its ashes. Woken by the dawn chorus, the others begin to sleepily disentangle themselves from their hammocks and mosquito nets. The sun is even slower to rise than they are, the night seeming to cling on as long as it can.

After a hurried breakfast, we find some abandoned tools from the last archaeological expedition and begin work on laying the booby traps: digging out the trenches into deep pits; filling others with wood and dry tinder; cutting vines and branches to cover the traps; setting up slingshots and tripwires in the plaza; and lugging rocks and loose masonry up to the top of the pyramid. We slave all day, driven by necessity and fear. We know this is our one and only chance to defeat Tanas and destroy her soul. Our one shot at saving the Light of Humanity.

By mid-afternoon we're sweaty and smeared with dirt but we're all set for the Incarnates' anticipated arrival. While the others take a rest in the shade, I use this last opportunity to practise wielding the Light. I'm keenly aware I've done little since my lessons with Vihan and hope I can refine my rough skills in time. Standing in the middle of the plaza, I channel my sister's aura exactly as Vihan taught me. The pressure of the moment seems to help me focus and I'm soon sending out blasts of energy at the gruesome-faced pillars. I discover that knocking off chunks of stone from them can be really most satisfying.

Once I'm confident with the direction and power of my strikes, I concentrate on setting fire to piles of tinder at ever greater distances. This requires a careful balance between force and heat. Too much force and I blow apart the tinder; too little heat and by the time my blast reaches its target, it fails to ignite the wood. The technique takes a great deal of practice, but eventually I manage to get the balance right.

Then, despite feeling exhausted from my efforts, I move on to conjuring Light shields.

'You should take a rest,' Mei advises when she sees me struggling.

'I don't have time to rest,' I reply, gritting my teeth and circling my hands again. Sweat pours from my brow and it isn't from the heat of the jungle. My aim is to produce a double shield again, one from my sister's aura and one from my own. After our last encounter with Tanas, I'm convinced I'll need it. To protect my friends.

'You don't want to burn yourself out,' Mei reminds me. She comes over and hands me a bottle of water. 'It's time for dinner anyway.'

Wiping away the sweat with the back of my arm, I down the water gratefully. 'What's for dinner?' I ask.

'Rice and beans, again.' She gives me a weak smile. 'I know, not much of a last meal.'

I look at my friend and see the fear behind her eyes, however much she tries to hide it. I admire her bravery. 'Mei, this won't be our last meal, I promise you. We *will* defeat Tanas. The Light *will* prevail.'

'How can you be so sure?'

I take Mei's hand and feel her nervousness but also her strength. 'Because Tanas doesn't have friends like you.'

54

We sit on the steps of the temple, quietly eating our rice and beans, as the sun sinks low over the ridge. No longer suffocated by ash, the sky is turning a twilit dark blue.

'The first stars should appear any time soon,' says Tarek. He glances at his watch. 'We've a little less than an hour before the conjunction.'

A fidgety Jude sets aside her bowl and picks up her shield and the spear taken from a guardian statue. On her hip is her loaded Taser. Her intense gaze sweeps the darkening jungle below us. 'I can't sit here waiting any more. I'm going for a scout.'

She heads off down the steps and into the jungle. Twenty minutes later, she re-emerges and carefully threads her way through the archaeological site, avoiding the traps, across the plaza and back up the steps.

'Any sign of Tanas yet?' asks Tarek. Jude shakes her head.

No one says anything. I stroke Nefe, who perches beside me on the step, her warm fur comforting to the touch. Tarek glances up at the sky, then at his watch, then back at the sky. I can tell he's getting nervous.

'She'll come,' I say, as much to convince myself as the others. I'm aware of a faint thrum in my chest, although I can't tell whether that's a sign of Phoenix drawing closer or just my stress levels.

'How can you be so sure?' asks Prisha. She cradles the lamp in her lap, its eternal flame casting a blue halo around her.

'She will,' I insist. 'Just like a moth to the flame.'

'Perhaps Pablo didn't call his master,' says Mei, fidgeting with one of the salt bombs.

'Then Phoenix will sense where I am,' I reply. 'I opened a soul link with him last night. I'm the bait, and Tanas has taken it –'

'Look!' interrupts Tarek. We all tense, expecting to see Tanas and her Hunters, but Tarek is pointing to the darkening sky. 'It's happening.'

We follow his finger as he traces a line across the heavens.

'Mercury is the faint one near the horizon,' he explains. 'Next is Venus, the brightest of them, followed by Mars, Jupiter and, way up there, Saturn.'

We gaze in wonder at the gradual alignment of the five twinkling planets. Within myself I feel a strengthening of the Light, subtle yet distinct like the current of a river. 'How long do we have?' I ask.

Tarek looks at me, the night sky reflected in his glasses. His expression is grave. 'The full alignment will last no more than a couple of hours, but it'll reach its peak in an hour.'

As the minutes tick by – and with no sign of Tanas – Jude becomes more restless. 'Let's face it – she isn't coming. This ludicrous treasure hunt has been an utter waste of our time!'

'Patience,' I plead.

'Patience is going to get us killed,' replies Jude. 'Once the alignment passes, we've no way of stopping Tanas.'

Nefe looks up, her ears alert and her body tense. She growls.

'Shh, they're close,' I say, the thrum in my chest building. 'I can feel it! So can Nefe.'

Shutting my eyes, I reach out with my mind to Phoenix. I've previously only managed a soul link in the half-state between sleeping and waking. But I'm hoping that with my growing control over the Light I'll be able to do it on command. The brightness of my First Ascendant soul should also act as a beacon to my former Protector. He'll be drawn to me, just as he has been for countless past generations. All I see, though, is darkness –

Then the leaves part and I glimpse a stone pyramid through the bushes. Behind the temple rises the lava-streaked sides of a volcano, its peak smouldering like the embers of a colossal bonfire. Standing on the steps of the pyramid are five silhouetted figures: one clasps a shield and spear, another holds a lamp with a blue flame –

I open my eyes, breaking the link. Nefe hisses and her tails bristles. 'They're here!' I cry.

At that moment, Tanas and her Hunters emerge from the jungle into the clearing, led by our former guide, Pablo.

From a distance, dressed in her black tactical assault jacket and darkened shades, and with her long black hair tied back, Tanas looks like a lethal black panther on the prowl. She even moves with dangerous feline grace, and I feel a fear so deep it takes all my willpower not to turn and run. *Who am I to think I am the hunter?* In truth, she will always be the predator and I the prey.

In her hand is a yellowed paper scroll. *Vihan's map!* She crumples it into a ball and tosses it away. Then she signals to her followers. As her Hunters fan out, I spot Phoenix with Damien and the other members of his gang. A semicircle of six hooded High Priests gather behind Tanas.

I force myself to stand straighter and throw my shoulders back.

'Get into position,' I order the others. We scatter as planned – Mei and Prisha retreat to the platform above, Nefe bounding after them; Jude and Tarek descend to the base of the pyramid, while I hold my ground halfway up the flight of steps.

Tanas and her followers advance across the clearing. Pablo falters when he notices the excavations have changed in appearance, but he's too late to warn the Incarnates. Several Hunters plunge through the thin layer of dirt resting on the lattice of branches and leaves we'd laid over the trenches. They plunge into the deep, dug-out holes, their cries of shock and pain sounding like the howler monkeys in the jungle.

Jude and Tarek pump their spears in the air, celebrating our first victory.

'STOP!' screeches Tanas, her voice echoing across the clearing. The Incarnates halt their advance. She gives out orders to her followers before proceeding far more carefully, this time with Pablo out in front. Tentatively testing the ground ahead with his machete, Pablo guides them through the archaeological site.

But we still have a few more tricks up our sleeve.

When the Incarnates are halfway across, I summon up several bursts of intense Light, aiming them at the other hidden trenches. The crackling balls of Light zip through the air and ignite the stacks of wood that we piled there. Fires burst into life around the Incarnates, the sudden heat and light sending them into confusion and panic. A number of Hunters are set on fire while others flee the flames and stumble straight into the trenches.

Our plan is working! Their numbers are dwindling. But Tanas and her four remaining High Priests fight their way through the flames, along with Damien and his gang and several other Hunters. This is more than we hoped would survive.

I notice that Phoenix is one of those who have made it safely across. My heart lifts, but I feel conflicted at the same time. *He's now my enemy*, I remind myself. *Unless we destroy Tanas's soul . . .*

The Incarnates stand at the entrance to the lost city, the two guardian statues greeting their former ruler. Tanas sends a pair of her Hunters ahead. Their dark eyes scan the plaza as they slowly make their way down the avenue of carved stone pillars. In the dying light of the day, however, they miss the tripwire that sets off sprung branches, which launch a hail of rocks across the plaza. The projectiles whizz through the air and hit their targets better than any of us could have expected. The two Hunters collapse to the ground.

With our trap sprung, however, Tanas is now safe to advance. The dozen or so remaining Incarnates cross the plaza unchecked and charge towards the pyramid. At the foot of the steps, Tarek and Jude bravely hold them off with their spears, but Tanas manages to slip through.

Just as we planned.

Up the steps she strides, in the bold manner of a returning ruler, her sleek black hair streaming out behind her. Three other Incarnates, including Thug, fight their way past Tarek and Jude's line of defence to join their master. I hurriedly retreat, leading them on to the top of the pyramid by making it seem I'm running scared. Once I reach the sacrificial platform, though, and with Tanas and her three Hunters committed to the climb, Prisha releases an avalanche of stones. The rocks cascade down the steps. By the time they reach Tanas, the missiles are hurtling at breakneck speed.

Tanas nimbly leaps to one side, shooting out a ball of pure Darkness to shatter a boulder heading her way. But Thug and the other two Hunters are less agile. They're wiped out by the avalanche, Thug catching a rock straight in the chest. He falls back, tumbling head over heels down the steps.

'Watch out!' I cry to Jude and Tarek, who jump aside at the very last second as the deluge of stones and the battered body of Thug hit the bottom. The immense effort of carrying those rocks up the pyramid has paid off.

Tanas is now all alone as she joins me at the top of the temple. She glares at me through her protective sunglasses. 'I bet you think you're clever . . . with your little booby traps,' she sneers. 'But while sticks and stones may break my Hunters' bones, it is *I* who am going to hurt you.' She nods at the black gleaming knife in my belt. 'Ah, I see you found the obsidian blade. Not that it'll do you any good. This night I promise you your soul will be snuffed out and the Light of Humanity extinguished forever!'

Tanas points to the horizon, where the orange-red embers of the sun are fading fast. 'Girl,' she says, addressing Prisha, who's retreated with the eternal flame to the altar. 'Look upon your sun, for this will be the last time you see its rays upon this earth. That precious flame of yours will be the last light your eyes will ever see.'

'I wouldn't be so sure about that,' says Mei, as she springs from behind the godhead and throws a salt bomb at Tanas. It bursts apart on impact, scattering salt across her face and neck.

Tanas takes a step back but then turns indignantly to Mei. She brushes the white grains off her assault jacket, the salt appearing to have no effect whatsoever. 'Are you serious?' she sneers with a derisive laugh. 'You're throwing dust at me now? You must be desperate.'

Mei stands her ground. 'It isn't dust,' she says. 'It's pure salt from Taghaza.'

Tanas flinches. 'What?' Gradually her face begins to twitch and her skin turns red, and then rapidly it starts to blister. Tearing off her sunglasses, she tries to wipe away the corroding salt with the sleeve of her jacket, but it's too late – the reaction has taken hold.

She becomes ever more frantic. She lashes out at Mei, knocking her aside, and Mei lands heavily at the base of the huge godhead. In her blind fury, Tanas is too distracted to notice me dash forward with the syringe. In one swift movement I jab the needle into her exposed neck. I inject the Soulsilver and watch as the ethereal liquid disappears into her veins. I jump away, elated that the hardest part of the ritual is complete.

Tanas yanks out the needle and turns on me.

'What have you done?' she screeches, as her skin smokes and peels from her pale smooth face.

'I gave you a taste of your own medicine,' I reply, thinking of the foul black potion she once forced down my throat.

Tanas lurches towards me, arms outstretched, her narrow dark eyes whirlpools of pure hate. 'You wretch! I will suffocate your soul and witness your body burn!'

But before she can seize me or wield the Darkness, Prisha takes out the mummified hand from the Canopic jar and places it on the altar. Then she opens up the lamp and sets the hand alight with the eternal flame. The taloned fingers blaze like blue torches, noxious fumes spiralling into the air. At once, Tanas forgets the salt that is searing her face and the Soulsilver that is coursing through her veins. She's no longer interested even in me. Instead, she stares in mute horror at her own left hand as it blackens and withers before her eyes. Tanas scrambles over to the altar, knocking Prisha and the lamp aside in her desperate bid to extinguish her previous incarnation's burning hand. She rips off her jacket to smother the flames, but, as hard as she tries, the fire refuses to go out. Eventually clasping her own shrivelled stump and writhing in agony, Tanas falls back on the altar.

I smile to myself. In her panic, Tanas has made herself vulnerable – she's no longer protected by her nano-carbonized jacket or her glasses. I draw the obsidian blade from my belt.

'Only your own death can defeat you, Tanas,' I declare as I stand over her, the black blade raised, just as she had stood over me with the jade knife all those millennia ago. Our roles reversed, I feel strangely empowered, the ancient pyramid seeming to focus my energies, while the rumble and roar of the volcano behind fuels the fire in my belly.

In contrast, the Incarnate leader appears weak and pathetic as she squirms before me, cradling her shrivelled hand, her gaunt, snake-like face scarred by the salt. For a moment, I almost pity her.

Almost . . .

Then I look into Tanas's foul eyes and I remember all the death she has brought upon this earth, all the lives and Light she has taken and the reign of Darkness she promises. *That Darkness that is so inviting . . . so tempting . . . so powerful . . . Imagine the power I'd wield if I embraced the Darkness . . .*

Mesmerized by Tanas's infinite gaze, I'm vaguely aware of the noise of fighting drawing closer and Tarek shouting, 'Do it now!'

Blinking hard, I break the connection with Tanas. There's a smirk on her thin lips. She was attempting to hypnotize me! I shake my head clear and raise the obsidian blade. With the blade poised to strike, I glance up at the night sky – the five planets are aligned. I turn back to Tanas on the altar.

'Now for me to destroy *your* soul.'

55

This one strike will end it all. Complete the ritual. Save the Light of Humanity. I bring the blade down, aiming for Tanas's heart, but my hand is stopped by another.

'NO! LET ME GO!' I shout, rounding on my assailant. Having expected Damien, I am stunned to see Phoenix instead, his pooling black eyes meeting mine. For a moment, time seems to stand still – the tip of the blade hovering centimetres above Tanas's chest, my mind unable to fathom that *my* Soul Protector, the one who has defended me through every one of my lives, is now protecting Tanas's soul!

'Phoenix, no!' I plead, tears of desperation in my eyes. 'You don't know what you're doing!'

'Nor do you,' he replies, his grip tightening round my wrist. 'The Darkness must prevail.'

My whole arm trembles as I try to force the knife down. 'I can save you . . . if you just let me finish the ritual,' I say through clenched teeth.

'Genna, I've already told you: I don't need saving.' He sharply twists my arm, sending a shooting pain through me and making me cry out. He yanks me away from the altar.

As we wrestle for control of the weapon, a bloody battle plays out around us. The temple platform has become overrun by Incarnates. At the top of the steps, Jude is fighting both Damien and Spider. Her Taser is spent and her spear broken in half, yet she doesn't back down. She smashes Spider in the knee with the spear's shaft, then using her shield as a battering ram she drives Spider and two other Incarnates over the edge of the platform. I hear the tattooed girl's scream, loud at first, then it fades away. But Jude's victory is short-lived, for Damien sweeps her legs from under her and she goes crashing to the ground.

Meanwhile, Tarek is surrounded by the vengeful Knuckleduster and the remaining two High Priests. Mei rushes to Tarek's aid, flinging salt bombs at the priests. However, apart from temporarily blinding them, they seem immune. Prisha, having taken cover with the lamp behind the massive godhead, has armed herself with a makeshift slingshot. She is peppering Blondie and another Hunter with stones, forcing them to retreat.

I continue to grapple with Phoenix, the fight as much a battle for the blade as for his soul. The pain of each strike, punch and kick that he lands is nothing compared to the hurt he inflicts on my heart. *How, after all this time, can Phoenix be my mortal enemy?*

As we lurch back and forth across the platform, I get a flash of the snowy courtyard in the Purple Cloud Temple, high up in the Wudang mountains. Just as we practised taiji together as Yuán and Feiyen all those centuries ago in China, we now fight one another, our arms entwined, our bodies swaying, each of us trying to gain the upper hand and take each other's balance.

Be like a reed, Feiyen taught me then. *Remember: the soft and pliable will defeat the hard and strong.*

Heeding my Soul Protector's advice from that long-ago time, I surrender myself to Phoenix's movements, sensing each push and pull and allowing him to become overconfident. Then, with a deft twist of my body, I throw him off balance and pin him against the statuesque jaguar godhead, the blade to his throat. 'Don't force me to kill you,' I beg.

'*Hǎo shēnshǒu!*' Phoenix praises me in Mandarin, evidently recognizing the taiji technique he himself taught me as Feiyen.

A spark of hope ignites in my heart. 'If you remember that, then you must remember who you truly are,' I plead. Eye to eye with him, I peer deep into the depths of his soul, wading through the Darkness, searching for that gleam of his true self.

'What are you trying to do, Genna? Hypnotize me?' he says with a contemptuous laugh.

'Yes, if that's what it takes.'

In desperation, I share some of my precious Light. A gossamer-thin, spectral thread passes between our eyes, joining our souls. At first the connection is tenuous, so fragile even a single breath could break it. Then gradually the strand of Light thickens. To begin with, I consider this a good sign – that I'm bringing my Phoenix back – but I rapidly lose control of the process and the Darkness draws out of me more Light than I intend, threatening to suck my own soul dry. Suddenly there's an explosion of pain and stars burst across my vision. There's a flash of blue, then darkness descends –

Slowly, I come round. My head hurts, and I realize someone must have struck me and knocked me out. A low, thunderous roar fills my ears and I'm aware of cold stone pressing against my back. The feeling is at once familiar and deeply unsettling. As I regain my senses, I discover I'm lying spreadeagled on the sacrificial altar. The pounding in my head is exacerbated by the heavy beat of a drum and, above the distant roar, I hear the ominous chant of '*RA-KA, RA-KA, RA-KA . . .*'

It's as if I've been transported back some five thousand years.

Diablofuego is once more erupting, the volcano spitting lava into the night sky, a fountain of fire against the darkness. Its unending rumble reverberates through the jungle. Upon its slopes the trees are ablaze and the ash-filled air reeks of fire and brimstone. A veritable hell on earth, just as I foresaw in my *su'mach* vision.

Under the flickering light of several flaming torches, I can make out hooded figures bowing and chanting before the colossal statue of the jaguar-faced godhead. Jude's bronze shield rests against its base, an offering to the fire god Ra-Ka. My concern for my friends spikes. Craning my neck, I'm horrified to discover that Mei and Prisha are bound to stone pillars on either side of the statue, while Jude and Tarek are on their knees, their faces bruised and bloodied, their hands tied. Knuckleduster and Blondie stand guard behind. In front of them, gaping open like the mouth of a huge fire-breathing monster, is the lava pit. Wreaths of sulphurous steam rise up and an ominous red glow emanates from the magma far below.

A serpentine face looms into view. Her once flawless skin is now ruined by salt burns as well as criss-crossed with scars, but she otherwise appears to have recovered from our botched ritual attempt.

'I'm glad you can join us,' says Tanas with as much warmth as a pit viper. Her withered left hand is now a black claw. In her right hand she clasps the jade knife. 'I'd hate for you to miss your own death – and those of your friends.'

She strolls over to Mei and Prisha and with the knife cuts an incision into each of their wrists. They twist and writhe against their bonds, crying out in pain as blood trickles from their wounds into a bowl at their feet. The rhythm of the drum now thuds like a heartbeat and the Incarnates murmur in a long-forgotten, ancient tongue, '*Rura, rkumaa, raar ard ruhrd . . .*'

Still groggy from my concussion, I try to rise, to summon the Light to stop Tanas and save my friends. But my head is swimming – and my arms are immediately pinned down by Damien on one side and Phoenix on the other. Two hooded priests seize hold of my ankles in a vice-like grip.

'Phoenix, let me go!' I beg. But he stares straight ahead, as rigid as a statue. Sheathed in his belt is the obsidian blade, black and gleaming just like his eyes. Despair wraps itself round me like an iron chain. My attempt to share my Light and bring back his soul has failed.

I turn my head to Damien. 'Jabali!' I cry, using his soul name. 'That part of you *isn't* dead. I've seen it, the spark of Light, from your life as a Hakalan warrior . . . as a Soul Protector. Don't deny your true nature! Fight the Darkness.'

Damien shoots me a scathing look. 'You're wasting your breath. My loyalty lies with Tanas.'

'Jabali, whatever I supposedly did . . . whatever made you decide to become an Incarnate . . . for that I'm sorry. Truly sorry,' I plead.

He snorts. 'Your apology comes several thousand years too late!'

'Why must I apologize, though? For what?' I ask desperately as Tanas cuts into her own withered hand and lets her blood mix with that of my friends' in the bowl.

Damien glances bitterly at Phoenix, then back down at me. 'You always favoured my First Brother over me. Whichever life I led, you only held my brother in your heart.'

I blink, stunned and bewildered by his explanation. Was he *jealous*? 'Of course I did,' I say. 'He's my Soul Protector!'

Damien laughs cruelly. 'Not any more.'

A flare of indignation rises up in me. 'So, what – you became an Incarnate simply because you felt rejected? I don't remember rejecting you, ever.'

'And there's the problem!' he snaps. He shakes his head in dismay at my apparent heartlessness. 'I could no longer go from life to life being ignored, being tortured by my unrequited love. The pain in my soul grew, until I could take it no more.' Tears appear to well up in his pooling eyes, or it could simply be the sulphurous fumes in the air. But the hurt look in his gaze is vaguely familiar. I think back to the brief Glimmer of myself as Tishala, my first incarnation on this earth, dancing round the fire with the other women of our tribe. Of feeling someone's eyes upon me. Of turning and expecting to see Asani, my Soul Protector, only for it to be his older brother, Jabali. Then of being whisked away by the dance, not giving it another thought.

But now, in hindsight, I recognize the deep longing in Jabali's eyes.

More past-life memories surface in my mind like ripples in a pond ... *The gift of a golden bracelet, one of many from suitors of the daughter of a powerful Mesopotamian king ... A duel fought between two tribal warriors in my honour, one of them an incarnation of Jabali ... A shy glance from a farm boy at a rice festival* ... Separately these moments were easily overlooked, but put together and revisited in the light of Jabali's declaration the message is clear.

'Jabali, I'm sorry I didn't acknowledge your love for me,' I say sincerely. 'Really I am. But why turn to the Darkness?'

Damien stiffens and blinks away the tears. 'As the Hakalan saying goes ... *A child who is not embraced by the village will burn it down to finally feel its warmth*.'

56

Tanas returns with the bowl of blood. I lie still upon the altar, stunned into submission by Damien's revelation. My nemesis – the Soul Hunter who has pursued me across lifetimes, who has tried to sacrifice me twice in this life alone . . .

He once loved me?

And then I think, *How could that unrequited love have turned into such hate?*

I try to fathom how his love could have soured into an unrelenting desire to destroy me and my soul . . . and the Light of Humanity along with it. But I'm left at a loss. The love that I hold for Phoenix is made of pure Light. How did Damien's love turn so bitter and twisted, so dark?

'I don't know about you, Genna, but I'm getting a strong sense of déjà vu,' Tanas says conversationally. A smirk plays on her salt-scarred lips as she swirls the bowl's morbid contents. 'I'm sure we've been here and done all this before . . . Oh, we have!' she adds jauntily, then her smirk contorts into a scowl. 'Except this time there's no Protector to save you and your soul will perish.'

Seizing my hair with the claw of her left hand, she lifts my head off the altar and I wince in pain. 'Your pathetic ritual attempt failed. Only *I* have the power to banish souls for eternity. Now let me show you how it's really done –' She puts the bowl to my lips and recites a fiendish hex: '*Ruq haq maar farad ur rouhk ta obesesh!*'

I splutter and gag as she forces the warm, bitter liquid down my throat. It burns and scalds my stomach and I feel its poison seep into my limbs. She sets the bowl aside and turns to her black-eyed acolytes.

'My loyal and patient subjects,' she says, addressing them over the thundering roar of the volcano. 'This night the last of the Light will be snuffed out. This night will be eternal. This night begins my reign of Darkness!'

The High Priests and Hunters holler their approval, sounding like a pack of ravenous wolves. The volcano rumbles, spewing forth more molten rock and sending rivers of red streaking down its blackened slopes.

'No! There'll be another dawn!' I insist, even as my limbs grow heavy and my soul's link to my body weakens. Desperately I try to summon a Light blast, but the ritual potion seems to be clouding my auras, blocking my ability to wield the Light.

Tanas bends her dark gaze towards me. 'Oh, really?'

I glare defiantly at her. 'Even if you sacrifice me, the Light will still shine on.'

Tanas laughs. 'Poor Genna. I think you're very much mistaken.'

She clicks her fingers and Pablo appears at the top of the steps, dragging a young girl into the wavering light of the torches. Her ice-blond hair is tangled, her clothes torn and smeared with blood and dirt. Her sparkling blue eyes bulge with fear. She clasps a toy rabbit in her arms, Coco, once my beloved childhood friend, now ripped and missing an ear.

'Tasha!' I cry. She is – was – the last hope for the Light. The Soul Survivor I was counting on if I am to die.

'Genna!' she sobs. 'They killed Steinar.'

'What?' gasps Jude. Her face blanches, seemingly unable to believe that the immense Norwegian Soul Warrior can somehow have been vanquished. Enraged, she launches herself at Blondie, headbutting him in the chin. As he reels away, stunned, Tarek struggles to his feet in a bid to join Jude in the fight. But, with their hands bound, they're both easily overcome, brutally beaten into submission by Knuckleduster's ringed fists and forced to their knees.

'Move another inch,' Knuckleduster warns Jude, 'and I'll kick pretty boy here into the lava pit.'

Jude stops resisting and Tarek goes still as Pablo hauls Tasha over to the pit opening. 'You want me to throw her in too?' he asks eagerly.

Her feet slipping on the edge, Tasha screams and lets go of Coco. The little floppy-eared bunny drops into the abyss, vanishing amid the wreaths of smoke. Picturing him burning to a cinder, I fear for Tasha and my friends and the gruesome fate that awaits them. But I'm powerless to do anything about it. With my limbs pinned and my strength sapped by the ritual, I can only watch as Tasha teeters on the edge.

Then I see a shadow with a white-tipped tail pounce

from the top of the godhead statue, and my heart lifts. Landing on Pablo, Nefe slashes at his face with her razor-sharp claws. Pablo shrieks in pain. He releases Tasha as he tries frantically to pull his attacker off. Recovering her balance, Tasha darts to safety behind the statue, as Pablo, blinded and bleeding, staggers to one side and loses his footing on the rim of the horrifying pool. Arms wheeling, too shocked to scream, he falls backwards into the pit opening, Nefe leaping off him at the last second.

'That darned cat!' Tanas snarls, but she makes no attempt to save Pablo from his fate.

Bounding past the furious Tanas, Nefe jumps on to the altar and lashes out in all directions. She rips into the two High Priests, forcing them to let go of my ankles. Next, she claws Phoenix, leaving deep scores in his hand. He cries out, his dead-eyed trance broken and his grip on me released. But when Nefe turns on Damien, Tanas grabs her by the scruff of the neck and hurls her into the night.

'*Nefe!*' I cry as she vanishes down the steep side of the pyramid. Anger and grief boil in me and I launch myself at Tanas. 'You killed my cat!'

But Damien, Phoenix and the two priests quickly restrain me, pinning me to the altar once more.

'Enough of this delay!' snaps Tanas. 'We end this NOW!'

She storms over to the godhead statue and seizes the jade knife. As she marches back towards the altar, I writhe and kick. Quickly exhausted by my futile efforts and the effects of the ritual potion, I look up at my Soul Protector. 'Phoenix! I beg you! Help me!'

He glances down, as if noticing me for the first time.

Tanas stands beside the altar and begins her final and fatal incantation: '*Rura, rkumaa, raar ard ruhrd . . .*'

The faintest starlit gleam shines in the corners of Phoenix's eyes –

'*Qmourar ruq rouhk ur darchraqq . . .*'

It grows brighter, the darkness receding like an ebbing tide –

'*Ghraruq urq kugr rour ararrurd . . .*'

Phoenix frowns, appearing confused and disorientated. 'Genna . . .?'

'*Qard ur rou ra datsrq, Ra-Ka . . .*'

Tanas raises the jade knife to the seething black sky above –

'*Uur ra uhrdar bourkad, RA-KA!*'

At the last second, Phoenix lets go of my wrist, draws the obsidian blade from his belt and drives it at Tanas's chest. But Tanas, moving with the lightning speed of a jaguar, deflects the strike and knocks the blade from Phoenix's grip. She seizes him with her clawed hand and holds the jade knife to his throat. 'Nice try, traitor. A long time may have passed, but you don't get away with that trick twice.'

'But I only just escaped your prison of Darkness! You couldn't have known,' says Phoenix as the two priests restrain his arms.

'Your eyes gave you away,' Tanas replies with a snort of a laugh.

She glances in the direction of the lava pool and a malicious grin spreads across her lips. 'To be a true phoenix, you need to burn!'

She nods a command to the two priests, who drag him over to the opening. Joining them, Tanas puts the tip of the jade knife to his heart. 'Let's make doubly sure your soul never reincarnates, shall we?'

'Genna!' Phoenix yells, as Tanas begins her ritual incantation. 'Your life with mine, as always.'

Fighting the potion's effects, I half jump, half scramble off the altar and crawl towards the obsidian blade lying on the floor. But Damien gets there first and picks up the blade.

'Let me finish him, O Lord and Master,' says Damien. 'He is my First Brother, after all.'

Tanas pauses in her ritual and muses on this a moment, then steps aside. 'Why not? You've more than proven your loyalty to me. You've stayed true to our pact and brought about the downfall of your former fellow Protectors. Now that we're so close to extinguishing the Light, I can gift you this *one* Soul.'

She hands him the jade knife. Damien faces Phoenix, the lava pool boiling below. Despair fills my heart as I realize the end has truly come.

Tanas hungrily looks on. 'One First Brother killing another . . . how deliciously dark. And to think all it took to turn one against the other was to lay the seed of jealousy.' She glances in my direction and smiles at her own cunning. In that instant, I understand how Damien's unrequited love for me became so toxic and how it poisoned his soul. Tanas's evil hand was behind his hatred.

Staring into Phoenix's starlit eyes, Damien raises the jade knife to strike his brother down. 'I've waited many, many lives for this moment.'

57

'What are you waiting for?' growls Phoenix as the knife remains poised in Damien's hand.

'This!' With a deft flick of his wrist, Damien switches knives, turns from his First Brother and plunges the obsidian blade into Tanas's heart!

I gasp, barely able to believe what I've just witnessed. Tanas stares uncomprehendingly at the blade protruding from her chest, blood oozing out black and thick like the sap of a diseased tree. She opens her mouth to speak, but only a strangled sucking sound issues from her thin, pale lips.

I watch with grim satisfaction as her narrow eyes shrink into pinpricks of darkness, her skin flakes and sheds like the scales of a snake, and her mane of sable black hair turns white as ash. The obsidian blade in her chest starts to smoke, curls of noxious black fumes rising up into the night sky. With a rasp of pain, Tanas staggers backwards and teeters on the lip of the lava pit.

The two High Priests holding Phoenix rush to save their master, but Phoenix gets there first.

'You say it is I who need to burn, yet you forget that a phoenix rises from the flames.' He kicks Tanas hard in the gut and she pitches over the side. 'But *you* won't! Not ever again!' he shouts after her, as Tanas plunges into the lava pool.

A long, tortured cry of agony echoes up from the inner chamber before fading into silence. For several seconds, no one moves or says anything. Even Diablofuego falls into a grumbling silence. Then, like a spell has been broken, I feel the strength in my limbs return and the effects of the ritual potion melt away.

Pulling myself to my feet, I stumble over to Phoenix. 'The ritual worked – it actually worked!' I shout.

We embrace, as much to hold each other up as to celebrate this miraculous moment. I'm shattered beyond belief. My body bruised and aching, I feel held together by adrenaline alone.

I glance across the opening of the lava pit and see Jude and Tarek escaping the clutches of the bewildered Knuckleduster and Blondie, and leaping in triumph. They dash across to the fearsome jaguar-faced statue, where they cut their bonds on the edge of Jude's shield. Then they free Mei and Prisha and tend to their wounds. Tasha peers nervously out from behind the statue, seeming not quite able to believe that Tanas has been defeated.

Phoenix looks me in the eyes. I'm relieved to see his are starlit and gleaming blue, my Soul Protector returned to me once more. 'I'm so sorry, Genna, for losing my way,' he says. 'I was forced to join the Darkness, to become a Hunter. The ritual that Tanas performed on me back in Haven wasn't meant to kill me. It converted me against my will. My soul was corrupted, my thoughts and actions not my own. It was a living nightmare –'

'Phoenix,' I interrupt, 'it's over. There's no need to apologize. Having the real you back is more than enough.' I hold him tighter. 'I thought I'd lost you forever. I shared my Light with you, and even then you showed no signs of coming back.'

'I almost didn't,' he admits. 'My soul was imprisoned in Darkness, the weight of it dragged me down as if I was drowning. I could see your Light though, far, far above. I tried to swim towards it, follow its pathway to the surface, but I was pulled down again and again. It was probably the shock of Nefe's sudden attack that sharpened my senses and enabled me to connect with your Light and return –' Phoenix glances around. 'Talking of Nefe, where is she?'

Tears prick my eyes. 'Sh-she's dead,' I stutter. 'Tanas killed her.'

Phoenix gently wipes away my tears. 'Don't grieve for her, Genna. Nefe *will* return in another life.'

'I know,' I reply, with a bittersweet smile. 'But loss is always hard to bear. I loved her so much.'

Phoenix returns my smile. 'Except now, with Tanas's soul gone forever, we can look to the future with hope. The Light of Humanity has been saved!'

I nod as the world-changing realization hits me. For the first time, our future lives promise to be very different. There'll be no more running, no more hiding, no more fear of Tanas and her Soul Hunters. And the one who broke that cycle, who ultimately saved the Light, is none other than . . . *Damien*.

We both turn to him. Phoenix's First Brother stands by the opening to the lava pit, his head bowed, the jade knife still in his hand. He appears to be contemplating the weapon as if baffled to have it in his possession.

'Damien,' I call gratefully, 'I'm so relieved you finally saw the Light. I know you've hunted me for all these generations, but now I understand that Tanas had twisted your mind and soul. She admitted to laying the seed of jealousy in your heart that turned you to the Darkness. That pitted you against your First Brother. That made you want to become an Incarnate, hellbent on destroying me and the Light. Yet, despite all that, I can forgive you – we can *all* forgive you. At the ultimate moment, when we truly needed you, you did the right thing! You ended Tanas's reign of Darkness before it could begin.'

Damien gives a strange snort of a laugh. 'What, you think I killed Tanas because I saw the Light?' He looks up from the jade knife and turns to us. There's a malevolent, twisted grin on his pale face. 'No, Genna. I killed Tanas so that *I* could rule the Dark.'

I feel Phoenix tense at my side. I can barely breathe myself. I see that Damien's eyes are still pooled, his gaze cold and murderous. It's only now that I'm aware of the surviving Hunters and High Priests remaining in their former state. *No one has changed.*

'B-but how?' I stutter. 'On Tanas's death, you should revert.'

'Not when I take Tanas's power for myself, though,' Damien replies. 'And you, Genna, with your ritual . . . *you* enabled that for me. By ensuring that Tanas's soul will never return, I ascend to her dark throne.'

'Not if I can help it,' snarls Phoenix.

He charges at Damien, but Damien is ready for him. Appearing to welcome Phoenix's attack with open arms, Damien embraces his First Brother and thrusts the jade knife into his gut. Phoenix grunts in pain and slumps against Damien's chest.

'Bye-bye, little brother,' says Damien, stepping aside and letting Phoenix fall through the opening in the platform.

'NO! NO! NO!' I scream as my Soul Protector disappears into the fiery abyss. Alerted by my cries, Jude and Tarek stop tending to Mei and Prisha's wounds, only to discover that Knuckleduster, Blondie and the other Incarnates have surrounded them.

I drop to my knees, peering into the chamber in the desperate hope Phoenix may have somehow missed the lava and survived. But there's no sign of my Protector on the hard temple floor or in the pool of molten rock. His body would have been incinerated in seconds.

Losing my soul love so soon after regaining him is too much for me to bear. My heart breaks into a thousand pieces and hot tears stream down my face as I let out a wail of grief.

Damien laughs. 'Oh, stop making such a fuss. Just like your stupid cat, he'll reincarnate, although it's a pity it'll be far too late to save you or the Light of Humanity.' He steps closer and offers his hand. 'Now, Genna, I give you a simple choice. Join with me in the Darkness as my queen . . . or perish forever.'

I look at his proffered hand with loathing. 'I'd never stand by your side,' I reply. 'Your hatred has made you into the devil incarnate.'

Damien slaps me hard across the face. My cheek burns. 'And your love for Phoenix has made you weak! No wonder the Light is failing.'

The two High Priests – now under Damien's dark influence – grab hold of me and drag me back to the altar. Jude and Tarek dash over, but Knuckleduster, Blondie and the other Incarnates pounce on them. After a violent tussle both Jude and Tarek are restrained.

Legs kicking, I'm hauled up and on to the hard, cold stone of the altar. Damien strides over and places the tip of the jade knife upon my heart and recommences Tanas's ritual: '*Qmourar ruq rouhk ur darchraqq* –'

As he utters the incantation, sulphurous fumes rise up behind him from the lava pit. They thicken and darken, swirling and coalescing into a forbidding shape. Damien raises the jade knife for the final, fatal phrase . . .

'*Uur ra uhrdar bourkad, RA-KA!*'

Suddenly a shard of pure Darkness bursts out of Damien's chest and he slumps to the ground.

As my mind races, trying to fathom what has just happened, I see a wraith-like figure step out from the wreaths of sulphurous smoke. A dark, twisted, nightmarish form of long limbs and claw-like fingers, it stalks towards me. I want to turn away from the freakish sight, but I'm too terrified to even move. Its head is unnaturally elongated, with a lipless mouth and lidless black eyes. A chilling demon of pure Darkness. Its breath is husky, hollow and harsh as a winter wind.

And then the Soul Shadow speaks: '*Only* I *have the power to destroy souls for eternity.*'

58

I've never been more afraid in this life, nor, I think, in any of my past lives. The vision is so horrifying it freezes my blood and stills my beating heart. The night sky appears as black as death, not a single star shining in the firmament. The temperature plummets and my breath frosts in the suddenly frigid air. All the jungle now reeks of ash and decay. My very life feels as if it is being sucked from me as the nightmare draws closer, ever closer.

'*Your ritual may have killed my body, stopped my soul from incarnating in human form, but my Darkness prevails.*'

'No, no, it isn't possible!' I gasp. I realize Tanas has returned, more powerful and more terrifying than ever before. The Incarnates all prostrate themselves on the temple platform, subdued by this fearsome apparition. Diablofuego erupts as if paying tribute, sending fireballs raining down upon the city and spewing forth a river of molten red rock that floods the plaza below.

The Soul Shadow peers down with its lidless eyes at Damien's dead body.

'*Let no one usurp my throne!*'

With its talons, the Shadow crushes Damien's body to dust. Then slowly, menacingly, it turns to me.

'*You, foe, you have plagued me long enough. It is time for a blade of pure Darkness to bring this to an end.*'

Muttering an incantation, the Shadow conjures up a long, dark, jagged blade. It raises its arm ready to strike – but before it brings it down on me a sudden, concentrated hail of salt crystals strike its spectral form. The Soul Shadow flinches, as if stung by a swarm of bees. Angered, it rounds on Tarek, Prisha and Mei, who hold their line and hurl the last of Mei's stash.

'Pathetic!' it snarls, shrugging off the attack. In retaliation, it fires a deadly barrage of black bullets. Jude manages to snatch up her shield in time to deflect the bombardment, while Tarek and Prisha dive for cover behind the godhead statue, but Mei is caught out in the open. She shudders as if whipped by an icy wind, before collapsing in a heap.

'*Mei!*' I cry.

I leap to my feet upon the altar and go on the attack. Channelling my Soul Twin's aura, I fire off a blazing ball of golden Light. The Shadow counters with an orb of pure Darkness. They collide mid-air, neutralizing one another in an ear-splitting explosion. I'm blasted backwards and thrown off the altar to the ground. I skid across the platform, narrowly avoid rolling down the pyramid's steep steps, and lie in a heap, winded.

Tarek rushes out from behind the impassive godhead statue, screaming a battle cry. He grabs one of the broken spears and charges at the Soul Shadow. He manages to drive the spear's obsidian tip deep into the sinewy leg of the monster. It howls in rage and pain.

'Master, I'll save you,' cries Knuckleduster. She leaps up and seizes Tarek from behind. The Shadow tears the obsidian spear from its leg, then brutally skewers Tarek *and* Knuckleduster with the blade of Darkness.

They both drop, limp and lifeless, to the floor.

I can scarcely believe the creature's ruthlessness. This thing, this abomination, is pure evil.

Blondie, seeing the fate of his fellow Hunter, makes a run for the pyramid's steps. With barely a glance, the Shadow throws the spear and pierces Blondie in the back. The young Hunter manages two more strides before tumbling away down the steps.

Ignoring the trembling Incarnates at its feet, the Soul Shadow sheathes the blade of Darkness and sweeps its lidless gaze across the platform until it spots Tasha cowering with Prisha behind the statue. It beckons to her with a taloned finger.

'*Come, don't hide your Light, little one.*'

The Soul Shadow strides across the lava pit. Prisha tries to shield the girl but the Shadow knocks her aside with one flick of its talons. My friend disappears over the edge of the pyramid.

'Prisha!' I scream, reaching for her.

As the Soul Shadow closes its claws round Tasha, I can take no more. I rise again to my feet in a fit of fury. 'LEAVE HER ALONE!' I punch out a spinning star of Light, then another, and another – and yet another. I know I risk burning out, but I cannot allow this Soul

Shadow – this abhorrent spectre of Tanas – to take Tasha's soul.

The shooting stars crackle through the air, leaving tracers of light in their wake. By some fortune, Tasha escapes the Shadow's clutches as it rapidly circles its taloned hand, conjuring up a Dark shield. On contact with this, the stars blink out one by one.

Then the Shadow strikes back.

A deluge of deadly darts like shards of black glass shoot towards me. I summon up a hasty Light shield, recoiling as the darts ricochet off. But one manages to bore its way through to hit me. All of a sudden my shoulder feels numb, and I struggle to keep my arm raised to generate the shield. I stagger away in pain, the Light shield fizzling out.

The Soul Shadow sends a second wave of darts and Jude rushes to my defence. She stands before me, her bronzed Athenian shield our only protection. The darts pummel the surface, leaving dents and piercing the polished metal.

'RUN!' she yells as another volley of darts rains down on us.

'Where? I cry, glancing around. The plaza is now completely flooded with lava and the surrounding jungle ablaze. 'There's no escape!'

The Soul Shadow launches a spiralling orb of Darkness. Jude braces herself, but her shield is no match for such a supernatural weapon. The orb hits her with its full force. Flung backwards, she crashes against the altar and loses grip on the shield. Almost immediately a shard of Darkness hits her squarely in the chest. I dash to Jude's side.

Her valiant defence has given me just enough precious time to recover from the Shadow's dart, and this time I succeed in creating a new Light shield.

'I've failed you,' wheezes Jude, coughing up blood, 'like I failed your Soul Twin . . .'

'No – you haven't failed me,' I insist gently. 'You *never* failed me. Nor Aya.' I place my hand upon her chest in an attempt to heal her Dark wound, but the shard is buried deep. She splutters up more blood and I sense that her end is very near. I choke back a sob. 'You did not fail. You have given your life for me. As a Soul Protector, there is nothing more that you can give. You are making the ultimate sacrifice, for me. You've redeemed yourself in every way –'

Jude manages a weak smile, 'So, see you in another life, perhaps . . .' Then the Light in her eyes fades.

I clutch her limp body to me and weep.

The Soul Shadow lets out a boom of laughter like a thunderclap. '*The last of the Soul Protectors is gone . . . Now nothing stands in my way. The Light of Humanity* will *be extinguished for eternity!*'

The Shadow lassoes Tasha with a chain of Darkness, binding her to the godhead statue. Then with its lipless mouth it appears to suck the girl's soul from her. A spectral white glow is drawn from Tasha's eyes and swallowed by the Darkness. Her soul sucked dry, Tasha's head flops forward and her body hangs limp in the binding of chains.

I scream, feeling the Light of Humanity fade to nothing more than an ember.

I am now the Soul Survivor.

Night descends around me like the final curtain on a play. As my eyes struggle to make out anything in the darkness, only the hellish glow of the lava pit and distant blaze of the jungle illuminate the scene before me. Upon the temple platform the remaining Incarnates bow and scrape at the feet of their master, too afeared to even look upon its odious face.

The Soul Shadow releases the chain round Tasha's body, letting it fall to the ground, then it turns to me. '*Come! It is time. Face the inevitable.*'

Drawn by its mesmerizing voice, I obediently place Jude down, rise slowly and take a step forward –

'NO!' I declare, forcing myself to stop mid-stride. 'Not while the Light still burns within me.'

Channelling my twin auras, I fashion a samurai sword of pure Light and call upon the last of my strength. I'm exhausted beyond all measure, my body bruised and battered and on the point of burning out. Yet, somehow, I find the will within me to fight this final battle.

The Soul Shadow conjures up a new blade of Darkness. '*Let us put that last Light out, once and for all.*'

We confront one another atop the temple pyramid, fireballs raining down around us. I try to steady my hand, seeking the courage I need. In my head I hear my Japanese sensei speak to me from my deep past: *Strike with the soul, Miyoko-san, and you will never miss.*

My sword flashing like lightning, I cut down at the Shadow. The strike is perfect, yet the Shadow is like smoke. It deflects my attack and slices its blade across my stomach. I leap away at the last second, feeling its ice-cold edge rip through my clothes and score a poisonous black line into my skin. Wincing in agony, I spin round to hack off its head. Again, my aim is true, my speed unmatched. But the Shadow manages to block my strike and counter with a thrust to my chest. I'm forced to bend like a reed in the wind just to avoid the lethal blade.

Sword and blade clashing in the night, we wield the Light and the Dark. Sparks fly like steel beaten in a forge. Yet, despite all my training through all my lives, I fear I'm not able to beat the Soul Shadow. The Darkness has inexorably grown too strong. As I slice for its wraith-like body, my sword and its blade become entangled. With a devious twist of its scrawny wrist, the Soul Shadow disarms me, and I watch distraught as my Sword of Light goes spinning into the lava pit.

Holding its dark blade to my throat, the Soul Shadow leans in close. '*Finally. The Darkness will reign eternal.*'

The Shadow opens its lipless mouth and beings to suck out my soul. Like a guttering flame, I feel my Light dim. The world grows dark around me. My body turns ice-cold. A desperate loneliness creeps into every part of my being, and I know . . . I know this is the end.

As the last dregs of my soul are siphoned off, I catch sight of a spark in the darkness.

The speck of light – blue, bright and flickering – appears to grow stronger. All of a sudden it streaks through the air like a shooting star and hits the Soul Shadow between its lidless eyes. The Shadow ignites! Spreading now like wildfire, the spark consumes its victim in a blazing ball of blue flames. The Soul Shadow, roaring in pain and fury, casts me aside and reels away.

Gasping in a shuddering breath, I feel my life return, my soul strengthen. Shakily I rise to my feet and discover Tasha standing beside the altar, frail and deathly pale yet mercifully not dead, her soul clinging on as a faint gleam in her eyes. On the ground are the shattered remains of the lamp. In that moment, I realize that the spark of Light I saw arcing towards the Soul Shadow, at the darkest point in our battle, was the eternal flame.

I turn back to our foe. The Soul Shadow blazes, a fiery volcano in itself, yet *still* it does not perish!

If it is not, even now, destroyed, and both ritual and prophecy appear to have failed, then what on earth can destroy Tanas's dark soul?

Tanas's boast was evidently right. Only she has the power. As the Soul Shadow lurches towards me, writhing amid the flames, my eye is drawn to the polished bronze of Jude's Athenian shield. The snake-haired head of the Gorgon, Medusa, gleams almost as if it's alive and I'm once more reminded of the legend of Perseus. This gives me one desperate, final idea.

'TANAS!' I shout. 'You have failed. My soul survives. The Light lives on!'

'*Not for much longer*,' roars back the Soul Shadow, conjuring up a spear of Darkness.

As it launches the burning weapon at me, I summon up the last of my Light. Using both my own aura and my sister's, I create a shield of such intensity that I am blinded by its brightness. The spear rebounds off the shield and shoots back towards the Shadow, where it buries itself in the wraith's chest.

I charge forward, driving the Soul Shadow to the brink of the lava pit. As we teeter on the edge, my body burns brighter than a thousand stars. Then, locked together, we plunge head first into the lava . . .

Darkness and Light entwined.

Epilogue

A century later

All is dark. All is silent. Gradually, almost imperceptibly at first, a faint halo of light appears in the far distance. There's a murmur of excitement. In the sky, five planets are perfectly aligned, glinting like diamonds. Then a warm, red glow pushes back the night and welcomes in the new day. A great cheer goes up as the sun rises above the horizon, its rays illuminating the dawn sky like a fiery crown.

I stand amid the throng of people, smiling as I relish the warmth on my skin. The Festival of Light always attracts a big crowd and none more so than the one on the banks of the Ganges in Varanasi. Marking the victory of Light over Darkness, this yearly festival is now celebrated around the world in honour of a new dawn in human history. An era that has seen an end to war, the eradication of poverty and disease, and the recovery of the planet that has healed beyond all expectations.

Gazing round at the countless happy faces bathing in the sun's golden rays, I catch glimpses of their souls in their eyes. Fresh, free and full of the Light of Humanity – yet blissfully unaware of the reason for this miracle.

I am one of the very few who know. I was there when the Darkness was vanquished, when Tanas's soul was destroyed for good. I turned thirteen when I had my first Glimmer, a vivid memory of being a samurai in ancient Japan. Yet it wasn't until my sixteenth birthday that I recalled my life as a young schoolgirl from England called Genna. Even now, I find it hard to believe. In fact, I sometimes question if what I remember is true. But I've met other people – other souls like me – who remember too.

That's why I'm drawn to this spot. Varanasi, the sacred City of Light, home of the eternal flame. It has a special connection for me. I know I was here once before, in a past life.

'You need a guide?'

I roll my eyes and sigh. This is the sixth person to offer their services already this morning, and the sun has barely risen!

'No, thank you,' I reply politely. 'I know my –' I stop mid-sentence and stare at the young man who's approached me. Dressed like a backpacker in beige cargo shorts, a checked cotton shirt and a navy baseball cap, he's clearly not a guide, nor a local either. In fact, he isn't even Indian. Tall, broad-chested, with short blond hair, a chiselled jaw and a worldly-wise grin, he looks more Icelandic. His eyes are glacier ice-blue and mesmerizing in their intensity.

For a long moment, I become lost in his gaze as a kaleidoscope of memories and lives flash before me: *learning from him how to track antelope on the African savannah . . . racing each other on camels across the Sahara Desert . . . practising capoeira in the Brazilian rainforest, my foot striking his jaw and knocking him out . . . performing together as circus acrobats in a Russian circus . . . speeding on a motorbike through London, my hands clasped round his waist, Damien and his Soul Hunters giving chase behind us . . .*

The Glimmers go on and on, a rush of recollections that sends my heart racing and my head spinning. Although this is the very first time we've met in this life, we embrace each other tightly, not saying anything, not *needing* to say anything, just feeling our souls reconnect as the crowds of chanting sunworshippers circulate around us.

Eventually we pull apart.

I smile warmly at him. 'Hi, I'm Sunstra,' I say, for some reason feeling the need to introduce myself.

'I'm Björn,' he says, grinning back. 'But call me Phoenix if you prefer, or Asani, or whatever you want.'

'How about . . . *late*?' I suggest teasingly.

He gives me a mock-wounded look. 'Believe me, I've been searching *everywhere* for you. England, Egypt, Japan, Fiji, Guatemala . . .'

'Well, now you've found me. And it only took you a hundred years!'

He laughs. 'Sorry,' he says with a shrug of his broad shoulders. 'Seems to have taken me a while to reincarnate.' His good-humoured expression turns serious. 'To be honest, I didn't know if I ever would. If *we* ever would. What happened? The last thing I recall was Phoenix being pushed over the edge into a lava pit by my First Brother.'

I take his arm and we stroll along the city's stepped ghats, wending our way through the dawn celebrations and away from the packed crowds. I realize that, for all my teasing, my Soul Protector must have been deeply worried as to my ultimate fate. I relate what happened after his death in Guatemala, telling him how our ritual failed to destroy Tanas completely. How she returned as a demonic Soul Shadow and executed Damien for his treachery. How Tarek and Mei were struck down by shards of Darkness, and Prisha was thrown off the pyramid. How Jude sacrificed herself for me and redeemed herself in every way. How the Soul Shadow almost conquered the Light by sucking Tasha's and my souls dry, and how, at the Darkest point in our battle, the spark was ignited and Tanas's soul was finally extinguished.

We pause beside a jetty, the sun glinting off the clear waters of the Ganges like a sprinkling of gold dust.

'So the Soul Prophecy proved to be true?' he says.

I nod. 'Apparently so, although I'd never have guessed it was Tasha.'

He frowns and gives me a questioning look. 'Tasha? From what you've said, I consider it to be *you* who fulfilled the Prophecy.'

'Me?' I shake my head. 'Tasha was the one to throw the lamp, to release the eternal flame and to ignite the spark.'

'Be that as it may, your soul shone brightest. You literally burned out to conquer Tanas.'

'But I didn't actually defeat Tanas. She defeated herself,' I argue. 'Remember how Tanas boasted that only she had the power to destroy souls? I figured that, if that was the case, then Tanas's soul might be destroyed by turning her power upon herself. A bit like Perseus holding up his shield as a mirror to defeat Medusa, I used my Light shield to reflect her spear of Darkness back at her. The Soul Shadow killed itself.'

Björn gives me a chiding look. 'I think you're doing yourself a great disservice. It was *your* bright idea to turn her power against her. *Your* Light shield that reflected her spear of Darkness. And *your* sacrifice that saved the Light.'

'But I couldn't have done that if Tasha hadn't ignited the spark,' I insist. 'Or without Jude, Tarek, Mei and Prisha's help . . . or *you*, my Soul Protector. The one person who sacrificed themself again and again, life after life, so that I could live, so that my soul and the Light of Humanity could survive.'

He smiles modestly. 'Well, whoever should take the credit, it clearly worked. We're here to live another life, and – for once – there are no Soul Hunters chasing us.' He pauses beside the river to admire a kingfisher dip into the water and fly off, then he buys us both an iced mango lassi from a passing vendor. Taking a long sip, he lets out a contented sigh. 'Bliss! Utter bliss . . . we can now truly relax and enjoy our lives, together.'

We continue our stroll along the riverbank, watching the flotillas of rowing boats glide up and down. 'And what about the others?' he asks. 'Have you managed to reconnect with any of them?'

I nod and take a sip of my lassi. 'Jude – I bumped into her on a beach in southern Thailand. She's on a yacht doing a round-the-world cruise. Tarek – he's an astrophysicist in Switzerland.'

Björn grins. 'Seems like they achieved their dream lives!'

'It was Tasha, though, who found me first,' I explain. 'She appeared soon after my first Glimmer in this life, drawn to me by my Wakening. She's a qualified doctor from Delhi and was helpful in reassuring me I wasn't losing my mind.' I gaze off at the river's rippling waters. 'She also eased my conscience over Mei and Prisha's fates. By some miracle, they survived the battle. She told me that Prisha landed on a ledge lower down the pyramid; her arm was broken but otherwise she was OK. Mei regained consciousness once Tanas was truly vanquished. She was weak, very weak. It took her several months to recover, but both my friends went on to lead peaceful, happy lives.' I give a bittersweet smile. 'I only wish I'd been there to share those times with them.'

'Don't we all!' says Björn. 'Do you happen to know if they've reincarnated?'

'Yes, I do – and they have! In fact, Mei was relatively easy to locate, since I'd shared some of my own Light with her. You won't believe what she's reincarnated as?'

'A comedian?'

'No – an archaeologist like her previous-life parents!' I reply, laughing. 'She has vague memories of our past incarnation together.' My laughter fades away. 'Prisha, though, sadly doesn't remember it at all. I recognized her soul reborn in a young waitress at a restaurant in Los Angeles. She waits tables while she trains to be an actress. I was so excited to reunite with her that I blurted out everything about our past life together, and unfortunately it completely freaked her out. So she's kept her distance ever since.'

'That's understandable,' says Björn. He raises an eyebrow at me. 'I've been in that same situation with you. It's very difficult to convince someone unless they have a past-life memory you can corroborate.'

I dump my lassi cup into a bin and sigh. 'I guess you're right. I'm just glad that Prisha's soul has come back. So many First Ascendants' and Protectors' souls didn't.'

Björn nods sadly. 'I like to believe their spirits still live on in the Light.' He glances up at the dawn sky; in the west, where twilight persists, the moon and a dusting of stars still shine in the heavens. 'That with each new star that appears in the night sky, one of them has returned and been reborn in a new soul.' His gaze returns to me, his eyes now glistening, with tears or the Light I can't quite tell. Maybe both. 'And what about Nefe? That cat of yours has nine lives at least. Surely she survived?'

I take out my phone and show him my screensaver of a young tabby cat perched upon my shoulder like a parrot.

Björn laughs. 'Nice selfie!'

'Thanks,' I reply. 'I found her as a kitten in an animal shelter. Or should I say she found me! As soon as they opened the cage, she jumped on my shoulder! I knew it was Nefe straight away.'

As I'm pocketing my phone, we pass a middle-aged couple disembarking from a tourist boat. Our eyes meet for the briefest moment, and I recognize their gentle souls. 'Mum! Dad!' I call out before I can stop myself.

They both look at me, somewhat bemused. In this life I've been born with Thai heritage. The woman looks to be

Japanese and the man European, perhaps English. 'Sorry, do we know you?' he asks.

I smile awkwardly. I want to express how much I miss them and how sorry I am for their suffering in the last life. But I know from experience this isn't the best way to handle such delicate matters. 'My apologies. I mistook you for someone I once knew.'

The woman regards me with a shrewd look. 'I feel I *do* know you. Are you sure we haven't met before?'

'Perhaps,' I reply, a warmth blossoming in my heart. 'If we have, it was a long time ago.'

The man chuckles. 'That's exactly what my Suzume said to me the first time we met.' He takes the woman's hand and squeezes it affectionately. 'In Japan they believe that an invisible red thread connects those who are destined to meet, regardless of time, place or circumstance.' He looks at me. 'Perhaps we are part of that same thread, too?'

I nod. 'I very much believe that.'

The woman smiles and bows. 'Well, my dear, I do hope our threads cross again.'

'So do I,' I say as I watch my parents from another life wander away, hand in hand. A peace settles within my soul, a wound finally healed. I turn back to Björn with tears of gratitude in my eyes at our chance meeting. 'You were right,' I say. 'My mother and father did reincarnate, and they found one another again.'

'It's strange how certain souls are drawn together,' he says, as he offers his own hand to me. 'Your life with mine . . .?'

I take his hand and hold it tight, vowing never to let go. 'As always.'

'Death is but the doorway to new life . . .
We live today – we shall live again –
in many forms shall we return.'

Acknowledgements

The universe works in very mysterious ways.

I've been a full-time author for some fifteen years and in that time I hoped the process of writing would get easier. Yet somehow it doesn't. Each new book is a new challenge, a new mountain to climb. And if *The Soul Survivor* was a mountain, then this book is my Mount Everest.

I have never struggled so hard to write a story in my life. To find the oxygen of words with which to breathe life into my characters. There were many, many times I thought of giving up, the path of the plot too complex, too twisting and too treacherous to tread. At one point it seemed I would need another lifetime in order to finish this book.

During the long arduous writing process, I caught Covid twice (its effects leading to months of writer's block); tore my upper left hamstring tendon (which prevented me from sitting at my desk); then, just as I started writing again, I fell on concrete and ended up with severe concussion – and as a result I forgot the entire book!

Still, I battled on, inching forward word by word, until I eventually completed *The Soul Survivor* on the weekend of the late Queen's Jubilee, 3–6 June 2022. But it wasn't the royal celebrations that made this completion date extraordinary.

As you now know, Tanas and the Darkness are eventually defeated in a ritual that must occur during a rare alignment of five planets visible to the naked eye in our solar system: Mercury, Venus, Mars, Jupiter and Saturn. As I sat at my desk writing those final chapters, that *exact* celestial conjunction was happening right above my head. This rare alignment began on the morning of 3 June 2022. It had not occurred since December 2004 and will not happen again until 2040.

The coincidence is beyond comprehension.

I wasn't aware of the alignment date until my father told me. I came up with the idea for the Soul series well over ten years ago. The project was delayed many times by writing commitments, significant personal life challenges and the reasons given above. Yet I finished this trilogy – and Tanas – on the day of the alignment. The odds must be literally astronomical!

I can only interpret the coincidence as a sign that, despite all the challenges, I was *meant* to finish the book on that date.

As I said, the universe works in mysterious ways.

My lesson from this? Trust in the universe. Everything happens for a reason, at the time and place it's supposed to.

Yet whatever cosmic influences there were, I couldn't have completed this monumental task without the help and support of some very special souls.

First and foremost, my Marcela. *Tu luz y amor me llevaron a través de los tiempos más oscuros. Tu aliento constante, creencia inquebrantable e infinita paciencia me permitieron continuar escribiendo. Te amo. (¡Yo lo dije primero!)*

My mum and dad for their understanding, love and tireless support. (Congratulations on surviving yet another tortuous writing process!)

Zach, Leo and Ollie for providing me with a soulful reason to keep on writing, and for always reminding me of the joy, laughter and love in life. I am blessed to have three such wonderful boys.

My Soul Sisters, Karen and Hayley, for their loving guidance, honest advice and eternal friendship.

Mary for her healing of mind and spirit. You have helped me to the top of the mountain.

All my brethren in the HGC; Geoff, Charlie and Matt; Rob, my cinema buddy; Brian, my fellow Tough Mudder; and the Dysons, especially my goddaughter Lulu.

Charlie Viney for your unwavering belief in me and for always fighting my corner.

My superb team at Puffin Books: Karen Ball, for taking up the editorial reins and navigating such a complex trilogy with enthusiasm, professionalism and incisiveness; Ben Horslen, for managing the project; Sarah Hall, for her meticulous eye for detail and excellence in polishing my words; and Wendy Shakespeare, for being the one editorial 'star' I can rely on orbiting my books.

Finally, a special mention to Diarmuid Mainwaring of Royal Belfast Academical Institution, who was the

Grand Prize winner of *The Soul Hunters* Lockdown Competition!

To all my faithful readers and librarians, thank you for reading *The Soul Survivor* and spreading the word among friends and family. You are the reason I write.

See you all in another life!
Chris

Fans can keep in touch with me and hear first about my next book series on Twitter @YoungSamurai or via the website at www.thesoulprophecy.co.uk, where you can also find a character list and glossary to the Soul series.

About the Author

As an author, Chris Bradford practises what he terms 'method writing'. For his award-winning Young Samurai series, he trained in samurai swordsmanship, karate and ninjutsu and earned his black belt in Zen Kyu Shin Taijutsu. For his Bodyguard series, he embarked on an intensive close-protection course to become a qualified professional bodyguard. More recently, for the Soul trilogy, Chris travelled extensively to experience first-hand the cultures featured in the story – from living with the Shona people in Zimbabwe, to trekking the Inca trail, to meditating in a Buddhist temple amid the mountains of Japan. His books have sold over three million copies, are published in over twenty-five languages and have garnered more than thirty children's book awards and nominations.

To discover more about Chris, go to
www.chrisbradford.co.uk

THE SOUL PROPHECY

DEATH IS ONLY THE BEGINNING . . .

An adventure that spans centuries.
A breathtaking fight for survival.

www.thesoulprophecy.co.uk